— THE —
FORGONE WAR

Nathan Smith

THE FORGONE WAR

The Story of the Brave Keystone Grenadiers

Nathan Smithtro

THE FORGONE WAR
THE STORY OF THE BRAVE KEYSTONE GRENADIERS

iUniverse books may be ordered through booksellers or by contacting:

iUniverse
1663 Liberty Drive
Bloomington, IN 47403
www.iuniverse.com
844-349-9409

Because of the dynamic nature of the Internet, any web addresses or links contained in
this book may have changed since publication and may no longer be valid. The views
expressed in this work are solely those of the author and do not necessarily reflect the
views of the publisher, and the publisher hereby disclaims any responsibility for them.

Any people depicted in stock imagery provided by Getty Images are models,
and such images are being used for illustrative purposes only.
Certain stock imagery © Getty Images.

ISBN: 978-1-6632-0125-6 (sc)
ISBN: 978-1-6632-0126-3 (e)

Library of Congress Control Number: 2020918657

Print information available on the last page.

iUniverse rev. date: 12/18/2020

INTRODUCTION

This story is based on historical facts about the Seventy Sixth Pennsylvania during their time fighting in the War of 1812. This story is about a young American apple farmer and his four best friends who were forced to fight against the British and Canadian armies during America's second war of independence. On June 18, 1812, America declared war on England and Canada. But on the same day, a veteran of America's earliest Indian Wars, Simon Smithtrovich, created the Seventy-Sixth Pennsylvania Keystone Grenadiers. His best friends—Celestia and Daisy Rose, Timmy Miller, and Brittany Benson—followed him into the War of 1812. Together they made up the staff of the brave Seventy-Sixth. Their friendships were challenged both physically and mentally in some of the war's terrible battles, such as the Battles of Lundy's Lane, Bladensburg, and New Orleans. They learned that they must rely upon themselves and the men and women that they commanded to carry on the fight where their families had left off at the end of the Revolutionary War. This is a story about a company of three hundred men and women who would stop at nothing to uphold the Keystone State's motto, which became their battle cry against the British and Canadian militaries: "Virtue, liberty, and independence!" Three hundred Pennsylvanian grenadiers would march into the War of 1812. Only One hundred and nine would live to the end of America's forgotten war. It has been 208 years since the War of 1812. This is a story about a simple apple farmer who wanted to serve in the US Army. He had four best friends who were like a part of his family. Simon Smithtrovich and his best friends created an elite crack company of grenadiers who stopped at nothing to help America stay free. The War of 1812 has been forgotten by many American citizens to this day. Many Americans do not realize how important the War of 1812 was. The men and women of the

Seventy-Sixth Pennsylvania were not like ordinary soldiers of their time. Never did a soldier of the Seventy-Sixth desert, and never did one of the grenadiers disobey an order that was given to him or her. Simon never gave his soldiers an order that would lead to the total destruction of the Seventy-Sixth on the battlegrounds. Major Simon Smithtrovich treated his grenadiers with firmness, fairness, compassion, respect, honor, and dignity, as though they were part of his family. The Seventy-Sixth Pennsylvania was well supplied and clothed during all four seasons. The Seventy-Sixth was well known for loving to sing songs. For them, singing was their best way to keep up morale before and after a battle. They created their own march that was in the tune of the British Grenadiers. Every grenadier was faithful, loyal and true to himself or herself as well as to the United States. Never did they fear an enemy that was too strong or had greater numbers. Even though they hated their enemies, deep down they felt sorry for all soldiers who fell in the war's terrible battles. They believed that their true strength came from the one thing they believed in the most—the power of friendship. Every Keystone grenadier was a great friend, and they all knew that in the heat of battle, the grenadiers right next to them would watch their backs. They had a common bond of brotherhood and sisterhood that was invincible. They fought in the name of unity not only for the Keystone State but also for the unity of the United States of America.

CHAPTER 1

"GRENADIERS, TO THE FRONT! FORWARD MARCH!"

The Battle of Chippewa
July 5, 1814
9:00 a.m.
Chippewa, Canada

The Americans under the command of Major General Winfield Scott led a brigade of 3,500 men to a piece of land called Chippewa. In the rear guard of the brigade was an irregular force of Pennsylvania called the Seventy-Sixth Pennsylvania Keystone Grenadiers. They were under the command of Major Simon Smithtrovich. He was a young and very daring man who was known for his battle tactics against any enemy that opposed his company. He was a veteran of the early American Indian wars. He was never afraid to march against any foe, no matter their size or how much firepower the enemy displayed. He was strong and fit with brown hair, and he had worn glasses ever since he was a child. He was accompanied by four of his best friends that commanded a part of the Seventy-Sixth. His second in command was First Lieutenant Celestia Rose, whose younger sister, Daisy Rose, was a first sergeant. They were two out of over two dozen female soldiers who enlisted in the Seventy-Sixth. They were not like other women of their time. They had always wanted to fight for their country. It was their right to serve, and they didn't waste a minute before enlisting. They were very strict with training new recruits. The third, a female soldier who commanded the company marching band, was Drum Major Brittany

Benson. She had always loved the marching songs that armies played. She came to be the drum major after displaying her potential at the birth of the Seventy-Sixth. Celestia, Daisy, and Brittany were young and very beautiful. Ever since then, Brittany had turned the Seventy-Sixth Corps Band into the best of the best from the state of Pennsylvania. Last but not least was Simon's male best friend, who was like a brother to him. Sergeant Timmy Miller was third in command of the Seventy-Sixth.

The Seventy-Sixth marches right behind a platoon of blue-coated soldiers on a dirt road. General Scott halts his men once they reach an open field.

"Battalion, take care! Halt!" he shouts.

Three companies back, Major Simon Smithtrovich orders the Seventy-Sixth to halt. Just then a sergeant runs up to Simon and says, "Major General Scott would like to speak with you. He has your battle orders."

"Very good," Simon replies to the sergeant. Simon turns to the Seventy-Sixth. "First Lieutenant Rose, you will be in charge till I return. I will be only a few minutes."

"Yes sir!" she says. They salute each other, and Simon walks to meet with the general. While Simon is walking through the ranks down the road. Celestia, Daisy, and Brittany have a small conversation.

"I hope we get to play today," Brittany says to Celestia. "My corps is getting really impatient to play our marches, ma'am."

"Do not worry; you will have your chance to play," Celestia assures Brittany.

"Besides, Drum Major," Daisy adds, "we couldn't ever have such great taste for battle without your music." Brittany smiles and looks down at her silver mace. She pulls out a piece of cloth and begins to polish the head of the mace, the head is what's called the crown. She chuckles a little bit. She looks up at Celestia and Daisy.

"You know, I actually had to use this mace to defend myself at a skirmish in lower Canada," Brittany says.

Celestia and Daisy look at each other, and Daisy says to Brittany, "What did you do to that mace? Did you bash a lobsterback's skull?" Daisy asks.

Brittany nods. "That is correct. We got overrun, and my corps had to use our instruments as weapons. I did not just teach how to march and play music. I taught them how to use their instruments as weapons." She shows Celestia and Daisy the top of her mace. Daisy points to a dent on top of the ball. "See that dent on the top there? I hit that lobster's head so hard that it made a dent. That, to me, is like a memory of knowing how close I came to capture or death that bloody day."

Celestia looks at her corps band, and she can see that they are hungry for the taste of music. Celestia smiles and then decides that they have been quiet long enough. She walks over to the band, stands at attention, and then speaks to them. "You have been quiet for long enough, so when we get our next orders, you can play us a song. Drum Major, do you have any tunes you can play for us?"

Brittany smiles as a march enters her mind. "How about our song— 'The Keystone Grenadiers'!"

Sergeant Timmy Miller and Major Simon Smithtrovich walk up the road, passing other American companies of regulars and militia.

"I sure hope we get to fight today," Simon says to Timmy. "The Seventy-Sixth has not seen battle for the past two months." He fixes his bearskin cap, making sure that the hair is perfect and his green plume is standing straight up. "We are a brave company of grenadiers. We belong on the front lines, by God."

Timmy tries to soothe Simon. "Well, sir, could it be possible that General Scott has been holding us back because we are a special force?"

Simon looks at Timmy and scratches the left side of his head. "My dear sergeant, you could be right. And I hope you are, because we are not parade-grounds soldiers. Even so, we do enjoy marching upon the parade grounds quite a bit. Would you not agree, Sergeant?"

"I do agree, sir. During that time, a soldier must be able to do his duty by fighting on the battlegrounds. I'm glad that the ladies came with us as well. Brittany, given the task to train our marching band—she is a genius."

Simon smiles and looks back at the Seventy-Sixth. He looks forward and smiles again. "That's why I chose her for the position of drum major. She is a great teacher, and she, along with the corps, loves music. I mean, who on God's green earth does not love music?"

Soon Simon reaches General Winfield Scott. Simon salutes him. "Sir, Major Smithtrovich reporting as ordered!"

General Scott salutes Simon and then gives Simon his new orders. "Major, you are to take your grenadiers to the front of our lines. You are to be our advance party so that the rest of the battalion can be deployed on the field."

Simon and Timmy get smiles upon their faces.

"Yes sir! My grenadiers will hold those redcoats in check, until you come, sir," Simon replies.

"I want your grenadiers to cross the bridge on the right side of the creek and, once you do that, march toward the center. The Ninth and the Twenty-Second Regiments will support you. Are your grenadiers up for the task, Major?"

Simon looks at Timmy and then looks down at the Seventy-Sixth. Simon and Timmy nod once at each other. Simon looks up to General Scott and says, "Sir, we will show you that we are up to the task. Sergeant Miller, let's return to the company. General, may we have a clear path?"

General Scott and his staff clear the road that leads toward the bridge.

"May God be with you brave Seventy-Sixth today!" General Hancock says.

Simon and Timmy salute Scott and march back to the Seventy-Sixth. The regiments cheer them on as the men and women of the Seventy-Sixth Pennsylvania Keystone Grenadiers wait for their orders to advance. They all smile as they ready themselves to march into battle. Simon and Timmy return to the unit. Simon takes a long look at his soldiers. After a deep breath, he gives his commands.

"Seventy-Sixth Pennsylvania, attention!"

The Seventy-Sixth stand at attention with straight posture.

"Seventy-Sixth, fix your bayonets!"

The Seventy-Sixth fix their bayonets to the ends of their muskets. The socket bayonets are fixed with a quarter turn.

"Seventy-Sixth, right-shoulder your firearms!"

The Seventy-Sixth right-shoulder their muskets. Then Simon turns his attention to Drum Major Brittany Benson.

"Drum Major Benson, to me, double time!" Brittany runs over to Simon. They salute each other.

Brittany salutes Simon with her mace. "Drum Major Benson reporting as ordered, sir! Sir, do you require a tune?" Brittany asks her commander.

Simon smiles and pats on her shoulder. He tries to think of a song to play, and then it hits him like a cannonball.

"Yes I do, Drum Major. play 'The Keystone Grenadiers' if you please."

Brittany smiles, and she fills with joy. She salutes him with her mace and marches back to the Seventy-Sixth Corps Band. The Seventy-Sixth Company is in this order: The band is in the first ranks. The band has twelve members in the corps: one drum major, three trumpeters, three fifers, four snare drummers, and one bass drummer. In the second rank is the Seventy-Sixth's color guard. There are two soldiers with muskets and two color-bearers. One carries the American flag, and the other regimental flag is carried by another man.

The Seventy-Sixth's regimental flag is the state of Pennsylvania's flag. Their American flag is unique. Where the white stars would normally be is a big white "76." This is the same flag that was carried during the Battle of Bennington during the Revolutionary War (1775–1783). The infantry of the Seventy-Sixth stand in rows of 5; there are 305 men in total. With their flags billowing in the breeze, the men are ready to fight.

Simon gives his final orders to advance. He shoulders his Brown Bess and shouts to the Seventy-Sixth: "The Seventy-Sixth Pennsylvania shall take care to advance! Grenadiers, to the front! Forward march!"

Drum Major Brittany Benson blows her whistle in a four-second note. Then she blows four quarter notes. The drummers play the cadence to the march. The Seventy-Sixth begin their march down the road. Brittany twirls her mace as she marches the whole unit down the road. The men of the Ninth Regiment begin to cheer on the Seventy-Sixth as they march onward.

Some of the men of the Ninth Regiment shout to the Seventy-Sixth.

"You go get those lobsters!" one regular shouts.

"May providence be with you all!" says another. "Give them the bayonet! Stick it to those red bastards!"

Several other American soldiers shout to the Seventy-Sixth as they march on past.

Simon looks back at his men and can see where the rest of the American army shall wait until they get the forces ready to attack. The few skirmishes in which the Seventy-Sixth Pennsylvania have fought in upper and lower Canada have been small. They have been ambushing supply convoys and attacking enemy camps during the day and night. Never had they taken prisoners in the raids Major Smithtrovich and his Keystone grenadiers had carried out in the past year and a half. The Seventy-Sixth's first major battle of the War of 1812 is about to test the men and women of the unit and their commanders' willpower to carry the day.

CHAPTER 2

"THOSE ARE REGULARS, BY GOD!"

The Battle of Chippewa Campaign
Chippewa, Canada
July 5, 1814
10:00 a.m.

The Seventy-Sixth reaches the bridge that crosses the Streets Creek. Simon marches up to Drum Major Benson with plans to order them to the rear.

"Drum Major Benson, you may retire your corps to the rear," he says to Brittany. But Brittany does not want to return to the rear.

"Sir, with your permission, we want to lead the Seventy-Sixth across the bridge. Our corps has always led our forces into battle. We cannot change that tradition, sir," Brittany states to her commander.

Simon knows she is telling the truth, and he himself is not a person to violate the value of tradition. But he has a bad gut feeling telling him that one of the soldiers in his marching band was going to either die or be wounded. He always had keen intuition. It seems to be his own conscience giving him warnings that predicted what was about to happen. But this time he softens and decides to let his band lead the Seventy-Sixth into their first major battle.

"Very well, Drum Major," Simon says. "I give you permission to lead us into the fray. I will have some skirmishers to escort you. But you still lead us. Lead the way."

"Thank you, sir," Brittany says. They both salute, and Simon returns to his position as he pats the shoulders of four of his men to direct them to head up to the front of the column. They rush up, and Brittany leads the way across the bridge.

On the other side of the bridge, Canadian militiamen take position in the trees. They see the Seventy-Sixth marching across the bridge, and they do not wait to resist. One of the militiamen aims his musket and opens fire without the orders of his commander. The bullet strikes one of the Seventy-Sixth's drummers in the chest. The drummer falls to the ground and cries out in pain. His fellow comrades help him to his feet. The drummer sees the wound in his chest and faints from the pain. Members of the corps band break ranks and retreat to the rear. The Seventy-Sixth infantry marches across the bridge despite the incoming enemy fire. The bullets whiz through the air as they cross the bridge. Simon spots a line of British regulars just about one hundred yards away. Commanding the British advance guard is General Sir Phineas Riall, leading fifteen hundred regulars. He sits upon his horse as he watches the Seventy-Sixth Pennsylvania form their ranks.

Simon gives his commands as he marches the Seventy-Sixth into a battle line.

"Seventy-Sixth to the left wheel, march!"

The Seventy-Sixth wheels left as they marched within one hundred yards of the British lines. Daisy looks over at the redcoats and begins to fill with hate. Celestia grips the flint of her musket. Celestia and Simon lock eyes with each other. They both smile, for they are in love, in a relationship that began before this war. Timmy marches right with the rear ranks of the Seventy-Sixth. Simon waits to halt the Seventy-Sixth till they are in line with the redcoats' lines. Once they are in line, Simon commands his men to form their battle line.

"Seventy-Sixth Pennsylvania, take care; halt! Seventy-Sixth, right face!"

The Seventy-Sixth face toward the enemy. Both sides eye each other with extreme hate. General Riall is confused by the green coats opposite him. He has a hard time trying to spot the enemy through the tall brush. He thinks that they are Canadian green jackets. But when he notices the American flag, he knows that trouble is about to begin.

Once both sides form their ranks, they begin to fire volleys into each other. With smoothbore muskets not being as accurate as flintlock rifles, the battle tactic of that era was to have soldiers form massive battle lines. They would often stand a mere one hundred yards apart. The point of this type of warfare was to break the enemy's line. Once their lines would break or begin to buckle, horsemen or cannons could break the enemy lines. The muskets were of calibers varying from .50 to .75 and fired lead musket balls.

"Seventy-Sixth, make ready! Take aim! Fire!" Simon shouts.

First they cock the hammers of their muskets. Next they aim their muskets downrange toward the redcoats. Once the triggers are pulled, the flints strike the steel and create sparks that ignite the black powder in the flash pans, in turn igniting the powder in the barrels and firing the muskets. The Seventy-Sixth fires a volley that erupts in white smoke and sparks. Simon, Celestia, Timmy, and Daisy fire their muskets alongside their troops. The bullets rip into the British advance guard. Three dozen British soldiers are shot. A dozen British soldiers are shot and killed, while others are wounded, getting shot all over their bodies. One British ensign who had the honor of carrying the British Union Jack is shot four times in the chest. He clutches the flag as he falls to the ground. A British sergeant grabs the flag and raises it high. The banner never touches the ground. The Seventy-Sixth reload their muskets as General Riall gives his orders to return fire.

"First rank, make ready! Present! Fire!" General Riall shouts.

The first rank of the British lines fires a volley into the Seventy-Sixth. The volley cuts down twenty grenadiers of the Seventy-Sixth. Five out of the twenty are killed. Both sides begin to reload their muskets. To reload their muskets, a powder charge is poured into the muzzle. This is followed by a musket ball rammed on top. More powder is poured into the firing pan. Finally, a hammer holding a flint is cocked. Now the musket is ready to fire again. Soldiers on both sides have been trained to fire three rounds a minute. Just as both sides are about to fire another volley, the Seventy-Sixth gets reinforced by the Sixth Infantry Regiment. The Sixth marches in front of the Seventy-Sixth, and they form two battle lines. The Sixth fires a volley into the British lines. The volley cuts down more redcoats.

General Riall is horrified and surprised by the discipline of these American regular soldiers.

"Those are regulars, by God!" General Riall exclaims as he watches his men getting cut down by the soldiers wearing green and gray coats.

Soon the Ninth, Eleventh, and Twenty-Fifth arrive on the battlefield and make contact with General Riall's troops. Both sides fire volley upon volley at each other. Dozens of American and British soldiers are wounded or killed. General Riall's soldiers begin to charge down toward General Scott's lines. Unfortunately, Riall moves his men into rugged terrain. They fire upon Scott's lines again and then continue to advance forward. Simon notices that General Riall has made a massive gap on the right flank, between the end of his line and the nearby woods. Simon pulls out his spyglass and shows Celestia the gap on the right flank.

"First Lieutenant Rose, do you see what I see?" Simon asks.

"Yes, that bastard has made a critical error in his right flank. We should take advantage of this before he fills that gap with a reserve company," Celestia says.

"Keep up the fire; I will inform the general."

"Simon, be careful," she says.

Simon shoulder's his Brown Bess and ignores a volley of redcoat fire. Simon runs through the American lines, and as he is running, a few Americans are cut down by redcoat musket fire. One in a gray coat is shot and falls in front of Simon. He trips over the soldier's body and looks back at the man's face. He sees that the man was shot in the nose and that the man's nose has been blown off his face.

"Poor bastard!" Simon exclaims.

Simon stands up and continues his run to General Scott. He manages to reach General Scott and informs him of what he has discovered.

"General, the right flank is wide open, sir. Sir, may I make a suggestion?"

"What do you have in mind, Major? This better be good," Scott says, looking through his spyglass.

"General, the enemy has left a gap in their right flank, sir. If you move your men against the right flank, they will be trapped."

General Scott sees the gap in Riall's line and decides to move against him. The British charge with their bayonets toward his line. The whole regiment fires a devastating volley at the charging redcoats. The volley checks the redcoat charge, and six cannons at the American rear fire solid shot. The shells scream as they soar through the air. They explode all over the British lines and begin to tear off the redcoats' arms and legs. One redcoat catches a shell in his chest that tears right through his body. His heart, lungs, and ribs are blown out his back.

General Winfield Scott unsheathes his sword. "Regiment, prepare to advance! Charge your bayonets and advance!" The Seventy-Sixth, Ninth, Eleventh, and Twenty-Fifth advance with their bayonets. They unleash a loud and scary battle cry that stops the British advance and the British begin to retreat.

"Whoo-hoo! Those lobsters are running, my friends!" Timmy screams.

The Seventy-Sixth utter a cheer, and they charge forward with their bayonets. A few redcoats straggle behind as they try to defend themselves against cold American steel. Simon catches three redcoats off guard. He manages to bayonet the first one in the chest without any trouble. The second one swings his musket like a club. Simon ducks and thrusts his bayonet into the man's chest. Unfortunately, the redcoat grabs Simon's musket as he falls. The final redcoat tries several times to bayonet Simon, but Simon manages to dodge every blow. Simon unsheathes his American eagle sword and begins to strike back at the redcoat. With one massive swing, Simon cuts the redcoat's left hand off, and the redcoat falls to the ground. He cries out in massive pain. Simon finishes the redcoat off by stabbing him directly in the heart. Timmy regroups with Simon, and they charge into another group of fleeing redcoats. Celestia and Daisy, along with the main body of the Seventy-Sixth Pennsylvania, fire relentless volleys into the fleeing redcoats.

Celestia spots General Riall, and she turns to the Seventy-Sixth. She points her finger at the British officer. "Seventy-Sixth Pennsylvania, fire upon their commander!" Celestia shouts.

"Cut that bastard down to size!" Daisy exclaims.

The Seventy-Sixth aim their muskets, and one young British officer with General Riall's staff spots the Seventy-Sixth. The young officer rides his horse in front of General Riall to shield him from the volley.

"Open fire!" Celestia shouts.

The Seventy-Sixth fires over one hundred muskets. The volley cuts down dozens of redcoats from the First Battalion of the Eighth Foot. The young British officer shielding the general is shot seven times in the back. Four of the bullets exit the officer's body. One bullet lodges into General Riall's coat. He decides that enough is enough and, with the guns of the Eighth Foot, retreats from the field.

General Winfield Scott watches with triumph as the redcoats retreat from the field. The American regiments erupt not with musket fire but with cheering, for they know that victory is theirs. The Seventy-Sixth stand and watch as the enemy runs away. This is their first taste of a major battle during the War of 1812.

The Rose sisters hug each other, filled with gladness that they have survived.

"Daisy, I am so darn proud of you, little sister! What did I tell you? You stayed with me and followed my orders! I will always watch your back—and you will do the same, right?"

Daisy smiles at Celestia. She salutes her big sister. "Yes ma'am! You have always taken care of me, and I am very glad that you're my big sister, ma'am."

Celestia rolls her eyes with a smile on her face. Daisy holds her salute, waiting for Celestia to salute back. Celestia brings her feet together, stands up straight, and salutes.

One hundred yards up the field, Simon and Timmy are walking across the battleground. Suddenly a patch of smoke appears, and then a voice comes from within the smoke.

"Please do not shoot us; we surrender! We surrender!"

Simon and Timmy aim their muskets at the smoke.

"Emerge slowly!" Simon shouts toward the smoke. "Our muskets are loaded, so don't be stupid!"

Five British soldiers emerge from the smoke with their hands raised; they are unarmed. Simon gives the five redcoats the following commands: "Keep your hands in the air! Get down on your knees, and if you bastards move, I swear I will skewer you where you stand!"

The five redcoats obey Simon's orders. Timmy moves in to begin a search, but Simon stops him. Then he asks the five redcoats a question.

"Before we take you lot in, can my sergeant perform a search?" Simon asks the prisoners.

They all nod once, which gives Timmy the right to search them. Timmy moves to the first one and pats the redcoat down. He grabs the redcoat's bayonet and throws it toward Simon. He then grabs the redcoat's pistol and tosses it to Simon, and while Simon keeps his eyes on the five prisoners of war, Simon keeps a bit of distance by standing fifteen feet off so he can see all the prisoners. If he were to stand too close to the enemy prisoners, they could try to grab his musket or try to stab him with a melee weapon. For ten minutes, Timmy confiscates munitions pouches, bayonets, three flintlock pistols, and two sabers.

Back in the rear ranks, the Seventy-Sixth's marching band has been comforting their fallen drummer. They manage to get him on a wagon along with the rest of the wounded. Drum Major Brittany Benson, along with the rest of the corps, watches as her friend is hauled to the rear. Brittany sheds a tear but wipes it off, and the color guard joins them. She turns to her corps and says, "Corps, reform on the colors!"

The band reforms on the color guard and prepares to regroup with the Seventy-Sixth. She blows on her whistle for three seconds. Then she blows her whistle three times.

"Hup!" the band shouts.

The band stands at attention, awaiting Brittany's command.

"Corps in cadence, mark time. Forward march!"

Brittany holds her left arm straight up, indicating to the band to start the song. The corps and the color guard march forward. Only the drums play a mid-tempo march. They march across the bridge and upon the field. They spot the Seventy-Sixth up on the field and march up the field to meet them.

Timmy gives a thumbs-up as a way of indicating the search has been completed. Simon was just about to give the prisoner's directions. But before he can speak, Celestia and Daisy bring up the Seventy-Sixth. The redcoat prisoners begin to get scared. One begins to shed a tear, and Timmy begins to harass him.

"Aw, what is the matter, lobster? Are you getting afraid that we might kill you? That all depends on you, buddy. If you listen to our orders, we will not have any right to thrust a bayonet into your tyranny-filled heart and carve it out just like a Thanksgiving turkey."

Simon walks over to Timmy. Timmy stops talking and backs off.

Simon kneels down near the redcoat and speaks to him in a calm voice. "Listen, my friend; we will not hurt you unless you try to escape. What is your name, my friend?" He pats the redcoat on the left shoulder.

The redcoat answers with a voice of pride and dignity. "Sir, my name is Corporal Brian Turner of the First Battalion, Eighth Foot. What would your name be?"

"Well, Corporal, my name is Major Simon Smithtrovich. I'm the commander of the Seventy-Sixth Pennsylvania Keystone Grenadiers. Seventy-Sixth staff, sound off!"

"First Lieutenant Celestia Rose!"

"First Sergeant Daisy Rose!"

"Sergeant Timmy Miller!"

"Drum Major Brittany Benson!"

Simon asks the Seventy-Sixth what their state motto is.

The Seventy-Sixth Pennsylvania shout out their state motto while standing at attention. "Virtue, liberty, and independence!"

The prisoners are shocked by the discipline, dedication, and loyalty of the Seventy-Sixth Pennsylvania. Simon sheaths his sword and slings his Brown Bess. He turns to his friends and the rest of the troops.

"Seventy-Sixth, we will be marching back to camp, and these prisoners will be coming with us. Now, these prisoners are not to be harmed, and if any grenadier disobeys this order, you will be court-martialed. Understand?"

"Sir, yes sir!" they shout.

Simon turns to the prisoners and gives them their orders. He then speaks to the corporal.

"Corporal, you lot will come with us, and you will not try to escape. I say again that if you try to, you will be shot. Do you understand?"

"Yes sir!" Corporal Brian Turner says.

The prisoners stand up, and their hands are tied with rope. Ten grenadiers guard them as they march back to camp. The Battle of Chippewa has ended. General Brown and Scott have suffered 61 killed and 225 wounded. Major General Phineas Riall has suffered 108 killed, 305 wounded, and 46 captured. The Seventy-Sixth Pennsylvania has suffered 10 dead and 14 wounded.

Who are the Seventy-Sixth Pennsylvania Keystone Grenadiers? The Seventy-Sixth Pennsylvania are not an ordinary military unit. They're an elite corps of special soldiers called "grenadiers." They call themselves Keystone grenadiers because they are from the Keystone State. Known as the spear tip of the US Army, they march into battle with cadence. They march with marching music playing loudly through the air. They have the best gear because they are the cream of the crop. They have the best weapons of their time and are the best-dressed soldiers on the battlefield. Their uniforms start with their headwear. They wear bearskin caps with twelve-inch green hackle plumes on the top left. On the front of each bearskin is an armor plate that displays the American eagle. The caps have chin straps so that during battle the caps will stay on their heads. A green cord is wrapped around the left side of each cap.

Their regimental coats are colored medium green with black cuffs and collar. The coats extend to the waist and have tails in the back. The pattern on the front of each coat is one of black military regulation lace, making the coats heavy on the chest and waist but light on the back. For the ranks of private to corporal, their epaulettes are a light green. For the noncommissioned officers from the rank of sergeant to sergeant major, the color of the epaulettes is medium green. For the officers from lieutenant to colonel, the color is black. The breeches are black with small amounts of green lace on the tops of the pant legs. The grenadiers also wear over-the-knee buttoned black gaiters and laced-up ankle-high boots.

The musicians wear the same uniform, but their coats are heavy on lace on the chests, from the shoulders all the way to the cuffs. Their headgear is the same, but they have dark green twelve-inch hackle plumes. When they march, whether it be on the parade grounds or into battle, they march with great discipline and passion. The sound of their march shakes the field of battle. Their snare drums sound like a constant roll of thunder. They are well armed with the best weapons.

There are five platoons that make up the whole company—the company marching band and four infantry platoons. They have been issued Brown Bess flintlock muskets. This is the longest-used firearm in British military history. Every single Keystone grenadier has fifty rounds each, issued along with a socket bayonet. The noncommissioned officers are issued sabers along with their Brown Besses. Each officer carries a

Brown Bess musket, a flintlock pistol, and a saber of thier choice. The Seventy-Sixth have even created their own regimental song, called "The Keystone Grenadiers." It is in the tune of "The British Grenadiers," which is one of Britain's most famous military marches.

July 5, 1814
9:00 p.m.

The men and women of the Seventy-Sixth Pennsylvania settle in for the night. Simon sits by the fire while he cleans the blood off of his saber. He dips a cloth into a bucket of water and begins to rub it on the blade. Water and blood drip off the cloth. He gently moves the cloth up and down the blade with easy strokes. Simon's saber is razor sharp, so he is careful that he does not cut himself. A few minutes later, Simon's sword is finally clean. He grabs his scabbard and sheathes his blade. His scabbard is made of metal. Simon feels a short burst of a summer evening breeze. He closes his eyes and smiles as he feels the wind flow right through his body as if he were a skeleton. He takes a deep breath and inhales the sweet, fresh air. He then feels a hand touching the back of his shoulder. Simon turns his head to see who was behind him. In the corner of his right eye, he sees that the hand belongs to Celestia Rose. Simon smiles at the sight of her. Not only is she the second in command of the Seventy-Sixth; she is also Simon's girlfriend. Celestia stands at attention and salutes Simon.

"Good evening, sir," Celestia says with a commanding voice.

Simon smiles, stands at attention and salutes his second in command. Celestia holds her salute. They meet each other's gaze.

"Good evening, First Lieutenant Rose," Simon replies to Celestia.

They both recover their arms, and they have a seat near the warming campfire. Celestia sits right beside Simon. Despite being soldiers in the US Army, they've a strong relationship of love that is impossible to break. No sword in the whole world could cut their love in half. Simon and Celestia enjoy each other's company.

"Celestia, how do you think the Seventy-Sixth did in battle earlier today?"

Celestia looks at the flames of the campfire. She thinks for a few moments as she tries to remember what she saw earlier in the day. Celestia finally gives her battle report to her commander.

"The Keystone grenadiers gave a flawless display of discipline and training today. They never broke from the field. They let the lobsters know that the Seventy-Sixth shall be a force to be reckoned with, this being the first major battle against British regulars."

Simon liked her answer, and then a thought hit him like a musket ball to the head.

"You're right. This was our first major battle, and it was against British regulars. That literally just crossed my mind just now that you said that," Simon says with amazement.

Celestia chuckles and wrinkles her face. She snorts and continues to chuckle. Simon laughs softly and then kisses her forehead. Celestia's cheeks blush, and she hugs Simon. Celestia pulls back and circles her right foot in the dirt, for she is flustered.

Celestia twirls her fingers for a few seconds as Simon puts another log on the fire. Simon then sits back down on the log.

"Simon, can I hug you tighter?" Celestia asks Simon with a loving tone.

Simon smiles and scooches closer to Celestia. They are so close to each other that their legs are touching. Simon grabs a blanket and wraps it around them. He then looks deep into Celestia's eyes. "Of course," he says with a welcoming tone.

Celestia wraps her arms around Simon's chest and back. She rests her head on his right shoulder, smiles, and sighs. She is so comfortable in that position. Simon puts his arm around her back and gently rubs her back. For a whole hour they sit on that log and listen to the crackling of the campfire. Celestia is so relaxed that she actually falls asleep. Simon doesn't notice for a whole half hour. When Simon finally notices that Celestia is asleep, he escorts her, partially awake, back to her tent. Simon helps her into her tent and tucks her into bed. But before Simon leaves the tent, Celestia says something to Simon that he will never forget.

"Good night, Simon. I love you," Celestia says as she yawns.

Celestia finally falls asleep. Simon kisses her on the forehead.

"Good night, Celestia. I will see you in the morning."

Simon exits the tent and heads back to sit on the log. The fire is still burning but is on its final log. Simon finds himself lost in thought. It is the first time in their relationship that Celestia has told him that she loves him. Simon doesn't know what to think about those three words Celestia just said to him. He has a blank expression upon his face. Then he recollects the facts of his past. Simon and Celestia have been dating ever since 1806. That was six years before the "War of 1812" even started. Simon finally goes to his tent. He takes his coat off, unbuttons his black over-the-knee gaiters, and unties his boots. He then lies down in his bunk and falls asleep as the other Keystone grenadiers sleep through the night. The next two days would come to characterize a war without any mercy.

July 6, 1814
8:30 a.m.

On a nice, warm summer morning, the sky is blue and everything is feeling so fine and dandy. However, the Keystone grenadiers are awakened not by the sweet singing of birds. They are awakened by the roaring of American artillery fire. Simon hears the cannons roaring like a terrible thunderstorm. He pokes his head outside and sees his Keystone grenadiers putting on their uniforms and preparing for battle. First Sergeant Daisy Rose dashes over to Simon's tent. Simon sees Daisy approaching and asks her what is happening.

"First Sergeant Rose, what the bloody hell is going on here?"

"Sir, there is a massive force of Canadian militiamen gathering at stone barricades just three miles away from here," Daisy says while trying to catch her breath. "The Seventy-Sixth, Ninth, and Eleventh Regiments are to form up and destroy the barricades. The Seventy-Sixth is ordered to destroy two barricades on the right flank, while the Ninth takes the center and the Eleventh attacks the left flank."

"Very well. Where in the world is your sister?" Simon asks Daisy.

"Sir, she is forming the company now. We are just waiting for you to take the lead."

"I will be ready in a few seconds. I need to get myself dressed. Have the company ready to march in five minutes."

"Yes sir!" Daisy says.

Simon then ducks back into his tent. He hurries to get his uniform squared away and to grab his gear. Four minutes later, he steps out of his tent and jogs to the front of the company. He reaches Celestia at the front of the column. They salute each other.

"Good morning, sir. It is quite a hectic morning so far," Celestia says.

"Yes, that it is. Are we ready to move out?" Simon asks Celestia.

"Yes sir. We are ready for the fight to come, sir. On your order, sir."

Major Simon Smitrovich gives his commands to the Seventy-Sixth.

"Seventy-Sixth Pennsylvania will prepare to march. Seventy-Sixth, to the front! Forward march!"

The Seventy-Sixth marches onward down the road. They march with their regimental colors waving in the morning breeze and their bayonets shining in the morning sun. The Seventy-Sixth has to march two and a half miles to where the American artillery is placed. The Seventy-Sixth arrives on the American right flank. From where they are standing, all they can see are two large hand-built Canadian barricades that stretch one hundred yards in length. The second barricade is about seventy yards behind the first barricade. The stone wall itself is made up of stones that are about knee high in height. The stone wall is covered with broken tree limbs and leafless bushes. The Keystone grenadiers wait for further commands from General Scott.

General Scott rides up to Major Simon Smithtrovich. Simon salutes General Scott as he approaches him.

"Major Smithtrovich, Seventy-Sixth to the front," General Scott orders. "You take your company and destroy those barricades. Once you have done that. We will march onward to their camp and destroy them as well. You will be accompanied with forty riflemen on your flanks. Godspeed and good luck."

Simon turns to his company. "Seventy-Sixth, to the front! Forward march!" The Seventy-Sixth marches past the artillery batteries and toward the enemy. The Seventy-Sixth begin to form their battle lines. Simon marches his platoon into position.

"First platoon, take care; halt!" Simon shouts.

First Lieutenant Celestia Rose forms her platoon on the left of the first platoon. Her troops form their ranks.

"Second platoon, take care; halt!" Celestia shouts.

First Sergeant Daisy Rose's third platoon marches into position on the left side of the second platoon.

"Third platoon, take care; halt!" Daisy shouts to her platoon.

Sergeant Timmy Miller's fourth platoon finally makes their final march into position. His platoon is the left flank of the battle line.

"Fourth platoon, take care; halt!" Timmy shouts to his platoon.

Finally the Seventy-Sixth Pennsylvania's Corps Marching Band marched into their spot on the battle line, at the center rear. The snare drummers are first in their ranks. The trumpeters are second in the ranks. And the fifers are last in the ranks. The American riflemen form up on the right and left flanks. The Seventy-Sixth's numbers consist of only 258 grenadiers. Their Battleline is two ranks deep. The Seventy-Sixth's own snare drummers play a slow tempo cadence. All the Keystone grenadiers can do now is wait, as soldiers do, for their next order. Celestia and Daisy stand in front of their platoons. They both look at each other. Celestia winks at Daisy. Daisy nods her head once. Drum major Benson and her corps stand and wait. Brittany pulls out a hand sized painting of her mother. She holds it in her hand and then brings it up to her lips. She kisses it and speaks under her breath.

"Mother, I love you very much. Should I die today, please take care of yourself and remember the sacrifice I made for the keystone state." Brittany puts her hand sized painting back inside her haversack.

On the enemy barricade just about 150 yards away from the Seventy-Sixth's battle line, Canadian militiamen prepare for the battle to come. Many are standing or kneeling at the barricades with their muskets aimed at the Seventy-Sixth. A group of ten Canadians are doing a last few minutes' prayer. They pray the Our Father and Hail Mary. After they finish with their prayers, they make the sign of the cross. Then they take their position at the barricade.

A French Canadian colonel up on his horse gives his orders to his countrymen. "Get to the barricade! Get to your positions! The enemy will soon be upon us."

The enemy opposing the Seventy-Sixth Pennsylvania consists of nearly four hundred men. They outnumber the Seventy-Sixth two to one. However, these Canadian militiamen are made up of citizens with little to no military training. The Keystone grenadiers, however, are well trained with the bayonet and saber. The Canadians are still confident because they outnumber the Keystone grenadiers. Only a small pocket of British regulars is at the barricade. They number thirty British regular soldiers. The Canadian militiamen have only two six-pound cannons at their disposal.

Back in the rear of the American artillery positions, American artillerymen fire one last barrage of cannon and mortar fire down upon the Canadian barricades. Some of the artillery pieces the Americans have to use is a French twenty-four-pound cannon and three thirteen-inch mortars. The shells whistle as they soar through the sky. The shells blow dirt and earth high into the air as they explode upon the ground. The sounds of the screaming shells send chills up several Canadian soldiers' backs. The Seventy-Sixth Pennsylvania waits for the clock to strike ten before they march into battle. Simon and his staff stand at the front of their platoons. Simon pulls out his pocket watch and waits for ten o'clock.

Celestia observes the enemy barricades. She sees that they are in the air. That means they are not nailed to any natural terrain. When the clock strikes ten, Simon gives his command to march against the enemy barricade. Simon takes off his bearskin cap and holds it against his chest. He looks up at the blue sky that has only a few small white clouds in it. He closes his eyes and prays.

"Dear Lord, may you keep us safe, for we are to face another foe. Keep us in your heart as we shall always keep you in ours. May we trust you to keep us safe as we commend our spirits to you now and forever. Amen."

Simon puts his bearskin cap back on his head and prepares to march his company into battle. He takes a deep breath and exhales. He then gives his commands to advance against their unseen foe.

"The Seventy-Sixth will take care to advance," Simon commands with a loud and stern tone. "Seventy-Sixth, to the front! Forward march!"

The Seventy-Sixth marches forward toward the enemy barricade. The Seventy-Sixths Corps Marching Band plays "Yankee Doodle" as they march.

The Canadian militiamen and their regulars aim their muskets as they wait for their advancing enemy to march within range. One militiaman who is just a boy aims his musket downrange. He begins to tremble with fear as if he were a jolted spring. His hands shake as if he has arthritis.

He is amazed but extremely terrified at the advancing foe. Two brothers have different feelings about the advancing American grenadiers. One is not afraid as he aims his flintlock rifle downrange; his face has an angry expression. His younger brother, who has not even reached puberty, is absolutely scared. The boy is crying softly, for he is worried for his and his brother's lives. The Canadian colonel brandishes his saber and points it at the advancing Keystone grenadiers.

"Hold your fire! Hold your fire!" the colonel shouts to his soldiers.

The Seventy-Sixth Pennsylvania is now within 110 yards of the barricade. The Canadian forces commence their defense.

"For king and country, fire at will!" the colonel shouts.

The Canadian militiamen commence firing at will. With their first shots fired, only a few Keystone grenadiers fall to the dirt. As fast as the first man is shot down, the next in the rear rank steps forward and takes his place. The Seventy-Sixth continues to march forward despite the enemy musket and artillery fire. The Canadian artillerymen fire their two six-pound cannons. The shells fly through the air and explode twenty yards from the Pennsylvania line.

Simon calls to his men, "Steady, lads! Keep your ranks!"

The American artillerymen fire another barrage of cannon and mortar upon the barricade. This time their shells find their targets. Two mortar shells pierce the middle section of the barricade. Several Canadian militiamen are blown off their feet and riddled with shrapnel. The militiamen land upon the ground in terrible agony. From the front of the American line, all that is to be seen is musket and cannon smoke that obscures the foe that inflicted the wounds upon the great beast that is the Seventy-Sixth, for every single Keystone grenadier that falls to the dirt is like a great beast shedding his own skin. But from the rear of the American line, there is a trail of dead and wounded grenadiers. A few grenadiers shudder as they try to find safety that is nowhere to be found. It is horrible for all the men and women of the Seventy-Sixth to see their friends and family fall to the ground. Nevertheless, they must press on, and now that they are fifty yards away from the barricade, it is their turn to unleash pure hell against their unseen foe.

"Seventy-Sixth, take care; halt!" Simon commands.

The riflemen take their position in front of the Pennsylvania line. They lay upon the ground, take off their shakos, and use them as bipods for their flintlock rifles. The riflemen open fire upon the barricade. Every single shot that is fired by the riflemen hits its mark. Canadian militiamen begin to get cut down. The riflemen's fire begins to make the enemy barricade buckle. But the worst is only seconds away. Simon and his staff fall in line with their platoons. They make a space for their platoon leaders to join the firing line.

"Present arms!" Simon shouts.

"Present arms!" Simon's staff shouts as they repeat to their platoons. The Keystone grenadiers poise their muskets in front of their bodies.

"Make ready!" Simon shouts.

"Make ready!" the staff repeated to their platoons. The Keystone grenadiers cock the hammers on their muskets.

"Take aim!" Simon shouts.

The front and rear ranks aim their muskets downrange.

"Fire!" Simon shouted with great energy.

The Seventy-Sixth fires a devastating volley into the enemy position. The volley cuts down 110 Canadian militiamen. The militiamen are shot all over their bodies, with wounds to their chests, legs, and heads. Half of those who are shot are killed instantly. And with one finally barrage of artillery fire, the first barricade is blown to pieces. Stone and wood explode all over the place. A British regular is showered with stones and dirt. A man behind him gets a face full of flames from an exploding shell. The man's face is burnt like an overcooked steak at a summer barbecue. He falls to the ground in severe pain. He immediately realizes that he is blind. His eyelids are severely burned from the intense heat of the explosion. He crawls upon the ground and cries out to his comrades.

"Help me! Help me, for the love of God! I'm blind! My eyes are gone! Somebody help me!"

The Canadian militiamen begin to retreat from the first barricade. However, some who attempt to run to the second barricade are cut down before they can even turn their backs. None dare to stay for their wounded or dying comrades as they flee for their own lives. The Canadian colonel brandishes his sword as he begs for his men to stand and fight.

"Remember that you're king's men! Stand your ground, lads! Stand firm!"

But none of his soldiers are even listening as they flee from the beast that fires restlessly into their lines.

Now that the Canadian forces are on the run. The Seventy-Sixth now marches forward with a bayonet charge.

"Grenadiers, advance your firearms! Charge your bayonets!" Simon shouts to his grenadiers.

"Huzzah!" the Keystone grenadiers shouted.

The Seventy-Sixth level their bayonets, waiting for the command to march forward, ready to introduce the retreating enemy to cold American steel.

"Seventy-Sixth, for virtue, liberty, and independence! Quick march!" Simon shouts to his company.

The Seventy-Sixth Corps Marching Band snare drummers play a march with a brisk tempo as the Seventy-Sixth marches forward. The riflemen stand up and run for the flanks. They march and fire into the remaining brave British redcoats. But when the smoke clears, the British redcoats decide to give up the fight. They run outside the barricade and put their hands in the air. One of the surrendering soldiers is the Canadian colonel. He thrusts his sword into the ground in front of him. His saber's grip points up toward the sky. He puts his hands up, for he doesn't want to fight anymore. Celestia looks at Simon and points at the surrendering redcoats. Simon glimpses the surrendering British soldiers. He then looks to the rear and can see the lifeless corpses of his company. Simon then meets Celestia's gaze and shakes his head from side to side. Celestia knows that Simon is ordering her that no prisoners are to be taken on this day. The British soldiers watch as the Seventy-Sixth Pennsylvania marched closer to them. Some of the facial expressions of the Keystone grenadiers show anger and pure hatred for the enemy in front of them. Simon marches forward just ten yards from his platoon. The colonel pleads for his life to be spared. He cries out to Simon to have mercy.

"We surrender! Please spare our lives! For the love of God, spare our lives!"

Unfortunately, Simon isn't listening to the colonel's plea for mercy. A few riflemen accompany Simon as if they are personal bodyguards. Simon reaches the Canadian colonel and, without a moment's hesitation, thrusts his bayonet into the heart of the enemy commanding officer. Simon thrusts the bayonet so hard that the tip of the bayonet exits out the colonel's back. Some redcoats attempt to pick up their weapons and fire at Simon, but they are all cut down by the American riflemen. Simon pulls his bayonet out of the officer's body and continues his march to the second barricade. The remains of the Canadian militiamen from the first barricade stand with their brothers. There they prepare for the final stand against the Seventy-Sixth Pennsylvania. The Keystone grenadiers march on past the first barricade. All around them are the lifeless and grisly remains of the enemy that attempted to resist them. The Seventy-Sixth soon reaches the second barricade, and many of the Canadians begin to retreat.

"Retreat!" one militiaman cries out.

"Run for your lives!" a second one screams as he is shot in the back.

"For the love of God, it's a bloody massacre!" a third militiaman screams out.

Some brave Canadian militiamen make a final attempt to stand, firing against the Seventy-Sixth, but it has no effect against the beast. The Seventy-Sixth crashes into the second barricade and begins to cut the enemy down with bayonets. Many of the Canadian militiamen have not been issued bayonets, leaving them defenseless in close-quarters combat. Many Canadian soldiers are bayoneted in their attempts to resist the Seventy-Sixth. The remaining Canadian soldiers retreat from the field in defeat. As the shattered militiamen run, the Seventy-Sixth halt in their positions. They all begin to cheer in jubilation, not only for their survival but also for victory against an enemy that outnumbered them two to one. The whole Canadian force has been beaten back. The battle is finally over.

July 6, 1814
11:00 a.m.

After one hour of intense and bitter combat, The United States is the victor. While the Keystone grenadier's loot the bodies of the Canadian militia, the staff of the Seventy-Sixth discuss the battle report. The staff sit upon the stone wall of the second barricade.

"First platoon losses are two dead and six wounded," Simon says.

Celestia then gives her battle report. "Second platoon losses are one dead and five wounded, sir."

"Third platoon suffered zero dead and four wounded, sir," Daisy says.

"Fourth platoon losses are two dead and zero wounded, sir," Timmy says.

"Sir, my corps are all accounted for, sir," Brittany says with a hint of relief.

Simon adds up the losses in his mind. Then he gives the final report to his staff.

"I have the final tally. Five are dead, and fifteen wounded. We have twenty casualties in total. Since there are five dead, we are going to each write a letter to the family of one of the dead. I want those letters on my desk before dinnertime."

"Yes sir!" the staff say to Simon.

The Seventy-Sixth reforms their ranks, and they load the dead and wounded onto two wagons. The Seventy-Sixth begin their march back to their encampment. No songs or music are played during the whole march, according to their tradition that should any of their comrades die in battle, no words are to be spoken and no music is to be played. This is their way of showing respect for the men and women who gave their lives to uphold their state's motto and to fight for their nation's freedom.

The Seventy-Sixth arrive back at their encampment just one hour later. Many go to clean their uniforms, clean their muskets, and cook their lunches, though many don't have an appetite for they were just on the field of battle. Simon and his staff each write a letter to a family of one of their dead comrades. Throughout the rest of the day, the Keystone grenadiers rest, for they know that the next battle will happen again at any moment. The Battle of the Stone Barricade was their calling card. It was not the last time the Canadian militiamen would face the Seventy-Sixth Pennsylvania. For many of the Canadian militiamen, it was their final battle.

July 7, 1814
Early morning

In the predawn hours of July 7, 1814, Simon was in his tent studying a map of the terrain. He is waiting for information regarding where the enemy encampment was. Despite his company being outnumbered and miles away from the main body of the US army, he intends to attack the enemy. But with what, and where at? Every single avenue leads to a road called Portage Road. It leads to an intersection called Lundy's Lane. Simon has a feeling in the pit of his gut that the turnpike leads to an open field. The field is a great piece of land for a large military force to encamp. The turnpike is concealed, making it a great option to lead a force to encircle the open field.

First Lieutenant Celestia Rose enters Simon's tent. She notices he has his eyes glued to the map. She sits down right on his bunk and speaks to him.

"Good morning, sir," she says.

Simon looks up and jumps. He holds his chest with his hand.

"Good God, Celestia, you scared me. I didn't even hear you enter my tent," he says with a laugh.

Celestia puts her arm around Simon's back. Simon continues to look at the map.

"What are you looking at, sir?" Celestia asks.

"I am trying to figure where those Canucks made their encampment. Last reports have them spotted up near this Portage Road. Then they just suddenly vanished. But everything keeps leading me to this turnpike that leads to an open field. It is about a half mile wide, and it would be a great place for an army to make camp. I sent Sergeant Miller to scout the turnpike just one hour ago. I sure hope he can find the location of the camp."

"Sir, I was actually coming here to tell you that the two companies of marines will be joining our camp, compliments of General Winfield Scott."

Simon looks up at Celestia with a look that only Celestia knows. Simon smiles at her with a pumped-up facial expression.

"I know that look. That is your pumped-up face. You have a plan, don't you?"

Simon nods. He then turns to the map and begins to discuss a risky plan with Celestia.

"If my suspicions are correct, we will march the Seventy-Sixth and the marines up Portage Road. Then we will split our forces in two. You and your sister will take your platoons to the southern edge of the camp. Sergeant Miller will take his platoon and attack from the north. Marine company number one will aid Sergeant Miller's platoon, while my platoon will attack from the west. Marine company number two will attack from the east. We will encircle them like a tightening noose."

Celestia is impressed with the strategy, but she is not so sure what the enemy fortifications are like. Just then they hear a horse rider approaching their tent. Celestia and Simon both run outside. They see Timmy reporting back from his scouting mission. Sergeant Timmy Miller dismounts from his horse and reports to Major Smithtrovich.

"Sir, by the living God, you were right about the turnpike. The enemy encampment is at the end of the turnpike. The whole Canuck force is encamped at the open field. They are vulnerable if we have numbers to encircle them."

Simon steps forward and grabs Timmy and gives him a brotherly hug. They both laugh. Timmy has done his job well.

"This is the best news I have ever heard in months. Now, once the marines arrive, we can move the whole regiment against those Canucks. First Lieutenant Rose, get the troops up and have them cook their breakfast. Sergeant Miller, you have done a great job. Both of you get some coffee and ready your meals. The marines will be arriving within two hours. Move it!"

"Yes sir!" Celestia and Timmy shout.

Celestia starts to wake up all the grenadiers. All the Keystone grenadiers wake up and prepare their breakfasts. Many of the grenadiers made musket balls and shine their bayonets. They clean their uniforms and make sure they have all their gear squared away for the attack to come.

July 7, 1814
7:00 a.m.

Just two hours later, the US Marines, under the command of Colonel Francis Peterson, arrive at the Seventy-Sixth's encampment. They march into the camp with fifes and drums filling the air with beautiful music. However, their presence as they march is very intimidating. Drum Major Brittany Benson and her corps are interrupted when they see the US Marines marching toward them. Brittany sees Colonel Peterson up on his horse, but she then looks behind him and sees a young drum major twirling his mace. Brittany's heart begins to race, for she becomes quickly attracted to that young man. The marines halt their march.

"Marines, take care; halt!" Colonel Peterson shouts to his men.

He dismounts from his horse. One of the marines holds his horse as he dismounts. Colonel Peterson then walks over to Drum Major Benson.

Brittany quickly orders her corps to attention.

"Corps, ten hut!" Brittany commands.

"Hup!" her corps shouts in unison.

Brittany salutes Colonel Peterson, and he salutes back. Brittany introduces herself and her corps to Colonel Peterson.

"Welcome to our encampment, sir. I am Drum Major Benson; I am the leader of the Seventy-Sixth's Elite Company Corps Marching Band."

"It is a great honor to meet you all. But we can have more time to chat later. Can you please tell me where your commander's tent is located?"

"Yes sir. Just six tents on the right side, sir. He will be expecting you, sir."

"Thank you, Drum Major."

Colonel Peterson walks away to go talk to Major Smithtrovich. Brittany watches Colonel Peterson walk away, and when she looks forward again, the marine drum major is right in front of her. The young man speaks to Brittany.

"Hello there. I am Drum Major Ivan Mattson. If I had ever seen such a beautiful face as yours, I would know your name. May I ask what a wonderful angel such as you be called?" Ivan said with a French accent.

Brittany hesitates as she giggles for a few seconds. Brittany then shakes her head as a way to get her mind straight. She introduces herself to Ivan.

"Excuse me; ahem. My name is Brittany Benson."

"It's nice to meet you Brittany, but please call me Ivan."

Brittany's eye twitches and she holds her head. She faints, but Ivan catches her in his arms. Brittany is completely out cold. Ivan asks Brittany's corps for help.

"Can one of you help me out, please?"

Just then Daisy runs over and sees that Brittany is out cold.

"Oh dear. I will take her. Just a bit of information—if Brittany faints on you, she thinks you're cute."

Ivan's eyes are wide open. He is flattered by the fact that Brittany has a crush on him.

Daisy and a few other members of the Seventy-Sixth's corps band carry Brittany to her tent. As they are carrying Brittany, Brittany is giggling and muttering under her breath. "That soldier was so cute. So handsome! He looks like a royal prince, and I would love to be his princess any day."

Daisy and the members get Brittany to her tent and lay her down on her bunk. Daisy and the band members exit the tent. Daisy then speaks to the band members.

"You three guard her until she is better. She is going through a lovestruck phase again."

"Yes ma'am. With all due respect, ma'am, you should get to that war meeting."

Daisy rushes to Simon's tent, and when she enters, the meeting is already underway. She joins in just as Simon begins to discuss the battle plan with the rest of the staff.

"We have a chance to end the Canadian resistance today, thanks to my scout, Sergeant Timmy Miller. He discovered the location of the enemy encampment. Their numbers were cut in half at the barricade battle yesterday. We showed them that they couldn't beat us when they had the numbers. Now we can show them how it feels to be outnumbered and outgunned."

Major Simon Smithtrovich turns his attention to Colonel Peterson. He begins to discuss the matter of ranks because Peterson is a colonel and Simon a major.

"Colonel Peterson, I know that you are a higher rank."

Before Simon can finish speaking, Colonel Peterson wants to state something right off the bat.

"I know I am a higher-ranking officer, but this is your plan. I will follow the battle plan. But I want to be very clear on this important fact: no one commands my marines except me. Do I make myself clear?"

"Yes sir. I understand crystal clear, sir. Now let us get down to business. Colonel Peterson, You and your marines will attack from the east and from the north. Sergeant Miller will aid in your attack from the north. Your second company will attack from the west, and my platoon will aid on the western flank. Now, First Lieutenant and First Sergeant Rose, your platoons will attack from the south. The main objective is to prevent them from escaping from either flank. We will then begin to tighten the grip on the camp just like a noose. Now, how many soldiers do we have?"

"My marines are numbered at two hundred men for each company. That makes our grand total at four hundred marines."

Simon smiles and then tries to remember how many grenadiers they have fit for battle. He pulls out his muster roll and adds up the number of grenadiers.

"We have two hundred fifty grenadiers. So that adds up to six hundred fifty grenadiers and marines that will take part in this attack."

"Permission to speak, sir?" Sergeant Miller asks.

"Permission granted," Simon says.

"Sir, in the middle of the camp there is a large white brick mansion with white columns right here."

Timmy places his finger upon the map that displays the open ground.

"The mansion is called the Miller House."

Simon then looks at Timmy with confusion. Timmy puts his hand over his face and sighs.

"Why in the world would it be called that unless … Sergeant Miller, is there something you are not telling me?" Simon says with a puzzled tone.

Sergeant Miller hesitates to speak as he looks down at the map. He then finally explains what he is hiding from the rest of the staff. And it is a very personal matter.

"This is my family plantation. My family owns this bloody land. We have owned it ever since 1782. When my father resigned his commission in the American regulars, he recovered this land and this house from a loyalist family."

Simon finally knows the reason why this attack is so personal to Sergeant Timmy Miller. Simon walks over to Timmy and reassures him that they will help him get his family's land back.

"Don't worry, Sergeant. We will help you in this battle. By all the things that are great and holy, we will help you get your home back. We will leave your home untouched."

Timmy smiles and hugs his best friend. He then says with a stern voice to his best friends, "Let's go kill these sons of bastards!"

Just fifteen minutes later, the American coalition of grenadiers and marines begins the ten-mile march to the Portage Road turnpike. The whole regiment moves out in silence with no marching music being played. The only sounds in the column are the sounds of marching boots. This is a very secret mission, and if the Canadians were to get a sight of the American Regiment, the plan would fail. But amazingly, the Canadian militiamen yet again have made another serious mistake. No scouts were ever sent to see if any enemy columns were coming to attack the camp. Once again, the boldness of the Americans is augmented by the foolishness of the Canadians.

July 7, 1814
11:45 a.m.

After four hours of marching through the lower Canadian countryside, the American regiment reaches its separation point at the turnpike. Once there, Colonel Peterson and Major Smithtrovich begin to deploy their companies. Simon gives the word to deploy.

"All right, we're taking back our territory! Grenadiers, marines— action stations!" Simon shouts to his staff and the marine NCOs.

With those words being said, the whole regiment begins to move silently down the turnpike that leads to the Canadian positions. The unsuspecting Canadian militiamen were cooking their lunches or engaged in rest and relaxation activities. The officers were discussing future battle plans inside the drawing room of the Miller House. From the highest-ranking officer to the lowest sentry never even knew about the hellish Colemanite that was about to befall them. Simon gets his platoon into position on the fringe of the trees. They have a clear view of the western side of the camp. Celestia and Daisy get their platoons into position. Sergeant Miller, along with his platoon and a platoon of the US Marines, gets into position as well. Colonel Peterson, along with his main body of his companies, gets into position. Within ten minutes, the whole American regiment is in position to attack the enemy camp. The American grenadiers and marines number six-hundred and fifty, while the Canadian militia number fewer than two hundred. Simon's platoon is to initiate the attack from their position on the western side of the camp. The first part of the battle plan is for Simon's platoon to draw the enemy fire. Once they have done so, Celestia and Rose's second and third platoons will open fire from their position. Then Sergeant Miller's fourth platoon will attack from the north. Then, once the Canadians realize that they are surrounded from the front, left, and right flanks, the enemy will begin to retreat, but that is when the marines will launch their attack. The Canadians will be surrounded on all sides.

Each of the American platoons has two snare drummers. All platoons are now in place, and the time to attack is only seconds away. Major Smithtrovich turns his head and looks at the snare drummers. Simon puts his left hand up and then waves it down. That is their signal to play a drum roll.

The roll is so loud that it is heard from inside the Canadian camp. Many Canadian militiamen hear the roll and spring from their tents. Some stand trying to listen and find out where the snare drum roll is coming from. One sentry hears from where it is coming from. The sentry screams and points his finger at the western side of the camp.

"To arms! To arms! The enemy is in the brush! Western flank! Western flank!"

A few of the militiamen grab their muskets and rush to the western flank of the camp. But before the Canadian militiamen knew what was upon them, Simon's platoon emerges from the brush and unleashes a devastating volley. The sentries that are in front of the western edge of the camp are instantly cut down before they can even fire a shot. Musket balls riddle the tents, and some of the Canadians that are still in their tents are shot. The tents are splattered with blood and flesh.

The Canadian militia rushes over to the western flank. They manage to fire a volley of their own. But they are soon riddled with another volley. When Canadian militiamen at the southern edge of the camp tumble out of their tents and grab their muskets, Celestia's and Daisy's platoons open fire upon them. A bugler sounds the call to arms. When the volley is fired, a musket ball shoots the bugle out of the man's hand, and he is shot in the left ear. Many more militiamen are cut down by the volley. Musket balls riddle the tents, and some musket balls even hit the columns of the Miller House. One Canadian militiaman is shot in the neck after a musket ball bounces off one of the columns. The Canadian militiamen are in complete and total chaos. None of them know what is happening. Some even try to run for the northern flank of the camp, toward the turnpike. Unfortunately, they are met with a volley by Sergeant Miller's fourth platoon. They volley cuts down over fifty Canadian militiamen within seconds. The main body of the Canadian militiamen begins to retreat into the mansion. They now know they are overrun by the Seventy-Sixth and the US Marines. Simon and his staff emerge from cover and charge toward the camp with bayonets drawn. A few Canadian units bravely manage to make a stand, but their flanks are soon overlapped, and they start to head for the rear. Only a platoon of twenty Canadian militiamen manages to take cover in the mansion, while the rest run for their lives to the eastern flank of the camp. As they are retreating, many of the militiamen fire backward at the advancing enemy that is nipping at their heels. A few militiamen fire back randomly and accidently shoot their own men. Thirty Canadian militiamen manage to escape, so they think. They take cover in the underbrush of the eastern flank of the camp. They think that they are safe until they hear muskets being cocked behind them. They turn around, and without a moment's hesitation, Colonel Peterson's marines open fire. The thirty militiamen are unable to fire a single shot or even have a chance to surrender. Colonel Peterson moves his marines out of the brush, and they rejoin the rest of the regiment. The whole regiment regroups as they begin to surround the mansion.

July 7, 1814

12:15 p.m.

The Miller Mansion

The situation is now very critical for the twenty Canadian militiamen hiding inside the mansion. They are now surrounded by over six hundred American soldiers. Simon regroups with Colonel Peterson just one hundred yards away from the mansion.

"Colonel Peterson, the last of the Canucks, are hiding in the mansion. We must smoke them out without causing any damage to my friends' home."

Colonel Peterson looks at the mansion and knows that the regiment is faced with a difficult task.

"I understand. But those bastards are dug in by now. We may have to level the mansion to get them out."

Sergeant Timmy Miller then runs over, and he overhears what Colonel Peterson is saying. He then begins to yell at the colonel. Timmy gets right up in Colonel Peterson's face.

"With all due respect, sir, if you even so much as put one cannonball inside my home, then I will put one in you!" Timmy screams threateningly.

Simon restrains Timmy and pushes him away.

"Sergeant Miller, that is enough! Just cool down. I gave you my word that your home will still be intact. We will give them a chance to surrender, but if they decide to resist even more. Then you will take your platoon and storm the house."

"Very well then," Timmy says as he walks back to his platoon.

A few minutes later, Colonel Peterson attempts to ask the remaining Canadian militiamen to surrender. Colonel Peterson stands out in the open at the front of the mansion. He begins to scream at the enemy inside the mansion. And while he is trying to ask them to surrender, a Canadian rifleman takes aim through an open window on the third floor.

"You inside the mansion, listen to this. You are completely surrounded! Please save yourselves! There is no further need for more bloodshed! Throw down yourselves and throw down your arms! Come out! You need to surrender! Surrender now!"

The Canadian rifleman aims and fires at Colonel Peterson. Colonel Peterson is shot in the chest. He cries out in pain as he falls onto the ground. His fellow marines are stunned and horrified. The rest of the Canadian militiamen open fire upon their attackers. A few US Marines try to run to their commander but are cut down before they can reach him. Sergeant Timmy Miller has finally had enough. He shouts to his platoon and the marines under his command to attack. He grabs his saber and utters a loud and scary battle cry.

"Kill those Canuck bastards! Take no prisoners!"

Sergeant Miller's fourth platoon fires a volley at the windows of the mansion. Timmy now has complete disregard for the destruction of his property. All he cares about now is smoking the enemy out of his home. The fourth platoon charges down the pathway that leads to the front door of his home. The battle cries send major chills up the spines of the remaining Canadian militiamen that are still inside. These Canadian militiamen know deep down in their hearts that they are going to die—but not before they spill more American blood.

Simon sees Sergeant Miller and his platoon charge at the mansion. "Cover Sergeant Miller, lads. Aim for the open windows!"

Soon the whole field that surrounded the mansion is obscured with musket smoke. Hundreds of musket balls strike the walls of the mansion. Inside, the Canadian militiamen make their final stand. Many struggle to return fire because every single time they attempt to fire, a bullet almost hits them when they peek out. Celestia's and Daisy's platoons fire upon five Canadian militiamen that are sniping at them from the third floor. One Canadian militiaman aims his musket but exposes his chest and head. As he fires his musket, he is riddled by a volley. He takes three musket balls to the chest and one to the head. The militiaman falls out the window and lands on the ground below. He was dead before his body hit the dirt. Sergeant Miller and his grenadiers manage to get to the front door of the mansion. They back themselves against the wall so they do not get shot from the floors above. Timmy prepares his men to storm the mansion.

"Follow my lead, grenadiers. They are up on the third floor. They will expect us to take the main stairs, but there is a secret passage to the third floor. I want the first squad to guard the main stairwell. I will take the second squad to the secret passage. Once you hear the sound of dying Canucks, storm the stairwell and join us on the top floor. Understood?"

"Yes, Sergeant!" Miller's grenadiers say.

Sergeant Miller takes the second squad, and they slowly enter the mansion through the front door. One by one, they enter the mansion's main lobby. When they first enter, they do not spot any enemy militiamen. Then Timmy decides to take the whole platoon up the stairs. They move slowly, step-by-step, checking all corners upon the stairs. Their bayonets are fixed, and soon they manage to walk up the stairs to the second floor. Sergeant Miller's platoon benefited from the musket fire covering the sound of their footsteps.

Just as they begin to cross through a long corridor, a lone Canadian soldier comes charging at Sergeant Miller. Timmy calmly kneels down and takes aim with his Brown Bess. He breathes normally and shoots down the charging enemy soldier. The soldier falls to the floor with a mortal wound to his chest. Timmy stands up and leads his grenadiers on through the hallway. As they march on past the dying Canadian soldier, the Canadian militiaman is coughing up blood, his wound spewing out blood like a water hose. One Keystone grenadier decides to put the man out of his misery, and he bayonets the Canadian in his heart. With one strike to the heart, the Canadian soldier is dead in seconds. The grenadier recovers his bayonet and rejoins his platoon.

Sergeant Miller and his platoon soon reach the secret stairwell. Timmy moves a painting down, and it reveals a wooden door.

One grenadier is amazed by the secret door. "Sergeant Miller, where do I get one of those for my home?" he says.

Timmy chuckles softly. He then opens the door and answers the question. "I do not know. When my father reclaimed this place, it actually came with it." He then speaks to all the others. "Now, only two will go at a time. Wait ten seconds, and then another two will go up. It is tighter than a lobster's purse in there."

Timmy's grenadiers laugh and commence their sneak attack. They move up the staircase—a spiral made up of twenty steps. They move one step at a time, trying to be as quiet as can be. Timmy is confident that his plan will work, but on the other hand he is hoping in his heart that he is not going to walk his grenadiers into a trap. Sergeant Timmy Miller and a fellow grenadier reach the door that leads to the third floor. He looks through a crack and is shocked to see several Canadian militiamen just fifteen feet from the door. Timmy makes the sign of the cross, and they prepare to breach the door.

A grenadier puts his hand on Sergeant Miller's right shoulder and pats it. "On your lead, Sergeant," the grenadier whispered to Timmy.

Timmy looks at the grenadier and puts his hand out. They shake hands, and then the grenadier hands Sergeant Miller a grenade. Timmy then lights the fuse and quickly opens the door so he can toss the grenade into the room. It rolls right between three Canadian militiamen. They do not have any time to react. The grenade explodes, and they are blown off their feet and out the windows. Their bodies land upon the ground outside. Sergeant Miller and his platoon stormed the third floor and spread out. The remaining Canadian militiamen are overwhelmed by the Keystone grenadiers. Close-quarters combat begins; both sides fire at each other with their muskets almost touching. Sergeant Miller runs into his own bedroom and sees a Canadian soldier reloading his musket. He tries to sneak up on him, but when he takes a third step, the floor creaks and the enemy soldier turns around. He sees Timmy and charges him with his bayonet. Timmy is able to dodge the blow and manages to throw the Canadian off balance. The enemy soldier lands on his back. The force of the fall stuns him just long enough for Timmy to bayonet him. Timmy bayonets the Canadian soldier three times in the chest. The Canadian soldier cries out in pain and agony. Then Timmy finishes his enemy off with a bayonet thrust to his forehead. Timmy can actually hear the blade pierce the soldier's skull with a crunching sound. Timmy then recovers his bayonet and picks up the Canadian and throws him outside the window.

On the outside, Simon sees the Canadian militiaman fly out the window. Simon then speaks to himself in his own mind. *"Good lord! Sergeant Miller sure has no mercy. I actually feel bad for those Canadians."*

After ten more minutes of close-quarters combat, the last of the Canadian militiamen have been killed. The Miller Mansion has been liberated for a second time in its history. A Keystone grenadier brings forward their regimental flag to Sergeant Miller. They take the flag onto the balcony above the entrance of the mansion. Some grenadiers and US Marines are still firing upon the mansion. Simon spots Sergeant Miller and orders for the regiment to stop firing.

"Seventy-Sixth Pennsylvania, cease fire! Cease fire!" Simon shouts.

The rest of the staff begin to repeat the same order to stop firing.

"Second platoon, hold your fire! Cease fire!" Celestia shouts to her platoon.

"Third platoon, Cease fire! The mansion is ours! Stop firing!" Daisy shouts to her own platoon.

The whole regiment ceases firing. Sergeant Miller brings their colors forward, and one Keystone grenadier tosses the British Union Jack flag from the balcony. He replaces it with their flag. Timmy's platoon stands upon the balcony and begins to cheer, for victory was theirs. The whole American regiment began to cheer loudly, for the battle was won and was also over. Drum Major Ivan Mattson and several US Marines bring a wagon forward and place their commander upon the wagon. They put a blanket over his body. Simon walks over to Drum Major Mattson and expresses his condolences for the loss of their commander.

"Drum Major Mattson, I am very sorry for the loss of Colonel Peterson."

They shake hands.

"Thank you, Major. Colonel Peterson was the finest officer we have ever had the privilege to serve under."

"How about your losses?" Simon asks Ivan.

"Sir, Colonel Peterson was the only one killed. We have thirty-five wounded."

First Lieutenant Celestia Rose runs over to give their tally of the dead and wounded.

"Sir, I have the tally. We only have five dead, times eight wounded. However, out of the forty wounded, we only have one that is severely wounded. One corporal lost his left eye."

Simon then begins to speak, but Celestia cuts him off because there is a problem.

"Sir, the corporal does not want to be sent home. He says that he can still fight. He wishes to talk to you in person, sir."

Celestia then takes Simon over to the wounded grenadier. He is being treated by two other Keystone grenadiers. They are holding a cloth over his shattered eye socket. Blood is dripping off the cloth. Simon and Celestia reach the wounded corporal. Simon begins to speak to the corporal. The corporal sees his commanding officers out of the corner of his right eye. He makes an attempt to stand up but is forced back down by his brothers who are treating him.

"Corporal, do not stand up. Now, what is this about you not wanting to be sent back to Pennsylvania?"

"Sir, I may have lost an eye, but I am still able to stand on the field of battle."

"Corporal, if you have had a wound that was able to be treated very easily, then I would say yes. But in your case, I am sorry. You will be sent home. But your good deeds and your blood that was shed here will never be forgotten."

But the corporal is not willing to lose this argument. He forces himself up onto his feet and begins to yell at Simon, trying to show his commander that he still has the willpower and strength to fight.

"You are not sending me home! Why in the hell are you going back on your damned word? You said to all of us, and I quote, 'The only time a Keystone grenadier should ever exit the battleground is when he is victorious or when that soldier makes the ultimate sacrifice knowing that he or she has done his or her duty to uphold the motto of Pennsylvania.' End quote. If you send me home, sir, then you are going back on your own damn word, sir. Are you going to abandon your word, or are you going to let me stay, sir?" the corporal shouts.

Celestia then begins to get angry with the corporal. She raises her voice to him. "You do not question the orders of your commanding officer, Corporal! You are way out of line!" she says with an angry tone in her voice.

Simon puts his hand up in front of Celestia. She stops yelling and retires two paces. Simon puts his arm down and walks over to the corporal without saying a word. He looks at the wound and he makes up his mind.

"You're right, Corporal," Simon says. "A true grenadier will continue to fight for a just cause until he dies on the field. You have just shown me that despite having a horrible wound, you are still willing to fight, not only for the commonwealth of Pennsylvania but also for the land that we call the United States of America. Therefore, I am giving you permission to stay and continue your military career." The corporal hugs Simon, who hugs him back. They salute each other. Simon begins to walk back. "You have heart, Corporal; I will be keeping my eye on you," Simon says with a joking tone.

The corporal laughs despite being in moderate pain.

"Har-har! That is very funny, sir!" the corporal says in a sarcastic tone.

Simon and Celestia regroup, and Simon gives his next orders to Celestia.

"First Lieutenant Rose, have our men begin to bury what remains of these Canucks. I want them to be buried on the northern flank of the camp. Just because they are the enemy, we will not dishonor them by not giving them a proper burial."

"Yes sir. I will have the company start burying them at once. Will we be encamped here for the night?"

"Yes, have the marines start gathering all the necessaries and supplies for both our companies: food, water, dry clothes, ammo, muskets, bayonets—everything! I will help out with that as well."

"Yes sir!" Celestia replies.

Throughout the rest of the day, The Keystone grenadiers and the US Marines scavenge any military supplies that they can find throughout the camp. They manage to find a lot of supplies that they need: fresh food, dry clothes, and ammunition stores of musket balls, cannonballs, and over fifty barrels of gunpowder. On the side, the US Marines and the Seventy-Sixth bury what is left of the Canadian militiamen. Major Smithtrovich and his staff help bury the dead right beside their own grenadiers. It takes almost till midnight to finally clean up the whole camp. After a long, hard day of marching and battling against a tough and determined enemy force, the Seventy-Sixth and their marine allies can finally rest. For the rest of the week, the Seventy-Sixth and the US Marines relax. They wait until General Winfield Scott arrives with his army. The US Army waits for their marching orders, and when those orders finally arrive, they will be marching into one of the bloodiest battles of the War of 1812.

CHAPTER 3

A TERRIBLE NIGHT FOR OFFICERS

Battle of Lundy's Lane
July 25, 1814
Early afternoon
Niagara Falls, Canada

The battle begins in the early afternoon when General Scott and the First Brigade advance upon the redcoats. Then the Royal Artillery fires upon the First Brigade. The shells explode all over the First Brigade. Dozens of American soldiers are struck by the shells. A few shells kill a dozen packed bodies in one blast. When the shells burst, grass, dirt, and fire are blown into the faces of the American forces. The First Brigade suffers mild losses, and General Scott sends the Twenty-Fifth Regiment to the right flank on a flanking maneuver. The Twenty-Fifth has found a disused pathway that leads to the Eighth King's Regiment and the Upper Canada Incorporated Militia Battalion. Both units are redeploying their lines and are completely unaware of what is about to hit them. The Twenty-Fifth forms a massive battle line, and they unleash a devastating volley of musket fire. Bullets tear into the Eighth King's Regiment. Eighty-five redcoats are cut down by the volley. Redcoats are shot all over their bodies. A young royal ensign trying to rally his men is shot three times in the chest. He falls off his horse only to have a cannonball strike him. The upper portion of his body is blown to pieces. The first rank begin to reload their muskets as the second rank take aim and fire a second volley. The second volley erupts, and the bullets

42

cut down more British and Canadian soldiers. Members of the Eighth begin to panic, but the commander of the regiment, Major Thomas Evans, dismounts from his horse and rallies the men.

"Hold your ranks! Stand! Prime and load your arms and fix bayonets!" Major Evans shouts.

The Eighth reform and dress their lines. They load their muskets and fix their bayonets. The Twenty-Fifth march forward with their bayonets at the ready. The Twenty-Fifth march to within range, and the Eighth return fire. The volley cuts down fifty-seven Twenty-Fifth regulars. One American regular is shot in the chest, and he falls back and his head is pierced by the bayonet of a regular right behind him. The bayonet pierces the skull, and the blade comes out of his forehead. The regular sees his friend's head on his bayonet, drops the musket, and falls to his knees. He throws up, and the second he looks up, he gets shot directly in the right eye.

The Eighth Regiment tries to reload, but the Twenty-Fifth charges into them with bayonets. Several British soldiers are bayoneted in their chests. One British redcoat is bayoneted by three American soldiers at the same time. Both sides are mixed together in hand-to-hand combat for ten minutes, until the Eighth Regiment begins to break and run. Then Major Thomas Jesup sends Captain Ketchum's light infantry to secure the junction at Lundy's Lane. General Phineas Riall tries to rally his men, but Captain Ketchum's men fire upon General Riall and his men. The volley checks General Riall's units, and he is also wounded in the process. He is shot in the arm as he is trying to ride to the rear. General Riall falls off his horse. His cavalry commander, Captain William Hamilton Merritt, tries to bring General Riall back to the lines. Suddenly they both have over a dozen American muskets and bayonets pointed at their faces. The two redcoats surrender without a hassle. The Twenty-Fifth takes them prisoner, along with hundreds of other wounded and redcoat messengers.

As the Battle of Lundy's Lane rages on, a company of the First Royal Scots Grenadiers under the command of two British captains, Captain William Brereton and Captain Alex Kurt, are marching their men toward a small patch of trees surrounded by a ring of green bushes. Cannon shells explode in the air, leaving white patches of smoke. The Royal Scots march to within fifty yards of the trees and bushes, but they have a hard time spotting anything, owing to the smoke from the cannon fire. What they do not know is that the Seventy-Sixth Pennsylvania is hiding in the patch of trees and thick bushes. The Seventy-Sixth's staff stand together and watch as the Royal Scots march into range. The Seventy-Sixth aim their muskets slowly through the brush toward the redcoats. They cock the hammers of their muskets. Simon aims at a British lieutenant up on a gray horse. Celestia aims at a British sergeant major. Daisy and Timmy aim at the two captains' horses.

Simon speaks quietly to Celestia and Timmy. "Pass the word: no one will fire except on my order."

Timmy and Celestia pass the order to both the right and left flanks.

"Wait for the order to fire," Timmy says

"Hold your fire. Wait for the command," Celestia whispers to her platoon.

The Seventy-Sixth waits for Simon to give the order. They stay as still and silent as the grass upon the land. Suddenly three redcoats break ranks and walk over to the brush. Simon pulls the barrel of his musket back into the brush, but a twig that is stuck between the muzzle and the ramrod snaps. The redcoat hears the twig snap and looks deeper into the brush. Suddenly the redcoat spots Simon's barrel, and Simon gives the order to fire.

"Fire!" Simon shouts.

Simon fires into the face of the redcoat. The brush erupts with white smoke and a thunderous roar of musket fire. The volley cuts down over fifty redcoats. Celestia fires at the British officer on the gray horse, hitting him directly in the throat. He grabs his neck as the blood spills out like water from a spigot. He falls off his horse while he holds his throat. The blood slips right between his fingers. He rolls on the ground like a log as he gasps for air.

Timmy's and Daisy's shots find their marks. Captain Kurt and Captain Brereton have their horses shot from underneath them. They fall to the ground but quickly get up on their feet.

Captain Kurt brandishes his sword. "First Regiment, dress your ranks and return fire!"

"First Company, make ready! Take aim! Fire!" Captain William Brereton orders.

The Royal Scots fire into the trees, but the redcoats aim a little high, sending a volley over the heads of the Seventy-Sixth. The Seventy-Sixth reload their muskets within fifteen to twenty seconds. They aim and fire a second volley. This volley is enough to make a few of the British grenadiers begin to break and run while the rest stand firm. Simon brandishes his own sword and gives his famous order: "Stand up, Keystone grenadiers! For virtue, liberty, independence, and for the Keystone State! Charge those sons of bastards!"

The Seventy-Sixth utters a loud, bloodcurdling battle cry as they charge out of the brush with bayonets fixed and ready for use. The First Regiment fills with fear and terror as the rest begin to panic and run. Only a small handful of British grenadiers hold their ground. One British officer faces down Simon with his saber. They clash with their swords. Celestia and Daisy fight back-to-back, bayoneting redcoats left and right. Timmy sits with a few other Keystone grenadiers, and they pick off retreating redcoats. One redcoat hiding in the smoke spots Simon fighting his fellow officer. The redcoat fixes his bayonet and charges through the smoke. Two cannonballs explode on his left and right sides, but he manages to keep running toward Simon. Timmy spots the redcoat charging at Simon. He aims his musket and fires, but he misses his shot. Timmy fixes his bayonet and takes off running to save Simon. While Simon is still fighting against the British officer, Simon parries the officer's saber and knocks the saber out of the redcoat's hand. Simon looks up and sees the redcoat charging at him. Suddenly Timmy thrusts his bayonet into the redcoat's chest. Timmy twists and turns the bayonet and then slides it out. Simon turns to Timmy. They hug each other.

"Thank you, Sergeant Miller; you saved my life," Simon says, out of breath.

Timmy smiles, pats him on the shoulder, and cleans the blood off his bayonet. "That was your training that just saved your life, sir," Timmy says.

Simon turns to his right and spots the British officer trying to sneak away. Simon drops his sword, aims his Brown Bess and fires. The musket ball strikes the redcoat officer in his back. The officer falls to the ground. The Seventy-Sixth regroups with Sergeant Miller and Major Smithtrovich. First Lieutenant Rose and First Sergeant Rose regroup with Simon and Timmy.

"Jesus! Are you two alright?" Celestia asks.

Simon smiles as he picks up his sword. He sheaths it and responds to Celestia.

"We are just fine. Sergeant Miller saved my life. Now where the hell is that lobster I shot? Oh wait; there he is. Grenadiers to me!"

The Seventy-Sixth forms up on the staff and stops the British officer trying to crawl away. The officer crawls slowly, leaving a small blood trail right behind him. The left side of his white trousers is covered with blood. Celestia uses the butt of her Brown Bess to turn the officer onto his back. The Seventy-Sixth surround the officer and aim their muskets at him. Simon notices that it is Captain Alex Kurt. Captain Kurt looks up at Simon with the utmost hate.

"Who in the hell are you bastards!" Kurt shouts at the Seventy-Sixth.

Simon aims his musket at Captain Kurt's face and speaks to him in a calm tone.

"We are the Seventy-Sixth Pennsylvania Keystone Grenadiers, lobsterback!" Simon says with confidence. "You think you bastards are going to win this war? You expect us to bow to your king? We have the spirit of freedom and the unity of friendship on our side. We are not some ragtag military anymore. We are a force that will not stop resisting until you are long gone from our land."

Celestia adds, "We are a loyal family of Pennsylvanians who will not stop fighting against your overpaid, overdressed monkeys of officers who spread tyranny all across this nation. And we will serve and protect our nation from tyranny, persecution, and the threat of extinction."

"America will never, ever, have to bow to any pompous king ever again," Timmy says with a threatening voice. "And we will take this war to your king's castle and fight hall by hall, door by door, room by room, one piss pot at a time, till we find your beloved king. And then once we do, we will hang him from the highest room of the tallest tower for all your royal subjects to see. And that is a fact!"

Captain Alex Kurt scoffs. "That to me sounds like a damn fantasy. You sound just like a bloody dreamer who reaches too high for the stars. You, sir, stick to reality, or Lord Wellington will stick it to your heart with his sword."

Daisy points her bayonet at Kurt's face. The bayonet is about five inches in front of his right eye.

"Permission to carry on and kill this lobster, sir?" Daisy asks Simon.

Simon looks down at the Captain. Simon recovers his Brown Bess, and the Seventy-Sixth do the same.

"Permission … denied. We will not kill you. We are honorable warriors who do not kill enemy officers in cold blood. We want you to go and tell your high and mighty Wellington that the United States is here to stay and we shall remain forever free."

Captain Alex Kurt begins to crawl away. The Seventy-Sixth create an opening in their circle so Captain Kurt can crawl through. He manages to stand, and he looks back at the Seventy-Sixth.

"God bless the lot of you. You are all honorable soldiers indeed," Captain Alex Kurt says. He walks away, disappearing in the smoke.

Major Smithtrovich turns to the Seventy-Sixth and smiles at them. "Grenadiers of the brave Seventy-Sixth, you have all survived today. Great work today. But do not go round-eyed. This war has only just started to get ugly. We will not quit this war until the last redcoat leaves the country peacefully or in a casket. Now I see we have several wounded. Tend to the wounded and gather any food, water, or other supplies before we head back to camp. Seventy-Sixth, fall out!"

The battlefield is littered with shell craters in the green grass, discarded muskets, abandoned knapsacks, smashed wagons, dead horses, destroyed cannons, and dead soldiers. Simon wanders the battlefield and discovers the carnage of war. The dead bodies litter the field. Small parts of the field are in flames. Black smoke rises into the sky, and the smell of death fills the air. The smell causes some soldiers to throw up. Simon sees Timmy standing over the body of a young redcoat teenager. Simon walks over to Timmy, and they both stand over the young redcoat. The redcoat was wounded by a musket ball to the leg. He is paralyzed by the pain. Timmy begins to feel bad for the young redcoat.

"You know, sir, I wish the young ones would not suffer the most through war. But I guess they knew what they were signing up for," Timmy says.

However, Simon does not share the same compassion for British redcoats. He has every good reason to hate them. "Signed up for? That is not true, because they fight for a duke. We do not fight for a pompous monkey who calls his own men, and I quote, 'Scum of the earth!' We fight for our freedom because of the tyrants this boy is serving."

Timmy scoffs. "Sir, this is just a young teenager. He chose to serve his king just like how we chose to serve our president," Timmy says.

Simon scoffs, and yet he is starting to realize that no matter what one fights for, one is still a human being.

"I know that he is just a teenager. He is still a redcoat nonetheless. Well, actually, he is a yellow coat, because he is a drummer. On the other hand, I do agree with you. He is still a human being."

Simon begins to show compassion. He leans down and takes a bandage out of his knapsack. The boy begins to tear up from the pain. Timmy helps Simon, and they begin to patch the redcoat's wound. Timmy patches the wound as Simon confronts the frightened teen.

"Don't worry. We will not hurt you. What is your name?" Simon says.

The teen gives his name while trying to talk through the pain.

"Private Oliver Adams of His Majesty's Royal Marines. What are your names?" Oliver asks with a painful voice.

"I am Sergeant Timmy Miller, and this is my commander, Major Simon Smithtrovich," Timmy says.

Simon spots three British soldiers walking toward them. A redcoat sergeant major is calling out for Oliver. Oliver notices that it is his father.

"Major, can you please pick me up and help me get to my father?"

Simon nods once, and he and Timmy pick him up.

"Sergeant Miller, can you find a white flag?" Simon asks Timmy.

"A flag of truce," Timmy says as he looks around and spots a white flag lying against a cannon.

Timmy runs over and grabs the flag and heads back to Simon. They escort Oliver, locking their arms with his. Timmy holds the white flag as they escort Oliver over to his father. The redcoat sergeant major spots Simon and Timmy carrying a white flag and carrying his son. Oliver's father and his two guards rush over to get his son. They stand ten yards apart as the exchange begins. The two guards drop their muskets and take Oliver. Oliver turns around, almost forgetting to thank Timmy and Simon.

"Major Smithtrovich and Sergeant Miller, thank you very much. God bless you!" Oliver says.

The two redcoats begin to help him back to their lines, and the sergeant major speaks to Timmy and Simon.

"My name is Sergeant Major Harry Adams of the Royal Marines Artillery. I would like to thank you lot for finding and saving my son." Then he recognizes Simon's face and utters a threat to Simon. "Major Smithtrovich, may God have mercy on your soul, for the great recompense will be upon you. And by the living God, we will meet again. Till then, cheerio." He then walks away.

Simon and Timmy are extremely confused, but then a memory hits Simon faster than a flying musket ball. They both head back to the Seventy-Sixth and see a wagon load of wounded grenadiers. The Rose sisters walk up to Simon and report their casualties.

"Major, I have the report," Celestia says. "We have seven wounded. Amazingly, no deaths today."

Daisy looks around the surrounding battleground. The sight of dead and wounded, which number in the hundreds, is truly a sight to behold.

"I wish I could say the same for the rest of our comrades. There are hundreds of them on the field," Daisy says.

Simon looks around. All he can see is death and the total destruction of a peaceful land. Simon sighs and is amazed deep inside his soul that his company did not suffer any deaths that day.

"What are your orders, sir?" Daisy asks.

Simon puts away his sword and goes to give the company some news that would lead to disaster of epic proportions for the United States in the war.

"My grenadiers in arms of the brave Seventy-Sixth, I have an announcement to make. I was given a letter from the president of the United States of America. The letter reads ..." He opens the letter and clears his throat. "To Major Simon Smithtrovich and his fellow soldiers of the Seventy-Sixth Pennsylvania Keystone Grenadiers. I am writing to inform you that you must march from Canada to the White House. A British invasion force has been spotted moving up the coast toward the Chesapeake Bay. I am ordering your company to march here to help defend the city. Make haste, and it will be an honor to make the Keystone State's finest my personal bodyguards. Signed, President James Madison."

All the grenadiers are shocked and give a loud cheer. The Seventy-Sixth retires along with the rest of the army to Fort Erie, and they settle in for the night, for they will have a ten-day march ahead of them. The Battle of Lundy's Lane ends right after midnight.

The result of the battle is a tactical draw. In some cases, it is a British strategic victory. The Americans had suffered 174 dead, 572 wounded, 79 captured, and 28 missing in action, for a grand total of 853 casualties. General Winfield Scott and General Jacob Brown were wounded in the battle. The British had suffered similar losses: 84 dead, 559 wounded, 169 captured, and 55 missing in action. The total is greater than the American losses by twenty-five casualties, at 878. Along with General Riall, General Sir Gordon Drummond was wounded. The Battle of Lundy's Lane would prove to be one of the bloodiest battles in the War of 1812.

CHAPTER 4

"WITH MUSIC AND BAYONETS ONLY!"

Central Pennsylvania Countryside
Present-day Jefferson County
August 1, 1814
Midday

The Seventy-Sixth Pennsylvania has set out from Fort Erie. As they march upon a dirt road that leads to a peaceful, quiet valley that stretches along a mile of open field, The clouds roll in and it begins to storm. Raindrops fall from the sky quite slowly at first, and then, within seconds, a downpour begins. The Seventy-Sixth look up at the sky and can feel the rain hitting their uniforms. Simon groans, but yet he does not mind the rain at all. He reaches and touches his bearskin cap to find it drenched. He looks back at his troops and says with a morale-boosting tone, "Keep on marching, lads; it is just a little rain."

Seconds later, a loud crack of thunder roars overhead. Celestia flinches because the thunder is so loud. She puts her finger in her ear. The thunderclap was so loud that she became partially deaf.

"For God's sake, my hearing is gone," she says as she twists her finger inside her ear.

Soon they reach a road that leads into the forest. That provides them with some dry cover from the rain. It is still dangerous because of the lightning but is better than being out in the open

The Seventy-Sixth continues to march in order despite the storm, which was dropping raindrops larger than .59-caliber musket balls. The Seventy-Sixth Corps Marching Band marches into the forest first, and the cover that the branches provide them is great.

"That is more like it," Brittany says. She grabs her bearskin cap and feels the bearskin. The fur is drenched. She squeezes it, and water squirts out of the fur. She then puts it back on her head. She wants to keep twirling her mace, but the lightning tends to strike tall objects that tower in the sky. She then puts her mace under her right arm as she marches in time. A few minutes later, the whole company is under the trees. Simon decides that they should take cover before moving on to their destination.

"Seventy-Sixth, take care; halt!" Simon shouts in a strong and loud tone.

The Seventy-Sixth halts, and the corps marching band stops playing their marching music. Simon about-faces and gives his orders.

"We will hunker here till the storm passes. Then we will march onward to Washington. Seventy-Sixth, fall out!"

His soldiers fall out of formation. Simon sits on a log, and Celestia joins him. Simon takes off his bearskin cap. He feels the fur and finds it wet to the touch. He then grabs a cloth from his knapsack and begins to dry the fur. Celestia takes off her boot and begins to rub her left foot. She rubs it with a massaging touch. Simon looks over at Celestia's face, for it is cold from the rain. Simon pulls out his own blanket from his knapsack and wraps it around her shoulders.

"Sir, that is really not necessary. I am not that cold," Celestia says.

"No, I insist," Simon says as he finishes wrapping her with the blanket.

Celestia smiles at Simon and then grabs his hand. She slides closer to him. "Thank you, sir. That was very thoughtful," she says to him.

She then begins to fix her hair, for the back of her head is wet. She hands Simon her bearskin cap, and he gladly holds it for her as she begins to dry her hair. Once her head is drier, she leans down, and Simon puts her cap back on her head.

"Does my hair look okay now, sir?" she asks.

"Your hair has never looked more beautiful. Nothing can ever take away your magnificent beauty," Simon says.

Celestia's cheeks blush bright red. She giggles for a few seconds and wiggles her fingers.

Brittany sits on a tree stump and sees a leaf that is dripping water. She grabs her mace and she puts the ball of the mace under the dripping water. The water drips onto it, and Brittany turns the ball so the whole thing gets wet. She then uses her sleeve to wipe the water off of the ball. She looks at the ball and can see the reflection of her face upon the ball. She smiles and then winks at herself.

"Hello, me," she says to herself. She laughs, and then she puckers her lips and smacks them. She blows herself a kiss. Her corps watches her, and they chuckle. She hears her corps chuckling, and she quickly looks up at them. They all turn and look in different directions. She smiles and chuckles herself. She then stands up and stands to attention. She marches in place and practices her twirling. At first she marches to no music, but then a drummer stands up and walks right next to Brittany.

"Are you doing your routine, ma'am?" the drummer asks Brittany.

"Yes. Can you give me a drum cadence?" Brittany asks.

"What tune do you have in mind, ma'am?"

Brittany thinks for a few seconds. "Play 'The Liberty song.'"

"Yes ma'am," the drummer says.

The drummer stands to attention with his heels together and his feet pointing out at a forty-five-degree angle. He cracks his knuckles and begins to play the march. Brittany begins to march in place. She twirls her baton in various ways. She starts twirling slowly and then begins to pick up the pace. She keeps her head straight, as well as her eyes. She stares at an imaginary spot and never loses sight.

While Brittany trains, other grenadiers begin to clean their muskets, eat food, and talk with one another. Daisy stands just near the edge of the trees, using her spyglass to scope the area. She spots a flock of birds flying around in the sky. She follows the birds and then comes across a sight that she did not expect to see. She spots a British Union Jack waving above a wooden fortress. She begins to view the ramparts. Only a few redcoats are standing on the northern rampart. She runs over to Simon.

"Sir?" she says with an excited tone. Simon looks up at Daisy.

"Yes, First Sergeant?" he says.

"There is a British fortress just one hundred fifty yards away," she says.

She grabs his hand and rushes Simon over to the spot where she found the fort.

"Bloody hell, First Sergeant. What kind of fortress are we talking about here?" he asks.

"Take a look for yourself, sir!" she says. Daisy hands him the spyglass and begins to explain what she has seen so far. "Major, that fort is lightly defended, and their artillery is very light. From what I can see, there are only two four-pound cannons on the northern ramparts."

Simon sees that she is telling the truth. He spots only ten redcoats upon the northern ramparts and considers what to do. Should the Seventy-Sixth attack the fort or continue their march to Washington? Simon looks down at his grenadiers and pulls out his bayonet. The whole unit awaits his command on what to do. He then fixes his bayonet and does a right about-face to the Seventy-Sixth. He gives the Seventy-Sixth the following commands.

"Seventy-Sixth, form double ranks on the road. Double time!" Simon shouts.

The Seventy-Sixth put their caps back on their heads and grab their muskets. They stand at ease till Simon gives the commands to prepare for battle. Simon stands in front of his company and takes one look back at the fort through the branches of the trees. He then looks at his unit and stands to attention. He takes a deep breath and gives his commands.

"Seventy-Sixth Pennsylvania, attention! Prepare to fix your bayonets!"

The grenadiers put their hands on their socket bayonets in their belts and wait for the next command.

"Grenadiers, fix your bayonets!" Simon shouts.

They grab their bayonets out of their belts and they fix them to the muzzles of their muskets.

"Shoulder your firearms!" Simon shouts.

The grenadiers shoulder their muskets, and then Simon unsheathes his sword. "My friends, hear my voice. You have proven yourselves in battle time and time again. Today will be very different, because we will take this fort with music and bayonets only! We need to save our ammunition for when we defend Washington. Drum Major Benson, I want you and your corps to play the loudest march that will ring across the land." Drum Major Benson salutes Simon with her mace. Simon continues his orders.

"This land that we are standing on is our home state of Pennsylvania. All of us were born and raised in this state. Now let's show these bastards that the Keystone State is not their home. Who is with me?" Simon shouts.

The Seventy-Sixth cheers, and the snare drummers play a drum roll. The staff stand fifty feet apart from each other across the battle line. Simon looks at his grenadiers and his staff. The color-bearers bring the regimental flag and the state flag forward. Brittany makes a sign of the cross. Timmy fixes his hat and checks his bayonet to see if it is secure on the muzzle of his musket. Daisy looks at Celestia, and they salute each other. Simon looks toward the sky and waits for the right time to advance.

A few minutes later, the rainfall begins to intensify. The raindrops fall harder and faster. Simon looks down at the open field and notices that the visibility has decreased. He had a plan that French army had employed during the attack of Fort Necessity back in the French and Indian war. He knew that if the redcoats at the fort tried to open fire upon them, their black powder would get wet. Attempts to fire their cannons and muskets would then be useless. Simon points his sword forward and gives his command to advance.

"Seventy-Sixth Pennsylvania! Charge your bayonets!" he shouts.

The Seventy-Sixth charge their bayonets forward and utter a battle cry.

"Seventy-Sixth Pennsylvania, to the front! Forward march!"

The Seventy-Sixth Pennsylvania marches forward, and the Seventy-Sixth Corps Band plays a loud march of snare drums and trumpets. The march was the tune that was played by the French Grand Armee, 'The French are coming!' But in this case, it is the Keystone grenadiers who are coming.

The music can be heard by the redcoats inside the fort. One redcoat spots the Seventy-Sixth marching toward them and shouts to his fellow defenders.

"To arms! To arms!"

The fifty redcoats inside the fort rush to the northern ramparts and open fire upon the Seventy-Sixth. They fire the cannons, and the shells explode all around the Seventy-Sixth. The Seventy-Sixth marches with pride and with great energy. The shells do not strike anyone in the Seventy-Sixth. The Seventy-Sixth corps band marches with passion and pride, knowing that providence is on their side. Every time the snare drummers pound on their drums, the water splashes off the drumheads. Timmy almost trips when he steps in a gopher hole. He recovers and continues pressing forward. Simon, with no facial expression, looks toward the fort. Once they are within fifty yards of the fort's gates, the redcoats fire their muskets at the Seventy-Sixth. Unfortunately, their powder is bad because of the rain. It is not strong enough to fire a bullet strongly enough to kill a man.

Once the Seventy-Sixth are close, Simon shouts, "Seventy-Sixth Pennsylvania, charge!"

The Seventy-Sixth scream out loud as they rush the gates of the fort. The redcoats make a desperate attempt to keep the grenadiers out of the fort. A tug-of-war battle begins. The force is too great for the gates. With one great heave by the Seventy-Sixth, the gates come loose and fall onto the redcoats trying to defend the fort. The weight of the gates crushes them, and more weight is added when the soldiers of the Seventy-Sixth run on top of gates. Two of the redcoats are crushed to death by the weight.

The grenadiers storm the fort. Simon and Timmy are the first officers in. Just as they get into the fort, they are met by the defenders. Simon instantly cuts down two redcoats with his sword. Simon slices one of the redcoats in the chest, and the second one is stabbed with a thrusting blow. The blade goes clean through the soldiers' body and out the back. Timmy knocks down one redcoat with a blow from the butt of his musket. He then stabs another one in the chest twice. He forces the second redcoat to the ground, and a third tackles him. The redcoat pulls out his pistol and is about to shoot Timmy when, before he can pull the trigger, a bayonet is thrust through his back and comes out of his chest. Blood splashes on Timmy's face. The redcoat falls to the ground, and Daisy recovers her bayonet. Timmy grabs her musket, and she lifts him back onto his feet.

Celestia enters the fort and is kicked by a redcoat officer. The force of the kick sends her back to the wall. The officer tries to stab her in the face, but she ducks and picks up a pike. She then dashes to the right side and has enough room to thrust the pike into the officer's gut. The officer screams out in massive pain as he falls to the ground. Celestia then stabs the officer for a second time directly in the heart. She lets go of the pike, and all the officer sees is a pike protruding out from his chest.

Drum Major Benson and her corps stand at the gate entrance and watch as their fellow grenadiers beat back the British redcoats inside the fort. They witness the horrors of war and the gruesome aftermath. Suddenly a hand rises from the destroyed gates. A redcoat is still trapped underneath. He pleads for their help, but he gets no sympathy from them. Brittany pulls out her short sword and stabs the redcoat in his chest.

As the battle reaches its end, so does the thunderstorm. The rain stops, the sun comes out and lets out a bright shine. Five redcoats are surrounded by the grenadiers, and they look at the sky and then at their muskets. One redcoat asks a question to Simon: "Parley, sir?"

Simon walks forward and touches the redcoat's chest with the tip of his sword. The redcoat trembles in fear and begins to beg for mercy. Simon tries to decide whether to kill these redcoats or to be a true officer and restrain himself from killing a surrendering foe.

"Please, sir? Have mercy, sir!" he whimpers.

He then throws down his musket, and the rest of the redcoats drop their muskets. Simon looks down at the ground and then looks back at his grenadiers. They all nod to him to spare the lives of the remaining redcoat defenders. Simon looks back at the redcoat. He then recovers his sword. The redcoat sighs in relief that his and his comrades' lives are being spared. Simon then speaks to the redcoat.

"I will let y'all have parole on one condition," Simon states.

"What would that condition be, sir?" the redcoat asks.

Simon goes and picks up the British flagstaff off the ground. The flag is dripping with muddy water. Simon shakes a bit of the mud off the banner. He then takes it over to the redcoats and hands it to them. The redcoat that spoke takes it and hoists the banner high.

"I want you to take this flag back to England, and you carry it with pride and with honor. Let your Duke Wellington know that you and your comrades defended this fort with bravery. You may take your fort's flag with you."

Before Simon can finish speaking, a Pennsylvania militia platoon marches into the fort. The commander of the militia platoon walks up to Simon. Before he speaks to Simon, he observes the carnage that the Seventy-Sixth have created.

"Good God, sir! You guys sure do know how to make a hell of a mess. I am First Lieutenant Ethan Loss of the Harrisburg Militia. We were on our way here to take this fort. I guess your troops saved us the trouble."

"My name is Major Simon Smithtrovich of the Seventy-Sixth Pennsylvania Keystone Grenadiers. The pleasure was all ours. Now, Lieutenant Loss, these redcoats are allowed to head home, and they can keep their colors. They are not to be furtherly harmed. Do you understand me, Lieutenant Loss?"

"Yes sir!" replies Lieutenant Loss.

Simon leaves the redcoats to the militiamen. He walks up to the redcoat and offers his hand. They shake.

"Thank you, sir. May providence be with you and your company," the redcoat says.

"May God be with you and your comrades," Simon says.

A few minutes later, the Seventy-Sixth reform their ranks, and they resume their march to Washington. The fort was taken in fifteen minutes of intense fighting. The casualties were heavy for the redcoats. The Seventy-Sixth Pennsylvania did not lose a single grenadier in the assault.

The five redcoats return to England, never to set foot in the United States of America again.

It takes the Seventy-Sixth Pennsylvania sixteen more days to march to Washington, where they have to face another challenge before their next battle. They have to train twenty new recruits in just four days.

CHAPTER 5

MEETING THE PRESIDENT

Washington, DC, Maryland
August 17, 1814
10:00 a.m.

In Washington, soldiers and civilians are preparing for the British assault. The townspeople are scrambling to pack whatever they can. They are throwing suitcases out their windows onto the street. Some grab muskets and rush to join the militia forces. American regulars and militia are marching across the city, trying to keep the civilians from panicking. The Seventy-Sixth Pennsylvania marches into the city and heads directly for the White house. President James Madison, along with his first lady, Dolly Madison, can hear the Seventy-Sixth's drums outside. They both walk outside, and they can see the Seventy-Sixth Pennsylvania in their best array. The Seventy-Sixth halt and present arms as a salute to the president. President Madison walks down the steps and greets Major Smithtrovich. Simon salutes President Madison, and then they shake hands.

"Welcome to Washington, Major," President Madison says.

"Thank you, Mr. President, it is a great honor to serve under you, sir."

Simon steps back, and then President Madison gives the situation that threatens the city.

"Seventy-Sixth Pennsylvania, hear my voice. The danger that threatens this city is real. The redcoats are on the march. My scouts have been tracking their movements since they landed at Benedict, Maryland. Their main objective is to capture me and the members of Congress. I brought you down here because we need extra muscle, and from what I was told, you men and women of the brave Seventy-Sixth are the best of the best."

Simon looks at Celestia and nods for her to speak on behalf of the unit. She marches two paces forward and stands at attention. She speaks with a loud and clear voice.

"Sir, we are well disciplined and battle hardened. We march to the beat of the Keystone's cadence, and that cadence marches us to victory. We may look like parade-grounds soldiers, but we are the toughest sons of guns in the state of Pennsylvania, sir! On behalf of the Seventy-Sixth Pennsylvania Keystone Grenadiers, we are very honored to serve under your command, sir!"

Just then, First Lady Dolly Madison steps down and begins to inspect the Seventy-Sixth. Simon orders the Seventy-Sixth to stand at attention.

"Seventy-Sixth Grenadiers, Attention!" Simon shouts.

The Keystone grenadiers stand as straight as flagpoles, while Dolly Madison inspects them. The grenadiers stand emotionless. She first inspects the Seventy-Sixth Company Corps Marching Band. Drum Major Brittany Benson salutes the first lady with her mace.

"Ma'am, it is a great honor to meet you," Brittany says.

"It is a great honor to meet a fine lady like yourself. You and your corps keep making America proud," Dolly says as she pats Brittany on her right shoulder. Dolly moves on to the Rose sisters. "You, First Lieutenant and First Sergeant Rose … as clean as a whistle. It is very amazing to see fine women such as you and your sister in such a fine uniform. Your family would be very proud of you two. I wish you two and all the females in this company the best of the future battles that you will fight."

Celestia and Daisy salute Dolly Madison, and she moves on to Sergeant Timmy Miller. Timmy stands straight with his eyes forward. Dolly looks at him, and he does not move a single inch. She moves on to Major Smithtrovich.

"So you must be the commanding officer of this company?" Dolly asks.

Simon salutes Dolly Madison. "Yes ma'am!" he says with great energy. "My grenadiers are trained and ready and are honored to protect you, your husband, and the rest of America from the tyranny of the British."

"Twenty new recruits will arrive here tomorrow morning, and you will have the honor of training them into elite grenadiers," the president states. "Major, will you train these recruits?"

"Yes sir!" Simon says to President Madison.

"Great. Now head to the encampment and settle in for the night. Till we meet again."

The Seventy-Sixth march down to the American encampment. They set up their tents alongside thousands of American regulars and militia. Just after they set up their camp, Simon decides to let his grenadiers go and enjoy the city.

"Seventy-Sixth Pennsylvania, now that your tents are set up, I am giving you permission to head to the city. Have a bit of fun. Still, there is a catch. I am giving you the right to drink, but I want every grenadier sober. If you come back to my camp dead drunk, I will have you flogged! And I want you all back before nightfall. Do you understand?"

"Sir, yes sir!" the Seventy-Sixth shout.

"Very well then. Seventy-Sixth, dismissed!"

The Seventy-Sixth break ranks. Some head back to their tents, while others go to the city for a while. Celestia and Daisy go to the city, while Timmy and Simon stay in camp. Timmy begins to clean his Brown Bess musket. Simon sits on a tree stump and pulls out his diary. He writes and remembers all the memories that he has shared not only with his close friends but also with all the men and women of the brave Seventy-Sixth.

> Dear diary: The months have gone by, and my troops have not lost hope in winning this war. I thought this bloody war would end in a very short time. I never knew that it would threaten our nation's capital. My grenadiers are ready to fight against whatever the lobsters are going to send our way. On our march down here, dozens of companies and regiments have been coming to the city. President Madison has been collecting such a force within the city that an attack would be suicidal. Our company's morale is very, very, high, however something tells me that will be a very different kind of battle. I really hope that this coming battle will not turn into another Brandywine creek. I just can't believe that the British are going to try to destroy this lovely city. I just hope that this nightmare that

the President has feared does not come true. Nevertheless, we are ready to uphold our state's motto, and we are willing to die defending it. Long live virtue, liberty, independence, and, most importantly, the power of friendship in America!

Simon puts away his diary and goes and sits right next to Timmy, who has just finished cleaning his musket.

"My musket is clean, sir," Timmy says. Timmy hands Simon his musket and he inspects it. Simon sees that it is freshly cleaned inside and out.

"Yep, freshly cleaned. Good man. Now it is about lunchtime. Are you hungry, Sergeant?" Simon asks.

Timmy's stomach roars. He grabs his gut. "Yes sir, I guess I am hungry. Some food would be nice right now. Would you join me, sir?" Timmy asks Simon.

Simon nods, and they walk over to the mess tent and get some food to eat. As they are having their meal of ham and chicken, they have a conversation about how far the Seventy-Sixth has come.

"I know that the enemy is knocking on the doors of the city, but the last time we came here, we came here for a summer vacation back in 1813," Timmy says.

"How can I forget? That was a great summer. We just decided to take a break from the war. We would not have had that chance to relax if we actually belonged to a general," Simon explains.

Timmy puts his plate aside.

Simon finishes his food and puts his plate aside.

Timmy thinks about one of their first battles that they fought two years ago. "Simon, do you remember that battle when we faced off against Canadian cavalry?" Timmy asks Simon.

Simon scratches his head for a few seconds, and then the memory pops back into his mind.

"Yes, I remember. By God, that was the first time we got ambushed."

"What do you remember about it? I only remember getting knocked out at the beginning of the battle."

Simon sits back and looks up at the sky. He tries to remember anything that he can about that battle.

"It is kind of vague. There are only a few things I can remember. We were marching in an open field. Suddenly a loud roar of cavalrymen sounded all around us. We were caught out in the open. Then a large force of cavalry charged at us." Timmy begins to laugh, and Simon looks at him with confusion.

"What the hell is so funny?" Simon asks Timmy.

"Sir, the second I saw those Canucks charge at us, I must have soiled myself." Simon begins to laugh as well. "Just their bloody war cries made us form a square without even being ordered to," Timmy says as he laughs. They both slowly stop laughing. "Seeing those horses circling us … They swarmed us like angry bees. Amazingly we killed every single one of those Canucks."

"I agree. You all made me very proud that day, by God."

"In what way?" Timmy asks.

Simon then stands up and looks in the direction of the White House.

"You all made me very proud for defending yourselves with a tactic that I never even taught you all, and for displaying calm under heavy numbers and heavy fire. That day was the defining battle that assured me that this unit can withstand any enemy that dares to oppose the Seventy-Sixth," Simon says. Simon turns and faces Timmy. He has a gut feeling that the next battle is going to be like none they had fought in the past two years. "I think that this next major battle will be a bit different though. Bonaparte is in exile, and now we have the redcoats' full attention once again. They will bring their finest soldiers on us like a hammer on an anvil."

Simon knows that if they lose, the city of Washington will be at the mercy of the British. Both of them know how much is at stake, and it is critical that they not lose. Timmy realizes that the Seventy-Sixth has not lost a battle for the past two years. He stands up and walks toward Simon.

"Sir, let us take a walk," Timmy says.

Simon and Timmy begin to roam about the camp.

"Sir, I realized that we have yet to lose a battle."

Simon thinks for a second and sees that Timmy is right.

"You're right. We have fought in ten engagements, and we still have yet to lose a battle. And I know that the best of the best have to lose once in a while, but this next battle is a battle that we must not lose."

"I know that, sir. We will either claim victory or this loss will be an investment in our future. Sometimes when you have very little and you face insurmountable odds, you must be ready to lose everything that you have. We must be ready to do this so this nation will win its right to mature, now and forever, as the United States of America."

Simon looks at Timmy and pats him on the back.

"Damn well said, Sergeant Miller. You need to write that one down."

Timmy chuckles. "No sir. I am no writer."

"We actually are all writers if you think about it for a few minutes. With every single battle we fight and every victory we achieve, we write the pages in the book that will be read by our grandchildren in the future."

"Amen, sir!" Timmy exclaims.

Celestia and Daisy walk around the city of Washington. Many other females look at them and are somewhat confused that women are wearing American uniforms. The Rose sisters walk into the Union Tavern. Inside they see only a few American Regular soldiers having a drink. Celestia and Daisy take off their bearskin caps and put them aside on the table as they take their seats.

A bartender walks up to the Rose sisters. "May I get you fine ladies some refreshments?" the bartender asks them both.

Celestia and Daisy speak in unison.

"Rum please?"

The bartender pours the Rose sisters some rum.

"Here you are. This is the finest rum, on the house. Today all American soldiers drink free of charge."

"Thank you, sir," Celestia and Daisy say.

The bartender goes to serve other American soldiers. Celestia and Daisy raise their glasses high.

"For virtue, liberty, and independence," Celestia says. "To the war and for Washington."

Daisy then adds more. "For the Brave Seventy-Sixth, and to our grenadiers in arms, and to our valiant commander!"

"Hear! Hear!" Celestia says.

Celestia and Daisy both drink their rum.

"Mmm! This is great rum," Daisy says.

"Indeed."

They both put their empty glasses on the table, and then they begin to have a conversation.

Celestia looks outside the window and sees the street filled with American soldiers.

She feels lucky to be a soldier deep down in the pit of her heart.

"I must say that a soldier's life is actually quite … interesting. I never even knew that I would be fighting alongside the best of the best from the Keystone State, let alone that I would be doing so with my little sister."

Daisy smiles. She feels flattered to have the same honor. "I am glad to be in the same company with my big sister."

Both Celestia and Daisy are loyal to each other as sisters. When they became grenadiers, they swore on their family's honor to protect each other.

Daisy looks at her bearskin cap. She picks it up and looks at the plate on the front of the cap. "You know, I always thought this would be uncomfortable during battle and heavy to wear while on the march."

Celestia grabs her cap and feels the fur with her hands. It has a softness to it. The fur makes her feel relaxed and calm. She loves touching the fur gently. "I never really felt the weight at all. I must say that it makes us look taller than we really are. I love the feel of this cap."

Celestia and Daisy focus on the positives and the negatives of the bearskin caps. Finally they come up with a matter that intertwines with the bearskin cap.

"I think we can both agree on one thing about this matter," Celestia says.

"What's that?" Daisy asks.

"That this bearskin cap makes us look like the best-dressed soldiers in the US Army," Celestia says with a proud tone. She puts her bearskin cap on her head, and Daisy follows suit. They both exit the tavern and take a walk. They soon walk up Pennsylvania Avenue.

They both feel the cool breeze on this hot summer day.

"Ahh, that breeze is so refreshing," Celestia says blissfully.

"How is your boyfriend, Lieutenant?" Daisy asks Celestia.

Celestia is hesitant to talk; her cheeks blush as red as an apple. Daisy keeps asking her to talk.

"Come on; we are sisters and can talk about anything with each other because we trust each other."

Celestia finally speaks about their love. "He is everything that I sort of expected. He listens to me, he cares for me, and he is an angel that was sent down from the clouds."

Celestia then begins to rant on about how wonderful Simon is to her, and she begins to get a little personal.

"I love how he is always there for me. He never has been mean to me ever since we started to date. And when he joined the army, I hated to see him go, but I knew that I could not hold on to him forever. He has to live his life like us. And when he returned home and dressed in fine blue and pipe clay, by the living God, I just wanted to tackle him and crawl all over his body—"

Daisy stops her from finishing that sentence. She puts her hand over Celestia's mouth. "Hey now! You're going too far. Besides, I asked about your love life, not your sex life." Celestia gasps and smacks Daisy's shoulder. "What? It's true. But between us, would you?"

Celestia knows what Daisy is asking. Celestia sighs and gives her answer. Her cheeks blush redder than ever before. "Yes, I would. I knew his blue uniform was handsome two years ago, but his grenadier uniform makes me melt like ice on a hot summer day. But for that day to come, it has to be a very romantic moment—a nice dinner and a dance underneath the gleaming stars, and then a nice night of romance." Celestia sighs in pleasure and then has a feeling down below. Celestia is aroused just thinking about that future day. She has butterflies in the pit of her stomach. Daisy rolls her eyes and chuckles. She knows that her sister is aroused. She then begins to talk about Sergeant Timmy Miller.

"Trust me, Celestia, I would love to date Timmy. But I have heard that relationships during war do not last long. I am afraid that if we date and we go to fight in a battle, one or both of us will be killed. I would never be able to go through with that."

Celestia puts her arm around Daisy's back. "You worry too much. I am sure that one day you two will get together. I have never been wrong about things in our lives before."

Daisy smiles. "You're right. I am thankful to have you."

They smile at each other and hug each other. They then break off and walk back to their encampment.

Once they reach the camp. Daisy goes to see Timmy, while Celestia goes to find Simon. When she finds him, Simon is in his tent, looking at a map. She walks over to his tent.

"Sir, may I come in, sir?" Celestia asks Simon.

Simon looks up and sees Celestia. "Yes, come in. I actually need your help on a serious matter."

Celestia enters the tent and sits down right next to Simon. Simon then explains what he is talking about to Celestia.

"I am trying to guess the route the lobsterbacks will take to get to Washington. Their navy could sail up the Potomac River. They will reach the city and then bombard with a cannonade. But one spot keeps pecking my worried nerves, I think they might land their infantry at Benedict, Maryland."

Simon points to it on the map. Celestia studies the possible path that the British might take once they land there.

"I agree. They will march farther north, and we must find a place where we can make a stand."

Simon then looks at a town just northeast of Washington. "If we are going to make a stand, I imagine that General Winder will make his stand right here." Simon puts his finger on top of the city.

Celestia reads the name of the town. "Bladensburg. That is a perfect place for a defense. I have been there before, and the redcoats will have to cross the East Branch Bridge."

"Exactly. The redcoats would be fools to try to swim the bloody river. Their only pathway will be across the bridge. We can create our own barricade and fire volleys into them. It will be like a bloody turkey shoot. We can only hope that they head for the town, but we haven't ever been wrong before."

The rest of the Seventy-Sixth enjoy themselves for the rest of the afternoon and the evening, but when the morning dawns, they will be faced with the challenge of training the recruits that will soon join the Keystone grenadiers.

CHAPTER 6

＊——•——＊

TRAINING

August 18, 1814
American encampment

The men and women of the Seventy-Sixth awaken from a deep sleep. What they do not know is that the new recruits will help transform the destiny of the Brave Seventy-Sixth. Simon and his staff, along with the members of the Seventy-Sixth Corps Marching Band, walk over to the parade grounds to greet their new recruits.

"How many men and women are in the Seventy-Sixth right now?" Sergeant Miller asks.

"Two hundred twenty and counting us, which makes it two hundred twenty-five," Simon answers. Celestia and Daisy are not so sure about the new recruits.

"Major, I think that we are in over our heads on this one. How in the hell are we going to train twenty recruits in four days?" First Lieutenant Rose says.

Daisy seconds the statement. "I agree. We will be marching off to who knows where on the twenty-second," she says with an unsure voice.

Simon tries to soothe the tension. "My friends, in warfare there will be many challenges that shall be faced by every army on this earth. That will test our mettles every single day. Now, First Lieutenant Rose, First Sergeant Rose, and Drum Major Benson, you three get the privilege of training these twenty recruits. I and Sergeant Miller will help you if you need it."

They reach the new recruits and are shocked to see them standing at attention without an order being given. Their uniforms are in perfect order, with not a button out of place. Simon and his staff are stunned and do not know what to say.

"Y'all seeing what I'm seeing?" Simon asks his staff.

"This is such a surprise," Celestia says.

"Well, this is a first," Daisy adds.

"Are these the new recruits? Because it would take about three or four weeks to train civilians to stand like that," Brittany states while she observes their posture.

"I am speechless, sir," Timmy says.

Simon then looks over at Sergeant Miller. "How can you be speechless? You just said something!"

Timmy chuckles at the joke.

The rest of the Seventy-Sixth fall in and form a column right behind the staff.

Simon steps out of the staff line and gives his introduction to the twenty recruits. "Ladies and gentlemen of the Seventy-Sixth Pennsylvania Keystone Grenadier platoon of volunteers, I am your commanding officer, Major Simon Smithtrovich. I commend you for enlisting in the Seventy-Sixth. I was told yesterday by President Madison that you would be here in the morning. Now let me tell you all a little about us. This company was created on the same exact day this war started, which was June 18, 1812. We may look like parade-grounds soldiers in a way. We do love that sort of thing from time to time. However, we are battlefield soldiers, and we sure as hell love the taste and feel of battle. I am here to tell you one thing, so you better listen to my voice. We are here to kill lobsterbacks and Canucks. I only allow the best of the best in my company. I do not tolerate layabouts, and there will be no room for cowards. The training will be hell on earth. Will you cry? Maybe. Will you quit? I sure as hell hope you don't! Will we march you so bloody hard that your bones inside your feet will break. Rest assured that has only happened once."

The twenty soldiers chuckle a bit. Then Simon turns to his female staff. "Ladies, they're all yours, I will be watching. Good luck."

Celestia fixes her bearskin hat, and the Seventy-Sixth band plays an introduction march. A trumpeter plays a fanfare. Celestia blows her whistle loudly, and the drummers play a six-second drum roll and then they play a rat-a-tat-tat drum cadence. As Celestia asks the standard questions to the new recruits, she marches over to the left side of the line and makes her way down to the right side of the line.

"So...you all think you have what it takes to be a part of the brave Seventy-Sixth?"

"Yes ma'am!" they shout. Celestia continues with her questions.

"Do you think that you have what it takes to march headlong into the fray? To take the bayonet to our nation's enemies that threaten our own way of life?" Celestia asks.

"Yes ma'am!" they shout again.

"Well, let me be the first to tell y'all that you don't! If you were grenadier material, you'd already be a grenadier. If you do not think you can handle this, then drop your musket and take off your bearskin cap and place them both in the dirt, for that bearskin cap you wear upon your head is not just given to anyone; it must be earned. I will give you thirty seconds to bail out now before you humiliate yourself in front of our company. If you decide to stay, you will endure training like you have never seen before, for you must be ready to serve and protect not only our state of Pennsylvania but also the United States of America."

She waits for thirty seconds, and none of the recruits make any moves to quit. Celestia steps back, and then Drum Major Benson marches forward and stands at attention. Her band members stand right behind her.

"My name is Drum Major Brittany Benson of the Seventy-Sixth Corps Marching Band. We only have two purposes in the Seventy-Sixth: to lead the brave Seventy-Sixth into battle and to fill the air with gallant music. Now, if there is anyone who wants to be a part of the Seventy-Sixth Corps Band, march two paces forward."

A brother and sister march two paces forward. Brittany marches over to them both.

"State your names!" Brittany says.

The sister goes first, and then the brother.

"Private Jessica Little, ma'am!"

"Private Devin Little, ma'am!"

"I guess you two are brother and sister?" Brittany asks.

"Yes ma'am!" they both say at the same time.

"Very well, follow me. Brittany commands.

"Yes, ma'am!" they both shout in unison, as they march behind Brittany.

Brittany takes them to drill with the band while Celestia begins to train the other eighteen recruits. Brittany begins with the Littles by showing them a demonstration.

"You two, pay attention to my instructions. The vets will do the routine once, and you will show me nothing less than perfection in my corps."

Drum Major Benson does an about-face and marches over to the Seventy-Sixth's members of the company marching band. They stand at normal posture. She stands fifteen yards away from the band.

"Corps, attention! Corps, in cadence, hut! Mark time; march!" Brittany commands.

Brittany brings her mace up to the carry position and begins to march in place.

"Corps, step off!" she shouts.

The corps begins to march forward, she marches them thirty paces.

"Left, left, left, right, left!" Brittany speaks in cadence.

Devin and Jessica are impressed by their style and form. Then the Seventy-sixth's band began to perform turns called obliques.

"To the left oblique … hut!" Brittany shouts.

The band turns at a forty-five-degree angle and marches to the left. The band marches in two square forms, doing left and then right obliques.

After the band finishes the squares, Brittany gives her final commands. "Corps, mark time … hut!" she shouts.

The band marches in place for ten seconds. She does an about-face and spins her mace. She holds both of her arms straight up to the sky and blows her whistle for a long burst, and the drums do a quick three beats. She gives the band orders to halt.

"Corps, take care … halt! Corps, parade rest!"

The band stands at parade rest by moving their left feet eighteen inches to the left. Brittany takes a breath and marches over to Jessica and Devin. They both clap at the demo that they just watched, and now it is their turn.

"I hope you two paid close attention. Now it is your turn. Are you two ready?" Brittany asks.

"Yes ma'am!" they both shout in unison.

Brittany marches them to the parade grounds, and they begin their test. One drummer accompanies them. Devin and Jessica look at each other and wink once at each other. Their trial begins. Brittany stands at attention and gives her commands.

"Detail, attention! Detail, mark time ... march!" Brittany shouts. Jessica and Devin march in place. Then they march in synced paces. The two teens give a flawless display of style and discipline. They performed the routine without messing up a single time.

"Detail, take care; halt! Stand at ease!"

Brittany and the Seventy-Sixth corps cannot believe what they just saw. Devin and Jessica stand at ease. Brittany marches over to them.

"How in the world did you two do that in one try?" Brittany asks.

"We're both quick learners, ma'am," Jessica says.

"Drum major, are you okay? Devin asks.

Brittany is spellbound with how fast they learned the routine. Her eyes are wide open, and her mouth hangs down. Brittany shakes her head from side to side quickly and then answers.

"Yes. I am just spellbound. No recruit has done that marching drill on the first try."

"I guess there is a first time for everything, ma'am," Jessica says.

Then they all laugh and continue learning new drills. Then they learn how to play their regulation snare drums.

Soon Simon and Celestia are training the recruits in the final course of how to fire and reload their muskets. She demonstrates for them first, and they get to do it themselves. As she is explaining to them what to do, she is doing it simultaneously.

"Now gentlemen," Celestia says, "the last thing that is most important about your training is how to load your musket. You remove your cartridge from your cartridge box. You bite off the tail and you pour a tiny bit of powder into the flash pan. Then you charge the cartridge down the barrel. You remove the ramrod, and you push the round down the barrel. Now this is a very important tip to remember: do not ever forget to remove the rammer from the barrel; otherwise, you will partially lose the ability to fire. But notice how I said 'partially.' You can also put the ball in your mouth and spit down the barrel, then tap the bottom of your musket to send the ball down. That will save you twenty seconds. Finally you pull back the hammer, and now you're ready to fire."

Then Simon gives instruction to the eighteen recruits. It is now their turn to show that they can fire three rounds a minute. "Gentlemen, form double ranks, and let's see if you all can fire three rounds a minute. Recruits, form double ranks! Time this, Sergeant Miller."

The recruits form two ranks. The front rank kneels, and the rear rank stands. Timmy pulls out his pocket watch and gives the men the order to load their muskets.

"Prime and load!" Timmy shouts.

The recruits begin to load their muskets. They get the first shot off within fifteen seconds. They begin to load again. Then, at the thirty-second mark, they all fire a second shot. Simon and his fellow staff are shocked with amazement. At the forty-five-second mark, they get the third shot off. Then, exactly at the one-minute mark, they manage to get a fourth volley fired.

"Four shots in a minute, sir," Timmy says with a shocked tone.

The eighteen recruits recover their muskets and stand at attention, knowing deep down they have impressed the staff of the Seventy-Sixth. Simon turns to Celestia.

"How in the world did they all do that? Lieutenant, first sergeant, whatever you did to these recruits, I am very impressed indeed," Simon says, sounding impressed.

"Thank you, sir. These recruits—or should I say grenadiers—were worth the training. I am proud to be their drill instructor, sir," Celestia says with pride.

Simon walks over to the recruits. He has a surprise for the new soldiers of the Seventy-Sixth. "Well, tomorrow you get to display them on the parade grounds in front of the unit. And in front of General Winder, along with the president."

The recruits utter a cheer.

Two days later, the new grenadiers get their dress uniforms on and are inspected by the Rose sisters and Drum Major Benson. The veterans of the Seventy-Sixth Pennsylvania stand in formation in front of the White House. President Madison and General William Winder are standing alongside Major Simon Smithtrovich. The twenty new soldiers are just down the road on Pennsylvania Avenue. They are in formation in ranks of ten. Drum Major Benson stands in front of Private Devin and Private Jessica Little. Drum Major Benson turns to the Littles and reminds them to remember what they have learned.

"Remember everything I taught you, and you shall do just fine. I have faith in you two. Now let's make some thunder!"

The Littles salute her, and Brittany salutes with her mace. Celestia gets in formation at the front of the platoon alongside Daisy. She faces the platoon.

"It is time for your initiation march. Let's show our commander what you have learned. Are we ready to strut our stuff?" Celestia asks.

"Yes ma'am!" the twenty grenadiers shout with pride and energy.

Then First Lieutenant Celestia Rose gives the commands to begin their graduation march.

"Platoon, attention! Left shoulder arms! Drum Major Benson, play 'Yankee Doodle!' Platoon, forward march!"

Drum Major Benson twirls her mace. Devin and Jessica sound off and then play a slow to fast drum march. The platoon marches down the avenue. Civilians and other soldiers watch the twenty soon to be Keystone grenadiers march toward the White House. Some of the people cheer with glee and happiness. Then the rest of the band begins to play, and the recruits begin to sing "Yankee Doodle."

"Platoon, sound off!" First Lieutenant Rose shouts.

> To meet Britannia's hostile bands
> we'll march, our heroes say, sir,
> we'll join all hearts, we'll join all hands;
> Brave boys we'll win the day, sir.
> Yankee doodle, strike your tents, Yankee doodle dandy,
> Yankee doodle, march away, and do your parts right handy.
> For long we've borne with British pride,
> and su'd to gain our rights, sir;
> all other methods have been tried;
> There's nought remains but fight, sir.
> Yankee doodle, march away, Yankee doodle dandy,
> Yankee doodle, fight brave boys, the thing will work right handy.

Soon will the toils of war be o'er,
and then we'll taste of bliss, sir,
on beauty's lip, which all adore,
we'll print the melting kiss, sir.
Yankee doodle, beauty charms, Yankee doodle dandy,
Yankee doodle, ground our arms. Our sweethearts are the
dandy.

(Original current version written by, Edward Bangs, 1776)

Right as they reach the White House, They perform a right wheel, with the right side of the rank swinging right. They swing like an opening and closing door. They march to the front of the White house. The veterans of the Seventy-Sixth Pennsylvania are very impressed with the style of the new grenadiers. Their marching and discipline are flawless. Major Smithtrovich is very amazed. He knows deep down that these twenty soldiers are going to do great things during the future battles to come.

"My God, they're so smart and shiny, just like a new steel bayonet," Simon says.

President James Madison is impressed as well.

"Major, I must say that your staff is very gifted in skills of training; you must be very proud of them," President Madison says to Simon.

Simon smiles with happiness.

"Yes, I am, sir! They, along with this company, have become my rock," Simon says.

The platoon marches in place with high steps for twenty seconds.

"Platoon, take care; halt! Platoon, right face!" Celestia shouts.

The platoon halts their march and pivots to the right.

"Platoon, present arms; salute!" Celestia shouts with a very commanding voice.

The whole platoon present their arms in a way of saluting. The platoon salutes their commander; General Winder and President Madison are very impressed. Major Simon Smithtrovich is extremely impressed with the recruits. Simon walks down the stairs and stands face-to-face with his new soldiers of the Seventy-Sixth. Celestia and the recruits salute Simon.

Simon salutes them back. Simon then speaks to the platoon along with the rest of the Seventy-Sixth Pennsylvania.

"I am very impressed with you all. I am glad to say that all the new recruits have finished basic training. Congratulations to all you recruits—or should I now call you soldiers of the Seventy-Sixth Pennsylvania Keystone Grenadiers. I have our marching orders. We will be marching to Bladensburg, Maryland. We will be under the command of Major General William Winder. So you new recruits get to test your skills in battle against the lobsters sooner than you thought. I am allowing you all to go into the city to celebrate. However, there is a catch. Do not—and I repeat, do not—get drunk. Is that understood?" Simon says.

"Yes sir!" the Seventy-Sixth shout.

"Seventy-Sixth Pennsylvania, dismissed! Okay, now the new recruits can celebrate." Simon says quickly.

The twenty grenadiers cheer at having passed training, and the whole unit disperses. Simon walks up to President Madison and General Winder.

General William Winder gives Simon his orders. "Major, have your company ready to march at 0800 hours. Do you understand?"

"Yes sir! May I ask how our militia forces are holding up, sir?"

General Winder sighs. "Well, they are doing all they can to hold those lobsters back, but a lot of them are suffering heavy losses due to their leader."

"Who is their commanding officer, General?" Simon asks.

"Their commander's name is Major General Robert Ross. He is a veteran of the British Army in the Peninsular War," General Winder says.

Simon thinks about that name, and then it hits him like a thunderclap. He knows that name, and he is filled with a bit of fear inside his body. He shakes it off and then leaves the White House and rejoins his unit.

Celestia notices that Simon is a bit scared. She walks over to him and hugs him. "Major, what is wrong?" she asks.

Simon looks at her and says with a fearful voice.

"First Lieutenant, I have a feeling that we will be facing our greatest enemy in this bloody war. May God have mercy on our souls!"

CHAPTER 7

THE STREETS ARE PAVED WITH AMERICAN BLOOD

The Chesapeake Campaign, Part 1
August 19 to August 25, 1814

The day the twenty new Keystone grenadiers graduated basic training was on August 20th. One day prior, the redcoats under the command of Major General Robert Ross, a fearless Irishman who was veteran of the Napoleonic Wars and the Peninsular War who had been given an expeditionary force to attack the United States, had landed at Benedict, Maryland, on. He landed with over 4,500 men.

Ross's force is made up of multiple regiments and companies, such as the Eighty-Fifth Regiment of Foot, the Twenty-First, the Forty-Fourth of Foot, and a detachment of Royal Marines. Most of the British soldiers under Ross are vets who fought against the French. They are battle-hardened and highly trained soldiers. Just as they land upon Benedict, Maryland, several militia platoons sneak to the landing zones and begin to attack. The militia open fire and with their first shots manage to cut down a dozen redcoats. Although they manage to catch the redcoats by surprise, they encourage the wrath of the Royal Navy. A few small sloops fire upon the militia positions. Solid shot begins to rain from the sky and overwhelm the militias. A cannonball with a fuse lands in front of a group of five militiamen. The fuse ignites the powder inside the ball, and it explodes, sending out its shrapnel of musket balls. It is like a grenade but bigger. The five militiamen are riddled with musket balls and killed instantly.

The sight of the sloops and the hissing of the cannonballs is enough to make some of the militia to turn tail and flee. A few brave militias make a stand, but the redcoats fix their bayonets, charge from their boats, and begin to push the militia away. One militiaman is shot in the right leg and falls to the ground. A redcoat charges with his bayonet and thrusts it into the chest of his enemy. He stabs with the bayonet and twists the blade inside the man's body. The American lad cries out in massive pain with every twist. The redcoat then recovers his bayonet and moves on, leaving the American soldier dying right next to a few of his already dead brothers in arms. The first wave of landing redcoats has managed to clear the way for the rest of their brothers to safely land and begin their march to Washington.

Major General Robert Ross lands with the Royal Marines. Just before noon, all the British infantry, artillery, and cavalry landed. They begin their northward march to the city of Washington. Hundreds of American militia fight like hell to defend their towns and villages from the torch. Just a few hours later, a company of the Eighty-Fifth Regiment of Foot comes across a farm with a massive barn. The Eighty-Fifth marches toward the barn. All seems quiet until a volley erupts from the barn. Two dozen militia have taken refuge inside. They fire in a panic from the doors and any of the few windows inside the barn. One of the riflemen on the second floor of the barn manages to cut down one British sergeant who is leading the Eighty-Fifth to the barn. The redcoat company of the Eighty-Fifth returns fire. The bullets riddle the walls of the barn. Three militiamen are shot by the volley. The American militia flee the barn, leaving their fallen friends behind. Another volley by the Eighty-Fifth cuts down several more militiamen. They are shot in their backs as they flee. The Eighty-Fifth pitch torches, and they set fire to the barn. Within seconds the whole barn becomes a raging inferno. One of the militiamen who was shot was still alive. He manages to make it outside, but as he looks behind him, he sees the front frame of the barn begin to buckle. One redcoat drops his musket and runs over to the militiamen and drags him away from the barn. He gets him out of the way in time as the barn collapses to the ground. The American militiaman is stunned to have been saved by a British soldier. He looks up at him long enough to say before he dies, "You saved me! I thank you for not letting me burn. God bless your soul!" he said.

The redcoat takes the hand of the dying American and says to him, "Burning to death is no way for a soldier to die."

The American soldier takes his final breath and dies. The rest of the Eighty-Fifth march to their location, and the company rejoins the main force.

August 20, 1814
8:00 a.m. to 4:00 p.m.

The British continue their march, and the first moment of battle takes place outside of a town called Aquasco, Maryland. A company of the Forty-Fourth Foot engages against two platoons of Maryland militia. The Forty-Fourth Foot march toward the militia with bayonets presented. The militia form their ranks in ranks of fifty men that stretch fifty yards apart. The left rank of the Maryland troops fires a volley into the left flank of the Forty-Fourth Foot. The volley cuts down fifteen redcoats. Ten are wounded, and five are killed by the volley. The right flank fired their muskets and cut down thirteen redcoats, including a British lieutenant. The officer is shot directly in the head. The bullet exits out the back of the man's head. A British redcoat directly behind the officer is showered with blood and brains. The blood gets into the redcoat's eyes, and he drops to the ground.

"Help me! Help me, I am blind, damn it all!" the British soldier shouts.

Two of his comrades use their canteens to wash the blood off their friend's face. Then one uses a cloth and wipes the blood away. The man opens his eyes and is glad to find that he is not blind. Then he sees his officer with the back of his head blown away. He faints and falls into the arms of his comrades. The Forty-Fourth Foot return fire, and they need only fire one volley. The volley cuts down sixty-five men of the Maryland militia. One militiaman is shot as he fires his musket. Another is shot three times in the chest. Dozens are shot while they are trying to reload. The volley is enough to scare the remaining militia into retreating from the field. The Forty-Fourth Foot march forward with their bayonets to drive the enemy from the ground. The Forty-Fourth Foot's drum and fife corps plays "The British Grenadiers." The march echoes through the air and fills the Forty-Fourth Foot with great energy. But it sends the American forces

79

into panic mode. Some of the wounded militiamen try to escape but are bayoneted by the redcoats.

The Forty-Fourth Foot's losses are light, while the Maryland militia lose two thirds of their numbers. The bodies rot in the sun as the British continue their march to Washington.

Just after lunch, a Virginia militia of twenty men runs through a woods that leads to a small clearing and then another patch of woods. A rocket detachment of the Twenty-Sixth Royal Artillery Marines escort their rockets and cannons through the passage. The Virginia militia, armed with rifles and not muskets, waits for the detachment to enter the clearing. The woods are about fifty yards from the main passageway. The Twenty-Sixth was being covered with Royal Marine infantry. The Twenty-Sixth enters the clearing, and without a moment's hesitation, the Virginia militia open fire. One Royal Marine looks in the direction of the woods and sees an eruption of white rifle smoke. The volley kills seven Royal Artillerymen and six Royal Marines guarding the cannons. The artillerymen fall off the cannons and the ammo crate wagon. The militia reload their rifles, and the British Marines take advantage and unleash flankers to snuff out the militia. The flankers' job was to push the enemy away from the flanks of the main columns. This was a dangerous and ruthless tactic. The Virginia militia spot the flankers and melt away into the trees. The Royal Marines march back to the main columns, and the Twenty-Sixth load up their wounded. Then they continue their march forward down the road.

Thirty minutes later, the same militia are set up near the edge of a woods, and they wait for a company of soldiers from Forty-Fourth East Essex. They wait until they are within range, but this time they will be trying to take out the commanding officers. One British sergeant major is carrying the regimental colors. A rifleman aims his rifle and fires. The bullet hits the sergeant major in the head. The flag drops to the ground. Another redcoat picks up the flag, and then another shot rings out and the colors are dropped again. Every single time a redcoat tries to carry the flag, he is shot by a rifleman hiding in the trees. The royal artillery of the Twenty-Sixth decide that they have had enough of their brothers getting picked off, and they set up their rockets and their cannons. They fire rockets into the trees, and the rockets explode. The cannons fire shells into the trees. The shells cut trees in half, and the Virginian militiamen are not able to escape. The rockets explode on the dry grass, which catches fire within seconds. The riflemen are trapped in a fiery ring of hell. The woods are a massive ball of fire, and the riflemen are burned to death.

Despite the resistance, the British continue their march to Washington. Major General Robert Ross is very angry and frustrated about the resistance. He and Vice Admiral George Cockburn began to perform a tactic that the Russians deployed on Napoleon Bonaparte's Grand Armee during the invasion of Russia in 1812. The tactic is called "scorched earth," and it involves every single house, farm, and town being burned to the ground. Farmers and townspeople can only watch as their homes and villages are burned by the British.

August 22, 1814

3:00 p.m.

The town of Marlboro, Maryland

Two groups of five militiamen get held up in a two-story house. They pry up the doors and windows with the household furniture. They all take positions in various parts of the house. The first group of the five militiamen head up to the top floor. There they look out the window, trying to spot the redcoats. Then the music of British drums and fifes fills the air. Then Major General Robert Ross rides into view right in front of a company of fusiliers. The redcoats are fifty yards away, and they begin to march past the house. The redcoats do not notice the militia inside the house. But then a militia corporal gets an itchy trigger finger. He breaks the glass with the butt of his musket and fires upon the British column. His shot kills a cavalry officer. The officer falls off his horse and dies before he hits the dirt. The fusiliers halt and open fire upon the house. The musket balls tear through the wooden walls. The militiamen open fire upon the column. They killed three officers and wounded five infantrymen. Major General Ross rides forward and commands the fusiliers.

"Foot guards, make ready! Take aim! Fire!" General Ross shouts.

The volley rips into the house and kills two of the five militiamen. Then the Twenty-Sixth Royal Marine Artillery rolls up a twelve-pound cannon.

The militia tries to take out the artillerymen. The militiamen fire upon them and kill three out of five of the royal artillerymen. Two more redcoats help load and fire the cannon. The shell strikes the house, and the whole house is destroyed in a massive explosion.

The redcoats cheer and taunt the militiamen. Just then Major General Robert Ross rides upon and sees the destroyed house. Two redcoats are escorting a militiaman that was blown out of the house. Ross gets off his horse and walks over to the militiaman and talks to him.

"So you must be the bravest of your dead comrades," General Ross says. "Now, I want you to tell me whether there will be any more resistance? Will there be or not?"

The militiaman spits blood onto General Ross's coat. In his blood is one of his teeth. "There you go, lobster-back. That matches your uniform. As far as the resistance, you will not be surprised, because for every single step that you march, there will be thousands of soldiers just like me who are not afraid to stand in your way. We will never give up, because we are not just cattle for the slaughter. We are not your loyal subjects anymore and will never be until the end of time. So why don't you do America a favor and tell your king to blow his brains out in front of his own subjects."

Robert Ross pulls out his pistol and hits the man in the head. Then he aims at the militiamen's head. "How dare you talk about my beloved king! You are nothing but a traitorous rebel and a sorry excuse for a human being. The rest of your country will be brought back to His Majesty's loyalty or you all will be dead. Your children and your so-called whores of America will be our king's slaves. But your men will either be fighting for the king or hanging from the streets of London. Luckily the rest of your country can make that choice. Sadly, you won't!"

General Robert Ross shoots the militiaman in the head. His body hits the ground, and his blood spills out onto the street. The redcoats push on toward the city; a few of them set torches and burn houses in the towns as they march past.

Colonel William Thornton rides forward and sees the major dead on the ground. He rides ahead and catches up with General Ross. He questions him about killing the American militiaman. "General, was that really necessary?" he asks. General Ross laughs. "That was just a warning to all those who believe that they can fight against the best trained and most professional army in the whole world."

CHAPTER 8

THE MARCH TO BLADENSBURG, MARYLAND

The Chesapeake Campaign, Part 2
Washington, DC
August 22, 1814
8:00 a.m.

Major Simon Smitrovich and his staff take their places within the Seventy-Sixth. The color guard stands right behind them. The Seventy-Sixth Company Marching Band is third in the ranks. Then the foot soldiers, in rows of six, stand ready to move out. In front of them is the Baltimore Regiment that is commanded by Colonel Joseph Sterrett. To their rear is the First Infantry Battalion, commanded by Lieutenant Colonel William Scott.

General William Winder rides in front of the main columns. "The battalion will prepare to advance. To the front, quick march!" he shouts. The Baltimore regiment marches forward.

"Seventy-Sixth Pennsylvania, attention!" Major Simon Smithtrovich orders. "Left shoulder your firelocks! Company by the left step! Forward march!"

Drum Major Brittany Benson blows her whistle. She orders a mark time and forward march with a moderate whole note and four quarter notes. The Seventy-Sixth marches forward, and Privates Jessica and Devin Little play a slow drum cadence.

Timmy speaks to Simon. "Permission to speak, sir?"

"Permission granted, Sergeant," Simon says.

"Sir, shall we play a song? The regiments will be more motivated if they hear music, sir."

Simon smiles and looks back at his troops. He can see thirst and hunger for music. Simon shouts, "Drum Major Benson, would you please play 'Over the Hills and Far Away'?"

"Yes sir!" Brittany shouts. She blows her whistle for the band to prepare the song. She then blows four times. Devin, Jessica, and the main drummers play a twenty-second cadence, and then the whole unit joins in unison. The Seventy-Sixth's steps are so loud that they sound like constant thunder.

"Seventy-Sixth Pennsylvania, sound off!" Simon commands his troops.

The grenadiers and some of the other American regulars begin to sing their version of the famous British military march. They sound like a military choir.

> "Hark! Now the drums beat up again, for all true soldiers gentlemen, then let us list and march I say. Over the hills and far away.
> O'er the mountains' dreary waste to meet the enemy we haste. Liberty commands, and we'll obey. Over the hills and far away. Over the hills with heart we go to fight the proud insulting foe. Our country calls and we'll obey. Over the hills and far away. O'er the mountains' dreary waste to meet the enemy we haste. Liberty commands, and we'll obey. Over the hills and far away. Whoe'er is bold, whoe'er is free, will join and come along with me to drive the British without delay. Over the hills and far away.
> O'er the mountains' dreary waste to meet the enemy we haste. Liberty commands, and we'll obey. Over the hills and far away. On fair Niagara's banks we stand with musket and bayonet in hand. The British are beat; they dare not stay. But take to their heels and run away.
> O'er the mountains' dreary waste to meet the enemy we haste. Liberty commands, and we'll obey. Over the hills and far away. For we shall march together, my dears. We march to battle with no fears. America is here to stay. Over the hills and far away.

O'er the mountains' dreary waste to meet the enemy we haste.
Liberty commands, and we'll obey. Over the hills and far away.
Through smoke and fire, and shot and shell. And to the very
walls of hell. But we shall stand and we shall stay. Over the
hills and far away.
O'er the mountains' dreary waste to meet the enemy we haste.
Liberty commands, and we'll obey. Over the hills and far away.
For if we go, 'tis one to ten. But we return all gentlemen. All
gentlemen as well as they, when o'er the hills and far away.
O'er the mountains' dreary waste to meet the enemy we haste.
Liberty commands, and we'll obey. Over the hills and far
away."

(Original version written by, Seán "Clárach" Mac Domhnaill,
1715)
(American version written by, George Farquhar, words
1755 - 1812)

After marching six miles through the heat, the American defenders
have made their march to the town of Bladensburg, Maryland. The
Seventy-Sixth Pennsylvania sets up camp just two hundred yards away
from the East Branch Bridge. Celestia and Daisy are drilling, while Timmy
and Simon are talking about each other's family. Celestia and Daisy are
training with their bayonets. Celestia leads the training by giving out
commands.

"Thrust! Develop! En garde!" she says.

They repeat this ten times, and then they stand to attention.

"Order arms! Section dismissed!" Celestia commands.

They both sling their muskets. They sit on a log near the fire and drink
from their canteens.

"I really love the bayonet. This is, in my opinion, the number-one
weapon for close-quarters combat," Celestia says as she holds out her
bayonet.

"I agree," Daisy says. "This bayonet has saved my life more than a
dozen times. However, it pains me to see the faces of our enemies when we
thrust into their guts. I have seen some horrible faces that those redcoats
make."

"I know what you're saying. It doesn't feel right to do, but that's how warfare is nowadays. I have bayoneted twenty redcoat foot soldiers and six officers. How many have you bayoneted?" Celestia asks Daisy.

Daisy scratches her head and thinks for a few seconds. She counts on her fingers and speaks silently to herself. "I have twenty foot soldiers and five officers; however, I would have had the same kill count as you had Simon given me permission to bayonet that captain."

Daisy is kind of bummed that she couldn't kill that British officer at the Battle of Lundy's Lane. Celestia assures her that in time she will get another chance. "There comes a time when you must be a true soldier," she adds, "and one of the qualities of a true soldier is knowing when to spare an enemy." She pats her sister on the back.

"I guess that's why you're my big sister. Besides our father, you're the only one in the family who looked after me. I wonder where our family is right now?"

The Rose family was divided during the American Revolutionary War. Their mother's side of the family was loyal to the British. Their father's side of the family remained patriots. During the Revolutionary War, two thirds of the thirteen colonies remained loyalists, and one third were patriots. After the war ended, 72 percent of the loyalists sailed to England, but some believed that one day America would be reclaimed by the crown.

The Rose sisters get back to their training. Simon and Timmy talk about what the Seventy-Sixth could be facing within the next few days.

"Something tells me that we are not going to be facing down average lobsters. I have been hearing from the scouts that the lobsters have been slaughtering our militias as they march up here," Simon explains to Timmy.

"Jesus Christ!" Timmy replies. Those damn savages! How can they just kill without reason? We are not killing for a king; we are killing because we have to. There is a major difference, and that's a fact."

"To be truthful, I really didn't want to go to war. However, I really wanted to be a soldier. My father was an American regular for the Second Pennsylvania Regiment during the Revolution, and his first battle was at Bunker Hill."

When Timmy hears "Second Pennsylvania," he remembers that his own father fought with the second as well.

"That's funny, because my father was at Bunker Hill as well. He also served with the Second Pennsylvania. I think both of our fathers were fighting alongside each other in the same battles."

They look at each other in disbelief. They both say at the same time to each other, "What are the bloody odds of that?" They both laugh.

"Sir, if you had to guess, what would you think the British are going to do, sir?" Timmy asks.

Simon stands up and looks down at the East Branch Bridge. Simon begins to think about a battle that made Napoleon famous—the Battle of Arcole.

"I have a great feeling that General Ross will try to pull an Arcole bridge crossing."

Timmy is confused and does not know what Simon means. So Simon explains what happened at the Battle of Arcole. "On November 15, 1796, General Bonaparte led eighteen thousand French soldiers to Arcole, Italy. Their main objective was to destroy the Austrian Army by any means necessary. They crossed through a wooded forest where a low-hanging fog blinded them. Bonaparte and his aide-de-camp, Jean-Baptiste Murion, scouted the bridge, and they decided that they had to take the bridge. However, the Austrians had that bridge covered with artillery. Nevertheless, they regrouped with their army, and Bonaparte grabbed the regimental flag and charged like a regular soldier. The Austrians heard their battle cries, and a platoon of foot soldiers blocked the bridge. Just as they started to cross the bridge, the Austrians fired volley after volley into the French. They were about fifty-five paces away from crossing the bridge. One of the volleys fired by the Austrians would have killed Bonaparte, but Murion shielded him. Murion was shot about four or five times in the chest. A small number of French and Austrian soldiers died during the battle. But this was just on the first day. This battle would drag on for two more days. The French suffered forty-eight hundred casualties, while the Austrians suffered sixty-two hundred casualties. History could repeat itself, but I feel that this battle will be completely different by comparison."

Timmy is spellbound and amazed by the story.

"How in the world do you know all that, sir?" Timmy asked Simon.

Simon chuckles. He sits right next to Timmy. "My friend, I read a lot of books. Plus my one year at Yale taught me a lot about studying military tactics. Now muster up the Seventy-Sixth. I need to give them their final orders before the fighting begins. We do not know when the British are going to arrive."

"Yes sir!" Timmy says. He stands up and speaks to the bugler.

"Sound the assembly!"

The bugler sounds the assembly call. The troops of the Seventy-Sixth rally and form their ranks. Simon stands in front of his troops. "Now the redcoats are going to arrive possibly by this weekend. They will come down through Bladensburg. They will go up the main bridge. Our main goal is to keep them from crossing the bridge at all costs. Now, if they cross the bridge, we will reconnect with US Marines and continue to defend the line. And if we get beaten back again, we are to retreat to Washington DC and help get the civilians out of the city. Most importantly, we must get the president and the first lady out of danger before the redcoats arrive. Do you all understand these orders?"

"Yes sir!" the soldiers of the Seventy-Sixth shout.

"Now, my friends of the brave Seventy-Sixth, I must tell you about what we are truly dealing with here. But first a little history. On April 19, 1775, a shot was fired that was heard around the world. On June 17, 1775, a rebellion turned into a declaration of war against the British Empire. For six long and bloody years. The world turned upside down for independence. Now that America had won its freedom, a question arose from the ashes of the battlefields that our families had fought upon: can we hold on to our freedom when that day arrives when we must step up and take the places of those who went before us and shed their blood, who risked their lives and gave up their lives not just for America but for future generations of American citizens and soldiers, and who will one day look back and learn about how the few stood against many? For the past two years, we have lost family, fathers, brothers, cousins, and true friends. Hell, this country is not even forty years old, and we are on the verge of extinction. We will not let this great nation become another British colony again. We are not their bloody slaves. We are the ones who will do the impossible to claim victory for our families back home. We are the ones who are not afraid to march into our destiny and never have any second thoughts or doubts. We earned our freedom, and now we must stand to face another foe that wants to destroy all that we love and cherish. We have one thing that those lobsters can only dream of—the unity of friendship!"

The Keystone grenadiers smile and murmur among themselves. They know that Simon is speaking the truth. Celestia holds her chest, for she is touched by the speech.

Simon looks at the young faces of his grenadiers and asks them a question. "My friends of the brave Seventy-Sixth, I ask you, what is our motto?"

For a few seconds no one says a word. Then Timmy speaks the famous Pennsylvanian battle cry. "Virtue, liberty, independence!" Timmy says with pride.

One by one, the soldiers of the Seventy-Sixth repeat the motto.

Simon gets a smile upon his face, and he wants to hear his brave comrades in arms say it louder. "Let's hear that motto one more time, and this time I want you to scream out, because we are Pennsylvanians. Now, what is our damn motto that represents the state of Pennsylvania?" Simon shouts.

"Virtue, liberty, independence!" the Seventy-Sixth shout with strong pride and energy.

The whole unit begins to cheer so loudly that their battle cries can be heard throughout the whole American camp. Simon and his staff stand together and watch as their fellow soldiers' spirits soar higher than the stars that shine bright up in the night skies.

The British Army, under the command of Major General Robert Ross, arrived at Bladensburg two days later, on August 23. On the final night before the battle, the Seventy-Sixth spends time with each other. Simon and his staff sit by the campfire and enjoy each other's company, knowing that tomorrow, one of them or all of them could be killed in the heat of battle. The heat of the fire keeps them warm. Simon and Celestia share a blanket, while Timmy, Daisy, and Brittany share one as well.

"Tomorrow will be the difference between whether our nation will finally defeat the British or whether they will be knocking on the door of the White House," Celestia says as she pokes a stick at a log in the fire.

Simon and his staff have mixed feelings about what the battle is going to bring.

"I am actually nervous, and this is the first time. I hope that the blood that will be shed will not be in vain," Daisy says with a hint of fear.

"No offence, but that is nonsense!" Timmy assures Daisy. "All our grenadiers that have fallen have not died for nothing. They all died to preserve our nation and to let those invaders know that we will not quit the war."

"Damn right, Sergeant!" Simon says. "Listen, we have come too far to give up the fight. Our nation needs us now more than ever. If we surrender, then all the blood that our families have shed in the Revolution would have definitely been for nothing."

Then Brittany remembers a memory from when they were kids. She smiles and chuckles. "Remember when we were kids and we used to play soldiers with our neighboring town friends? We created our own forts, and we fought for hours on end. I miss those days—the glory days of our childhood."

They all think about the memory in the backs of their minds, and it soothes their worries a little bit. But they all realize that this is the real deal and any one of them can be killed at any second, whether in the first moments or the final moments of battle. Celestia looks up at the stars and sees a shooting star soaring through the clear sky. Simon spots the shooting star as well.

"What do you wish for, sir?" Celestia asks Simon.

Simon looks at Celestia's eyes, and they kiss.

"Aww, that's so lovely." Brittany says.

"That is my sister's first kiss. Congrats, big sister. I actually had mine back in 1812," Daisy says.

"Get a tent, Major!" Timmy says jokingly.

Simon and Celestia unlock lips. "I wished that all of us, including our troops, would live to see the end of this war," Simon says. "But deep in my heart, I know that possibly that will not come true." He looks to Celestia. "What did you wish for?"

"I wished that this war shall be over soon. However, this war has brought us closer than ever before. This has been a real adventure, and I will miss these blessed nights."

Simon looks at his pocket watch. "It is ten minutes till midnight. We had better get some sleep, because if I miss my prediction, tomorrow is going to be one hell of a day. Good night, my friends," Simon says.

"Good night, sir!" his friends reply.

They douse the fire and head off to bed in their tents. They all lay in their bunks and wonder about what tomorrow was going to bring. Eventually, they all finally fall asleep.

CHAPTER 9

THE BATTLE OF BLADENSBURG

The Chesapeake Campaign, Part 3
Bladensburg, Maryland
August 24, 1814
Noontime

The British invasion force awaits their orders from Major General Robert Ross. Ross, in many ways, is the ideal combat commander. He is very aggressive, he is very brave, and he always leads at the front of his troops. He is never afraid to do something that no higher-ranking officers or junior officers will do in a battle. He and his staff see the American forces, and all they can do is laugh and jeer at the defenses that the Americans have made. Ross gives his junior officers the orders to begin their attack.

"Wow! How very intimidating these pathetic American barricades they have constructed are. This will be easier than we thought. Now, are your men ready to attack, Colonel?" Ross says to Colonel William Thornton.

"Yes sir, my men will make those Yankee Doodle bastards turn and run like rabbits," Colonel William Thornton assures his commander. "They have been itching to take on those Yanks. If the god of war couldn't beat my men during the Peninsular War, I can't imagine what these Americans can do to our troops. They will never stop us, sir."

"I shall hope not, for your sake, Colonel. Now to business, Colonel. You may attack. My orders to all commanders: commence the attack!"

With that order, the British begin their advance against three American lines on the other side of the bridge. The American forces have three lines on both sides of the bridge. The Seventy-Sixth is stationed at the one in the middle that covers the East Branch Bridge. Colonel William Thornton salutes General Ross and rides toward his men waiting in the center of town. "The Eighty-Fifth will advance toward the front. We will begin the attack by crossing the East Branch Bridge. Light Brigade to the front! Shoulder your firelocks; quick march!"

The Eighty-Fifth Light Infantry marches forward down the Annapolis road toward the East Branch Bridge. The drummers and fifers play "The British Grenadiers" On the other side, the American forces stand ready for the British attack. The American officers in the middle section of the American line are made up of the Seventy-Sixth Pennsylvania Keystone Grenadiers and the Baltimore Regiment. The Pennsylvanians stand ready at the front of the bridge. They hear the sound of drum and fife music coming from the British lines, and they know that the battle is about to begin.

Simon calls to his men. "Listen to my orders and you shall see the sun rise tomorrow morning. No one shall retreat without my order. Anyone who runs away will be shot by me. Rely on your training and, most importantly, the fellow soldiers all around you. Do you all understand my orders?" Simon says to the Seventy-Sixth.

"Yes sir!" the Seventy-Sixth shout.

Sergeant Miller spots the Eighty-Fifth Regiment of Foot about to cross the bridge. "Here they come!" he shouts.

"Seventy-Sixth, prime and load! Once you are loaded, wait for my order to fire," Simon orders his men.

All the grenadiers of the Seventy-Sixth load their muskets very fast. They can see the redcoats marching towards them. Some of the soldiers in the Seventy-Sixth are new to the war.

One Keystone grenadier gets scared, but Timmy pats the soldier's back. "Be not afraid, lad. We are with you, for here we face our fears together. Remember that you are not alone, my friend. Now make your family and your nation proud by standing your ground." Timmy speaks with a calm voice that helps his fellow grenadier get his confidence back.

In the rear of the lines with the Eighth Maryland is Colonel Joseph Sterrett. "Cannons one through three, prime and load your pieces!" he shouts to his artillerymen.

The process of loading a cannon cannot be rushed; however, during battle that rule sometimes goes out the door. First, a leather thumb jacket, which is a leather piece that you put your thumb into and place it on the vent hole that you would light the fuse, seals the back of the hole as the barrel is cleared of any debris. A damp sponge creates a vacuum that kills any live embers. Then the black powder charge and cannonball are inserted and carefully rammed. A vent pick pierces the charge, and the hole is packed with more powder to ignite the shell.

Colonel Joseph Sterrett gives his orders to open fire. "Cannons one, two, and three, prepare to fire. Target the bridge. All cannons open fire!"

The three cannons open fire, and the shells fly through the air. The Eighty-Fifth hear the cannon fire, and they see the shells flying toward their direction. The shell impacts on all sides of the bridge. The shrapnel strikes several British soldiers. A spray of blood showers other redcoats. Despite the cannon barrage, they keep marching across the bridge. They step over their fellow soldiers as if they are logs of wood. A platoon of redcoats manages to march across the bridge, and the Seventy-Sixth and the Baltimore Regiment are waiting for them.

Major Simon Smithtrovich shouts, "Seventy-Sixth Pennsylvania, make ready! Take aim! Fire!"

They aim their muskets accurately and fire a volley that makes a terrible roar like a crack of thunder. The volley makes a thick blanket of white smoke. Ten British soldiers are hit by the volley; three are shot in the head, five are shot in the chest, one takes three musket balls to his left and right legs, and one is shot directly in the groin. Several British soldiers fall off the bridge and land in the water. The Eighty-Fifth halts its advance. The redcoats of the Eighty-Fifth raise their muskets and return fire. After firing their volley, the Seventy-Sixth reload their muskets. This takes them fifteen to twenty seconds.

The foot guards of the Eighty-Fifth halt their march and return fire.

"Eighty-Fifth, take care; halt! Foot guards, make ready, present, Fire!" Colonel William Thortan shouts to his men.

The British advance party of foot guards fires a volley that erupts a white smoke. Both sides reload their muskets and they fire at will, where they reload and fire at their own pace. Soldiers on both sides get cut down. The chaos of battle begins to get intense as the Seventy-Sixth and the Eighty-Fifth fire upon each other. Both sides fire relentlessly at each other. The musket fire sounds like a terrible thunderstorm. After a few minutes the Eighty-Fifth begins to retreat. The British cannons open fire on the Seventy-Sixth Pennsylvanian positions. Several cannons fire, and the shells explode all around the lines of the Seventy-Sixth. Suddenly the British unleashed a new type of weapon that was used in the Napoleonic Wars, the Congreve rocket. These rockets were filled with explosive ordnance and were used to target ammo depots and start fires in camps.

The redcoats fire several rockets, and the rockets scream while they fly through the air. Two of them land on Colonel Sterrett's cannons.

"Incoming!" Colonel Sterrett shouts.

They explode, and one of his cannons blows up, killing a dozen artillerymen, Then Simon sees the whole American left flank break and run away from the field. They retreat, and a few American soldiers get shot in their backs. The American left flank is covered with retreating American soldiers. They are engulfed by British artillery fire. Shells land on the ground and explode. The explosions kick up earth, dust, and dirt. The American soldiers run through the field. The shells explode directly in their faces. Simon is appalled upon seeing his fellow countrymen retreating. One American militiaman has an explosion of fire blasted right into his face. He falls to the ground with a severely burnt face. Simon looks through his spyglass. He cannot believe what he is seeing.

"Holy lord, there goes our left flank! Who in the hell gave that order?" Simon shouts.

Sergeant Timmy Miller runs over to Simon as a bullet whizzes right past his head. Simon and Timmy duck down below the barrage of hot lead.

"Major, what the hell do we do now, sir?" Timmy shouts to Simon.

Simon answers Timmy immediately.

"We got orders. They told us to beat these bastards back, and that is what we're going to do!" Simon shouts.

Simon stands up and looks at the bridge despite the heavy musket fire. He can see the British soldiers beginning their second assault. He pauses for a few seconds and pulls out his bayonet. He looks up, and his men wait for his next order. He speaks with a normal tone to his fellow grenadiers.

"Grenadiers, fix your bayonets!" Simon says.

The Seventy-Sixth fix their bayonets and wait for the redcoats to get close. A British officer gives his orders to his cannon crews to fire chain shot. One artillery crew places a chain shot load, which is two cannonballs connected by a chain, into their cannon. The chain shot flies through the air, and two American soldiers are hit by it and are both decapitated. Their heads explode in a shower of blood and brains.

Simon and Timmy were watching as those American soldiers lost their heads. Simon has a face full of fear, but he gets a grip in a few seconds.

Timmy is horrified at the sight of his soldiers getting slaughtered in that manner and screams at the redcoats, "You murdering bastards!"

The British unleash their second infantry assault. The redcoats storm across the bridge and soon reach the Seventy-Sixth Pennsylvania line. The sight of the redcoats scares the Keystone grenadiers deep inside their bodies, but they do not outwardly show the redcoats any fear. Simon calls to his grenadiers to prepare for the bayonet charge.

"Here they come, my friends. Give them the cold steel! Hold the line!" Simon shouts.

The Seventy-Sixth Pennsylvanian Keystone Grenadiers are met with a British bayonet charge. Several Seventy-Sixth soldiers are stabbed in their chests by the bayonets. Several redcoats are bayoneted as they charge over the wall. Simon bayonets a redcoat as he vaults over the wall. Both sides get entangled, and a bloody melee begins. Timmy can't grip his musket, as it is covered in blood and sweat. A redcoat charges him with a bayonet, but Timmy picks up a pistol and shoots the redcoat in the chest. Another redcoat charges at him. Simon sees the redcoat charging at Timmy, and he unsheathes his sword and throws it like a javelin. The sword strikes the redcoat in the chest. Part of the blade sticks out of the British soldier's back. The redcoat falls to his knees, gasping for air as he looks at the sword inside his body. Simon runs over to the redcoat and pulls his sword out of the redcoat's chest. Simon reaches his hand out to Timmy and pulls him onto his feet.

"Thank you, sir," Timmy says as Simon hands him his musket.

"You're welcome," Simon says.

Other Seventy-Sixth grenadiers struggle to hold their own against the relentless redcoat assault. One grenadier and a British soldier try to bash each other's head with the butts of their muskets. The redcoat grabs the grenadier's musket and manages to land a savage punch on his enemy's throat. The grenadier drops to his knees and grabs his neck. He gasps for air, but he is soon stabbed three times in the chest by a British bayonet.

A British officer is surrounded by four American regulars. The officer circles around with his sword out in front of him. He tries to keep his foes at a distance. One American soldier manages to thrust his bayonet into the officer's back. The officer screams and swings his sword and slashes the American soldier's throat. The Yankee has his jugular slashed. Huge amounts of blood spill out from the Yankee's throat. The British officer gets bayoneted to death. More American soldiers get killed or wounded, and other redcoats march into their lines to continue the fight. Both sides fire their muskets up close and personal. Soldiers are shot in their chests, legs, arms, hands, and even in their faces.

The Seventy-Sixth Pennsylvania begins to run out of ammo. They see the redcoats begin to gain the upper hand and begin to panic, but Simon manages to keep them from running. One tries to run away from the battle, but Simon grabs the young lad by his coat. He yells at the lad's face, "You're a grenadier! You go back to your place in line or I will cut you down!" Before the American soldier can answer, a bullet strikes the soldier's head and he falls to the ground. Simon spots the redcoat shooter and aims his musket and fires. Simon kills the redcoat with a bullet to his right eye. The redcoat falls backward and puts his hand over his eye. Simon looks down at the boy and can see blood spilling out of the lad's head. He feels a twinge of sadness, but he has to save it for after the battle. He turns to his men and quickly thinks about an order that he has never given to his grenadiers since the war started. He orders them to retreat, but not before they fire one more volley into the Eighty-Fifth.

The twenty new Keystone grenadiers stand with the Seventy-Sixth Corps Marching Band, defending them from British bayonet attacks. Every single time a group of redcoats attacks them. They manage to beat them back. Drum Major Benson stands with her corps. Among them, Jessica and Devin comfort each other amid the hellish sight of battle.

Suddenly the right flank begins to fall. The redcoats on the right flank march upon the Seventy-Sixth and the Baltimore Regiment. They fire a volley and knock down a dozen redcoats. Suddenly the British cannons fire upon the Pennsylvania and Baltimore units. Dozens of shells explode all around the center US line. One cannonball strikes one of the American cannons. The five artillerymen manning the cannon die from the blast. Simon and Timmy are blown off their feet by a cannonball exploding near their feet. They are covered in dirt and grass. Amazingly, they are not wounded, and they brush off the dirt and grass. They stand up and continue to fight.

The redcoats reach the second line of defense, and once again the Pennsylvanians and the Baltimore Regiment are mixed into hand-to-hand combat. Men are stabbing, shooting, and using their muskets as clubs. Simon swings his sword and engages redcoat soldiers. A redcoat lieutenant fights Simon sword-on-sword. The redcoat fights in the style of a duel. He has his left hand behind his back, while Simon fights with both hands on the grip of his sword. Both of them try for a kill. However, Simon is able to overpower the British officer by knocking the sword out of his hand. He chops and strikes the redcoat in his left shoulder. The sword strike cuts the redcoat's arm almost completely off his body. Huge amounts of blood spill out of the redcoat's wound. Simon withdraws his sword, and the redcoat falls to the ground dead.

Sergeant Miller and other Seventy-Sixth Grenadiers are fighting to defend the cannons. They stand right beside the artillerymen as they continue to fire their pieces. When the artillerymen begin to reload a cannon, the grenadiers fire into the British lines. They fire at a section of the Eighty-Fifth Light Infantry. They exchange volleys at close range. The redcoats fire a volley, and a bullet hits Timmy's bearskin cap, and it flies off his head. The force of the bullet throws him back on his butt. Timmy picks up his hat and sees how close the bullet was to hitting his head. He rubs the top of his head. Amazingly, he is not wounded. He gets up and he continues the fight. He guns down the redcoat execution-style. Blood squirts on Timmy's face. He wipes the blood off his face with his sleeve. The Seventy-Sixth Pennsylvania regroups along with the Baltimore Regiment. Just then, Colonel Joseph Sterrett and Major William Pinkney rally their men, but with the sight of the massing redcoats, they decide to break and run. Major Pinkney urges his fellow defenders to retreat calmly. Most of them run away as though they are being chased by the devil himself. The whole Baltimore Regiment breaks from the field. The Seventy-Sixth Pennsylvania Keystone Grenadiers fall back as well to the third line. They fire backward at the redcoats, hitting only a few of them. Just as the Seventy-Sixth reaches the American third line of defense, Commodore Joshua Barney arrives with 114 US Marines and two hundred naval infantry forces. He is horrified to see the American defenders in complete disarray.

Simon, Timmy, and a few other grenadiers drop to the ground, exhausted. But Simon gets back up as the commodore rides up to him, maintaining discipline in the presence of a superior officer.

"Sir, those lobsters are marching close behind us, sir," Simon says, trying to catch his breath. "They have managed to get across the bridge. They fired Congreve rockets at us. The rockets cut our men down. Half of the men are dead or wounded, sir."

The rest of the American regulars and militia rally around Commodore Barney. The marines and naval forces perform a defense around the final line.

Commodore Barney calls out the American defenders. "Catch your breath, my friends. We shall steady ourselves and prepare to defend. Face the British and do not be intimidated. Give all those bastards everything you have, my brave Americans!"

Little does he know that his words are not going to be enough to stop the Bladensburg races.

The redcoats march toward the American third line. Some of the redcoats are beginning to suffer from heat stroke just trying to keep up with the American forces. A few redcoats are unable to weather the fatigue and fall to the ground dead. The British continue their march and see the American third line. The Battle of Bladensburg continues.

As the redcoats advance upon the American forces, the third line of the American defenders make a desperate last stand against Major General Robert Ross's veterans. Despite the final stand, the redcoats under Ross are amazed by the pitiful resistance. One British corporal says, "I expected more from Yankee Doodle."

The Pennsylvanians' firing line erupts in white smoke. The volley tears through the British line; fifteen redcoats are hit. A few seconds later, the whole American line fires at the advancing redcoats with muskets and cannons. Cannonballs explode all around the British line. One cannonball lands in front of the British line, and the explosion cuts down several redcoats at once. The volley cuts down ten more redcoats, with wounds to their heads, chests, legs, and arms. The British soldiers halt their advance and return fire. From the rear, the second platoon of the Seventy-Sixth Pennsylvania arrived and formed up with the rest of the unit. The Rose sisters march forward and look straight ahead with faces that show no fear. Their fellow grenadiers form up their lines right behind the Seventy-Sixth. First Lieutenant and First Sergeant Rose walk over and salute Simon. Simon salutes them back.

"Lieutenant Celestia Rose and First Sergeant Daisy Rose, glad y'all could make it," Simon says.

Celestia rallies up with Simon. They look at each other and smile. Daisy stands right beside Timmy.

"Well, sir, I would say that you have seemed to miss me. Well, I missed you too, sir."

Celestia looks at Simon's dirty uniform and sees the blood on his face. "Jesus! You look like shite! Is the fighting that bad today?" she asks.

Simon uses his musket as a stand to keep himself from falling down. Simon and his 1st platoon are exhausted, but they are keeping up the fight. "Yes, it is! We have never faced redcoats like this before. They must be Napoleonic redcoats."

"He is not lying, ma'am," Timmy agrees. "Those redcoats are the toughest bastards we have ever fought. Nonetheless, we are going to continue to resist."

Simon and Celestia grab their muskets and form up with the rest of the unit. The American soldiers wait for the British to advance, but for five minutes there's no sign of the redcoats. The redcoats continue their advance, and the American soldiers prepare for their last defense. Just then a volley of musket fire erupts from the trees. The volley cuts down ten American regulars and two officers on horseback. Seconds later, the redcoats emerge.

"Marines, make ready! Take aim! Open fire!" Barney orders his marines.

The United States Marines fired a volley into the British line. The bullets cut down twenty-five redcoats. Despite the volley, the redcoats charge with their bayonets. Once again both sides are entangled in hand-to-hand combat. The British run their bayonets through the defenders in the most furious manner. They stab the American soldiers in their chests, legs, and necks, and even through the heads. The Seventy-Sixth Pennsylvania Grenadiers are overrun by the Eighty-Fifth light infantry. Both sides clash with bayonets. Simon and Celestia fight back-to-back, trying to defend themselves against the onslaught of the British. A redcoat charges at Timmy, but his chest explodes in a fine mist of blood. Timmy looks behind him and sees Daisy with her pistol aimed down toward him. The barrel of her pistol is smoking. Both of them run to the rear of the line. The rest of the American lines begin to panic and retreat back to Washington.

Simon sees that the redcoats will not stop and he fears for the rest of his company's safety. For the first time in his military career, he has to issue an order that he never thought he wouldn't have to order. "Grenadiers, reform and prepare to retreat. We must cover the retreat."

The Seventy-Sixth reforms and forms a rear guard as the rest of the American forces retreat in a hellish panic back to Washington. First Lieutenant Celestia Rose orders the Seventy-Sixth to retreat in a professional manner.

"Do not show your backs to them. Retreat facing the enemy! Steady marching pace!" Celestia shouts to the Seventy-Sixth.

The grenadiers retreat facing the enemy, slowly marching backwards. They fire back at the redcoats. Sergeant Timmy Miller and First Sergeant Daisy Rose gather other Pennsylvanian grenadiers and form them up to cover the rest of the retreating soldiers. The Seventy-Sixth Grenadiers form a barrier, but soon they get entangled with retreating militiamen. The redcoats fire their rockets and muskets, and the retreat turns into utter chaos. The British slowly march with their bayonets presented. The remaining American regulars and militias retreat in primitive terror. One American regular is running with the American flag as he is blasted by a cannon shell. The flag flies into the air, and a militiaman catches it. He tries to run, but he is shot. The flagstaff hits the ground, and the soldier clutches the flag. Then another American blue coat grabs the flag. As he tries to carry the colors, he is shot and falls to the ground. One by one, seven American soldiers try to carry the flag to safety but die before they can run. As the final soldier falls to the ground, Daisy runs and grabs the flag. She looks at the redcoats and spots three of them taking aim at her. But before they can fire, Simon, Timmy, and Celestia rush right beside her and fire at the three redcoats. Their shots find their marks. Celestia grabs Daisy's arm and begins escorting her back to the main force. The Seventy-Sixth Pennsylvania retreat facing the enemy back to Washington. The redcoats reform their ranks and do not chase after the retreating American soldiers. The Seventy-Sixth manages to escape, but several units are still falling behind. Simon looks at the companies that are accounted for. Two companies are still missing.

"Wait a minute. Lieutenant Rose, there are two companies missing. Wasn't there a company of regulars and militia in front of us?" Simon says.

"I thought they were in front of us," Celestia says.

Then Celestia spots the two missing companies running through a field. She opens her spyglass and sees the terror and fear on their faces. Then she sees the Twenty-Sixth Royal Marine Artillery. They fire their cannons and Congreve rockets.

"Oh, God!" she exclaims.

She drops her spyglass. The Seventy-Sixth can only watch as the Royal Artillery bombards the two companies. Dozens of cannonballs land all around the open field. Dozens are struck by shells as they explode in huge fireballs. They are overwhelmed by the fiery blasts. Some of the soldiers are hit, and their body parts are blown off their bodies. Legs and arms are strewn, and blood fills the air every time an American soldier is hit.

After one hour of battle, the American forces have been driven away. They run so fast the redcoats suffer heat stroke trying to keep up with them. This battle will later come to be known as the Bladensburg Races. On the British side, Major General Robert Ross rides up with Colonel Arthur Brooke and watches the last of the American soldiers running away from the field. General Robert Ross sees an American officer on the ground with a bullet deep in his thigh. He rides over to the officer and sees it is Commodore Joshua Barney. He gets off his horse and comes to

Barney's side. They both speak famous lines that will be inscribed into history books.

"Sir, I am very glad to see you again, Commodore," Robert Ross says.

"I am very sorry that I cannot return the compliment, General," Barney says very weakly.

The two smile and shake hands. Then Ross turns to Colonel Brooke.

"I told you it was flotilla men, sir," General Ross says.

"Yes, you were right, sir," Vice Admiral Cockburn says. "Though I could not believe you. They gave us the only fight we have had."

Colonel Thornton rides over to General Ross. He is very upset and filled with hate for the Seventy-Sixth Pennsylvania.

"Sir, here is my report. My casualties are fifteen dead, times three wounded, sir. Some of my men died from the damned heat, sir. Those godforsaken Seventy-Sixth Pennsylvanians were here again, and they tore my men apart, sir."

General Ross tries to calm his junior officer down.

"Silence, Colonel! First: I will get your men the ammo and water they need. Second: what unit were you fighting against, Colonel?"

General Ross then looks down at a bearskin cap that was left behind. It belonged to a Seventy-Sixth grenadier. He looks at the armored plate and then looks up the road. "It was the Seventy-Sixth Pennsylvania, sir. Their commander is Major Simon Smithtrovich, sir. Word is, sir, that he was one of the men who helped set fire to the Canadian Parliament building last year in April, sir."

Major General Robert Ross looks out into the distance and then gazes upon the dead and wounded upon the field.

"Sir, shall we chase down this fox?" Colonel Thornton asks.

"No, Colonel! I shall hunt down this fox myself. Get the men moving, and get Commodore Barney to a surgeon immediately!" General Ross says.

British soldiers rush over and help Barney onto a stretcher and carry him to the surgeon. The redcoats continue their advance toward Washington. Most of the American Army retreats back to Washington DC. However, not all the American forces retreat. The Seventy-Sixth Pennsylvania Keystone Grenadiers continue to fight back, and their next attack will show General Robert Ross that the Seventy-Sixth Pennsylvania will not give up so easily. The Seventy-Sixth Pennsylvania retreat down a dirt road and come upon an abandoned eight-pound cannon with a powder wagon right beside it.

Celestia stops and looks at the cannon. "Wait, everyone; I have an idea on how we can slow them down!" she shouts.

Simon stops for a few seconds and tries to decide whether to stay or keep his promise to the president. He decides to stop the company.

"Seventy-Sixth Pennsylvania, halt. Kneel down and form a defense. Staff officers, form up on me!"

First Lieutenant Rose and First Sergeant Rose, Sergeant Miller, and Drum Major Benson rally upon Simon just ten yards away from the cannon. The Seventy-Sixth forms a defensive cul-de-sac to watch the road for the British. As Celestia begins to explain her plan, Simon could see what Celestia had in mind.

Celestia has a sinister look on her face as she explains. "Sir, we have six barrels of black powder, and I was thinking we can trick the redcoats into trying to take the cannon. Once they try to take it, we'll blow the gunpowder and blow the road apart. A massive fire will consume the road and stop them in their tracks."

Timmy adds, "Also, with our green uniforms, we can hide in the trees and fire right into them. We can use the trees to conceal us."

Daisy steps in with a good extra part to the ambush plan. "We can fire into the smoke. And there will be so much smoke from the fire they won't be able to tell where it's coming from."

Simon likes the plan but feels that the musket fire is a very sketchy part of the plan. "Hmm, I like that idea. With all due respect, Lieutenant, have you spit your bit or something? Our muskets are loud as the percussion section of our marching band."

Simon looks around at his surroundings and then looks at the cannon and the barrels of black powder. Then the idea hits him like a lightning strike during a thunderstorm. "Unless we fire at the exact moment the powder goes off. The explosion will cover our gunshots. Okay, once the powder blows, fire exactly one second after the blast. Then fire a second volley for good effect. And then fall back. Understood?"

"Yes sir!"

Three grenadiers grab three powder kegs and pour the powder all over the cannon and onto the road. The rest of the men hide in the bushes alongside the road. Celestia pours a line of gunpowder toward the other side of the road so it will light up on the right-hand side. After a few minutes, everything is set.

"Okay, that is done," Simon says. "Grenadiers, into the trees and bushes. Wait for my command to open fire. We must time this just right."

Timmy runs over to Simon. "Major, I do have a secondary extra we can put on the field. I have five grenades. And since we are grenadiers, we shall let those bastards know."

Simon and Celestia laugh.

"That will do just great," Celestia replies. "Sergeant, give four other men one grenade each." Timmy hands four other grenadiers the grenades. Soon they hear drums coming from down the road. Soldiers finish pouring the gunpowder on the road and run to their positions. All of them hide in the trees in a cul-de-sac formation. All the Pennsylvanians hide to the left and right sides of the road and aim their muskets down the road.

The Royal Marine advance party is being led down the road by Sergeant Major Harry Adams.

"Royal Marines, take care; halt!" Sergeant Major Adams shouts to his men.

Sergeant Major Harry Adams and two British soldiers walk over to the cannon. Then Major General Robert Ross rides up to the front of the advance guard. He sees the cannon and then speaks to Sergeant Major Adams.

"Sergeant Major, what is the bloody holdup?"

Harry salutes General Ross. "Sir, this cannon is blocking our way. My guess, sir, is that those Yankees forgot it. The cannon looks like it's in perfect condition. Shall we take the cannon, sir?"

"Very well, but be quick about it, we must get to Washington before nightfall."

Major General Robert Ross rides back to the middle of the British force. Several British soldiers walk toward the cannon, and other British soldiers walk in front of the cannon to guard it.

The Pennsylvanians wait in the trees. They do not speak as they wait for the command to spring the trap. One American grenadier accidentally steps forward and snaps a twig on the ground. A redcoat looks up the road. He sees nothing and continues to get the cannon hooked up.

"Hold on, men; wait until they surround the cannon. Celestia, throw the grenade, you do it, wait until they surround the bloody cannon."

Celestia grabs the grenade from Simon and waits for the right moment. The powder kegs are not visible, because the redcoats are in front of them. Then one redcoat walks to the right side of the road. One powder keg is wide open. Celestia lights the fuse and she throws the grenade. The grenade flies through the air and lands in front of the barrel of powder. The keg explodes and starts a chain reaction, which causes the other kegs to blow up. One redcoat has another powder keg in his hands, and it explodes in his arms. His arms blow off his body, and his chest erupts in a pool of blood. Other redcoats are struck by shrapnel from the kegs. Several redcoats are blown off their feet and flung into the air. The cannon, which still had a shell inside of it, fired in the explosion. The shell flies through the air and explodes in front of the main British section. A fireball erupts in the redcoat line. The Seventy-Sixth Pennsylvania fire immediately after the powder kegs explode, with the thick smoke blocking the redcoats' view. The Seventy-Sixth's muskets' smoke mixes with the powder's smoke. The Pennsylvanians open fire upon the redcoats. The volley cuts down ten redcoats. They are shot in the chest or the face. Two wounded redcoats fall into the flames and catch on fire. They roll on the ground, crying out in major pain. The Pennsylvanians reload their muskets as fast as they can. The smoke continues to obscure the view of the redcoats. Confusion fills the British ranks as redcoats from the rear ranks begin to fire randomly into the trees. Officers try to calm their men. The Pennsylvanians fire again. The volley cuts down seven more redcoats. The redcoats can't see where the volleys are coming from. Timmy and the other four grenadiers throw their grenades. The grenades land in front of several soldiers and explode. A dozen British soldiers are wounded or killed by the bombs.

Simon utters a threat: "Welcome to America, you sons of bastards! How do you like them apples!"

The Pennsylvanians emerge from cover and retreat down the road. They run fast toward Washington DC.

Robert Ross rides forward and screams to the Pennsylvanians, "If you can hear me, Smithtrovich, I will hunt you down and you shall pay for what crime you have committed against Canada! We will burn your Capital to the ground. You will watch the flames light up the sky over your beloved city. Mark my words, you will pay for what your country has done against our allies!"

Celestia stops and hears Robert Ross yelling. She wonders what he means. Daisy runs to her and to her and grabs her right arm. "Come on, sister; we don't have time to look at the red roses. We've got to go now. Let's go!"

Sergeant Major Harry Adams walks over to a dying redcoat teenager. The redcoat teenager reaches his hand out to Harry. Harry grabs the lad's hand and grips it hard. The teen dies, and his hand falls to the ground. Harry looks at his left hand and sees it is covered in blood.

"Those damned Pennsylvanians!" he says as he observes the carnage all around him. "Colonel, I have dealt with this kind of thing before during my time in the Peninsular War. The French ambushed us in forest areas like this. But God damn it, this is inhumane. How can they kill my men so savagely like this?"

"I do not know, sir. But sir, we must press on; we have more of a reason to burn their capital now. Sir, shall I lead the men to Washington, sir?"

Robert Ross looks around and sees his own men in pain, and he is filled with frustration. He kneels down next to a wounded redcoat and grabs an apple from his pouch and gives it to him. He looks over at Colonel Brooke.

"What is your order, sir?" Colonel Arthur Brooke asks General Ross.

General Ross wants to send Brooke, but he turns to Vice Admiral Cockburn to lead the troops. "Lead the advance party. I will follow with the main body once we get the wounded on the wagons. May providence be with you, George. And once you get to the city, if you see any Yankee soldiers, kill them all! No mercy shall be shown to those bastards if they are going to show no mercy to my men." They salute each other, and Cockburn leads the advance party to Washington.

The advance party of the Eighty-Fifth and the Scottish regular soldiers march down the road toward their target, with nothing else to stop them from the unavoidable destruction of the American city of Washington DC.

At the end of the battle, both forces had suffered casualties in the hundreds. The Americans suffered two hundred killed, wounded, or captured. The British invasion forces suffered two hundred and fifty killed or wounded.

CHAPTER 10

—————◆—————

THE DESTRUCTION OF WASHINGTON, DC

The Chesapeake Campaign, Part 4
Washington, DC
August 24, 1814
Early evening

The Seventy-Sixth Pennsylvania, alongside dozens of American regulars, marines, and militiamen, gather around the White House. The city's remaining civilians are gathering their belongings and evacuating the city by foot or by horse. Simon and the other men take a minute to catch their breath. Timmy notices a patch of blood on Simon's left arm.

"Major, your left arm is bleeding. Are you hit?" Timmy asks.

Simon looks at his arm and sees the blood. He silently gasps and then touches it. A short burst of sharp pain runs through his body. "Yes, I am skimmed in the arm. I'm alright. Where the hell are Celestia and Daisy?"

Celestia and Daisy run up to them, out of breath. They are sweating bullets from their hair. Simon and Celestia run up and hug each other. She notices the blood on Simon's arm and pulls out a bandage from her haversack. She binds his arm.

Simon grunts in pain from the wound. "Thank you, Celestia, but this wasn't necessary. I'm glad you're all okay. That was some nice shooting, all of you. We really put a dent in their force."

"Yeah, but we didn't make them retreat. We just prolonged the hell that this city is gonna endure," Timmy says.

"I know, Sergeant. I know y'all don't want to hear this. I'm sorry to say that the destruction of Washington is inevitable. The only thing that we can do now is make sure everyone gets to safety."

Celestia finishes bandaging Simon's arm, and then the Seventy-Sixth begin to help the remaining soldiers and civilians out of the city, including the first lady, Dolly Madison. But before she leaves, she heads for a national treasure—the original portrait of George Washington. The frame is broken down, and the painting is wrapped. Dolly personally takes the painting into her carriage. The Seventy-Sixth escorts guard her carriage with every remaining grenadier that has survived the battle.

Just as the Celestia and her platoon begin to escort the carriage. Celestia see's a little girl crying while clutching onto her doll. The little girl's cries make Celestia's heart begin to break.

"Daisy, command my platoon and get out of the city," Celestia says to her sister, "There's a little girl crying over there. I'll catch up in a few minutes."

Celestia then runs to the little girl who was crying. The little girl looks up and she see's Celestia coming towards her. The little girl gets scared but Celestia assures her that she wants to help her.

"Hello there, what's wrong, darling?" Celestia asks the frightened child. "It's okay, don't be afraid. I'm here to help you."

The little girl looks up at Celestia and she cries even harder. She hugs Celestia with a tight grip. Celestia hugs the little girl. She didn't even know why the little girl was crying but she was heartfelt sorry for the poor child. Seeing little children in distress was one of those things that breaks her heart. The girl finally speaks to Celestia.

"I cannot find my mommy, I don't know where she is. Can you please, please, please help me?!" The little girl says as she continues to cry. Celestia hugs the child and picks her up, and carries her to safety. "Don't worry, my little dear. I'll help you find you're mommy. Just keep calm and tell me what she looks like, okay?" Celestia says with a soothing and calming voice.

Celestia wipes the tears from the little girl's eyes. The little girl then explains what her mommy looks like. "She has brown hair and she wears a red and black dress. Her name is Annie." The girl says as she tries to hold in her tears.

"Okay, that's a start. You have a really great memory." Celestia says with a calming voice. "What is your name, darling?"

"Lilly. What's your name?"

"I'm First Lieutenant Celestia Rose of the Seventy-Sixth Pennsylvania Keystone Grenadiers, but you can call me Celestia." Celestia says to the girl.

The little girl smiled when she heard Celestia told the child her name.

Celestia marches with the rear of the Seventy-Sixth. When the rear of the guard reaches the outskirts of Washington, Lilly spots her mother. her mother was asking other people and soldiers if they had seen her daughter.

"Over there. That's her." The little girl shouted.

Celestia dashed over to the mother. The mother saw her daughter being carried by Celestia. The mom cried out with happiness as she ran over to Celestia. Celestia handed Lilly over to Annie. Mother and daughter both hugged each other and cried tears of joy as they were reunited. The mom looks up at Celestia.

"Thank you very much. Thank you for finding my daughter. How can I ever repay you?

"There is no need, ma'am. I'm just a soldier just fulfilling one of my daily duties, to protect and serve the citizens of the United States." Celestia says with a proud tone, knowing deep down in her heart that she has done a great deed. Lilly then looks up at Celestia, she walks over to her.

"Thank you for helping me find my mommy." Lilly says with a thankful tone.

Celestia kneeled down, "You're very welcome, Lilly" Celestia says. Lilly then smiles and hugs Celestia one last time. Celestia hugs Lilly. Celestia then stands up and escorts the mother and child to safety. Lilly holds Celestia's hand as they exit the city limits.

All the American civilians and soldiers have fled the city, and now the nightmare that the United States has been fearing is about to come true. The next twenty-four hours will be filled with terror and utter destruction for Washington. Little do they know that the redcoats will be facing destruction as well—not at the hands of any human force, but at the hands of mother nature herself.

The British Army marches toward the US Capitol. Vice Admiral George Cockburn leads his marine platoon toward the building and gazes at it. He then turns to his men. "Gentlemen, this building is yours to ravage. My brave brothers, let's clear this building out. Go have some fun," he says.

The Royal Marines march up the stairs and storm through the doors of the Capitol. They start to plunder the rooms and hallways of everything they think is valuable or worth taking. The items that the redcoats get their hands on are the following: fine china, silver, extra food, paintings, and cask upon cask of rum. Major General Robert Ross enters the city with the main body of the invasion force. The redcoats fall out of the Capitol and set torches. They line up in front of the building and throw the torches through the windows. The fire quickly spreads. Flames shoot out of the windows, and smoke flies hundreds of feet into the sky. British soldiers cheer and shout. Soon the redcoats turn their sights to the most important building in Washington DC, the White House. They begin to loot the White House and steal items including a ceremonial sword and a pair of rhinestone buckles. Robert Ross takes President Madison's love letters to Dolly. The redcoats set torches and throw them into the windows of the White house. The fire erupts throughout the whole house, and the windows explode into flames. The redcoats are filled with cheer and joy, knowing that revenge has been paid to their enemies.

Harry Adams stands spellbound at the horrible sight. He sits down and pulls out his own diary and begins to write his thoughts about this event: "For what the Yankees have done to my home country has filled me with anger and vigor. I waited for this moment to arrive, and now that it is here, well, I just don't know how to feel now. This is not to be a military victory but a major mistake that we have made, and the question I ask myself now is, if I should die on the battlefield, how will my lord and savior forgive us for what we have done on this day? I pray to my lord to forgive our men, let alone myself. Indeed, we will be paying for this in the future. If that shall be my destiny, I will be ready to accept my fate either by hanging by the neck or with thirty-two inches of cold American steel piercing my heart."

He puts away his diary and embraces the heat of the roaring flames. All the redcoats stand and watch America's buildings burn to the ground. They also set fire to the US Treasury and the US Department of War building; only a few buildings are spared the torch. On a hill overlooking Washington, the Seventy-Sixth Pennsylvania, along with the president and the first lady, watch the black sky turn a fiery orange. The other Pennsylvanians watch in utter disbelief, listening to the crackle of flames as the city burns through the night.

President James Madison sits on his horse as he watches the sky take on an orange color. "Those damned rascals!"

Simon and his staff stand with their grenadiers as they watch the city burn. They fill with sadness, but mostly they fill with pure hatred. The fuel of pure rage and hatred for the redcoats gives the Seventy-Sixth more reason to keep up the fight. But on this night, the Seventy-Sixth feel as though they have failed their mission to save the city of Washington. Timmy stands with Daisy and Brittany. They fill with rage and anger toward the British.

"Those red bastards are going to pay for this dearly!" Timmy says with hate.

"You're goddamn right!" Daisy agrees.

Brittany growls angrily and kneels and drops her mace. She puts her hands over her face and begins to cry. Private Devin comforts Private Jessica as she begins to cry as well. Major Smithtrovich and First Lieutenant Rose stand beside each other as they watch the orange sky. Simon collapses to his knees and begins to have a breakdown. Celestia kneels on her right leg and hugs Simon. She shows sorrow, but she tries to hold it in. The sorrow eventually gets to her, and she begins to shed tears as well.

"My worst nightmare has come true," Simon says with pain and regret. "Why the hell did this have to happen? For what did we do to deserve this unholy sack of horse shite?"

"Sir, I heard General Ross screaming at us when we were running away after the ambush. He said something about the Canadian Parliament building. I remember hearing about an American attack on the city of York. Do you know anything about that?" Celestia asks Simon.

Simon looks at the orange sky and has a flashback rush through his mind. What his friends don't know is that back on April 27, 1813, Simon was sent with the First American Rifle Regiment to York. They had orders to destroy the Canadian Parliament in retaliation for the destruction of Fort York, which had been destroyed in a massive explosion from the powder magazine. The British defenders of the city had sabotaged the powder and rigged it to explode. When Simon came upon Parliament, he and the riflemen he was assigned to pitched their torches. Simon stood at the front of the building and he walked to the main entrance, gripping his torch. He whispered to himself, "For virtue, liberty, and independence. I am a grenadier of the Brave Seventy-Sixth Pennsylvania, and I shall follow orders till I die with honor. This is for burning my apple farm, you sons of bastards."

Simon threw the torch onto the roof. The roof began to catch fire. The other American soldiers threw their torches onto the roof and through the windows. In ten minutes, the whole Parliament building erupted in a blazing inferno. Through the smoke and intense flames, Simon knew that in his heart that he had made a giant mistake. He spoke to himself within his mind. *"I just hope that this wasn't a mistake. And if it was, then by God this will come back to kill me. This is going to put my company in great danger. I shall never tell them about what I have done here. With Jesus as my witness, I shall protect my grenadiers from my sins."*

Simon knows that he is not going to be able to hide this and that he will have to tell his staff what happened. This will put their friendship to the ultimate test. But first the wrath of God will be unleashed upon the British Invasion force. The British are about to be introduced to an American force of nature.

Thus, the Battle of Bladensburg ended. The losses were not too heavy, but the greatest loss was Washington. The Seventy-Sixth Pennsylvania had 245 at the beginning of the battle. In the end, the Seventy-Sixth was cut down by a third at Bladensburg and on the way to Washington. That means they suffered eighty-eight killed or wounded. This was the heaviest loss they would suffer during the War of 1812.

CHAPTER 11

THE FINGER OF GOD CLAIMS ITS BOUNTY UPON AMERICA'S ENEMIES

The Chesapeake Campaign, Part 5
Washington, DC
Early afternoon
August 25, 1814

As the British invasion force continues to loot and destroy buildings within the city, what they do not know is that things are about to take a dramatic and terrifying turn for the worse. The redcoats are already being downed by the infernal heat, which has soared up to one hundred degrees—a potentially deadly situation given that they are wearing full wool uniforms and knapsacks. During the Battle of Monmouth Courthouse back in 1778, The American and British soldiers suffered more heat casualties than soldiers dying by natural causes of battle.

From out of nowhere, thunderstorm clouds begin to roll in. The redcoats see the clouds and think it's just a normal storm. A light shower of rain begins to fall from the sky. The redcoats run into houses that are not destroyed or burned to get shelter from the rain. The rain continues for two hours without stopping, dousing most of the flames burning in the city. The civilians that remain in the city know something that the redcoats do not. All they have to do is look up at the sky, the color of which is dark green. Today is the day that the British will have their first and last sighting of America's most majestic and most deadly weather phenomenon.

As Ross, Cockburn, Harry, and Harry's son Oliver wait in a tavern for the rain to lift, the wind begins to pick up. Harry begins to get a bad feeling in his gut. He was born in the American colonies and had served with the British Army ever since the American Revolutionary War. He is hoping that what could happen is not going to happen. A few seconds later, the rain stops and the wind dies down. All the redcoats step out into the streets and look up at the sky. The whole British force grab their gear and prepare to march back to Benedict, Maryland. But with every minute that passes, the storm gets worse.

By Two o'clock, the storm had gone from bad to disastrous. The wind begins to howl. Major General Ross looks down toward the road of Constitution Avenue. Harry and Oliver stop and look in the same direction. Calmness fills the air, and then lightning cracks open the skies and thunder roars. Then they hear the sound of a terrifying roar like the constant pounding of bass drums. Harry hears a noise that is far too familiar to him.

"That noise ... Oliver, stay right next to me," Harry says.

"Father, what the hell is happening?" Oliver shudders, holding on to Harry's arm.

Their hearts begin to race, and the adrenaline begins to take over. The lightning gets worse, hissing like a snake, and the thunder is so loud that the ground begins to shake. Suddenly a massive cyclone drops from above and touches down on Constitution avenue. The cyclone is a mile wide, and has extreme wind speeds. The cyclone begins to suck up what is left of Washington, DC. Houses and buildings are ripped off their foundations, and trees are ripped from their roots. The British soldiers are shocked, and they all stand frozen with fear. Major General Robert Ross sees the funnel but does not know what it is.

"What the bloody hell is that!" Ross says under his breath.

Harry runs over to Ross. "General! General! It's a cyclone! Sir, we need to get away now!"

Harry sees the cyclone and panics. He screams at the top of his lungs to his men. "We've just made Mother Nature mad! *Everyone get out of the city now!*"

"Father!" Oliver screams in terror.

Harry runs to Oliver and grabs his arm, and they make a mad dash to find cover. Dozens of British soldiers are frozen with terror at what they are looking at. Their officers yell frantically at their men to get into cover. Oliver is scared out of his mind.

"Oliver, do not let go of my hand!" Harry shouts.

The howling wind is loud, and he must scream so his son can hear him.

The cyclone is a tall wedge-shaped funnel, and it has a massive ring of debris. When the cyclone is finally visible, the observers see it has a dark brown coloring to it. Massive amounts of lightning strike around the cyclone. The cyclone moves slowly but, after a few minutes, begins to pick up speed. The Cyclone's thunderous roar sends the redcoats into panic mode. Hundreds of redcoats flee from the city. The cyclone begins to destroy every single building in its path. Oliver and Harry stop to breathe for a few seconds. They watch the cyclone destroy what is left of the city. Suddenly, the cyclone shifts east and heads straight toward the rear of the British lines. Harry looks at the massive finger of God and thinks that it is standing still. That is a very big mistake. It looks as if it is standing still, but it is heading his way. It takes Harry a few seconds to realize this, and he then looks over his shoulder and sees a large barn in the distance.

"Father, it is just standing there," Oliver says.

But Harry now knows it is heading right for them. The cyclone destroys a tavern within seconds. The roof is blown off, and the walls explode in different directions.

"Oh, shite! Oliver, run!" Harry screams.

They both take off running down the road with the cyclone nipping at their heels. Other British soldiers begin to have trouble because they are carrying too much gear. The weight of the gear slows them down. Some British soldiers drop their muskets and their packs to unencumber themselves. The redcoats run like hell to get away from the finger of God.

As the cyclone clears the city limits, it begins to tear up the countryside. Fences are ripped apart and turned into airborne missiles. A few redcoats are impaled in their backs by the fence posts. Trees are ripped from their roots and tossed in the air or broken in half like matchsticks.

Dozens of other redcoats try to run through a cornfield along with Harry and Oliver. They see the cyclone's massive size. The cyclone unleashes a massive roar that scares the redcoats even more. Lightning strikes occur by the dozens in the cornfield. Several British soldiers are struck by lightning. The cyclone rips the corn stalks out of the ground. The rear of the British ranks is terrorized by the cyclone. It sucks up trees, rocks, cannons, wagons, and even a few British soldiers. They try to grab the walls as they're being sucked up by the wind, but some are not strong enough to hang on. The storm brings terror and death with a mix of lightning that splits the sky in two. The cyclone rips up trees and whole houses as if they are children's toys. Many trees are struck by the lightning bolts. They explode in showers of sparks and wood splinters. A few redcoats hide underneath the trees, which is the wrong thing to do during a thunderstorm. One tree snaps in half and crashes upon a British soldier. He is struck in the head, and it cracks his skull open. A tree explodes, and a redcoat is showered with wooden splinters all over his body. He falls to the ground in tremendous pain and then is sucked up by the monster cyclone. His body twirls around in the air as if he is a human toy. He then disappears into the massive vortex. Meanwhile, Harry and Oliver, alongside twenty American loyalists, run like hell to the barn. One unlucky redcoat is struck in the back by a fence post. The fence post is thrust through his body, and it sticks out through his chest. Several fence posts strike the barn. One American loyalist screams to his comrades to get inside.

"Get in the barn! Get in the bloody barn now!" one loyalist shouts.

"Close the doors! Close 'em! Close them!" another one shouts.

The loyalists struggle to shut the barn doors. The wind is so intense that the doors refuse to close. Seconds later they see a massive tree that has been uprooted from the ground. It flies through the air toward the barn. The loyalists panic and try to shut the door before the tree hits the barn. They're too late. The tree impacts the barn and shuts the door by slamming into the barn doors.

"Jesus! Stay the hell down! Keep your heads down, men!" Harry shouts.

Father and son take cover under a table, and they can see the massive cyclone through a small window. Oliver gets more scared, and he wants to get out of the barn. He knows that if they stay, they all will die.

"Father, we will die if we stay in this barn. We need to keep moving. We will be sucked up," Oliver says.

Suddenly a musket with a bayonet attached comes flying through the window and strikes right between Harry and Oliver. The bayonet sticks out through the other side of the wood post. They both look at each other and take off out of the barn. They manage to get out and run one hundred yards away from the barn. The cyclone heads straight for the massive barn and strikes it. Windows are blown out, and glass flies in every direction. Pieces of wood fly through the air and impact walls. Bricks are hurled through the air like cannonballs. The twenty loyalist soldiers are sucked up into the vortex. The walls of the barn blow out in all different directions. Harry and Oliver pause as they watch the cyclone destroy the barn. The cyclone gives another massive bone-chilling roar as the barn finally gets ripped from the ground and consumed.

"Holy mother of God!" Oliver says as he watches the cyclone destroy the barn.

Other redcoats try to find whatever cover they can find. Some even drop flat upon the ground so they won't get sucked up. Harry and Oliver, along with three other American loyalists, manage to take cover in a ditch, and the cyclone sideswipes them at a distance of 120 yards.

Soon after, the storm subsides. The British Army has suffered unknown losses—possibly more than they suffered at Bladensburg. This day will haunt them for the rest of their lives. The city of Washington is completely destroyed by the cyclone. All the flames have been doused by the rain.

The men in the ditch stay put until the next morning, when they begin their march back to Benedict, Maryland. They walk down a long stretch of dirt road, their uniforms covered in mud and their coats ripped by debris. Oliver is so shell-shocked that he wants to head back home. "I think I am ready to head back to England now. How in the hell did you know what that thing was?" he asks his father.

"That was a cyclone or what I like to call it, "The finger of God', and that was the biggest one I have ever seen. That was the third cyclone I have seen in thirty seven years. I saw one when I was just ten years old. That was back in 1777. Then, in 1785, I saw another one in Virginia. And now, in 1814 … and it was the biggest one."

"Well, what do we do now, Sergeant Major?" Oliver asks.

Sergeant Major Harry Adams explains to his son and his fellow loyalists, "We will regroup with the main force back in Benedict, Maryland. Just stay alert for any of our brothers—or worse, any American soldiers."

Oliver looks down the road and spots the Seventy-Sixth Pennsylvania marching down the road just a quarter of a mile away. The loyalists slowly pursue them for five miles and watch as the Seventy-Sixth makes camp in Rockville, Maryland. They stay and spot Major Simon Smithtrovich and decide to wait for the chance to capture him. They wait for their moment to pounce on Simon.

CHAPTER 12

———◦————◦———

FRIENDSHIPS FALL APART

Rockville, Maryland
August 26, 1814
Midday

At a camp just outside the town of Rockville, Maryland. The Seventy-Sixth Pennsylvania is still reeling from the destruction of Washington DC. Tensions begin to run high. Anger and hate fill the veins of the Seventy-Sixth Grenadiers. Simon and his staff begin to lose themselves. They are only minutes away from the biggest fight these best friends would ever have in their lives. Simon and Timmy are sitting by the fire, cooking their lunches. Celestia and Daisy are talking in their tent. Daisy is confused and wonders why Simon didn't tell the truth about what happened in Canada.

"Daisy, I have been thinking about Simon. Could he have lied to us? I mean, why wouldn't he tell us about what he did during the York campaign?" Celestia asks.

"I know how you feel. I mean, it is not as though Washington was his fault. Although he was probably one of the causes of it happening."

Celestia smacks Daisy's hand for that comment. She doesn't want to hear that nonsense. "Don't say that. This was caused by many reasons; it can't just be caused by one man. I do not believe that to be true. I mean, he could have been given an order to burn the building."

"Bollocks! That is an immoral order. And by the articles of war, no soldier needs to obey it. What if I had done something like that? I would tell my friends. I know it's not my place, but I really want to know." Daisy gets up and walks out of the tent.

Celestia tries to stop Daisy. "Wait; stop! No, don't! That's an order. Oh, Jesus, this is going to end badly."

Daisy walks over to Simon and speaks with a frustrated voice. "Sir, may we have a staff meeting?" she asks Simon.

"Yes, of course. What would you like to know? And are you mad about something? You seem to be angry. Just to let you all know that we're all angry at the British. Rest assured, we will make those lobsters bleed dearly for what they've done."

Daisy and Celestia sit on a log right beside Timmy and Simon. Daisy doesn't mince words and cuts straight to the chase. Thus begins the great fight between grenadiers who fight not only for freedom in the United States but also for the power of friendship in America.

Celestia sighed and began to interrogate her commanding officer. "Simon, we are not here to talk about them. We're here to talk about you and what you've done. I want you to tell me the truth. Why didn't you tell us earlier about what you did up in York, Canada?"

Simon knows he can't avoid this conversation any longer. He knows he has to talk about it or risk losing his staff's trust. He takes a deep breath. "What I did during the Battle of York is what I have told you already. And to be honest, why are you all so damn concerned about it?"

Celestia considers that he is holding back the truth. She is prepared to find the truth, either with words or using the sort of pliers doctors use to dig a musket ball out of an open, rotting wound. "What I recall is that you told us that your orders were to look for documents at the compound. Did you get any orders to burn the damn building, or did you do it of your own free will?"

Simon sighs and takes a deep breath. He takes off his bearskin cap and realizes that he must tell the truth. "When the battle was raging, we were about to attack the city, but the redcoats sabotaged the powder magazine at Fort York. Seconds later, the whole fort was blown from the face of the earth. Our commanding officer was killed, and in retaliation for that, we burned the whole city to the ground. We did it as a message to Canada to warn them that more harm would come to their land if they continued to fight back. I did what I was told to do. I am a soldier, and I obey orders.

We did what we needed to do, and I have no regrets. The reason I never told you is because I wanted to protect you from the British."

The rest of the staff gasped when they finally learned the truth. Timmy stands up and walks up to Simon. He gets right up in his face. "You lied to us!" he exclaims.

"I did it to protect y'all!" Simon says.

"Why would you do that, sir? We are a damn team. There should be no secrets. What gives you the right to hide that from us?" Timmy says angrily.

All five of them begin to get really angry. Simon claps his hands and tries to defuse the situation before things get too out of hand. "Look for what you think is the truth, but you must understand that what's done is done and nothing can change that. End of conversation. Let us all stop this bollocks arguing right now, before one of us says something that he or she will terribly regret. Staff dismissed." Simon stands up and tries to walk away.

Celestia stands and yells at Simon. She does not want him to run off. "Don't you walk away from me, sir. If you are a true officer, just tell us the truth, and we'll forgive you. That is what friends do, sir. If you are a true friend, you will tell us what the hell happened!"

Simon turns back around and looks at them. Celestia walks up to him and stares him straight in the eyes.

"It is not enough to just know the truth," Simon says. "We can't just march into the battle like the noble Duke of York's ten thousand men and fight the redcoats. It is not enough. Our tactics are the things that are stopping us from ending this war. And now that Napoleon is in exile, the whole British Empire is gonna be on our asses once again. Those redcoats we faced at Bladensburg were veterans of the Peninsular War. They were not your average lobsterback shite kickers."

"Why in the hell do you keep repeating the same bullshit that we already know, sir?" Celestia says. "If you want my honest opinion, sir, the only thing that is stopping us from defeating them is you."

Simon was horrified by what Celestia had just said to him. And after all they have been through, not only through the war, but from here all the way back to their childhood.

"Oh really, Lieutenant? Maybe you don't know how it is to be a commander. Do you know how many soldiers have died under my command? Take a guess. Go on."

Celestia shrugs. "I do not know how many, sir. We've lost so many that I've lost count, sir."

Due to Simon's anger that was building within his heart. He was starting to become self centered. Due to that, Simon was not acting like himself and his staff knew that.

"We created this company two years ago, and we had 300 soldiers under my command from the very start. We lost eighty-eight grenadiers at Bladensburg. We have had over a hundred of our grenadiers killed in action in our company now. A few of them died right in my arms. You would not know how it feels to see all your loyal soldiers dying right in front of you. The burden is all on me. It always is on the commanding officer. Every day I hate to send many loyal Pennsylvanians to fight, marching them to their deaths."

Celestia looks back at her sister, and then things begin to get more heated. "Simon, I know how you feel. I have blood on my hands as well. I have my sister to worry about. My father told me to keep her alive even if it means sacrificing my life."

"Yes, I understand that, but you guys are like family to me. Now how is that gonna make me feel if I see you all get killed? And now that Washington, DC, is destroyed, the country's morale is gonna drop lower than the depths of hell itself. We almost lost the Revolutionary War because the redcoats took New York and then, a year later, Philadelphia. We lost over a thousand soldiers in each of those battles, and the morale of the patriots was almost enough to cost us the war."

Daisy jumps into the argument, attempting to defend her sister from her own commander, whom she has entrusted her life with, but she believed that her family honor came first above all else. "Yes, that is true, but we defeated the British Army at Saratoga, which pleased the French. Once we got their support, we were able to defeat the British. If not for the bloody French, we wouldn't be a free nation."

"Well, we do not have the French backing us up this time!" Simon yells. "We are standing alone. This is a test that we need to pass; otherwise, our nation is gonna become a goddamn colony again. If we lose this war, all the blood that our fathers and grandparents spilled will have been for nothing."

"Sir," Celestia says, "what is very important right now is keeping our company's morale up."

Then Simon says something that leaves the staff shocked. "Nothing is more important than that? Beating the redcoats is more important."

Celestia gasps, as she cannot believe what Simon just said. "I know you didn't just say that about our grenadiers."

Brittany realizes that the conversation is turning heated. She could see that her commanders were not in their right mind set. Tempers are flaring and almost out of control. "You guys, stop this right now!" she shouts at her commanders. This is not like you two at all."

"Sir, let me speak my mind. When we stopped for that ambush, to be honest, sir, I would have rather kept going. In my own free will, I thought we should do anything to keep our city alive for a little bit longer. We almost didn't get the first lady out of the city in time. The only one who told us to stop was you. You could have chosen not to listen to my idea and just kept running back to Washington like the bloody coward you are."

Simon is shocked at being called a coward by the woman he loves. "Coward? A Coward! How dare you speak to your commanding officer that way! If you were not my friend, I would have you hanged from the nearest tree."

Daisy gasps and runs over and tries to break up the fight. "How dare you speak to my sister like that, sir! Let's stop this now, before things get out of hand. You both stop this right now!"

The whole Seventy-Sixth Pennsylvania can hear their own staff officers arguing, and they gather around. But they keep a safe distance and do not say a word so that no wrath will befall them. The argument continues, and it gets worse.

"Well, I am doing my very best," Simon says. "It is all on me. I am the one that Robert Ross wants. Do you know how it feels to have a five-hundred-pound bounty on your head? Do you suggest I turn myself in? I didn't tell you because I wanted to protect you all from the lobsters. You guys do not know what the hell I went through in York. I went through pure hell, and if they had got a hold of you all … I wouldn't know what the hell to do if they captured you."

Simon and Celestia begin to lose their tempers, and then they both finally snap. Celestia yells at Simon with a strong voice. Simon turns his back to Celestia and slowly walks away. But then he stops.

Celestia finally boils over. "No, I don't want you to do that. However, you are also the one who doesn't trust his own soldiers—especially his best friends and, most importantly, the one best friend who loves him. And that would be me. But apparently you are better off without your grenadiers. Would you rather be fighting the redcoats alone? Would you be better off that way, sir? And if you keep lying to us, you are not just lying to us; you are also lying to your own grenadiers and to those who have died. And worst of all, you have put the life of my sister in danger! Honest to God, how could I have been marching into a war side by side with a lying, worthless, weak, pathetic excuse for an American?"

Timmy gasps and realizes that Celestia has just made a mistake. "Oh, shit!" he says to himself.

"Wow!" Brittany says to herself as she puts her hand over her face.

"I didn't see that coming," Daisy says with a surprised tone.

Simon begins to fill up with massive anger and rage. He growls softly, clenches his fist, looks down at his pistol, and grabs it. He looks up at the trees and notices a bush moving; a small patch of red is visible. He puts his right hand on the grip of the pistol and starts to pull it out.

Timmy notices Simon's hand on the grip of his pistol and begins to get scared. "Simon, don't even think about it. Put your gun down!" Timmy says quietly. He begins to get scared that Simon might do the unthinkable—shooting someone or himself.

But then Simon holsters the firearm. Instead he finally snaps and turns around, and then he yells at Celestia, walking over to her fast. "You know what, Celestia! Maybe I would be better off without a grenadier like you! It would be nice not to have a damn stubborn wench telling her commander what the hell to do. I don't know why I fell in love with a stupid harlot of a patriot like you! You're just a stupid wench who loves to have smoke flow up her chimney. Let me tell you something; I wished with all my heart and soul you died in Bladensburg so I wouldn't have to listen to your bloody mouth, and look at your shite-filled face ever again!"

Celestia Rose gasps in super-sad shock. She looks down and begins to tear up. Her heart breaks in a million pieces on the inside.

※

Harry, Oliver, and their men are shocked. They all cannot believe their own ears. Harry is furious.

"My God, that is horrible!" Harry says in an angry tone.

"Sergeant Major, let's capture this bastard and teach him a lesson about respect, and let's also make him pay for his crimes," Oliver replies.

Timmy and Daisy drop their muskets in horror. They cannot believe what Simon said to Celestia. Timmy's mouth drops, and Daisy has a super-angry look on her face. Simon's eyes open wide; he is horrified by what he has said. He knows in his heart that he has made a major mistake. Possibly the worst mistake of his whole entire life.

Celestia turns her back and runs back to her tent. She begins to cry hard. She closes the tent shades and sits down. She takes off her bearskin cap and puts her hands over her face and cries. Her white gloves were soon drenched with her tears.

Simon tries to walk over to Celestia's tent, but Daisy stops him and punches him in the face. Daisy unleashes her bone-chilling fury upon Simon. "Who in the bloody hell do you think you are? You can't talk to my sister like that. You broke her heart. You know she has a very sensitive heart. You are not just a sorry excuse for an officer, you are a sorry excuse for a best friend. She says that she loves you, and then you roar at her, you damned bastard! You can go to hell! And as far as our friendship, it is over! We will have our resignations on your desk by nightfall."

She storms off back to her tent and goes to comfort her sister. Simon can hear Celestia crying in the tent, and his heart sinks. Simon runs out of the camp, and the other grenadiers run over to see what is happening. Timmy runs after Simon but loses him in the woods.

※

A few seconds later, Harry and his men follow close behind as they wait to pounce on their target.

※

Timmy wanders the forest looking for Simon, and then he hears Simon crying near the edge of the Potomac River. Simon is looking out at the water. Timmy walks to Simon and stands behind him but gives him some space.

"Sir, it is okay?" Timmy says to Simon. "I know you are very sorry. We'll find a way to win this war."

"No, we can't! There's no way to save America now. It's all my fault. And how in the hell could I yell at the woman I love? And she said that she loves me. How can she love a man like me? How can you still be my friend? I am the worst officer in the US Army. I sent eighty-eight of my brothers and sisters to their deaths. I killed them all!"

"Sir, this is not your damn fault! You're being way too hard on yourself. You have taken us this far, and we all make mistakes. And she will forgive you. You just need to give her a chance."

"No, she won't, and I don't blame her. She trusted me, and I wished that she had died. There's no way she will forgive me for that one. I cannot believe that I said that to the woman I love the most in this world." Simon then weeps like a baby. He stands up and says in a normal voice as he looks at the water of the Potomac River, "I'm going to surrender myself to the British."

Timmy is horrified by this. "Major! Now you are just talking shite. You will not turn yourself in, because they will kill you. We will be even sadder if they kill you. We will miss you. Sir, you need to just cool down, and then we can go back and talk to Celestia, okay?"

Two redcoats sneak up slowly to Timmy and prepare to grab him. They do it so quietly that Simon does not even hear the British loyalists grab Sergeant Miller.

Simon continues to feel sorry for himself, but he does not hear his sergeant being held against his will.

"I have failed you all. This is all my fault. I'm sorry that I let y'all down, Timmy. Timmy?"

When Simon turns around, he sees two redcoats restraining Timmy by putting his arms behind his back. One other redcoat puts a rag over Timmy's mouth. Timmy is able to shout to Simon, "Simon, watch out!"

Simon pulls out his pistol and tries to fire. Suddenly a gunshot is fired from the trees. Simon takes a pistol bullet in the palm of his right hand. The force of the impact knocks the pistol out of his hand. Simon's palm erupts in a small mist of blood.

"Ow, my hand!" Simon falls onto his knees.

Seven other British soldiers run out of the trees. They run over to Simon with their bayonets fixed on him. Then Sergeant Major Harry Adams walks over to Simon and looks down at him.

"You!" Simon growls.

"Major Smithtrovich, is it not? At last we finally meet. I told you that we would be meeting again. Well, I am here to tell you that it is time to recompense for the damage and the lies. Major General Robert Ross has some business with you. You will be coming with us. We can do this the easy way or the hard way. The choice is up to you."

Simon glances up at Harry Adams with a painful look on his face. He continues to resist against his captors.

"I don't know what 'recompense' means, but if you're gonna kill me, you may as well do so now. I am ready to die, so just do it, you worthless shitfaced wanker."

Timmy shouts out to Simon to just cooperate with their demands.

"Simon, shut the hell up!" Timmy shouts. "Don't be a bloody idiot!"

One redcoat punches Timmy in the gut twice. Timmy groans in pain. Simon tries to fight back, but Harry hits Simon in the face with the butt of his pike. The force of the blow knocks Simon out cold. Simon's body falls down to the ground.

Timmy tries to break free, but he is restrained.

Harry walks over to Timmy and points his pike at Timmy' chest. "Stop that right now! If you do that once more, I will run you through, so help me. Now, are you gonna let me talk, or will I have to blow your commander's head off? It is your damn choice. Oh, I'm sorry." Harry pulls the cloth from Timmy's mouth, and Timmy looks up at him.

"Speak, lobsterback!" Timmy says with an angry tone.

"First off, I'm sorry about shooting his hand. Speaking of which, someone wrap up his hand before he bleeds out. The general needs him alive. I was actually aiming for his pistol. I guess my aim has been terrible lately." Harry chuckles.

Two redcoats go over to Simon and sit him up. One uses a roll of bandages to bind his right hand. They manage to stop the bleeding.

Harry continues to speak to Timmy. "Secondly, I am sure he told you about what happened in Canada, did he not? And we knew where your camp was and the fight that you five had. Honestly, I was actually sad about the way he yelled at her like that. Never in my entire life have I yelled at my men like that, let alone a beautiful woman. I might as well tell you where we are going to attack next. It is a city that is nearby. You may take a guess. Go on."

Timmy thinks for a few seconds about cities that are nearby. He thinks of the next destination to suffer the same fate as Washington.

"Baltimore, Maryland!" Timmy says.

"Correct. We will send your leader back when we feel good and ready. Now, if you agree, we'll send him back to you in one piece. Do you agree to these terms, or will I have to kill your best friend right in front of your own eyes?"

Timmy sees his best friend lying facedown on the ground with several muskets pointed at his head. Timmy has no choice but to agree to Sergeant Major Harry Adam's terms.

"I agree, Sergeant Major. But if you hurt my friend, I swear I will hunt you down. When I find you, I will rip out your heart and feed it to the Indians."

The threat makes the redcoats laugh.

"You Yankees are so funny," Harry says. "All right, we will let you go, but I must warn you, if you try to mount a rescue, I will kill your major. Do you understand me, Sergeant?"

Timmy looks over at Simon again, having no choice but to let the redcoats take him.

"I do," Timmy says.

"Very well then. Let him go and get the Major on the wagon immediately. And I will say this one last time: if I see any American regulars or militia following us, your major gets it."

130

Three redcoats lift Simon and carry him out of the forest. Two other redcoats are waiting by the wagon. Timmy stands and watches as they take his best friend away from him. The redcoats put Simon on the wagon and ride off down the road. As the redcoats fade out of sight, Timmy runs back to the camp. He runs as if he is running away from an enemy bayonet charge.

Back at the camp, Daisy is comforting Celestia, who is crying hard in her tent. Daisy rubs Celestia's back, trying to calm her down, but she is having a difficult time doing so.

"Why did he say that to me?" Celestia asks as she sobs. "What did I do wrong? He called me a wench. How the hell could he say that to me? Why would he wish me to be dead?"

"Shh, just don't think about him. I'm sure he didn't mean what he said. It is okay; Deep down he still loves you. But do you still want to be friends with that bastard?"

Deep down in Celestia's broken heart, she still has feelings for Simon.

"Yes! But I risked my life, and this is how I get treated. Who's gonna love me? I want him to come back to camp and say he is sorry."

Timmy runs back into the camp, tripping on the grass and the dirt road that leads to it. He screams at the top of his lungs, "The major has been captured!"

The Seventy-Sixth Grenadiers gasp and run to Sergeant Miller.

"Listen up, grenadiers. The redcoats ambushed me and Simon, and they knocked him out. Some sergeant named Harry Adams told me that they will not hurt him unless we try to mount a rescue. That means no one can try to save him. I also have the location of the next target the British are going to attack. Believe it or not, the redcoats told me that they are going to attack Baltimore. So now we are to march to Baltimore and go to Fort McHenry. Is that understood?"

"Yes, Sergeant!" the Seventy-Sixth shout. All the grenadiers rush to break down their tents and grab their gear.

Timmy Miller walks over to Celestia and Daisy's tent, where Celestia is still crying. Timmy enters the tent and kneels in front of them.

131

"Come on, you two. We have an emergency here. We have to move out!" Timmy says.

"Timmy, your emergency can wait; Celestia is upset, Daisy says. "Her heart is broken. Can you help me cheer her up? I have tried for two hours. Did Simon tell you anything at all?"

"Well, with all due respect, Commander Celestia Rose, we need to march to Fort McHenry over in Baltimore and prepare the city for the next invasion. Celestia, look at me." Celestia looks up at Timmy and dries her tears. "Before he got captured, I found him crying at the Potomac River. He was very upset about what he said to you. He felt really bad, and he is very sorry. He loves you, and he can't think of another woman in the whole damn country that he would want to fight beside in a battle. And deep down, he would do anything to see you again. I know that you still love him, too. And don't even try to lie, because deep down, you do still love him. Our damn friendship cannot be broken over a pitiful damn fight. So our friendship is not over—not by a long shot!"

Celestia smiles. She knows deep down that this is still true. She wipes her face with her sleeve, and then Timmy accidently speaks of his true feelings for Daisy.

"Celestia, you still love Simon just as I love your sister."

Daisy gasps and hugs Timmy.

"I never thought you ever would, Timmy," Daisy says with joy.

"Yes, I still love him, and if I ever do see him again, he better apologize to me and ask something that I have been waiting for him to ask me," Celestia says, fixing her uniform. Timmy is confused by what Celestia is saying. He thinks of it but does not say it out loud. "Wait; let's back it up a bit. Did you say 'Commander,' Sergeant?"

"Yes, I did," Timmy explains. "You are the highest-ranking soldier here right now. So what are our orders, Commander?"

Celestia stands up and looks at Timmy and Daisy. Just before she speaks, Brittany comes into the tent.

"Timmy," Brittany says, "the Seventy-Sixth is awaiting orders. Wait a minute; if the major is gone, then who is in charge of the Seventy-Sixth?"

Celestia puts her bearskin cap on her head and speaks in a very commanding voice. "Sergeant Miller, you and I are going to follow the

British. We need to make sure that they do not hurt Simon. First Sergeant Rose, you will be in charge of the company till we both return."

Timmy scoffs at her orders.

"Celestia, I was given direct orders from that redcoat to not follow them; if they see us, they'll kill Simon," Timmy says.

Celestia hammers her fist on the table three times and then raises her voice to Timmy. "Dammit, Sergeant! Since when do you take orders from a lobster back?" Timmy stammers as he tries to speak in a complete sentence, and Celestia gets up in his face. "That lobster may have given you an order. Well, I am giving you a direct order. You and I are going to check on Simon. If they kill him, then we will mourn him, and then we will make sure that those bastards pay dearly for his death on the next battleground."

"Yes ma'am," Timmy says.

Both of them grab their muskets and their knapsacks. They exit the tent and run down the road as Daisy and Brittany watch.

"I sure hope they know what they're doing," Brittany says.

"I know my sister. She will do anything to get him back. I just hope that they're not too late. I also hope that Simon will be smart and not do or say anything stupid. But knowing Simon, he will be defiant against them. He will do anything to keep himself alive. The only thing that scares me is that his defiance could possibly kill him."

CHAPTER 13

FACE-TO-FACE WITH THE ENEMY

British encampment
Benedict, Maryland
August 26, 1814
Late afternoon

After a few hours of running through the woods, Timmy and Celestia finally catch up with the British prisoner escort. For the rest of the afternoon, Timmy and Celestia trail close behind the rear guard of the British invasion force. They finally make it to Benedict, Maryland. They hide in the brush about sixty-five yards away from the British camp. At the camp, the redcoats are cleaning their uniforms and their muskets, or drilling. At the surgeon's tent, a surgeon is tending to Simon's hand wound. Simon has been restrained to the bed with chains on his wrists and his legs. The tent is guarded by ten British soldiers, including Sergeant Major Harry Adams. Major General Robert Ross walks to the tent.

"Ten hut! Present arms!" Harry shouts to the guards.

They salute him, and Robert Ross salutes them back.

"At ease. Now, is he in there, and what is his condition?" General Ross asks Harry.

"Sir, he suffered a bullet to his right palm. He is very well alive and ready to talk, sir. But he has not woken up yet, sir."

"Well, I would like to talk to him. It is time for him to confess his crimes against the crown."

The surgeon is cleaning the blood off Simon's hand and arm when Simon's eyes begin to open up. The doctor looks at him. Simon looks up at the doctor and is very confused. The surgeon walks out of the tent.

"Sir, the prisoner is waking up," the surgeon says to General Ross.

Major General Robert Ross and Sergeant Major Harry Adams walk into the tent and see Simon beginning to wake up. Simon wakes up in a daze and then feels a sharp pain in his right hand. He looks up and sees chains on both of his arms and legs. The chains are attached to the bed.

"What is going on here? Ow, my hand! Hey, wait, where the hell is Timmy?! And why the hell am I in chains?! What the hell am I doing here?!"

A British guard runs in and aims his musket at Simon's chest.

General Robert Ross grabs the soldier's musket and aims it high in the air. "Stand down, Private! That is not necessary. This man is not to be harmed unless I order it. Now get the hell out of here."

The British soldier recovers his musket and walks out of the tent. Simon fills with anger and horror. Robert and Harry turn their attention back to him.

"Don't you dare try to get out of those chains, because if you try to escape or fight back, we will hang you. We want a word with you, Major," Harry says to Simon.

Simon is confused and begins to resist them in any way he can think of. "So let me get this straight. You hunted me down like I am some kind of wild animal, you put a bounty on my head, and I have thousands of redcoats trying to kill me. Then you finally take me prisoner—all so you can have a word with me?"

"Well, there is a little more to it," Harry says. "And since I did capture you, I have gotten paid. I thank you for that, Major."

"You expect me to thank you for that?" Simon says to Harry. "Why didn't you bastards just settle for a flag of truce at the Potomac River? Oh, that's right! I would have ambushed you two, mutilated your bodies, and buried what was left of you in the Potomac, *and that's a fact!*"

Ross unsheathes his sword and points it at Simon's chest. "Hold it right there. If you do that once more, I run you through. I swear to God. Now, are you going to cooperate, or should I just kill you now? Because it all depends on your bloody attitude. Make your choice, Major."

Simon realizes that he will not be able to escape. He cools off and decides to hear what the general has to say.

"Now, if you will act like a respectable officer, we would like to have a word with you, Major."

Simon scoffs. "A word? You suppose that the pain of taking me away from my best friends will make me weak. The anger I am feeling right now gives me energy to take all you bastards out with just my bare hands. And even given the tragic state of Washington, this is no way to detain an officer. And after our little word, you will just shoot me anyway. So what the hell are you waiting for? To be honest, I am ready to meet my maker— but not before I kill the two of you and hundreds of your lobsterbacks first. So give me my effects back and unchain me so we can go outside and dance, you cold blooded, pompous piece of shite."

Ross and Harry laugh at Simon. Robert Ross sits down in the bed to the right of Simon. "I know that you can destroy us. I can tell that you are a true warrior. However, there is a difference between a soldier and a killer. A soldier fights for his rights and beliefs. A killer is a person who kills just because he gets off on it. I see that you are a man of honor and recently have committed an atrocious crime against the crown and against Canada. But that is only one of two reasons why I have brought you here. The second reason is so simple that any soldier can do it. I know you were involved in the burning of Parliament during the battle of York last year. All you have to do is confess your sins, and the truth shall set you free. When you do that, we will happily send you back to your unit. Do you understand me, Major?" Harry asks Simon.

Simon leans up and looks at the general. He speaks right into his face with a defiant attitude. "Confess! I will confess when hell freezes over. And it can't be that simple. Do you bastards take me for a fool?" Simon does not believe what they are saying. He doesn't think that they will send him back to his company. It is hard for him to believe because hundreds of Canadian and British soldiers have been trying to capture him for over a year.

"Major, I am serious. It is that simple. You are only making this harder for yourself. Just confess! When you do, we will happily return you to your fellow patriots' bloody and wretched hands," Ross says to Simon.

However, Simon still does not believe that he will be released.

"You see right there—that remark. That is how I know you're lying to me. Why don't you bastards cut the bullshit and understand that you've already lost the bloody war? I speak on behalf of the US military when I tell you to surrender. Otherwise you will join your fellow brothers that have died by my bayonet, general."

"With all due respect, Major, you're in no condition to make threats. You are the one who is chained to the bed. And you are looking at a higher-ranking officer. Now you will obey, or dammit, I will kill you. And truthfully, I do not want to kill you. Major, you are the only one who is digging the grave deeper than it really needs to be."

"You may be a general. However, I do not salute lobsters. I would rather eat burned apples from my torched orchard back home. You bastards burned my fields, and my family lost our apple farm. I will not stop resisting until your redcoats are beggin on your knees, wishing you never left your castles. Do you understand that, you pathetic worm?"

"Oh, we understand what you're saying," Harry says. "We are sorry about that. And now you see how simple it is to apologize for our allies destroying your farm. Now why can't you say you're sorry for burning down Parliament? And another thing: if we wanted you dead, I would pull out my pistol and blow your head off right now without a moment's hesitation." He grabs his pistol, cocks it, and aims at Simon's head.

Simon leans his head into the barrel with a flat facial expression. He cockily eggs him on to pull the trigger. "Do it, you son of a bastard! Go ahead and do it if you want to have the honor of murdering an enemy officer in cold blood!"

Harry hesitates for a few seconds and then pulls the trigger. Simon flinches. The pistol is not loaded, however. Harry then recovers his pistol.

"Okay, so I was wrong. You do have the guts … for an English bastard. So are you actually going to load it and shoot me? Because I cannot believe that anyone can take lobsters like you lot seriously nowadays."

Harry begins to realize that talking is not going to be enough. He decides to go to plan B. He slaps Simon in his face.

Simon ignores the pain and continues to be cheeky. "Really? You hit like that? You hit like a pompous, blimey overdressed sorry excuse for a king's man!"

137

Harry Adams fills with anger and punches Simon five times. Simon does not give Harry the satisfaction. He spits out one of his teeth onto the table.

"I've felt worse!" Simon says. I am willing to die for my core beliefs. And I am willing to die as a grenadier."

Harry grabs his key and unlocks Simon's shackles.

Simon smiles. "I must tell you about your odds. You may have been fighting the Grande Armée, but we Americans do not run away like bunnies being chased by dogs. We stay and fight for our freedom or die trying. You may have beaten us at Bladensburg, but we will adapt and learn how to destroy your scum of the earth. We've beaten you bastards before and we will do it again, by God. You bastards will never win this war! Never!" Simon laughs as they unlock his chains.

Harry grabs Simon from the bed. He clutches Simon's coat and throws him against the desk. Simon falls to the ground. Harry runs over and grabs Simon and forces him up against the desk. Harry finally loses his temper. He puts his bayonet up against Simon's neck and begins to tell about the hellish nightmare he and his best friend faced during the battle that turned the colonial uprising into the American Revolutionary War—the Battle of Bunker Hill, also known as Breed's Hill.

"You smart-mouthed bastard. You listen to me. I was dodging militia bullets at Bunker Hill before you were even conceived, boy. You never know what it really means to have a true loss of friendship. My best friend, Oliver Piper, was a drummer boy just like me. During the Battle of Bunker Hill, he was killed by a cannon blast. You rebel bastards killed him!" Harry presses his bayonet up against Simon's throat, slightly cutting Simon's skin. A few drops of blood run down Simon's throat.

Simon feels bad about how Harry's friend perished in a brutal battle that killed seven hundred redcoats at point-blank range. Yet they still took the hill after three assaults.

"Well, it is painful to see a friend slaughtered. And I know how it feels to see true friends die. My family has been killing redcoats ever since the French and Indian War. I must know—how was your friend killed? Can you please give me all the details?"

As he explains to Simon, Harry sheds one tear. "We were marching up for the second assault on Breed's Hill. We were in the rear with our drums, and all we could see was our comrades dropping instantly to the dirt. The cries of the wounded were louder than the sound of our drums. I looked up the hill and saw a cannon fire. The second I looked at Oliver, a cannonball cut him in half right in front of my eyes. I saw his guts spilled out on the grass. Your countrymen gave my friend no damn mercy. So tell me why in the hell I should give your Yankee bastards any mercy from me?"

"I am sorry about your friend. I have lost countless brothers in arms. Since you told me this story, I will confess to you lot. First off, please put that bayonet down. You will cut yourself. And why would you want to kill the man who saved your only son?"

Harry lets go of Simon and puts his bayonet back in his sheath. Simon then utters a cheeky remark that he soon regrets. "I confess that … my father's friends were not able to end your childhood any sooner. Because honestly my father would have been happy to end it for you. Now my friends will have the opportunity to end your pitiful life. There, I said it. Is it tea time yet, Your Majesty?"

Simon laughs, and then Harry snaps. He punches Simon so hard that Simon falls to the ground. Then the guards come into the tent and grab him and throw him out of the tent. The guards pick him up and escort him to the firing range. They escort him through the camp, and other British soldiers watch as he is dragged. The other redcoats follow right behind them as he is taken to the firing range. Celestia and Timmy see Simon being dragged upon the ground. They fill with terror, not knowing what the British are going to do with him.

"Jesus. What the hell are they doing with him?" Celestia asked.

"I do not know. Just stay the hell down, and do not make a single peep," Timmy says.

They put Simon on a post, bind his hands, and tie a belt around his head.

Celestia trembles in fear. She knows in her heart that Simon is only moments away from being executed. They watch as the guards march into a firing line.

Just then Colonel Arthur Brooke speaks to Simon. "Major Simon Smithtrovich of the Seventy-Sixth Pennsylvania, you have been found guilty of major crimes against the nation of Canada and His Majesty

King George III. You are hereby sentenced to death by firing line. If the condemned have any last words, please speak them now."

The redcoat guards load their muskets. Simon stares at General Ross with a fearless facial expression. Simon finally breaks down and confesses, knowing that he might be able to save his own life. He takes a deep breath and screams at the top of his lungs. The entire camp can hear him.

"Okay, you bastards, I confess that I aided in the burning of Parliament. I burned it! But you bastards made me do it because you blew up Fort York! You bastards killed our commanding general! I understand why you bastards wanted revenge. You got your bloody revenge. I also confess that I am the worst American officer in my country's history. I never should have ever yelled at my best friends—especially the woman I love and cherish. I love you, Celestia, and if you can hear this, I am sorry that I treated you like a piece of shite. I am sorry, my lord and savior, that I have sinned, and I pray that you forgive me for my sins. If I die today, I am ready to meet my maker. There, I said it, you bloody bastards! Is that what you want, you lobsters?"

All the redcoats are shocked by what he says. Celestia's mouth hangs open from shock. But her shock is soon to turn to pure sadness and pure, bitter hate for the British. Harry Adams pulls out his sword. Simon closes his eyes. Robert Ross walks over and whispers to each of the guards. Then he steps back.

Simon whispers to himself, "Celestia, I will always love you. I will always cherish your friendships, my brave Seventy-Sixth."

"Guards, make ready! Take aim! Fire!" Harry shouts.

The redcoat guards aim high, sending a volley over Simon's head.

But from Timmy and Celestia's point of view. It looks like the redcoats have shot Simon in his head. Celestia then tries to run to Simon, but Timmy holds her back.

"No! No! No! No! *Noooooo!*" Celestia screams as Timmy puts his hands over her mouth, making her scream muffled.

Timmy holds her down below a bunch of logs. She tries to break free, but Timmy keeps a very firm grip on her. They both sob so hard that no sound comes out. Celestia bites Timmy's hand, and she then takes off running back toward their own encampment. They run about two miles without stopping before Celestia collapses to her knees. She is breathing heavily, still crying and remaining speechless.

Timmy manages to catch up with her. He drops his musket and falls to his knees out of exhaustion.

Celestia looks back at Timmy with tears and sweat all over her face. Timmy looks at her face, and he can see in her eyes that she is thirsty for the blood of the ones who took Simon from her and the company, despite Simon's having made his terrible insults. Anyone can hold a grudge, but it takes real courage to forgive. Celestia was willing to forgive Simon, but now she is not going to have that chance—or so she thinks. What they don't know is that the redcoats have tricked Simon and his friends.

Celestia then stands up and looks forward. She mutters a declaration of total war against Major General Robert Ross's army. Celestia's face makes her look like a bloodthirsty killer. She has a face of pure evil.

"For virtue, liberty, and independence! Those bastards will pay dearly for Simon's death!" Celestia screams.

Timmy stands right beside Celestia and nods once. "You're damn right about that. Let us get back to camp."

They begin to walk down the road, and then a question pops into Timmy's head. "Lieutenant, what are we going to tell the grenadiers?" Timmy asks Celestia.

Celestia's eyes open wide, and she knows that she couldn't hide this from them. She feels she needs to tell the Seventy-Sixth, but she knows it could go in two different ways. Either they will lose the will to fight or their will to fight will soar higher than the stars in the sky.

On the way back to their camp, Celestia thinks of what she will have to say to the company.

In the British camp, Simon slowly opens his eyes and can see the guards aiming high through the smoke from their muskets. Robert Ross walks over to Simon. Simon looks down at his coat and sees no wounds. He has not been shot. General Ross looks up at Simon and smiles.

"Congratulations, Major. You have been forgiven for your sins," he says.

Simon tries to talk, but he is very confused. He finally gets the words out of his mouth. "Can you please explain what the hell this was all about? This is not making any sense. What are you bastards playing at?"

Major General Robert Ross explains what happens when a man is shown the errors of his ways. "My fellow soldiers, listen and learn a lesson that this American has finally learned. This is a man when he is instantly rehabilitated, for what he has done in his life can be forgiven by his enemies and also the Lord himself. By the end of the week, we will send you back to your unit. Until then you can talk with my men, and they can teach you about friendship. Now guards, cut him down and take him to a spare tent. And tonight you may dine with me and my fellow officers, Major."

Simon then notices that he has done the unthinkable. He actually was so scared he soiled himself.

"Yes, General. Thank you very much. General, I need to use the latrine."

Major General Robert Ross smells something funny coming from Simon. He takes a few sniffs and realizes what has happened. He begins to laugh. "Major, did my redcoats scare you so badly that you soiled yourself?"

"Um, yes! You bastards were going to execute me. You guys scared the shite out of me—literally!"

All the British soldiers drop to the ground, laughing out loud. Simon looks at all the laughing redcoats and feels very embarrassed. This is one memory that he is determined never to tell his friends if he makes it back to the Seventy-Sixth. Harry and two other guards walk over to Simon and untie him. They escort Simon to a spare tent overlooking the general's tent. Harry hands him a pair of black breeches. Harry Adams begins to walk away, but Simon stops him.

"Harry, can we speak, please? I'm serious. Just let me change, and then we can talk. Jesus, that was so embarrassing!"

"Very well, and be sure to burn those pants," Harry chuckles.

Harry pulls up a chair from the tent. He grabs another one and gives it to Simon. Simon changes his pants and walks out and throws his soiled breeches into the fire. They sit in the chairs and begin to have a real conversation with each other.

"First off, Sergeant Major, I am really sorry about what I said about your best friend. It was wrong. I am just a dumb bastard. I always had a hatred for you redcoats. But now I realize that you lot are humans just like me."

"Major, I must tell you that you are a Yankee bastard. However, you are an officer who is quick to learn from his mistakes. To me you seem to be fighting for more than just your country. What are you fighting for?"

"Well, my home state of Pennsylvania's motto mentions virtue, liberty, and independence. The main thing I am fighting for is friendship in America. The best thing that keeps soldiers together during war is friendship. Do you agree?" Simon says.

Harry smiles, takes off his shako, and puts it on his lap. "Yes, I do agree, Major. All of these soldiers here are dear friends to me. Only a few of them are like family to me. When I saw you and your friends arguing, to be honest, that broke my heart."

Simon is shocked that Harry watched that whole episode with his staff.

"Oh my God! You watched that? I knew I saw a redcoat hiding in the bushes."

"Yes, it was very heartbreaking. And that is why you grabbed your pistol?"

"Yes. I know I just don't know that my unit will ever forgive me. Especially Celestia. She is the love of my life. We have been best friends since we were babies. Then, in school, we started to date, and she is the woman that I want to spend the rest of my life with. She is so beautiful. And she is the best fighter in my unit. I would give anything to see her again. I really want to marry her."

"Major, hear my words. Even in the darkest times in war, friendship can be found from unlikely people—or, in your case, your nation's enemies. When I fought at the Battle of Badajoz, I wasn't there just to kill French soldiers. I was there to save one! Yes, you heard me correctly!"

"Really? That is interesting. Whom were you trying to save?" Simon asks Harry.

"My cousin, Phillip Martin. He was a major with the French Old Guard. He was trying to desert the French Army, but he was imprisoned. When we were able to storm the ramparts, it was mad chaos. I could see French and British soldiers tearing each other apart. Then a French officer forced me to the ground. We looked at each other for a few seconds. It was Phillip. We both got up, and three frogs charged us with bayonets. We both cut them apart. I escorted him out of the fortress. I took him to Lord Wellington, and he spared him. Before I left for America, he was serving alongside Wellington as part of his staff." He looks at Simon's uniform and recognizes the style. "May I ask … Does your company represent the French Old Guard?".

"I was waiting for someone to ask that question. Who knew that it would be a man who actually fought against the real Old Guard? Yes, we dress like them. They are our idols, I guess you can say. We train like them, march like them, and fight like them. I left my bearskin hat back at camp. And wow, that is a great story, Harry. So a family member who was on the opposing side came to you for help?"

"Yes sir! So, in the end, should your destiny be shown to you, never let it out of your sight. Do not let your sins return and destroy all that you have worked so hard to create. When you return to your unit, give your honest apology to her and propose to her. Do you have a ring to give her?"

"No, I do not. Besides, I may be getting a major's pay, but it is not enough to buy a classy ring for a beautiful woman like her."

Harry pulls out his haversack, grabs a massive ring, and puts it in Simon's hand. Simon looks at the ring and is shocked to see the size of the diamond.

"Well, Major, you should give her this. This is a ring that I found at Badajoz from a dead French captain."

"Jesus! This is the biggest rock I have ever seen," Simon says with amazement.

"Major. I will give this to you as a gift. That is a ten-carat diamond. I am sure Celestia will love it."

Simon is amazed and happy. He puts the ring in his pocket. He smiles and puts his hand out for a handshake. "Thank you, Harry. I don't know what to say."

Just then a drummer walks over to Harry and salutes him. "Sergeant Major, I have orders from the general. He says that our forces will be sailing to Baltimore in a few days."

"Very good, Private. Simon, this is my son, Oliver. This is our American prisoner, but now I am proud to call him a friend."

"Hello there, Major. Long time no see," Oliver says

At first Simon does not remember the drummer. "Let me guess. You heard about me having a bounty because I aided in the destruction of the Canadian Parliament?"

"Well, that too. I am referring to your unit at the battles of Chippewa and Lundy's Lane, and your battle cry: 'Virtue, liberty, and independence.' I must say that your soldiers are very brave."

"Thank you very much. That battle cry is our home state's motto. And I am glad you are alive and well. Ugh, I cannot believe what I'm saying about my enemy. May I ask you a question, Sergeant Major?"

"Yes, you may," Harry says.

"Did you name your son after your best friend who was killed at Breed's Hill?"

"Yes, I did, and he is the best drummer in the Royal Marines. I could not be prouder of my son."

"Thank you, Father. And I would like to thank you, Simon, for saving my life," Oliver says.

Simon scoffs and chuckles, stands up, and fixes his coat. "Well, there always comes a time when one must know when to spare an enemy. Me and my brave warriors do not fight for vengeance or hate. We march to serve and protect our beloved state of Pennsylvania."

"Well, we appreciate you talking to us," Harry says. "We will come get you when it is time for dinner. Just relax in the tent. You must remember that you are still a prisoner. If you want to roam about the camp, you will have two guards around you at all times. Do you understand?"

"Do not worry. I will not try to escape … even though I can wipe out you lot in a few seconds."

Sergeant Harry Adams brandishes his sword and points it at Simon's chest. Simon freezes in his tracks.

"Do not forget I am sparing your life because you saved my son. A life for a life. Now we are even."

Simon looks at the blade as it touches his uniform. He looks up at Harry and chuckles. "That is fair enough. I'll see you at dinner."

They shake hands. Harry and Oliver and walk away. Simon looks at the sky and prays to the heavenly father that his sins will be forgiven.

Later that night, Simon dines with General Ross and his staff. They have a meal of fruit and turkey. Simon sits right next to General Ross.

"General Ross, this meal is great. My compliments on your hospitality, sir. But I will not compliment the fact that I was almost killed. But I forgive you."

"You're very welcome, Major. Now, have you ever dined with English soldiers before? And how is your wound feeling?" Major General Robert Ross asks Simon.

Simon feels his wound; it does not hurt him anymore. "No sir, I have not! This is my first time. And my hand is feeling fine, thank you. I'm just glad that the Sergeant Major was not a better shot. Now this is a joke, General; I thought you trained your soldiers to make their shots count, huh?"

For a few seconds they all are mute, and then they all laugh. Some officers tap on the dinner table.

"You have a point, Major! Good joke! Would like to join us all by the fire later tonight?"

"That would be nice, sir. I would be glad to attend."

All the redcoats join one another around a massive bonfire. They all sing and dance around the fire, and then Colonel William Thortan utters the song 'Rule Britannia.' Simon listens to them sing, and he feels a sense of happiness. The whole British garrison begins to sing. Colonel William Thortan sings the verses while the rest of the soldiers sings the chorus.

> When Britain first, at heaven's command,
> Arose from out the azure main,
> Arose, arose, arose from out the azure main,
> This was the charter, the charter of the land,
> And guardian angels sang this strain:
> Rule, Britannia! Britannia, rule the waves.
> Britons never, never, never shall be slaves.
> Rule, Britannia! Britannia, rule the waves.
> Britons never, never, never shall be slaves.
> The nations not so blest as thee
> Must in their turn to tyrants fall,
> Must in their turn to tyrants fall,
> While thou shalt flourish, shalt flourish great and free,
> The dread and envy of them all.
> Rule, Britannia! Britannia, rule the waves.

Britons never, never, never shall be slaves.
Rule, Britannia! Britannia, rule the waves.
Britons never, never, never shall be slaves.

(Original version written by, Thomas Arne, 1740)

They all cheer, and then Simon walks over to them and offers to sing along with the next song that the British were going to sing.

"Ah, Major Smithtrovich, care to join in the next song?" Colonel Arthur Brooke asked Simon.

"What one will it be, colonel?" Simon asked.

"British Grenadiers." Sergeant Major Harry Adams proudly said.

"I don't know. It's really your nation's song."

"Oh, come on, major. You're a grenadier. Come and sing with us. Besides, your country already stole yankee doodle and Hearts of Oak, since you're from a grenadiers company, then this one should fit you." Major General Robert Ross insisted on Simon.

"Oh, all right," Simon said as she rolled his eyes and stood next to Harry Adams and his son. "I cannot believe that these words are coming out of my mouth, but let's sing to His Majesty's grenadiers!"

"Huzzah!" The british soldiers shouted in unison.

The drummers play beginning of the march, followed by the fifers and the trumpeters. Simon along with the grenadiers of Major General Robert Rosses army sings.

Some talk of Alexander, and some of Hercules
Of Hector and Lysander, and such great names as these
But of all the world's great heroes
There's none that can compare
With a tow, row row row, row row row
To the British Grenadiers.

None of these ancient heroes ne'er saw a cannon ball
Nor knew the force of powder to slay their foes with all
But our brave boys do know it and banish all their fears
Sing tow, row row row, row row row
For the British Grenadiers.

When e'er we are commanded to storm the palisades
Our leaders march with fuses, and we with hand grenades;
We throw them from the glacis about the enemies' ears
Sing tow, row row row, row row row
For the British Grenadiers.

And when the siege is over, we to the town repair
The townsmen cry 'Hurrah, boys, here comes a Grenadier'
Here come the Grenadiers, my boys, who know no doubts or
fears
Sing tow, row row row, row row row
For the British Grenadiers.

So let us fill a bumper, and drink a health to those
Who carry caps and pouches, and wear the louped clothes
May they and their commanders live happy all their years
Sing tow, row row row, row row row
For the British Grenadiers.

(Unknown origin, suspected origin linked to John Playfords,
dance tunes collection of 1728. Turned British military march
in 1689-1702)

They all cheer and shout, and then the whole garrison go to their tents. But several guards walk with General Ross, Ross walks over to Simon and sits with him. The guards watch over their leader.

"Well, General," says Simon, "I bet we can agree on one thing—that the sweet melody's of music can really bring the bond of friendship together. Even among foes from opposing sides."

"I agree, Simon."

They both sit by the fire and watch it begin to burn out. Simon never expected to be having friendly conversations with the enemy that his family has been fighting against since the French and Indian War. Major Simon Smithtrovich is the first person in his family tree to have met the enemy and actually made a friendship with the British.

The next day, Simon wakes up and can see the clear blue sky. He puts his uniform on and steps outside. Two British armed guards stand with their muskets in hand.

Simon looks at them and greets them both. "Good morning."

"Good morning, Major," one of them says. "My name is Private Sean Hale."

"And my name is Corporal Ryan Hale. We have been ordered to guard you for the time you are here in camp. You are free to roam around the camp and talk to the other British soldiers."

"Do you understand these rules, Major?" Private Smith asks Simon.

"Crystal clear. I do want to take a walk. It is always a part of my morning routine," Simon says.

Simon begins to walk with Sean and Ryan guarding him. Simon can see their bayonets are fixed. It makes Simon scoff, but he nevertheless makes sure he obeys their rules. As Simon roams around the camp, he observes the other British soldiers. He pulls out his diary and his pencil. Simon writes down what he observes of the British camp.

> Dear diary: I find myself in a very strange situation. For the past few months, I have found myself being hunted like a fox in the wild. Instead of shooting me, my predators let me live to continue a fight in which I oppose them on the field. I guess these redcoats are not as evil as I imagined. They are very well trained and extremely disciplined. Every redcoat is polite, and they respect their officers. When they are in drill, I am left spellbound by their passion for perfection on the battleground. I was expecting these officers not to care about the men they command. The officers actually engage in conversation with their men. Many of these soldiers are blood related or treat each other like family. I have learned that to be a good soldier you must know when to spare an enemy. I will never disrespect the desire of these redcoats to serve their own nation ever again. They are loyal and true to their king, just as we are loyal and true to the motto that my company fights for. I now see the honor that both sides display on and off the battlefield. I hope that one day in the distant future we will be not opposing each other but fighting on the same side against a common foe. But when will that day come? Only God of heaven and earth knows that answer, and he will probably decide when that will happen.

The guards take Simon to the far side of the camp near the lake. They reach the lake, and Simon is treated to an amazing sight. He is awestruck by the sight of clear water and the greenest trees on the Chesapeake Bay.

"Wow! This is an amazing sight to behold," Simon says.

"We both come out here every morning after drill. We just sit for an hour and gaze at this beautiful water," Private Sean Hale says.

Sean and Ryan want to use this chance to get to know their prisoner. They all sit down side by side and have a conversation.

"Major, we would like to get to know you. What can you tell us about yourself?" Private Hale says to Simon.

Simon clears his throat. "I was born in Philadelphia, Pennsylvania. I am twenty-four years old; I was raised as a proud apple farmer since I was eight years old. Then, when I turned eighteen years old, I joined the US Army, and it took me three years to command my first platoon. We marched across Ohio and into the Indiana territory. I fought my first battle in July of 1811. We were marching down a long dirt forest road, and we were ambushed by Mohawks. That battle lasted for two days. We marched with over three hundred men, and by the end of the battle, my platoon was the only one that survived. Our major was killed, but the Mohawks lost many of their brave warriors."

"That uniform is unknown to us," Ryan says. "We have never seen a uniform like that. We have seen some green uniforms that the frog officers have worn, but nothing like yours, Major."

"I like it. Did you make that yourself, Major?" Sean says.

"Yes. I used some of my money my family has been saving since my parents began the apple business in 1795. I was also funded by our nation's government to help get the bearskins from France. I and my staff supplied the uniforms, but when we enlisted our grenadiers, almost all our troops brought muskets with them."

"That is very interesting, sir."

"Tell me about you two," Simon says.

"We were born in London," Sean said. "We enlisted in the army in 1800, when we were both thirteen years old. It was really hard to leave our family. We were the only kids our mother had. But she died three weeks after we enlisted."

"She was shot in a home invasion," Ryan added. "Two bandits broke into our home and stole some food. They were caught just two hours later and were shot on sight. We never found out she was dead until we graduated from training."

Simon put his hand over his heart. He felt sorry for their loss of their only parent.

"I am very sorry that happened to the two of you. My parents are in Philadelphia, living with my grandparents. The last time I saw them was just before we marched to the Battle of Chippewa. We made a quick stop at the city before we began our march into Canada for the fourth time in two years."

The brothers were shocked at the fact that Simon had been to Canada four times.

"You have marched your men to Canada four times in just two years?" Ryan asks.

Simon nods. "What battles have you two fought in?"

"We fought in Talavera, Badajoz, and Vittoria. Those frogs gave us a hell of a fight in every single battle," Ryan says.

Simon then asks them if they ever fought against the Old Guard before.

Ryan and Sean look at each other, trying to remember whether they have or not.

"I cannot recall that we have," Ryan says.

"Why do you ask?" Sean asks.

"I have a cousin who is serving in the Old Guard. He has been serving since the early 1800s," Simon says.

"How many family members do you have fighting against England?" Ryan asks Simon.

Simon chuckles at the question. "Just me and my cousin at the moment. I have had two other family members battle against the British since 1754. My father fought his first battle when he was just eighteen years old. He was a militiaman fighting for the French. He fought at the Battle of Monongahela.

"Can you tell us about what happened from your father's point of view?" Sean asked.

Simon then tries to remember the exact words of what his father had told him. He looks down at the water and begins to talk about what his father did during the battle.

"The British were moving down the Monongahela River with a large force of infantry and artillery. My father and four of his friends were part of the French scouting parties. My father ran through the woods just about fifty yards from the British columns. He said they were marching with music playing and colors flying proudly, as if they were on a parade ground. He thought it was quite a sight to see so many young men who were not afraid to march into the utter destruction that was about to befall them. They ran past the main body and began to harass the advance party under Major Thomas Gage. He was armed with a Brown Bess and a tomahawk. He moved through the underbrush, and he and his men began to attack British skirmishers. He sneaked up on two of them and sliced both of their throats. He then ducked back into the trees. He went to pick up his musket, and then a British lieutenant who was up on his horse saw him. He aimed at the officer, fired, and killed him with a musket ball to the head. More and more redcoats began to pour into the area. He saw French footmen marching right beside him, and they fired at the pickets. Several redcoats were cut down in a second, and the French regulars pressed on. He ran ahead of them and could see the British advance columns begin to panic and retreat. He and his men chased after them down a road that led to the main body. Once he and his men got to the main body, they saw the British in a state of panic. They were firing back randomly. He saw the enemy form battle lines, and seconds later the whole forest erupted with musket fire. British soldiers began to drop by the dozens. He was horrified to see so many young men just standing out in the open and getting blown away. He saw Colonel Washington's horse get shot. He aimed his musket and killed a British officer who was trying to free his leg, which had been crushed by a horse.

"For the rest of the battle, he never fired another shot. He felt so sorry for all those British soldiers who died that day. When the British were driven away, he walked along the forest. All he saw was the landscape strewn with red-coated bodies. Many were scalped, while others were mutilated. And from that day forward, he would have respect for those men who fell that day.

"He then fought at Fort Ticonderoga in 1759. Again he witnessed the redcoats marching toward him in a frontal assault. He fought against them and killed about fifty redcoats on his own that day. When the French abandoned the fort, he decided to resign his commission as a captain. Sixteen years later, my father picked up his musket and rode to Boston after hearing about the Battles of Lexington and Concord. He fought at Bunker Hill, and he would later join the Second Pennsylvania Regiment and serve as a captain. He fought from Long Island all the way to Yorktown. He was wounded four times but still kept fighting. Finally he swore never to fight again and resided in Chadds Ford, Pennsylvania. Since then, my father and I have created an apple farming business."

Ryan and Sean like the story that they just heard. Hearing that story is definitely a trip down military memory lane for them. And it shows them that the terrors of warfare at the time prove that men who could have brought new joy or terror to the world may never get that chance.

Simon stands up, and the Hale brothers escort him back to Simon's tent. Just before Simon enters the tent, the Hale brothers thank him for having a conversation with them.

"We both appreciate you talking to us, Major," Private Sean Hale says to Simon.

Simon smiles, and he puts his hands forward. "I am proud to make your acquaintance. I hope that you two will live to see the end of this war."

The Hale brothers shake Simon's hand. Simon enters the tent and lies down on the cot. He closes his eyes and falls into a deep sleep.

During that whole week, Simon spends his time with the redcoats. He chats with other soldiers and even trains with them. Some of these British soldiers treat him as if Simon is one of their own comrades. Simon is transformed into a new man and is ready to continue the fight, but he has a new lease on life, as well as a new lease on the power of friendship.

CHAPTER 14

COMPANY OF LOYAL GRENADIERS

Seventy-Sixth Pennsylvania encampment
Maryland countryside
Five miles from Baltimore, Maryland
August 28, 1814
Early morning

The Seventy-Sixth are eating their breakfast and preparing their gear for their march to Baltimore. The unit still wonders about whether Simon is still alive or whether he has been killed by his captors. Nevertheless, they must keep their heads up and march onward and save their feelings—not just for the enemy but also to help their comrades' morale. A few of the grenadiers that in the Seventy-Sixth have family members that live in the city of Baltimore. Jessica and Devin have their grandfather, who is sixty years old and lives on his own. They both begin to worry about what could happen if Baltimore suffers the same fate as Washington. The Littles sit with Drum Major Brittany Benson and talk.

"I really hope that our grandfather is okay, Devin," Jessica says as she shudders in fear.

Devin is worried about him too, but he does not show it. He comforts his frightened sister as Brittany gives them the gift of courage. She expresses her feelings for someone she knows that lives in the city as well.

"Jessica," Brittany explains, I am feeling the same amount of fear for our loved ones too. It does hurt right to the core, but we must hold up our heads and keep on drumming. I have someone in the city that I am worried for too."

"Who would that be, ma'am?" Jessica asks.

Brittany pulls out a hand-size portrait of her mother that she keeps inside her bearskin cap. She hands it to Jessica and begins to tell a short story about her mother.

"This is my mother, Sarah Benson. She is fifty-five years old, and she is my whole world. We are extremely close, and I have not seen her for three years." As Brittany continues to talk about her mother. She begins to feel homesick. "She raised me ever since I was just a baby. She always had a saying that she would tell me every single night before I went to bed: 'The second you open your eyes on a new day, stand up and fight to seize your victory in any way.'"

Brittany cannot control her emotions, and she cries. She puts her hands over her face as she sobs softly. Devin and Jessica sit right next to Brittany and hug her.

"Don't worry, ma'am," Devin says. "That quote was beautiful, and I'm sure you have made your mother proud."

"We'll be marching for the city soon, and you will get to see her again," Jessica says.

Brittany looks up at them and smiles at both of them. She dries her tears and begins to fill with joy. "Thank you. You two are very great friends. I'm so glad to have not only you two but also this noble corps of brave warriors."

They all feel touched and hug each other. On the other side of the camp, Sergeant Miller and First Lieutenant Rose sit by the fire, cooking their breakfast. They have yet to tell their company about what happened to Simon, and today is the day that they must give the terrible news about their commander. But they must hide it till the proper time comes.

Daisy brings a basket that contains apples, oranges, and bananas. She places it on the cooks' table, and the cooks give it to the men and women of the Seventy-Sixth. Daisy brings some of the fruit to her sister and Timmy.

"Hey, sis. Do you want an apple? I have plenty of others to go around," Daisy says to them.

"Where did all that fruit come from?" Celestia asks Daisy.

"This was a gift from a farmer just down the road. I was finishing my patrol, and a farmer called out to us and gave us all this food."

"Wow! That is very great."

Daisy hands her sister an apple and Timmy a banana.

"Thank you, Daisy," Timmy says.

"Thank you, little sister," Celestia says before she takes a bite.

"You both are very welcome."

After they eat their breakfast, they get down to military business.

"Gather the unit. It is time for them to know about Simon and our orders," Celestia says to Timmy and Daisy.

Timmy and Daisy stand up and walk out of the tent. They tell the men to get into formation in a field next to their camp. Celestia walks out in front of the unit. The unit is lined up in rows of thirty.

"Grenadiers, attention!" Celestia shouts. The Seventy-Sixth stands at attention, and she gives a speech to boost the company's morale, but not before giving them bad news that could break their will to fight on. "My friends of the Seventy-Sixth Pennsylvania, hear my voice. I know that we have been through a lot. The times have been very tough. I want to say that I apologize. I have yet to tell you all about our commander." Something in her mind tries to stop her from telling her grenadiers that Major Smithtrovich is dead, but she manages to speak, and she immediately wishes she had remained silent. "Grenadiers, I regret to inform you that the British have executed Major Simon Smithtrovich."

Many of the grenadiers groan in pain and loss. Some have angry faces. Many shed a few tears, but Celestia tells them not to let their emotions get the best of them, as they still have a war to fight. She speaks sternly, turning her sadness into energy that she and her company can use against the British in the upcoming battle.

"My comrades in arms, it hurts me to say those words. My staff knows how much it hurts. But we must let our sadness turn into much-needed strength. The major would not want us to feel ashamed for what has happened. He would want us to march onward and continue fighting in his honor. Sergeant Miller informed me a few days ago that the lobsterbacks' next target is the city of Baltimore. That is where we're marching to next. We cannot let this sadness and fear tear us apart. We must raise our heads as high as the sun in the sky. We must hoist our colors high. We must let our citizens know that there is still a fight on. This is a fight that we need them to join. Right now, the United States is on the very slimmest of edges of becoming extinct. We must show to the whole world that America is not a nation of pirates, disease-ridden degenerates, or sorry excuses for human beings."

All the grenadiers begin to have their faith restored in the cause. Celestia hoists the regimental flag into the sky with her left hand. Her voice becomes more inspirational and much louder.

"To those lobsters and Canucks, this is just another piece of land that they think is rightfully theirs. This flag does not belong to us as much as it doesn't belong to the army; it belongs to our great nation—a nation full of citizen soldiers who braved thousands of redcoats from Bunker Hill, Long Island, Trenton, Brandywine Creek, Saratoga, Monmouth Courthouse, and the Siege of Yorktown. This is our land; our families inherited our freedom. Now we must take their place. We must fight until the British and the Canadians realize that they cannot win. Burning down Washington is one thing, but now they have taken away a man we knew as a friend, a soldier, a leader, and, most importantly, a member of the family that shall remain forever as the Seventy-Sixth Pennsylvania Keystone Grenadiers!"

She takes the flag staff by both hands and waves the regimental flag from side to side several times.

"Huzzah! Huzzah! Huzzah! Huzzah! Huzzah! Huzzah!" the grenadiers of the Seventy-Sixth shout with pride and energy.

One hour later that day, the Seventy-Sixth is ready to march to defend the city of Baltimore.

Celestia stands at the front of the company and gives the orders to march to Baltimore, Maryland. "Seventy-Sixth Pennsylvania, attention! Right shoulder arms! The Seventy-Sixth shall take care to advance! Drum Major, play 'War and Washington'! Company, Forward march!"

The Seventy-Sixth begin their march, and as they march, they all sing a song to the tune of "The British Grenadiers" called "War and Washington."

Celestia shouts to the unit, "Heads high, grenadiers. March with pride. All together now. Let those heavens know that Major Smithtrovich and

Washington shall not go without consequence." She swings her sword and points high to the sky. "Keystone Grenadiers, sound off!

The Seventy-Sixth begins to sing with great pride and with passion.

> Vain Britons, boast no longer with proud indignity
> By land your conquering legions, your matchless strength at sea.
> Since we, your braver sons incensed, our swords have girded on.
> Huzza! Huzza! Huzza! Huzza for war and Washington!
> Great heaven! is this the nation whose thundering arms were hurl'd
> Through Europe, Africa, India? Whose navy ruled a world?
> The luster of your former deeds, whole ages of renown,
> Lost in a moment or transferred to us and Washington!

As the Seventy-Sixth marches through Brookville, Maryland, civilians can hear the sounds of drums, fifes, and trumpets coming toward them. People who are in their houses go outside and hear the music. Some of the people sit upon their fences and watch as the Seventy-Sixth marches toward them. They cheer them on as the Keystone grenadiers march on past. Daisy sees a mother and her daughter waving at the column. Daisy breaks ranks, runs back to the wagon, and grabs a bearskin cap. She heads to the mother and daughter. Daisy kneels down and she hands the little girl the cap. The little girl smiles and she puts the cap on her head. She then hugs Daisy. Then the mother speaks to Daisy.

"Thank you for serving our country."

Daisy looks up at the mother. "It is my pleasure." She then speaks to the little girl. "I want you to know that you can be anything you want to be when you grow up. Because we live in the United States of America. We choose what we want to be. And in this nation, we are all soldiers who will battle any tyrant who wants to spread tyranny. I want you to hold down the fort in this town because you're a junior Keystone grenadier now."

"Thank you very much," the little girl says happily.

"You're very welcome," Daisy replies.

"I will not let you down, ma'am," the little girl says. She then salutes Daisy. Daisy stands at attention and salutes the little girl.

Celestia looks at the rear of the column and sees Daisy doing a good deed. Celestia smiles and blows her whistle three times. The drummers play a cadence, and that is a signal for Daisy to rejoin the ranks. Daisy then marches back into the column, and the little girl watches the rear of the column march on past. As the Seventy-Sixth enter the center of town, they continue to sing the song. More and more civilians cheer for them as they sing.

> Should warlike weapons fail us, disdaining slavish fears,
> To swords we'll beat our ploughshares, our pruning hooks to spears,
> And rush, all desperate, on our foe, nor breathe till battle won;
> Then shout, and shout 'America!' and 'conquering Washington!'
> Proud France should view with terror, and haughty Spain revere,
> While every warlike nation would court alliance here.
> And George, his minions trembling round, dismounting from his throne,
> Pay homage to America, and glorious Washington!

> (Original song written by, Jonathan M. Sewall, American Revolutionary war)

First Lieutenant Celestia Rose is leading the company down the road, until they soon see American militiamen emerging from the trees. They rush in front of the company and down the road. A few minutes later, they see a platoon of the US Marines marching towards them. The marine's military band was playing Yankee Doodle Dandy. The US Marines begin to sing the lyrics of the original song.

> Yankee Doodle went to town,
> A-riding on a pony,
> He stuck a feather in his hat
> And called it macaroni.
> Yankee Doodle, keep it up,
> Yankee Doodle dandy,
> Mind the music and the step
> and with the girls be handy!

Father and I went down to camp,
Along with Captain Goodin',
And there we saw the men and boys
As thick as hasty puddin'
Yankee Doodle, keep it up,
Yankee Doodle dandy,
Mind the music and the step
and with the girls be handy!
And there we saw a thousand men,
As rich as Squire David,
And what they wasted every day,
I wish it could be saved.
Yankee Doodle, keep it up,
Yankee Doodle dandy,
Mind the music and the step
and with the girls be handy!

(Original song written by, Edward Bangs, 1776)

The Seventy-Sixth Pennsylvania followed behind the US Marines and several other platoons of militias as they all marched towards the city of Baltimore. The staff of the Keystone grenadiers knew that Washington, despite the city being destroyed by the British was evil, cruel, and a terrible crime against the United States, it wasn't enough to break the will of the people that lived in America. Instead, it was considered a call to arms against the British army. All the grenadiers could see dozens of militiamen, regulars, marines, and naval soldiers rallying from the countryside, just like the militia forces that rallied to Concord after the Battle of Lexington on April 19th, 1775. Not many had uniforms and not many had a musket or a sword, but they were ready to defend Baltimore, even if they had to fight with their own bare hands. The American forces have regained their strength, their passion, and their will to continue the fight. Now they are more determined to defeat the redcoats at the next battle—or, rather, next battles.

CHAPTER 15

"I'M TELLING YOU HOW THE CABBAGE GETS CHEWED"

Baltimore, Maryland
Fort McHenry
September 10 to 11, 1814
Midday to morning
12:00 p.m. to 7:00 a.m.

The whole city of Baltimore prepares for the attack. But two years earlier, the people of the city did not want to go to war. Violent anti war demonstrations flooded the city's streets. Now the whole city is readying for a battle that will transform the destiny of the United States. The defeat at Bladensburg has taught the citizens of Baltimore a great lesson. Baltimore's time is now, and they are refusing to let their city become char and ash at the hands of the British. The Battle of Baltimore will be either the beginning or the end of the United States of America.

Regular and militia forces flow into the city from all over while the main force is over at Fort McHenry. Civilians are helping the soldiers make defenses. The new command of the American defenders of the city of Baltimore falls under a man by the name of Major General Samuel Smith, who is a veteran of the American Revolutionary War and the Whiskey Rebellion. He is the commander of the Maryland militia and has one problem that he has to conquer before he can fight the British. He has to handle the dispute between himself and Major General William Winder. General Smith knows that General Winder is a more direct threat to his authority than the redcoats. He knows that Winder must step aside so that Smith can avoid another disaster. The dispute between them stems from General Winder being a regular officer and General Smith being a militia officer. So inside Fort McHenry they battle it out over who is to be the commanding officer of the defense of Baltimore.

"Gentlemen," General Winder says, "we are on the narrow ropes of extinction. The redcoats will not stop until we are slaughtered as my men were at Bladensburg. We ran like sheep chased by bloody dogs. And now they could do the same thing here. I say that we evacuate the whole city."

General Smith knows that if their men will stop running and fight, victory shall be theirs. "No, General. If we turn tail and run, you will be a laughingstock through the whole damn country. No more running away from a bunch of lobsters. Our men are much stronger than you think, General."

They continue to go back and forth at each other.

"I don't even have faith in our regulars, let alone the militiamen," General Winder says.

"How dare you not have faith," General Smith states with an angry tone. "Your men didn't even try to fight back at Bladensburg. And with that, you also almost lost your old friend Commodore Barney. I have fought my heart out during the revolution. I trained my men well, and they are itching to take on the British."

"Old history is not important. We must make a choice on what we are going to—"

General William Winder doesn't even get to finish his sentence before General Smith pounds his hand on the table and utters his famous quote.

"I'm telling you how cabbage gets chewed!"

General William Winder stops talking and leaves the headquarters, and Sam and John get down to business. General Samuel Smith pulls out a map of the city of Baltimore and points to the northern side of the city, indicating a hill called Hampstead Hill. They both know what they will face if the redcoats take over the city. General Smith knows that Fort McHenry will be the target of the naval attack and Hampstead Hill will be the attack by the British Infantry.

"We will build fortifications at Hampstead Hill," General Smith explains. "That will cover the whole northern side of the city. That should be about a mile in length. There could be a possible attack through North Point. So we will use a force of infantry and artillery batteries. This should be a mile stretch of entrenchments."

Then an officer by the name of Major George Armistead walks into the room.

"Sir, you wanted to see me, sir?" He walks to the table

"Yes, Major. I have your orders. Your men are to build two earthworks at the front of the Eastern tip of the fort. I will give you extra artillery pieces. How many men do you have in this fort?"

"Sir, I have a regiment of regulars, militia, and artillerymen. We have enough black powder to hold this fort for the rest of the year."

Another officer joins them at the table. His name is Brigadier General John Stricker. He will be ordered to take charge of the infantry at Hampstead Hill.

The Seventy-Sixth Pennsylvania Keystone Grenadiers finally arrive at Baltimore, and they march over to Fort McHenry, where they can see hundreds of regulars preparing the fort for the British assault. The Seventy-Sixth are stunned by the fortifications of the fort and the determination of the citizens of the city. As they enter the fort, they witness a moment they will never forget. A massive garrison flag that is made out of light wool bunting and that measures thirty feet by forty-two feet is hoisted into the sky. The Seventy-Sixth stand spellbound as they watch the flag wave in the sky. The garrison flag and a storm flag were created by Mary Pekkersguild. She was paid by the War Department a total of $574.44 for the two flags. She worked day and night to create them.

The Seventy-Sixth gaze upon the garrison flag as it billows in the breeze.

"That is a big flag!" Celestia says with astonishment.

"I have never seen one this big before. I cannot believe this. Those lobsters will have no bloody trouble seeing that flag at all." Timmy says.

"Grenadiers, stay here until I come back. Understood?" Celestia says to the unit.

"Yes ma'am!" the Seventy-Sixth shout.

Celestia falls out and sees the commanding officers' quarters. She walks over to them, and then Major George Armistead walks out of the headquarters. She walks up to him and introduces herself to him. She salutes him.

"Major, I need to speak with you. I am First Lieutenant Celestia Rose of the Seventy-Sixth Pennsylvania Keystone Grenadiers."

"Hello there, Lieutenant. My name is Major George Armistead. Welcome to Fort McHenry. I am pressed for time, so what do you need?"

"I need to speak to Major General Smith. I have been given direct orders from the president to march here for the defense of the city."

Celestia hands him a paper that states the orders. Major Armistead reads the letter and then escorts her to the headquarters.

"Wait out here. I will let you in shortly if he wants to talk," Major Armistead says.

He steps back in and speaks to General Smith. "General, the Seventy-Sixth Pennsylvania has arrived, and their commander wishes to speak with you. And their commander is actually a female, sir."

"Very well, Major. Send her in, please," General Smith says.

Major Armistead opens the door, and Celestia walks in. She stands at attention and salutes General Smith and General Stricker. They both salute Celestia, and she explains to them about her orders and about Simon being captured.

"Sir, I am First Lieutenant Celestia Rose of the Seventy-Sixth Pennsylvania Keystone Grenadiers. My company is here to help defend the city, sir."

"Welcome to Baltimore. Are your grenadiers ready to fight?" General Smith asks First Lieutenant Rose.

"Yes sir. Where do you want us stationed, sir?" Celestia asks.

He then shows Celestia on the map where the Seventy-Sixth will be placed to help defend the city. "We need infantry on Hampstead Hill. The redcoats will probably attack up at North Point. There is where the infantry battle will be, while their navy will bombard this whole fort with everything they have. If we lose Hampstead Hill, the whole battle could be lost. If they do break through, I want you and your company to fall back to the city and barricade the city streets. But stay on that hill unless we order you back. Is that understood, First Lieutenant?"

"Yes sir. Clear as day, sir."

Celestia salutes, and she exits the headquarters. She walks back to the Seventy-Sixth.

"What is the news, ma'am?" Sergeant Miller asks Celestia.

Celestia stands in front of her unit. "We have orders to march to Hampstead Hill and build an earthwork. The Redcoats will attack at North Point. If they do take the hill, our orders are to retreat to the city and barricade the streets. Fight block by block if we have to, by God. However, that will not happen because we won't let it happen. We will hold that damn hill till the last grenadier dies or until the last bullet is fired. Then we will fight with bayonets, if our bayonets break, then we will fight with our bear hands. I swear that we will hold that hill until death. Now, are there any other questions about the orders?".

"No ma'am!" they shout.

"Very well then. To Hampstead Hill we go. Keystone grenadiers, ten hut. Shoulder firelocks! Right face! Forward march!"

The Seventy-Sixth begin their march to Hampstead Hill. A few minutes later, Brigadier General John Stricker leads his men to the hill. His unit consists of a group of regiments of the Maryland militia, a small militia cavalry from Maryland, volunteer rifle companies, and an artillery battery of six eight-pound cannons.

As the Seventy-Sixth march through the city of Baltimore, the citizens cheer for them. Some citizens grab shovels, pickaxes, and muskets and march right beside them. To inspire the citizens of the city even more, Celestia calls back to Brittany to have their band play a song.

"Drum Major Benson, play 'The Liberty song.'"

"With pleasure, ma'am!" Brittany shouts.

She turns and instructs her corps to play the march. The citizens of Baltimore and the defenders join in and sing.

> Come, join hand in hand, brave Americans all,
> And rouse your bold hearts at fair liberty's call;
> No tyrannous acts shall suppress your just claim
> Or stain with dishonor America's name.
> Brave and free are our hearts.
> Brave and true are our men.
> We're always ready, steady lads, steady.

We'll fight and we'll conquer again and again.
Then join hand in hand, brave Americans all,
By uniting we stand, by dividing we fall;
In so righteous a cause let us hope to succeed,
For heaven approves of each generous deed.
Brave and free are our hearts.
Brave and true are our men.
We're always ready, steady lads, steady.
We'll fight and we'll conquer again and again.
With muskets and cannon and banners they come.
They march on our towns to the beat of the drum.
And through all the clamor and smoke of the fight,
There's Liberty's torch burning steadfast and bright,
Brave and free are our hearts.
Brave and true are our men.
We're always ready, steady lads, steady.
We'll fight and we'll conquer again and again.

(Original written by John Dickinson, 1770)

The whole city begins to dig fortifications at Hampstead Hill. The American soldiers and civilians arrive at Hampstead Hill and begin to build fortifications that stretch a mile in length. Cannons and small arms are placed at the hill. The hill is fortified by soldiers, as well as men and women both young and old, and black and white. The merchants of Baltimore sunk their ships on the left of Fort McHenry, which blocked the entrance of Baltimore Harbor. Only small sloops were able to get through the water barricade.

On the night of September 10, 1814, the whole city was ready for the fight. The only thing they can do now is wait. At Hampstead Hill, Celestia is sitting on the ramparts and watching the stars. Then she looks in her bag and spots an unopened letter. She looks at the front of it and sees it is addressed to her. "Open when the time is right, the front of the letter says. She opens the letter and she begins to read it in her mind. The letter says reads as follows:

Dear Celestia Rose, I am writing you this letter because I'm afraid I might not make it to the end of this war. I have had too many close brushes with death in this war, and I do not know if my time will be up soon. Should I fall in the heat of battle, I would want you to take command. I cannot think of anyone who could fill in the boots. I want you to remember these final words should I be killed in the battle of freedom. For the past year and a half, I have always thought about you. You are the one person that has truly become my diamond. From the time we were children and when we marched onto our first battleground. You are the one person that has always been there for me as I have done the same. The friendship that we have shared was so amazing. You have given me a wonderful life. It was such a great honor to have been your teacher, your leader, and, most importantly, your friend. I will always love you and will never stop loving you even when I take my final breath on the battlefield. And anything that I do in this war, I may or may not agree with my actions, but I will do it to protect my family, my friends, my country, my flag, our company, but most importantly, I will do anything to protect the most beautiful rose flower in the world, you Celestia Rose. Till we meet again in the Keystone State or in the garden of the Lord.

Your best friend and true love forever,
Simon Smithtrovich

She holds the letter close to her chest and looks up at the stars as a shooting star flies overhead. She begins to shed tears and sniffles a bit. She cries herself to sleep along the wall of the ramparts. She holds the letter in her hands as she sleeps through the whole night.

The next morning, Daisy wakes up and sees that her sister is not in the bed on the other side of the tent. She gets up, walks out and looks around, and heads to the ramparts. She spots Celestia sleeping against the wall. She walks over to her slowly and is very confused. She kneels and wakes her up.

"Celestia? Did you sleep out here all night?" Daisy asks her sister.

Celestia wakes and stands up. She puts the letter in her pouch and stretches. "Yes. I must have," she says as she yawns.

"What was that letter in your hand?"

"That letter was from Simon. I have just learned that he was telling the truth. He did this to protect us. Oh, my Lord! What have I done!"

Daisy hugs her sister. "Celestia, we need to save our sorrows after the battle. I do not believe he is dead. Deep down I know he is alive. Simon would not go down like a sitting duck."

Celestia is confused by what Daisy is saying. She has two voices inside her own head. One is saying that Simon was murdered. The other voice is saying that Simon is still alive. She doesn't want to think that he is dead, but in so many cases in life, human eyes trick thousands of people, and this could be another case of blindness.

"When Simon returns," Daisy continues, "this is something that you and he need to figure out. We will make sure of it, and there is no getting out of it. You two will face each other and deal with this even if we have to do it from night's dark to day's light. Understand me?"

Celestia looks up at her and is stunned by her younger sister giving her orders.

"First Sergeant Rose, are you giving me orders? You are way out of line."

Daisy begins to yell and rant at her as she tries to get Celestia to understand what she means. "I am not speaking as a soldier! I am speaking as your sister who wants only the best not only for herself and her friends but also for the one sister that she loves and cherishes with all her heart, and who has always stuck by you through good times and, recently, the bad times that have plagued our nation. So you and Simon will face each other and solve this problem together. I will not say this again. Do you understand me?"

Celestia stands petrified and then finally responds. "Yes, I understand you. Thank you for caring about me, Daisy."

They hug each other and begin to cool down. They look over and see that the whole unit is looking at them.

Timmy stands and walks over to the Rose sisters. "Um, is everything okay?"

"Yes, Timmy, everything is fine," Celestia says. "We were just having a family conversation. Go and ready your breakfast. We will begin inspection in one hour."

The Seventy-Sixth disperse and ready their breakfasts. The tension between the Roses cools, and throughout the rest of the day, the Seventy-Sixth drills hard to prepare for the battle, which would leave a great historical mark on the British and the United States.

CHAPTER 16

———◆———

FROM PRISONER TO SPECTATOR

The Chesapeake Bay
September 10, 1814
Evening

The Royal Navy sets sail up the Chesapeake River with a force of five thousand regular soldiers and nineteen warships. On board the British flagship, Major Simon Smithtrovich paces under heavy guard. He watches the forest pass by as they draw near to Baltimore. Major General Robert Ross walks out on deck. All the sailors and soldiers salute him. He walks over to Simon and leans on the planks of the ship, looking at the forest.

"How are you doing this evening, Major? Ross asks Simon.

"I am feeling okay, sir. I am just waiting to get back to my unit. I have some major damage that I need to fix. And I would actually like to thank you, General, for giving me that chance of redemption. I bet you don't usually give this treatment out to many other prisoners of war, sir?"

"That is a good question. I fought against Napoleon Bonaparte for a few years, and I have seen so many prisoners of war—too many to count—but only a few get my respect."

Simon looks up at General Ross, seemingly confused. "Respect, sir?"

"Yes, respect! For you and your Keystone grenadiers standing firm like a mountain during Bladensburg was very brave. Anyone who is willing to stand against the best trained, most professional military in the whole world earns respect. Major, you have earned my respect. That is why when we arrive in Baltimore, I will allow you to return to your unit."

Simon's eyebrows rise in amazement. "General, I am honored to say that even though we are enemies from a military point of view, beyond that I am proud to call you a friend. If one thing keeps me going during a battle, it is knowing that no one can destroy the power of friendship. Thank you, General. You have my respect as well."

The two smile and shake each other's hand.

Just then Vice Admiral Alexander Cochrane walks up to Robert Ross. "General, we are about twenty miles away from Baltimore, and an American truce vessel will make contact with us, sir. A lawyer named Francis Scott Key will be making a trade for the two prisoners you have, sir. With the prisoners that they have, sir."

"Very good, Admiral. Thank you. Major Smithtrovich, once we make contact with the truce vessel, you will be allowed to leave."

Simon is filled with happiness deep inside. He feels that something will still be keeping him from his unit.

"Understood. But it seems like there's a catch to all this," Simon says with suspicion.

"Yes. You will have to wait till after the battle is over to return your unit. I am sorry, but these are orders, and these terms are nonnegotiable."

Simon's heart falls into his gut, and now he has to sit by and watch as the battle unfolds.

His happiness turns to sadness, but he accepts the terms.

"Very well, General. Now I'm gonna go and get some rest. Tomorrow seems like it's gonna be a long day. Good night, General."

Simon walks to the bottom deck and finds a spare rack. He lies down and fills with fear at the prospect of not seeing his unit again—or, most importantly, his four best friends and the love of his life, Celestia Rose.

The Royal Navy sails up the river through the whole night.

The next morning, an American scout walks around on the side of the river until he sees the British forces sailing up the river. Fort McHenry's cannons fire one shot each. The cannon fire is a warning that the redcoats are arriving. Some citizens panic and flee the city, while others rush to Hampstead Hill or to Fort McHenry. One by one, the British set their ships in position. Soon the whole Royal Navy has completely blocked off Baltimore Harbor. The Seventy-Sixth Pennsylvania Keystone Grenadiers station themselves at Hampstead Hill. There, along with General John Stricker, regiments of militias, riflemen, and artillerymen wait and watch as the British forces sail into the harbor.

Down at the Baltimore dock, Francis Scott key sets sail with his ship, the USS *President*. He sails toward the British blockade. He raises the white flag and docks right beside the HMS *Hornet*. Francis Scott Key climbs aboard the *Hornet* with another man by the name of Colonel John Skinner, who is the man who made the exchange possible. They are both welcomed by the crew. Major Simon Smithtrovich and another American prisoner, Dr. Beane, a medical doctor who treats American soldiers, are under guard by British Royal Marines. Both of them watch as the meeting takes place.

"Good morning, General Ross," Francis says

"Good morning, Mr. Key. I believe that we have some business to attend to. Please have a seat. And you are, sir?"

"My name is Colonel John Skinner. I am the one who established this prisoner exchange. My rank should be noted. I have the British soldiers who were arrested here on the boat too."

Two other crewmen from Key's ship bring the British soldiers that were arrested onto the *Hornet*.

They all sit down for a nice breakfast, and while they eat, for an hour, they discuss negotiations. Finally the transfer of the prisoners begins.

"So," Ross says, "you have two of my men. And I have one doctor. And since you have two of my men, I'll add this American officer to go with you as well."

Francis Scott Key looks at Simon and walks up to him. "Hello there," Mr. Key says.

"Hello there," Simon replies.

Before Simon leaves with Francis Scott Key, he gives his goodbyes to his captors and friends. "General Ross, thank you for helping me change, sir. I bid you farewell, and I am hopeful that once this conflict is over, we shall meet again."

"Goodbye, Major Smithtrovich. It will be nice to meet again. Good luck."

"You too, sir."

The redcoats release Simon and Dr. Beane to Francis Scott Key. Then the redcoat prisoners are given back to Ross. Before Simon walks across the board connecting the two ships, Simon looks back at Ross and salutes him. Ross returns the salute, and Simon boards the USS *President*. Simon is so relieved to be off the *Hornet* and happy to not be a prisoner of war. He runs over to Francis Scott Key and shakes his hand.

"Sir, I can't thank you enough. This is a real gift from the hand of God," Simon says.

Francis tells Simon that they must wait for the battle to be finished before they can return to the city.

"Major, unfortunately we must wait here until the battle is over."

Simon gasps, angry that he is eight miles away from his company. "That is absurd! I have a company out there in the city without their commander. Who knows; they probably think I am dead. And they will be facing down the wrath of the British regulars and their massive navy. They have massive bomb boats that can fire one-hundred- ninety-pound cast-iron bombs into that fort. If that hits a wall of the fort, it will crumble like an egg. As for my unit, I sure hope they can hold out. If I know Celestia, she will do everything she can to make sure they do not lose. May God have mercy on those brave defenders."

The whole day, both sides stand ready for the fight. The two days will mark the turning point for the British military and the United States in the War of 1812.

CHAPTER 17

THE BATTLE OF BALTIMORE BEGINS

Hampstead Hill and North Point
Baltimore, Maryland
September 12, 1814
Dawn

As dawn breaks over the city of Baltimore, the British forces begin the first part of their battle plan. The plan is for Major General Robert Ross to lead five thousand regular soldiers over to North Point. Their main objective is to march toward the northern part of Baltimore while their navy fires upon Fort McHenry until the Americans surrender or the fort is completely destroyed.

Celestia wakes up, gets her uniform on, and grabs her Brown Bess. The second she steps outside. She begins to sweat. The morning is abnormally hot. She wipes the sweat from her head and fixes her bearskin cap, making sure the plume is pointing straight up toward the sky. She shoulders her Brown Bess and marches toward General Stricker's tent. As she passes, she spots Brittany up and ready. Celestia walks over to Brittany and greets her.

"Good morning, Drum Major Benson."

Brittany stands at attention and salutes with her mace. Celestia salutes Brittany in kind.

"Good morning, ma'am. My word, it sure is hot this morning. Just like the Battle of Monmouth Courthouse back in 1778, wouldn't you agree, ma'am?"

"I do agree. I can see your uniform is neat and tidy. That is very good. You never seem to disappoint."

"Thank you, ma'am. I always want to look very well dressed for the enemy. If I am going to die on the field, then I shall die with style," Brittany says proudly.

"I would like to thank you for being our drum major. You and your corps really know how to drum up some great marches. Personally, I feel that an army that doesn't march to any music—their morale will drop and there will be no reason to keep up the fight."

Brittany smiles and looks at her mace, seeing her face in the mace's reflection. "Thank you, ma'am. It is a great honor to march into battle with you, ma'am." Brittany looks at the troop tents and gazes upon the sky as the sun's rays begin to shine through the clouds. "Shall I wake up the troops, ma'am?"

"Not yet. Let them sleep for a few more minutes. They will need the extra energy today. I must report to the general."

"Very well, ma'am."

Celestia marches off to General Stricker's tent to receive her first command. She marches like she's on a parade ground. In her mind she imagined the sound of a snare drum beating the tempo of 'The Keystone Grenadiers'. She begins to hum the song, but not too loud. The Seventy-Sixth Pennsylvania Keystone Grenadiers are still asleep while Celestia reports to Brigadier General John Stricker's tent. Celestia stands at attention outside.

"General Stricker, sir. First Lieutenant Rose reporting as ordered, sir!" Celestia shouts.

General Stricker gets up from his bed and walks over to his table. He rolls out his map.

"You may enter, Lieutenant."

Celestia walks in and salutes him. He salutes her in return.

"Sir, you have orders?"

"Yes, I have your orders. You must take your unit to the edge of North Point. The redcoats will be landing at the tip of the Chesapeake Bay. Your job is to engage Ross's forces and draw them back to North Point. We will be there with the main body of our troops. You must not get entangled in their lines. Remember: I want you to fire a volley and then fall back. Keep doing that, just as our comrades did at Lexington and Concord. Do you understand?"

"Yes sir. We will not kill all the lobsters. We will bring the main course to your men," Celestia says.

"Very well. I have faith in your grenadiers. I am sorry to hear about your commander, ma'am."

"Thank you, sir. He was a very fine officer and, most importantly, my best friend. My troops are hoping that he will be with us again soon. But the war comes before friendship."

General Stricker grabs two chairs. They each take a seat, and then they both talk about friendships during wartime and the Seventy-Sixth's true dedication to their nation.

"Lieutenant, please sit down. There is something I would like to talk about before you move out. Do you really think war is more important than friendship? From what I have heard, that is what you and your fellow soldiers are fighting for. Is it not?"

"Yes, that is true, sir. We fight not just for our freedom and liberty; we fight for the power of friendship, because our friendship that runs within our ranks is what keeps our troops' morale high. We trust each other that we will watch the backs of the soldier right next to us."

"That is true dedication, and this is why the Seventy-Sixth are marching to the front first. I have heard about what your unit did during the Battle of Bladensburg. You stood your ground for almost an hour against the Eighty-Fifth. You withstood two bayonet charges. And when you were ordered to retreat, your grenadiers carried your dead and wounded back to Washington. That is very impressive."

"Thank you, General. We do not ever leave our wounded or dead for the enemy to either steal their personals or mutilate them. We all march to victory or die in each other's arms, knowing that we have done our best to preserve our nation with our blood, sweat, and tears."

"Before you set off, I have one more thing to say. When you believe that what you think you're fighting for is worth the price of your own blood, and when the ones who will follow you down that road believe in the same cause, then you all realize that you shall prevail over tyranny. Whatever you do on the battlefield, never end the battle for what you all think is right. Now go and make your commander proud. Dismissed, Lieutenant.

Both of them stand up. Celestia salutes and says her goodbyes.

"Thank you, sir, and may providence be with you."

John Stricker salutes Celestia. "May Providence be with you too."

Celestia leaves the tent and heads back to the unit, who are sleeping in the trenches and in their tents. Sergeant Timmy Miller hears Celestia's footsteps, wakes up, and grabs his musket. Celestia walks up to him.

Timmy stands at attention and salutes Celestia. "Good morning, ma'am."

Celestia stops in front of Timmy Miller and salutes him. "Good morning, Sergeant. You may stand at ease."

Timmy stands at parade rest, wiping a few sweat drops off his forehead. "Good, God, it seems like it is going to be a hot day, ma'am. Do we have orders, ma'am?"

"Yes, Sergeant, I have noticed that too. but we shall not worry about the heat. And yes, we do have our orders. I will give the orders once all the men are awake. So wake them up and get them in formation. We will be moving out in a few minutes, so we need to get them up quickly. Do you have any ways to get them up fast?"

"Yes ma'am," Timmy says excitedly. "I have a fast way of doing that. Watch this. I have always wanted to do this."

Timmy walks among the unit and steps up on top of the redoubt. He smiles and cocks his Brown Bess and aims it in the air. He looks at Celestia, who can see what he is going to do. She nods at Timmy in a way of telling him to do it. Timmy aims his musket high and pulls the trigger. A loud boom from his musket is loud enough to wake up the whole unit. They jump and grab their weapons. Then they see Timmy up on the redoubt.

"Oh good, you're all awake. I hope you all had a great night of dreams. Now form up in front of the redoubt. First Lieutenant Rose has our marching orders."

The grenadiers get their uniforms on and grab their muskets. They rush to form their ranks in front of the redoubt. They step over the redoubt and form their ranks fifty feet from the walls. Once they have formed their ranks, Celestia addresses her company.

"Keystone grenadiers, attention!" Celestia shouts.

The Seventy-Sixth stand at attention. They stand straight like professional soldiers as they ready themselves for battle.

"Good morning, my fellow grenadiers," Celestia says to her troops.

"Good morning, ma'am!" the Seventy-Sixth shout.

Celestia now begins to give her fellow grenadiers in arms the battle orders that will take them from a simple grenadier unit to a unit that shall shine brighter than the sun. Before she gives the orders, Celestia observes her fellow soldiers. She can see their faces as they face forward, not speaking a single word. She feels in her heart that today some of these fine men and women will not live to see the moon's shining light. She takes a deep breath and gives the orders of battle. She also preaches about what is at stake should they lose this battle.

"Today we are going on our first major raid. We have orders to invade the enemy as they land their troops at North Point. Our main job is to cause hell to their landings. Once we are done with that, we will fire and then retreat one hundred yards. We will repeat this until General Stricker can bring up the main forces to North Point. Now then, our rules of engagement are that no man will fire without my order. Is that clear? Now don't worry about breakfast, because today we will be having a special meal. We will be having hot and juicy lobster. How does that sound?"

The whole company laughs at her joke.

"That sounds very tasty, ma'am," says Daisy. "I love seafood. But ma'am, since when did we turn into cannibals?"

The joke makes the soldiers laugh again. Celestia rolls her eyes and continues to speak to the Seventy-Sixth. Her tone is serious, motivational, and heroic.

"Har-har, Daisy! Real funny. Now let us get down to real business. Now, I know this will be the first time we will be fighting a battle without our commander. I know that I cannot be a replacement. This is my very first time I lead you all into battle. I hope that you bear with me on this. I definitely know that he wants us not to worry about him. He would want us to keep our heads up high and never let our nerves get the best of us. This is what our commander has prepared us for over the past two years. We all know that the time has come to step up and let our nation know that there is still a fight. We will display to the great citizens that we will not stop fighting till we all take our final breaths. Now that we have our orders, who is ready to show those red bastards what the Keystone grenadiers can really do?"

"We are, ma'am!" the Seventy-Sixth shout in unison.

"Are we loyal to the United States of America, to our president, to our families, to our freedom, and to friendship?" Celestia shouts.

"Yes ma'am!"

"Are we proud to be Keystone grenadiers of Pennsylvania?"

"Yes ma'am!"

"Are we going to honor our fallen leader by upholding his name and everything he stood for?"

"Yes ma'am!"

"Grenadiers, shoulder your firelocks! Left face! Seventy-Sixth to the front! Forward march! Celestia shouted with a very strong commanding voice.

The Seventy-Sixth Corps Marching Band drummers play a strong drum cadence and begin their march to North Point. The sound of the drums awakens the other sleeping American soldiers. They look at the Keystone grenadiers as they march onward to the fray. They all begin to cheer. Throughout the camp, all the soldiers begin to wake up because of the pounding of the drums from the Seventy-Sixth.

They rush out of their tents, and some make way to the redoubts as they watch the Seventy-Sixth march away from the hill. They begin to cheer the Seventy-Sixth in a supportive manner. The Seventy-Sixth can hear their comrades' cheers, and it fills them with energy that they never even knew they had. Daisy marches right beside her sister. Timmy marches right behind them, while Brittany marches in front of the company.

"It is time to make our commander proud, wherever he is," Daisy says.

"I am sure he is praying for us," Timmy says.

Some of the grenadiers begin to hum a song based on a folk tale referenced in a song called "Springfield Mountain." This song, one of the first American ballads, portrays a man named Timothy Myrick, who was bitten by a rattlesnake and died on August 7, 1761. But the Seventy-Sixth turned the balled into a marching song.

Brittany turns to her corps. "Band, make ready! Now this is a song that we have not practiced, but let's give it a shot."

"We are ready, ma'am," Jessica says.

"On your cue, Jessica," Devin says.

Jessica cracks her fingers and begins to play the drum cadence. After ten seconds, Devin joins in and the rest of the corps begins to play the march. Celestia about-faces and commands the unit to sound off.

"Keystone grenadiers, sound off!"

"One!" Daisy shouts.

"Two!" Timmy shouts.

"Three, four, five, six, seven, eight, nine, ten!" the Seventy-Sixth shouted with cadence.

The Seventy-Sixth march in rows of five and columns of ten. The drumbeat is so loud that it shakes the ground beneath their feet. The Seventy-Sixth begin to sing in unison with pride and with strong energy. They sound like a mighty orchestra of voices. After every two verses, they hum the tune and then continue the verses.

"We Yanks go marching off to war, hurrah, hurrah.
We butcher lobsters just for laughs, hurrah, hurrah!
We Yanks go marching off to war, hurrah, hurrah!
We'd rather die than surrender, hurrah hurrah!
We Yanks go marching off to war, hurrah, hurrah!
All for one and one for all, hurrah, hurrah!
We Yanks go marching off to war, hurrah, hurrah!
Together we shall make our stand, hurrah, hurrah!
We Yanks go marching off to war, hurrah, hurrah!
Down with tyranny, up with freedom, hurrah, hurrah!
We Yanks go marching off to war, hurrah, hurrah!
Never shall we admit defeat, hurrah, hurrah!
We Yanks go marching off to war, hurrah, hurrah!
Our banner billows in the breeze, hurrah, hurrah!
We Yanks go marching off to war, hurrah, hurrah!
We thrive to serve and protect, hurrah, hurrah!
We Yanks go marching off to war, hurrah, hurrah!
Those that live shall fight again, hurrah, hurrah!
We Yanks go marching off to war, hurrah, hurrah!
God save the brave Seventy-Sixth, hurrah, hurrah!"

The Seventy-Sixth sing so loudly that the whole American camp can hear them from a mile away. General Stricker and his staff can hear the Seventy-Sixth singing. He thinks about the passion of the Seventy-Sixth.

"I have never heard a unit sing with such passion for battle. Good luck and Godspeed you brave Seventy-Sixth," he says to himself.

Down at Old Road Bay, the first of the British regulars make landfall, and they can hear the sound of music. A British lieutenant steps off his boat and hears the singing, and he knows that the enemy is quickly approaching. Sergeant Major Harry Adams and his son, Private Oliver Adams, are among the first to head ashore. Harry pulls out a spyglass and tries to look for the American forces that are heading their way. He is unable to see them, but he has no trouble hearing them. Harry is confused as to why the Americans are still willing to resist the British.

"My God!" Harry says to his son. "Well, so much for the element of surprise. I thought those bastards would still be sleeping. How can those Yankees still be in such high spirits?"

"Those Yankees should be begging on their knees for mercy to spare their nation from further destruction," Oliver says with a devious voice. "Those Americans never seem to know when to bloody quit. Well, today shall be the day that we destroy the last of the American pigs."

Harry is not so quick to think that the United States have given up the fight yet. He feels that this battle will be very different than the one just a few weeks earlier.

"I fear that we have plucked too many feathers of their beloved American eagle. And now we must be ready for the consequences. I believe that this will be a very different battle than Bladensburg. But do not worry, my son." Harry grabs Oliver's shoulders. "Now, when the fighting begins, you just make sure to stay by my side. You do not leave my sight. Do you understand?"

"Yes, Sergeant Major! But you have to give those Yanks some credit."

"What kind of credit would that be, son?"

"They do have some pretty great music," Oliver says. "I love you, father."

"I love you too, Oliver. Do not ever forget that, my son." Harry says as he hugs his son.

Soon dozens of boats loaded with men from the Second Battalion of His Majesty's Royal Marines begin to land at Old Road Bay. They land with a few six-pound cannons.

It takes the Seventy-Sixth one hour to march to Old Road Bay. There they can see the Royal Navy. They are shocked by the might of the navy, but nevertheless, they are ready to stand and fight. The Seventy-Sixth stand in the trees and look at the Royal Navy. The ships of the line that are in their view are the main fleet where the USS *President* is observing. The ships of the British fleet at the battle are made up of five bomb vessels: the HMS *Volcano*, HMS *Meteor*, HMS *Aetna*, HMS *Devastation*, and HMS *Terror*. There is one rocket ship, the HMS *Erebus*. Seven frigates of the line are present: the HMS *Surprise*, HMS *Severn*, HMS *Eurylans*, HMS *Hebrus*, HMS *Madagascar*, HMS *Havannah*, and HMS *Seahorse*. And three schooners make up the last of the fleet: the HMS *Cockchafter*, HMS *Wolverine*, and HMS *Rover*. The whole fleet is under the command of Vice Admiral Sir Alexander Cochrane.

The Seventy-Sixth is shocked by the sight of the redcoats' massive navy. The staff rally together and they discuss the second part of their orders. Celestia gives her orders.

"Daisy, you are to keep an eye on the fleet, and we will be setting up in the bushes one hundred yards to the rear. There is an open field about thirty yards right behind it. If we get pushed back that far, we will retreat and then open fire again."

"Just like Lexington and Concord, ma'am?" Timmy asks.

"Exactly! This time we will be doing this until General Stricker can bring up his regiments. Now, I will take the first platoon. Timmy, you will take the second platoon, and Brittany, you will take the third platoon."

Brittany hesitates at the fact that she will be commanding a platoon. "Ma'am, I have never taken command of a combat platoon. I'm just a drum major; I'm not a combat soldier."

Celestia offers her a musket and urges her to take it. "Brittany, you may be our drum major, but today we're all combat soldiers. I wouldn't want you to fire this musket if I didn't think you were capable of fighting. You said to me at the beginning of the war that you can fight just like us. Well, this is your chance."

Brittany hesitates but then takes the musket. She looks at Celestia.

"You're ready. We trust you and your corps. Do you trust me?" Celestia says.

Brittany looks back at her corps and can see that they are being issued with their own muskets. They salute her, and Brittany utters a statement that fills her corps with more passion to fight.

"Let those who are willing to steal our nation come to meet their fates at the hands of those who are born forever free."

Brittany's corps rally around their leader; they pat her on her back and hug her.

"We will not fail you, ma'am," Devin says.

"You have trained us well, ma'am," Jessica says. "We trust you to lead us as you have led us into battle—not with just muskets, but also with the great music you have taught us."

Brittany smiles and hugs her corps. "Thank you, everyone."

"Not to break up a tender moment but we do have a battle to begin," Celestia says to the Seventy-Sixth. "Grenadiers, to your battle stations!"

Celestia places her platoon in a heavily wooded area near the bay. Timmy marches back with the main force one hundred yards behind Celestia's platoon. They set themselves up for the ambush. Celestia checks on each of the men. Timmy does the same thing with his men. Daisy stands near the water, looking at the Royal Navy with a spyglass.

On one of the British men-of-war, one redcoat officer looking through his spyglass sees a faint flash in the trees. Daisy spots the British officer and begins to get scared. She puts away her spyglass. Vice Admiral Cochrane spots her and yells to his gun crews, "American infantry in the trees. Roll out the cannons! You may fire when ready!"

The crew of the HMS *Surprise* roll out their cannons, and Daisy watches as they do so. The sight of the cannons sends her running deep into the woods, and then she hears the thundering roar of the cannons. Seven eighteen-pound cannons open fire. Huge explosions erupt all over Daisy's position. Some cut trees in half. A few fall short and explode in the water. One cannonball ricochets off a tree and almost strikes Daisy. The cannonball flies past her and rips into a tree. The whole tree falls and almost lands on Daisy. She pauses for a few seconds, trying to catch her breath. The surrounding area is covered with dense smoke, and the land is filled with exploded trees and scattered branches. She grabs her musket and runs back to Celestia's first platoon. The first platoon watches as the woods are almost destroyed by the bombardment. Celestia worries for her sister, not knowing whether she was able to escape. Then they see a figure walking out of the smoke. Daisy runs to them and rejoins the platoon. Celestia runs over to her sister.

"What in the name of God happened?" Celestia says in a worried tone.

Daisy falls to her knees and looks up at Celestia. She speaks as she tries to catch her breath.

"I think the Battle of Baltimore just began, ma'am!" Daisy says.

Major General Robert Ross begins to land the rest of his forces. The last British regulars come ashore, and so far, the Pennsylvania grenadiers are out of sight. As soon as Robert Ross heads ashore, he is accompanied by his second in command, Colonel Arthur Brooke.

"We must get underway immediately, Colonel Brooke. Those Yankees shall not stand if we press them as we first make contact," General Ross says.

"Sir, the majority of their troops are militia. About eighty-five percent of their forces is my guess, sir," Colonel Brook says.

"I don't care if it rains militia!" Major General Robert Ross utters to his staff.

General Ross is overconfident about his overwhelming victory at Bladensburg. He decides to press on. He rides alongside a light infantry platoon, and the redcoats begin their march down the road. Little does he know that he is once again walking into a trap set by the Keystone grenadiers. Ross's advance party is two hundred yards away from the ambush point.

＝＞|＋|＜＝

Celestia and Daisy's first platoon of fifty grenadiers can see the advance party of redcoats marching toward them. The British drum-and-fife corps can be heard all the way from the trees. The redcoats march as if they were on parade grounds.

Celestia paces behind her troops. "Those lobsters are coming. Stand ready. Do not fire until I give the order."

＝＞|＋|＜＝

The foot guards of the advanced party cannot see what is within the trees. Some of the redcoats begin to get a little nervous. Some have never faced this kind of terrain, and some do not know about how the United States military fights. Many of these British soldiers will be facing American guerrilla-style soldiers.

＝＞|＋|＜＝

Once the foot guards are within one hundred yards of the trees, Celestia prepares her platoon to open fire. She speaks just loudly enough for her platoon to hear her commands.

"First platoon, make ready! Take aim!"

The first platoon cock the hammers on their muskets and aim at the advance party of redcoats. Celestia aims her musket at a British officer on a horse in front of the British advance party. She is breathing slowly. "This is for you, Simon," she whispers.

Timmy begins to mumble the Hail Mary under his breath as he watches the redcoats advance toward them. When the British are at fifty yards, with one mighty shout to her platoon, Celestia gives the command to unleash hell.

"Fire!" Celestia shouts.

The brush explodes in white smoke. The bullets whiz through the air. Celestia's shot strikes the British officer in the mouth as he is taking a breath. The bullet tears through the back of the officer's neck in a mist of blood. He falls off his horse. Eight other British soldiers are shot in the head. A redcoat sergeant is shot right between the eyes, and another redcoat is showered in the sergeant's blood and flesh.

In the rear ranks, General Ross hears the musket fire and looks through his spyglass. He sees through the musket smoke the familiar flag of the Seventy-Sixth, and he feels a very cold chill crawl up his spine.

"Bugger, not these bastards again! Oh dear, oh dear!" he mutters to himself.

Sergeant Major Adams rallies his platoon and returns fire. His men see small movements in the trees and small patches of white smoke. Sergeant Major Adams points to the trees and directs his advance foot guards to open fire.

"Second Battalion of His Majesty's Royal Marines, return fire. Prime and load! Fire when ready, lads!"

The redcoats form up by tens and fire upon the trees. The bullets tear into the brush. One bullet hits Celestia's bearskin cap, and it flies off her head.

"Yikes, my cap!" Celestia shouts.

She retrieves her hat and notices that her green plume has been shot in half, and it seems another bullet tore through the middle of her hat.

"Well, I'll be damned!"

She puts her hat back on her head. The redcoats are getting too close to the trees. Celestia gives the command to fall back to the second line.

"First platoon, retreat to the second line. Prime and load as you go. Fall back!"

The whole first platoon runs out of the trees, and the redcoats regroup their lines and continue to march.

Just then Major General Robert Ross rides up and sees his soldiers lying dead on the road. The redcoats are firing upon the Americans but are not hitting anything. The Seventy-Sixth's first platoon has managed to escape to the second line. Ross urges Harry to keep the advance party pushing forward. From behind the Seventy-Sixth Pennsylvania, one Maryland militia company and two companies of cavalry and riflemen come to aid the Seventy-Sixth. The Seventy-Sixth reform their ranks near a second line of trees to their backs. In front of them is a wooden fence that stretches the whole open field from north to south. The Seventy-Sixth take positions along the wooden fence and wait for the redcoats to advance upon them. Celestia gives her commands to the Seventy-Sixth and the riflemen that are at the fence.

"First platoon, kneel! Second platoon, stand! First Company, make ready! Present arms! Hold your fire until I give the order!" Celestia shouts.

All the men aim toward the road. They can hear the sounds of drums approaching. Soon they see the British Union Jack waving through the trees. The British main body marches toward the Seventy-Sixth. Instead of returning fire, they form their ranks. The redcoats dress their ranks and calmly march into formation. The Redcoat drummers and fifers fill the air with "The British Grenadiers." The Seventy-Sixth wait in dead silence, focused, as they watch the redcoats form their ranks. Celestia paces back and forth through the rear ranks, making sure the men are steady and calm.

The redcoats form their ranks with one hundred men in the first rank, and then they set up a six-pound cannon in the middle of their battle line.

The sight of the cannon sends chills up some of the grenadiers' spines. Two grenadiers standing right next to Timmy shiver at the sight of the British cannon. Timmy looks at them and pats them on the back one at a time, trying to keep them both calm and stop them from panicking.

"Steady, friends. You shall not fear the hot lead. We will endure for our freedom and friendship. Do you trust me?" Timmy says.

Both of the grenadiers nodded at the same time.

Just as the redcoats form their ranks, a British officer rides forward in front of his troops and gives the Seventy-Sixth a chance to surrender.

"You Yankee doodles listen to this: The United States has no chance against the might of His Majesty's Army. No one shall ever forget your fool's courage for defending your nation's broken dreams. We want to save your lives, but we cannot do that if you continue to resist. This is your final chance to lay down your arms, and we will make sure that you will be given a fair trial!"

Some of the Keystone grenadiers look at each other, but they know that the lobsterback is bluffing. They know deep in their hearts that the redcoats want them to be slaughtered. The British officer continues to plead the Seventy-Sixth to surrender.

"You have done all that the honor of war has asked of you, but it is time to lay down your weapons."

Celestia steps out of the ranks and lets the British officer know that the Seventy-Sixth will not surrender.

"We will never bow to a pompous bastard who calls himself a king," she shouts at the officer in a rebellious tone. "We are not a colony of people who cannot be ordered around with the penalty of death. Let me tell you lobsters something about those dunkers on the horses who dare call themselves officers. They would let all of you march to your deaths while they prance and get dead drunk. They are happy to let you all die. They are not true officers. They would rather take advantage of fine ladies in the American taverns."

Daisy then steps forward and stands side by side with her sister. "You all have been misled to your fates," she says. "Our officers lead from the front. A true officer is a figure that will never let their troops die in vain. We cherish our fellow soldiers like family. We never treat our soldiers like they are property. That is what all you lobsterbacks are a bunch of overdressed monkeys sitting upon horses."

Those words fill the British soldiers with rage. They can't believe that the American forces are insulting their leaders right in front of them.

Just then Timmy and Brittany join the rest of the staff.

"We will not let Washington and our Major's death be in vain," Timmy says. "You lobsters will pay for what you have done. Should we fall today, there are thousands of other Americans who will honorably take our place."

"From night's dark to day's light," Brittany shouts, "America will fight on the land and on the sea! We will fight in the bitter cold to the intense heat, no matter whether we are outnumbered or outgunned. Let it be known that the United States will never bow down to a tyrant who rules over his subjects who thrives to spread tyranny across the earth."

"For virtue, liberty, and independence!" every member of the Seventy-Sixth shouts. "God bless the United States!"

The British officer scoffs. "Very well! You bastards had your chance," he says.

The Seventy-Sixth's staff run back to their ranks, and the English officer returns to his men. The Seventy-Sixth commence their attacking defense. With no hesitation, they unleash pure hell on the redcoats.

"Keystone grenadiers, fire at will!" Celestia shouts.

The Seventy-Sixth and the Maryland militia open fire. The volley tears through the British line. Thirty-five redcoats fall to the ground. Those redcoats are shot in their chests, faces, and legs. One redcoat has three bullets tear through his left leg, blowing it off. The volley cuts down the artillerymen while they are loading the cannon, but four other British regulars pick up the rammer and finish loading it. The redcoats return fire as hotly as they have received it. A redcoat lights the fuse, and the cannon launches a shell toward the fence. The shell bounces upon the ground and tears a grenadier's right leg off his body. Then it explodes behind a few other Maryland militiamen. The explosive force sends shrapnel flying into the backs of three soldiers. They fall down to the ground with huge open wounds in their backs. The cannon blast lifts two Keystone grenadiers into the air, mortally wounding them. The soldiers on both sides are forced to the ground by the concussion of the explosion. They manage to get back up and keep fighting.

The advance guard of Sergeant Major Harry Adams's marines prepare to fire another volley of muskets. The front rank of the British battle line kneels. The rear rank stands up and reloads. Harry Adams looks over and sees Timmy Miller. Through the fog of battle, Timmy can even see Sergeant Major Harry Adams for a few moments. The two make eye contact.

Harry gives his commands to his men. "Second Company, make ready! Take aim! Front rank, fire!"

The British volley cuts down ten grenadiers and ten militiamen. Bullets tear through the line. One American soldier has a bullet rip through his right eye. One has a bullet strike his groan. One is hit in the shoulder, and blood from the wound splatters Celestia's right cheek.

"Second rank, take aim! Fire!" Harry shouts.

The second British battle line opens fire. The volley cuts down fourteen more American soldiers. One grenadier is shot six times in the chest. Celestia realizes that the Seventy-Sixth is beginning to be outnumbered, but then she begins to suffer from a once-in-a-lifetime event: the thousand-yard stare. While the Battle of North Point rages on, Celestia looks around and sees her soldiers getting wounded or killed. She looks at her sister while she is reloading her musket. A bullet grazes Daisy's left shoulder. Daisy falls to the ground and covers her shoulder. Blood drips from her fingers, and she cries out in pain. She looks over at the soldier who lost his leg. The soldier grabs his leg as blood spills out. He cries out in massive pain.

Celestia notices that Daisy is on the ground, wounded. She runs over to her, and Daisy begins to lose it.

"Daisy, are you wounded?" Celestia asks.

Daisy manages to stop her bleeding while she is crying from the pain. She appears to be extremely scared. She looks up at Celestia, and Celestia sees tears rolling down her sister's face. She is really scared from the sounds, smells, and terrible sights of battle all around her.

"Celestia, I am scared! I want to see Papa again! For the love of God, I cannot fight anymore!" Daisy says, losing control of her emotions.

Celestia tries to comfort her and get her back in the fight, but to no avail.

"I am scared too. You're going to be alright. Calm down!"

Daisy cries out to her sister in pain and terror. "I don't want to die here! Not like this! Please! I want to go home!"

Daisy cannot hold her emotions in, and she blubbers like a baby from all the terror of the battle all around them. Celestia hugs Daisy. She looks over her shoulder and watches her fellow grenadiers being severely wounded or killed. Celestia breathes heavily, and the crying of her frightened sister scares her to the core.

Three American bluecoats standing right behind the Keystone grenadiers are trying to reload their muskets, and then an exploding shell erupts in a fireball. The three bluecoats are engulfed by the blast. Their uniforms catch on fire, and they drop to the ground and roll, trying to put the fire out. One stands up after taking his coat off but is shot directly in the heart. One grenadier is crawling around on the ground, looking for his leg. He finds it and tries to reattach it. Two other grenadiers are hiding behind a tree. Bullets skim the front of the tree. One of them gets shot in the neck. He falls to the ground with blood spilling out. The second grenadier tries to stop the bleeding, but the soldier dies. He yells out toward the sky. Seconds later, he is shot directly in his temple. The side of his head blows out in a mist of blood and brains. Another one tries to crawl away from the battle because he has lost both of his legs. Pieces of flesh drag on the ground and leave a blood trail on the grass behind him. Finally, a redcoat stabs a wounded militiaman in his chest three times and then bayonets the soldier in his head. There is a crunch when the bayonet pierces the skull. Then the redcoat is shot directly in the groin. Timmy runs over to Celestia. Halfway there he gets knocked down by a grenadier who has been shot in the face. The soldier's left cheek is gone, and blood from the wound spills out onto Timmy's face. Timmy pushes the soldier off him and makes it to Celestia, who is still hugging her sister.

"What in the name of God do we do now, ma'am!" Timmy shouts.

Celestia slaps Daisy in the face to help her come to her senses. She slaps her three times before she finally snaps out of it. Celestia then speaks to her, letting her know that she will not be left behind.

"Daisy, listen to the sound of my voice. We are both gonna see our father again. I promise you that you will see our family. But I need you ready to fight. You're my little sister, and I promise that I will keep you alive. Do you trust me?"

Celestia wipes Daisy's tears from her face. Daisy smiles. "I trust you, big sister. I love you," Daisy says with a cracking voice.

"I love you too, Daisy." Celestia says.

Both of them get to their feet and look to the rear through the trees. General Stricker has finally arrived with the main body of troops.

Celestia knows it is time to move. The Seventy-Sixth have done their part, and they begin to retreat. But what the Seventy-Sixth does next is something that will never be forgotten. Ever since the first battle they fought in the early years of the War of 1812, they had never left a fallen comrade abandoned on the battlefield. The normal routine was to carry the dead and wounded away after the battle. Instead, the Seventy-Sixth carried their dead or wounded off the field while the battle was raging on. Celestia gives the command to retreat and to get their wounded off the field.

"Grenadiers, carry back our dead and wounded. Don't leave them behind. Get back to our lines as fast as you can!" she shouts.

Sergeant Timmy Miller hands his musket to a fellow grenadier and picks up their regimental flag off the ground. Then he picks up the wounded flag-bearer.

Daisy sees a wounded drummer boy. The boy looks at his drum and sees it has been destroyed by a cannon shell. She runs over to him and picks him up. He has been shot by two muskets balls in the left leg. She stumbles while trying to carry him along with her musket. She manages to carry the boy back to their lines. Other Keystone grenadiers sling their muskets and run to their dead or wounded grenadiers-in-arms. They pick up their friends and help them get back to their lines. Drum Major Brittany Benson runs over to a wounded fifer who lost his leg. Brittany picks him up and runs away from the battle. The redcoats try to shoot the troops of the Seventy-Sixth. They try to stop them from getting the wounded out of the field, but the American bluecoats cover them. Celestia runs to a wounded grenadier who was shot in the spine. The soldier is crying out in pain.

"Help me! I cannot move my legs! Ma'am, get me out of here!" the grenadier shouts.

"Don't worry! You're going to be alright. Let's get the hell out of here!" Celestia says to him. She picks him up, but as she tries to run, a bullet strikes the wounded soldier in his neck and severs his spinal cord. Then another bullet rips through Celestia's coat, and she falls down to the ground on her knees. She groans in huge pain, and then she looks down and sees blood spilling out of the grenadier's neck. The soldier is dead. But she still manages to carry him out of the field. For every step she takes, she can feel a massive surge of pain in her side. Once back to their lines, American surgeon's rush down to the Seventy-Sixth and help them get the wounded. Celestia hands the dead soldier to a young surgeon. She looks down at her coat and can see that the area from her gut to her black breeches is covered in blood. Soon Timmy and Daisy catch up, and other American soldiers run to both of them and take the wounded grenadiers and the militiamen to the medical wagons, where they will be taken back to Hampstead Hill. Daisy, Brittany, and Timmy regroup with Celestia. They all see a hole ripped in Celestia's uniform. And they see all the blood on her green regimental jacket and breeches.

"Ma'am, are you hit?" Timmy asks Celestia.

Celestia feels around her gut for the hole in her uniform. She notices that she has been wounded in her belly. Then another sharp pain races through her gut.

"Oh God! I am hit!" She cries out in pain.

Celestia falls on her knees and puts her hand over her wound. Timmy and Daisy help her to the rear ranks. They sit down near a tree stump. Celestia takes her hand off the wound and looks at it. Her whole hand is covered and dripping with blood. Daisy pulls out a bandage from her haversack and looks at Timmy.

"Excuse me, Sergeant Miller. Can we have a little privacy?" Daisy says.

"Yes," Timmy replies. I will let you two handle this. I will go check on our grenadiers." He runs off.

Daisy tends to Celestia's wound. Daisy unbuttons her jacket, revealing that Celestia has been shot in her side. Small amounts of blood are bleeding out. Daisy grabs a pair of pliers and digs for the bullet. Celestia groans in pain, and a few seconds later the bullet comes out.

"Thank you, Daisy. I never knew that getting shot would hurt this much," Celestia says through the pain.

"It is only a scratch, be lucky the bullet didn't go deeper into your belly. Besides, a tough woman like you should not be stopped by a little lead ball. Your soul is bullet proof, just like our friendship."

Another Keystone grenadier brings a pail of water and some clean bandages. Daisy dumps a clean cloth into the water and begins to clean the wound. Celestia then begins to cry softly from the pain. Tears rolled down her cheeks. She whimpers from the pain. Daisy looks up and sees that Celestia is in great physical pain.

"Celestia … I'm sorry! I will try to be more gentle. Does it hurt?"

"Yes … it does."

Daisy then finally cleans most of the blood around the wound. But what Daisy doesn't know is that her sister is also crying from the mental pain—the pain of missing their father, whom they have not seen since the war began. Celestia is still crying softly, but she is trying to hold herself together.

"Ma'am, what's wrong?" Daisy asks.

Then Celestia asks a question that Daisy will never forget till the day she takes her final breath.

"Do you think Father would be proud of us?"

Daisy drops the washcloth and the bandages. She begins to stammer, and her eyes grow full of tears. Daisy then grabs her sister, and meets each other's gaze.

"Celestia, Father would be so proud. And Simon would be so proud of us as well. Don't you ever forget that! I'm very proud of you. I know that you can be overprotective, but that is because you are my older sister. You have been a role model for me for many years. I will always continue to look up to you for guidance and knowledge. Our company will continue to look to you as well. We all love you just as much as you love us all. I love you very much, Celestia."

They hug each other very tightly. Both of them sigh when they hug each other.

"I love you too, Daisy. By God, that will never change!"

Timmy comes back over and sees them hugging and crying in each other's arms. He stands there and holds his hand over his heart. "Aww, that is a sight to see. Now that is true family honor if there ever is any, by God."

The Battle of North Point continues. But what happens next during the Battle of North Point will change the course of the War of 1812 for the British and the American militaries.

CHAPTER 18

SINGLED OUT

Battle of North Point, Part 2
September 12, 1814
Noontime

More American reinforcements march toward North Point. Both sides eye each other with no word of command. General Robert Ross enters the battleground in front of his troops along with his officers. Before the fighting even resumes, two American riflemen—Daniel Wells, eighteen, and Henry McComas, nineteen—sneak into the woods. They have been ordered to target British officers and what they are about to do will earn them a place in the books of history for years to come.

"Daniel, climb up that tree and tell me if you have a view of that lobster on the white horse," Henry McComas says.

"Already climbed up. Can you please hand me my rifle?" Daniel says to his friend.

Henry hands Daniel his rifle, and then they both notice Major General Robert Ross riding in front of his troops. Major General Ross rides forward to lead his men. He turns to rally the light infantry, and a British officer witnesses the unthinkable.

"I have sight of the lobster. Permission to take the shot?" Daniel asks Henry.

"You have the permission to send that bastard straight to hell! Take the shot when you are ready."

They both cock their rifle hammers and aim at Robert Ross. Daniel slowly breathes, and then, without a moment's hesitation, he pulls the trigger and shoots Robert Ross. His rifle is true to the mark as the bullet tears through Ross's arm and enters into his side. Robert Ross falls from his horse. Other officers, including Colonel Arthur Brooke, come to his side. One officer picks his head up. Growing weaker, Major General Robert Ross issues his final order.

"Colonel Brooke, you are in command."

Ross takes his final breath and dies. Seconds later, a British volley overwhelms the American riflemen. Daniel takes a musket ball to the chest. He grabs a tree branch to prevent himself from falling. Henry fires one more shot and kills a foot soldier. Then he himself is shot down by another British volley. Up in the tree, Daniel slowly loses his grip on his rifle, and it falls from his hand and lands on the ground. With one bullet, Henry McComas and Daniel Wells would never know how they both had changed the course of the War of 1812.The death of Robert Ross sent shock waves through the British ranks. The redcoats fire a volley into the American lines which cuts down two dozen American regulars and militia. A few seconds later, a loud roar erupts from the British lines. The redcoats then charge at the Yankee lines. With anger and hate, the redcoats fight like devils. One redcoat bayonets an American soldier so hard that his barrel is thrust through the body and out the Yankee's back. One militiaman tries to charge the redcoat. The redcoat fires his musket and shoots the militiaman in his head. The soldier dies before he hits the ground. Both sides are entangled in close-quarters combat. Soldiers fire from the hip or aim down their sights to kill their targets. One blue-coated private stabs wildly at British soldiers, stabbing them in their chests and necks, and he thrusts his bayonet into the forehead of a redcoat. A British officer unsheathes his sword and begins to fight several American soldiers on his own. He swings his sword, cutting off hands and legs. He stabs wildly like a madman. After a few minutes of hand-to-hand combat, Colonel Arthur Brooke blows a whistle. Only a few redcoats begin to fall back to the main line. The rest still are fighting hand-to-hand with the American soldiers.

Colonel Arthur Brooke rides to his artillerymen. "I want you to open fire on their lines," he orders the artillery officer. "Use cannonballs and our Congreve rockets. Blow those bastards apart."

The artillery officer is hesitant to fire upon their troops. Colonel Brook raises his voice at the officer to get him to obey his commands.

"This is how we are going to break our forces off. Do not question my damn orders. Now unleash hell on those American pukes!"

"Yes sir!" the artillery officer says.

As Colonel Brooke rides back, the artillery officer begins to shed tears because he knew that he was going to be killing his own men. Brooke rides back to his staff. The Americans continue to defend their lines until the sound of Congreve rockets is heard by the American lines. The rockets land on top of the American and British forces. Dozens of rockets explode between all the soldiers. A dozen soldiers from both sides get struck. Shrapnel strikes their bodies. The American soldiers begin to panic and retreat from the field. One American wagoner comes racing down toward the American lines, carrying bullets and gunpowder. A rocket flies through the top of the wagon. The wagoner looks behind and sees the rocket inside the back. He grabs his sword and manages to free the horses. The horses ride free, and he quickly jumps clear. Seconds later, the whole wagon erupts in a massive explosion. Bullets fly out in all directions. A few American soldiers are caught in the blast and are riddled with several musket balls. Four American regulars are killed instantly. The Seventy-Sixth Pennsylvania watches from the rear of the American line as the British artillery fire begins to destroy General Stricker's lines. Timmy is appalled by the devastation he is watching.

"My God. How can those men take any more? We need to regroup at Hampstead hill.

"Those unholy bastards. How can they kill their own? Should I run to General Stricker and request to retreat?" Daisy asks Celestia.

"Negative. We must wait for our orders. We have done our part for now."

A few minutes later, General Stricker had enough. The American infantry and the Seventy-Sixth Pennsylvania retreat back to Hampstead Hill. But unlike the militia that retreated at Bladensburg, General Stricker retires his men in good order. The Battle of North Point was finally over.

The losses on both sides were not heavy. The United States suffered 24 killed, 139 wounded, and 50 captured. The British suffered 46 killed and 295 wounded. But the greatest loss was Major General Robert Ross. The tragic death of loss affected the British Army in a massive way. He was a trusted officer, and he was loved by his men, whom he had marched to victory in his previous battles over in Europe. British soldiers who really loved that general were shattered. Had Major General Robert Ross lived through the battle, he would have become a well-known figure. That honor, however, will be given to the lawyer Francis Scott Key, who is still detained on the USS *President*, where Major Simon Smithtrovich is being held.

CHAPTER 19

THE DEFENSE OF FORT MCHENRY

Baltimore, Maryland
September 13, 1814
Morning

On board the USS *President*, Major Simon Smithtrovich and Francis Scott Key are having breakfast and can see the Royal Navy getting ready for a second battle. The USS *President* stays while the British gunboats and bomb vessels move up the bay toward Fort McHenry.

"Thank you for the meal, sir," Simon says to Francis. "So, you are a lawyer? Because I come from a family of lawyers myself. We own our own business up in Pennsylvania. But I chose to be an apple farmer. We had the best apples on the western side of Pennsylvania."

"You're welcome, Major. And that is very interesting that you come from a family of lawyers. But how come you did not want to follow in the family business?"

"Well, I wanted to take my own path. But when the Canadians raided my family farm, they threatened my parents and my friends. The bastards stole all our produce. Then the bastards decided to burn my orchard to the ground. I learned one thing that day: if those lobsters are not gonna treat my countrymen with respect, then I will treat them like the savages they truly are."

"How long have you been in the army, Major?"

"I joined the army in 1808, when I was eighteen years old. I was ranked a sergeant major. I fought my first battle on July 5, 1811, This was in northern Indiana Territory. We were marching down a road that led to a clearing in the middle of the forest. It was about one hundred yards from the woods. Once we crossed into the clearing, a gunshot rang out on our left flank. One of our men dropped. Then more shots were fired at us from all around. Everywhere I looked, there were clouds of musket smoke. I saw two dozen of our men killed or wounded in the first five minutes. Then we had Mohawk Indians right in our faces with tomahawks. They hacked away at our men. The blood was everywhere, and the screams of my brothers made me shudder. I kept my mind straight, but the second I killed one Indian, I had another one in my face. Those bastards were relentless. Our commander, Major Franklin Thomas, gathered me and fifty other men, and we rushed down the road into another open field and took cover behind a stone wall near a mansion. We fired right into them. They charged the wall, screaming the most terrifying war cries I have ever heard in my life. Our commander was shot three times, and I saw they were about to finish him, so I ran blindly through the smoke and managed to kill his attackers. I managed to fight off twenty Mohawks with just my saber. We beat them back, but the damage had been done. Our battalion had been caught off guard, and we lost two hundred men in just one hour. I watched as our commander died right in my arms. But before he died, he gave me the rank of Major. In order for me to command my own company, I had to prove myself on the battlegrounds, and so I did. I did not want the command, but I was forced to accept it. I formed the Seventy-Sixth Pennsylvania Keystone Grenadiers on the same day this bloody war started—June 18, 1812. I have fought in battles from Chippewa to Bladensburg. And you already know that I was taken prisoner by the English."

Simon gets up from his seat and walks to the port side of the ship. He looks down at Fort McHenry. Then he looks up at the British ships. He worries more about his company.

"Listen, Major; I know how bad you want to be with your unit," Francis explains. "Trust me; I think we are here for a reason. Destiny has a way of making things happen through history. Maybe you were meant to be captured and to be on this ship for a reason."

"That is true, but the only thing I worry about is whether my unit withstood the fighting yesterday. Now that I think of it, this is a pretty good test. This is a company that was trained to be an elite unit. They are without their commander and are being pitted against the British Empire. Yeah, the best trained most professional army that is made up of the scum of the earth."

Both of them laugh. Suddenly their laugh is interrupted by the Royal Navy, which is only minutes away from the bombardment of Fort McHenry. The ships begin to roll out their cannons. One by one, the cannons are pointed at the fort. The bomb vessels aim their bomb cannons. Hundreds of cannons are aimed at the fort.

"Mr. Key, you might want to cover your ears. Things are going to get really, really loud."

"Why is that, Major?" Francis asks.

Seconds later, there is a massive roar of cannons being fired, and thus the battle of Fort McHenry has begun. Francis falls out of his seat and observes the spellbinding firepower of the Royal Navy.

"Jesus, Mary, and Joseph!" Francis exclaims.

"That is why. And I swear those cannons get louder every single year. I am so surprised I have not gone deaf yet," Simon says.

Both of them are shocked at the display of firepower that the Royal Navy has. Simon looks down at the fort and can see the shells exploding all around it. He slams his fist on the planks of the ship, and the only thing he can do is watch the battle unfold.

Ten minutes before the bombardment, the defenders inside the fort are preparing for the battle to come. What they do not know is that the battle to come will be the most intense and most awe-inspiring battle in the city's history.

Major George Armistead turns to his men. "Gentlemen, prepare to open fire!"

A captain named Frederick Evans, the commander of the Evans Company Corps of American Artillery, readies his men. He has a few cannons at his command.

He shouts to Major Armistead, "Sir, Evans Company is ready. But the enemy is out of our range."

"Give all cannons full elevation. We will defend this fort till the day that the hottest pits of hell shall freeze over!" Major Armistead shouts.

All the cannon crews elevate their cannons to max range. All the men are eager or scared about the battle to come. Some officers look down their spy glasses and see the British ships running their cannons out. Major General Samuel Smith knows that time is running out. General Smith stands right beside Major Armistead. They both look at the fleet. A few seconds later, they see the HMS *Volcano* fire its cannons. He turns to his men and screams, "Gentlemen, it's begun! Fire all cannons!"

The British cannonballs fly toward the fort. The bomb vessels begin to fire 190-pound cast-iron bombs. The shells explode all around the fort in massive fiery blasts. The American defenders fire their cannons. American Infantry soldiers hide from the cannonballs on the outer ditches of the fort. They try to get as close to the wall as possible. They watch as shells explode dozens of feet away from them. The shells explode and send shrapnel flying all over the fort. One American soldier is crushed by a wagon that is blown apart by a shell. Three other soldiers rush to him and manage to help the soldier get the wagon off his body. Congreve rockets whiz through the sky toward Fort McHenry. One American sergeant is killed by one of the bombs. A piece of shrapnel that is about the size of a dollar passes through his body.

The scream of a rocket can be heard by all the American soldiers inside the fort. Despite the heavy bombardment, the American soldiers continue to defend Fort McHenry. Seconds later, a mortar shell lands in the powder magazine inside Fort McHenry. The shell crashes through the roof, and American defenders run for cover. Some soldiers duck down. But nothing happens. Three American soldiers run into the room and they see the 190-pound bomb sitting in the middle of the room. The shell was steaming but had not exploded.

"Why the hell didn't the shell explode?" the sergeant says.

"How in the hell should I know?" the corporal says. "It must be a dud. Someone go get a bucket of water. We must cool it down."

"I will run and grab a bucket of water," a private said.

The private rushes out of the room and grabs a bucket on the ground and runs to the horse water tub. He dunks the bucket in the water and fills it up. Once it is full, he rushes back to the powder magazine and pours the whole bucket of water on the mortar shell. The shell steams from the cold water.

Amazingly, the shell does not explode.

"That was way too close. Now, should we get the powder out of here just in case?" the sergeant asks his men.

They look through the hole in the roof where the shell crashed through, and they see another shell exploding overhead. Then they all look at each other and say the same sentence in unison: "Let's get the powder out of here ... Agreed!"

Several American defenders gather three wagons, and they all start grabbing powder kegs and putting them on the wagons. They take them to the barracks and officers' quarters. One wagon goes around the fort, giving each cannon station another round of gunpowder.

Had that 190-pound bomb exploded, Fort McHenry would have erupted in a massive explosion from the quarter of a million pounds of black powder being stored inside the fort. The fort would have fallen, and possibly the city of Baltimore would have fallen as well.

A half hour later, a terrible thunderstorm erupts over the skies of Baltimore. The rain comes down thick as cannon shells. Lightning strikes crack open the sky, and the sound of thunder roars through the air. Captain Evans feels the raindrops hitting his uniform. He looks up at the sky and sees raindrops and lightning.

"Shite! That is not good. Men, keep that powder dry any way you can."

His soldiers grab blankets from their sacks and cover the kegs of powder, protecting them from the rain.

Major George Armistead looks up at the sky and can feel the heavy raindrops hit his coat. "Jesus Lord! Things have just got a lot more difficult."

"Easy, Major. There may be a storm brewing, but we are still in this fight. I want you to spread the word throughout the city to douse lights," General Smith says.

"What for, sir?" Major Armistead asks.

"So that the redcoats cannot see any landmarks. Send out several couriers—and also send one to Hampstead Hill. We need to know how they are holding up there."

"Yes sir!" Major Armistead says.

Both sides fire shell after shell at each other. The American defenders stand fast and continue to fire their cannons. Five riders set off to Baltimore and inform the citizens to douse their lights. Within fifteen minutes, the whole city has been visibly erased from the face of the earth. The British try to distract the American forces with a flotilla of twenty gunboats armed with artillery. However, the Americans do not fall for the trap. The American cannons fire upon the boats. They set up their cannons outside the fort and upon a small hill on the southern part of the fort. five Yankee eight-pounders fire and destroy the gunboats one by one. The gunboats explode because of the powder kegs on board their boats. The British artillerymen, along with a dozen of their cannons, get blown into the water. The attack is beaten back, and the battle of Fort McHenry continues deep into the night; the bombardment of the fort does not relent. Colonel Arthur Brooke prepares for the final assault on Hampstead hill.

Hampstead Hill
9:00 p.m.

The Seventy-Sixth tend to their wounded men. Some soldiers have gruesome wounds. One soldier has an open chest wound that has left one of his intestines hanging out of his body. Some of the soldiers have missing legs or missing arms. One has had his left eye shot out of his head. Other soldiers have massive cavities on their legs or on their chests. Celestia and Daisy are helping tend to those wounded soldiers. Daisy holds one soldier's hand as the man's leg is about to be amputated. Celestia is whispering to him, trying to keep him calm with the soothing sound of her voice. The soldier is losing blood from his leg, and his body temperature is starting to drop.

"Someone help me, please! I am cold! So bloody cold!" he says while he severely shivers.

Celestia grabs a blanket from her knapsack. "Here put this blanket across him. We need to warm him up," she says to Daisy.

Celestia and Daisy put the blanket across the soldier's body. They try to warm him up.

The soldier shivers still, and he can feel his body temperature decrease even more. He looks up at Celestia. Celestia watches the soldier's face become paler by the second.

"Why in the hell am I so cold?" he says.

"Your blood is running out of the leg. We need to amputate," she says.

The soldier begins to panic and tries to get off the table. Celestia and Daisy hold him down as the doctor grabs the bone saw.

Celestia whispers to the soldier, trying to calm him down. "Soldier, stay with me! Soldier, listen to me. This is gonna be over before you know it. Just stay calm and take the pain. Here, grab my hand. Squeeze it as hard as you want to."

The man grabs her right hand, and the doctor begins to cut his left leg off his body. The man screams loudly. The pain is too much for him to take. He tries to get off the table. Celestia puts her arms across his chest and forces him back down. Two other soldiers come to the table and restrain both of the soldiers' arms. A few seconds later, the soldier's leg is cut off. The doctor grabs bandages and wraps them around the man's left knee. Celestia looks down at the man's face and sees that the soldier was dead. He bled out from his wounds.

"Doctor, it is no use. The poor lad is dead," Celestia says with a sad tone.

Celestia and Daisy tend to other wounded soldiers. Celestia looks around and sees the wounded crying out and surgeons tending to them. Celestia walks out of the tent and heads down to the redoubt. She stands up on the redoubt and she can see the bombardment of Fort McHenry. She can see the bombs exploding in the air. She stands spellbound by the scene.

"Well, what a truly beautiful sight. But why does destruction and death have to be so beautiful?" she says.

Just then Daisy stands on the right side of Celestia.

A few seconds later, Timmy walks over and gives them their muskets back. "Here you go. They have been cleaned. Also, I have the count, ma'am. We have thirty-nine casualties. Twenty dead and nineteen wounded. We have a head count of one hundred eleven soldiers left. Also, a sniper shot and killed Major General Robert Ross."

"Well, that is very good news," Celestia replies. She then wonders, "*If Robert Ross is dead, then who is in charge of their infantry?*"

Just then one of the messengers arrived at the hill. He dismounts his horse and looks for General Stricker. He stops and sees the Keystone Grenadiers. He runs over to them, salutes Celestia, and delivers his message.

"First Lieutenant, compliments of General Smith. He wishes to know the condition of your position on the hill and whether you can hold it?" the messenger says to Celestia.

"Corporal, inform Major General Samuel Smith that our condition is not critical and we will hold this hill for as long as we can," she informs the rider.

"Very well then. I will inform him when I arrive back. Godspeed to you all."

"Likewise, Corporal," Daisy says.

They salute each other, and the corporal mounts his horse and sets off back to Fort McHenry. Just then, there is a sound of snare drums coming from the bottom of the hill. Celestia walks over to the redoubt wall and grabs her spyglass. She sees a company of two hundred British regulars marching toward the hill. Celestia calls to the grenadiers of the Seventy-Sixth Pennsylvania.

"To arms! To arms! The enemy is on us! Grenadiers, to the redoubts!"

The grenadiers run out of their tents, grab their muskets, and run to defend the redoubt. Daisy and Timmy take twenty soldiers and man the six cannons. The grenadiers aim their muskets down the hill.

One hundred yards away, the British soldiers march toward the American positions. They march with high steps, and their colors fly proudly, as if they are on a parade ground. Colonel Arthur Brooke leads his men up the hill. He can see the hill is packed with American soldiers that are well armed with artillery.

"First company, halt! Foot guards, make ready! Take aim! Fire!" Colonel Brooke shouts.

The front line of the British foot guards aim their muskets uphill. The American soldiers duck behind the redoubt walls. The British fire, and the bullets strike the front of the redoubt, kicking up dirt. None of the American soldiers are shot. The Seventy-Sixth stand up, and they return fire at the British foot guards. The first volley cuts down fifteen redcoat foot guards. A British officer rides in front of Colonel Arthur Brooke and takes three bullets to the chest. The officer falls off his horse and dies before he hits the ground. Daisy and Timmy manage a cannon, and Daisy lights the fuse. The cannon fires a solid shell. The shell flies into the air and strikes a British soldier. The shell decapitates the redcoat in a shower of blood and flesh. Other redcoats use their arms to protect their faces from the blood. Colonel Arthur Brooke fills with anger. He cuts down a retreating redcoat with his pistol, shooting him in the back. The redcoats make it to about fifty yards from the hill before they begin to retreat. But this is just the first assault.

Celestia pats her sister's back; they think the attack is over.

"They're falling back! Hold your fire!" Celestia shouts to her grenadiers.

Drum Major Benson and her corps are on the right flank of the hill. Devin and Jessica try to spot the redcoats to see whether they are retreating or just regrouping. Just then Jessica spots the redcoats at the bottom of the hill, and they charge their bayonets. She shouts to Celestia, "Lieutenant, they're coming again! They're coming again!"

"They're coming back!" Brittany shouts.

"Open fire! Do not let them storm this bloody hill!" Celestia shouts.

The Seventy-Sixth opens fire once again as the redcoats charge with bayonets. Several redcoats are hit by the first volley. As the first line charges up the hill, the soldiers of the Royal Marines arrive to attack. Sergeant Major Harry Adams and his son, along with their company, form their ranks. They form two ranks of fifty men each.

"For the glory of the marines! First company to the front. Forward, march!" Harry shouts. He charges his pike forward with his son by his side. The Royal Marines march up the hill. Oliver beats his drum as loudly as he can, and he can see the flashes from the Seventy-Sixth's muskets. Deep inside, he is filled with fear, but he keeps his cool as he marches up the hill.

Harry shouts to his men as they march upon the hill, "Hold the line! Keep your ranks! Do not show any fear, lads!"

As they march up the hill, they fire their muskets, but most of their shots strike the redoubt of the hill. The only sight the redcoats have is the flashes of the American's muskets and the cannon fire.

Back up on the hill, the Seventy-Sixth holds fast. The Seventy-Sixth's corps marching band pours relentless musket fire onto the charging redcoats. Brittany reloads her musket and then takes aim at a British officer on a brown horse. Her mace is on the wall to her right side. One Royal Marine halts and kneels on his left leg. He aims for what he thinks is an American soldier and pulls the trigger. The bullet ricochets off the mace and skims the right cheek of Brittany's face. She shouts out in pain and falls to the ground. Devin and Jessica see Brittany on the ground and run over to her aid.

"Brittany, are you okay!" Devin asked.

"Oh no! You're hit, ma'am!" Jessica shouts.

Brittany feels her face and sees blood, but she notices that it was not a fatal shot.

"I'm okay, lads. It's just a skim in the face."

She then grabs her mace and notices a dent on the top of it. "Holy mother of God!" she says.

They grab their muskets and continue to fire on the redcoats. Brittany spots the redcoat who fired the shot. She aims and fires, shooting the marine in the neck. The marine grabs his neck as the blood squirts from it. The rest of the redcoats halt their position about fifty yards from the top of the hill and fire a massive volley from over two hundred muskets. The volley hits the top of the redoubt. Some of the bullets find their marks upon the Maryland militia. Several of them are shot and killed. Celestia grabs her musket, looks down the hill, and sees Sergeant Major Adam's company leading the advance guard. She looks down at the lock on her musket. She knows that it is loaded. She cocks her hammer and aims downrange. Her iron sights are fixed upon Harry Adams. She breathes slowly as she aims. A British Congreve rocket soars through the air, and the glare lights up the hill for a brief moment. Harry Adams becomes visible, and without a distraction, she pulls the trigger. Sergeant Major Harry Adams is shot in the neck. He falls to the ground with his hand around his neck and drops his pike. Blood spills out of his neck.

Oliver sees his father on the ground with a gruesome neck wound. "Father, *noooooo!*" Oliver shouts. He drops his drum and runs to his father's side.

Harry rolls on the ground, choking on his own blood. The redcoats march right over his body as if he were a log of wood. Oliver kneels right beside him. Blood squirts out and lands on the front of his son's drummers' uniform. Oliver grabs his father's hand as Harry speaks his final words.

"My son, it is okay. I love you very much and do your duty for our king!"

"I love you too, father," Oliver says as he begins to cry.

Seconds later, Harry's arms fall to the ground and he takes his final breath.

"Father! Father! Please wake up! For the love of God, do not go!" Oliver sobs. Oliver falls to the ground and puts his head over his father's chest and cries.

Celestia then steps onto the rampart and yells out at the redcoats. "Now you bastards know how it feels to have your hearts ripped out from your bloody chests!"

A few of the redcoats open fire on her but miraculously miss her. She steps backs down and continues to fight. She yelled at them because at that point they had lost Major General Robert Ross and half of their staff officers.

Realizing that they will not be able to penetrate the American defenses, the redcoats begin to retreat from the hill. They run past Oliver and his father's lifeless body. Two Royal Marines grab Oliver. Oliver fights his own comrades, for he does not want to leave his father's side. It takes four redcoats to restrain Oliver and bring him back to their lines. As Oliver is being dragged away, he cries out loudly. Oliver's cries of pain at the loss of his father sound scarier than the deepest battle drums. Even the drums that were beating the retreat.

Colonel Arthur Brooke has no choice but to take his infantry back to the boats.

Oliver marches back with his comrades, and he takes one last look at the hill. He takes off his shako and looks inside it. At the bottom is a painting of him and his parents. He then speaks to himself.

"I swear to my family ... those bastards will pay dearly for killing you, Dad. You just relax in peace now. Take care of my mother for me."

The American defenders up on the hill cheered very loudly and began to chant an insulting war cry at the British redcoats.

"Burn your flag! Burn your flag!" The American defenders shouted in unison

Oliver can hear their cheering, and he begins to fill with bitter hate and rage. The American forces have beaten back the infantry attack.

The Royal Navy continues its bombardment of Fort McHenry. Major Simon Smithtrovich and Francis Scott Key sit on the deck of their ship and watch the bombardment of Fort McHenry continue. Both of them are dazzled by the bombardment. They can see the bombs exploding in the sky. The American flag waves over the fort. The shells explode, and the two men can see the light glaring through the flag. Simon grabs his diary and writes about what has happened to him and the progress of the defense of Fort McHenry.

> Dear diary: The past few weeks have been very hectic. I have learned a lot, even during my time in captivity. The enemy has even taught me things. Yet I have much to learn, especially about friendship. I pray to the lord that I love and cherish. I pray that my best friends are still alive. Something tells me that they are alive. So far in my life, my instincts have been right to me. For the whole day, I have been watching the bombardment of Fort McHenry. If anything can be beautiful when there is so much danger, I think it is the sight of our Stars and Stripes lighting up with every bomb that explodes. I give high respect to those brave American defenders over at Fort McHenry. Shall we win this day? This will be marked down in our country's history. We will never ever bow to any pompous king ever again. We are Americans, and we do not bow to our nation's enemies. We will win on the battlefield or die and take our seat at the right hand of God.

Simon puts his diary away in his haversack. He stands up and walks over to Francis Scott Key.

Francis is amazed by the fireworks exploding over the fort. "I cannot believe this display. Yet I wonder if we have suffered any losses," he says.

Simon scratches his facial hair and wonders the same thing, but he is more worried for his company's safety.

A few minutes later, Simon says, "Damn! I can't see the fort. The smoke is too thick. The sun is beginning to set. How much more can that damn fort take?" Simon says.

"I pray that the bombardment keeps going," Francis says.

Simon looks over at him. "Why is that?"

"If the cannons stop, there could be a possible surrender of the fort, or the Royal Navy might give up the battle. We might not know who won the battle till morning."

Simon feels a pain in his heart. "Well, I don't know what is worse—that the redcoat cannon fire has probably killed a lot of defenders or that my forces are inside that fort."

"Major, if you expect the worst, that is what you will get. I am worried as well. I am worried for all the citizens and soldiers of that city. But we must stay strong and pray that they can hold."

Simon knows that Francis is right, and he accepts and has to pray that his company can rely on his training to survive on the battlefield.

"You are right, Francis. We will have to let fate decide the conclusion of this hell storm."

The defenders of Hampstead Hill watch as the bombardment continues. The Keystone grenadiers sit on the redoubt as they are spellbound by the barrage of the fort. Celestia and Daisy stand on the redoubt, where they have a clear view of the fort. With every bomb exploding in the air, the explosion lights up the city and the countryside. The Seventy-Sixth are amazed by the bombardment.

"I have never seen such a thing," Celestia says. "It's been over twelve hours, and that fort hasn't suffered a scratch. How in the hell is that possible?"

"You've got me, sis. This is a beautiful sight to see. If we win this battle, this will mark our names down in the history books; no doubt about it," Daisy says.

The American infantry stationed at Fort McHenry are hiding behind the walls of the western redoubts, spellbound by the rocket glares. They see the US flag waving in the storm's breeze, and with every single bomb and rocket exploding in the sky, the flag glows as brightly as the sun for a few short seconds.

Some of the defenders find happiness through the intense bombardment. The three American soldiers who doused the bomb in the powder magazine gaze up at the flag.

"That, by God, is the most beautiful sight I have ever seen—our flag's rays of light," the sergeant says.

The corporal does not take notice immediately and thinks that his sergeant is losing his mind. "What in the world are you talking about? This is hell on earth!" the corporal says.

The Sergeant points up to the flag, and the corporal is awed by the flag and the explosions. His eyes open wide, and he has a smile upon his face.

"My God in heaven! Am I dreaming?" the corporal says with amazement.

"No. This is the real deal. How can hellish firepower make something so bloody beautiful?" the private says.

"If we have died in battle and this is heaven, then this was truly worth fighting and dying for," the sergeant says.

"I don't know what is scarier—this bombardment or being next to a friend of the Almighty?" the corporal says to the sergeant.

The private smacks the corporal's arm. "Hey, we all go to the same church. And to answer your question, it would be this bombardment."

Three more bombs explode right next to the flag. They duck their heads and look at each other as they speak in unison.

"Agreed!"

Throughout the rest of the night, the bombardment continues without end. By morning the Royal Navy is still bombing the fort. But soon the redcoats begin to run out of ammunition. The Royal Navy fires one last salvo, and the shells fly toward the fort. They explode in the sky with a massive blast of fire and smoke that conceals the fort. Neither the British nor the American soldiers on Hampstead Hill can see Fort McHenry. The defenders of Fort McHenry continue to fire their cannons, but an American officer stands up on the ramparts and sees the British cannons stop firing. Just then Major Armistead stands up right beside him and looks through his spyglass. He sees a British bomb vessel beginning to set sail. The other British vessels begin to raise their anchors and set their sails. He turns to the cannon crews, claps his hands over his face, and yells at the crews.

"Cease fire! Stop firing! No more! Stop your fire!" Major Armistead shouts.

Throughout the fort, the American cannons fall silent. American defenders climb up onto the ramparts. They see the Royal Navy beginning to leave the bay. American soldiers are amazed that they have done the impossible. Some soldiers drop their muskets and stand spellbound. A few soldiers begin to cry tears of joy. Major General Samuel Smith stands alongside Major Armistead. He smiles and utters a loud cheer. The men of Fort McHenry cheer so loudly that the cheer can be heard by the American soldiers on Hampstead Hill. The defenders on Hampstead Hill wake up and run to the eastern section of the redoubt see the most amazing sight of American soldiers upon the ramparts of Fort McHenry, cheering and shouting. The Seventy-Sixth begin to cheer. General Stricker rides on his horse, and when he looks through his spyglass, he spots the American flag still flying over the fort. He sees the defenders celebrating the victory over the British war machine. Timmy begins to cry in amazement. Celestia and Daisy hug each other and cheer. The Seventy-Sixth celebrate, and a few fire their muskets into the air.

The Royal Navy can hear the cheers from the city of Baltimore and the American lines. On board the USS *President*, Simon and Francis can hear the cheering, but the mist on the bay is so thick that they cannot see whether the Americans have lost or won the battle. Simon and Francis pace the deck of the ship. Looking down their spy glasses, they try to see whether the fort has the Stars and Stripes or the British Union Jack flying over it. Both of them fear that the American defenders have lost the battle.

"Can you hear all that cheering? I pray to God that it is the Americans," Simon says with a worried tone.

Francis Scott Key has a tough time trying to see whether the American forces have defended the fort or whether it has been taken by the British. A few minutes later, the mist begins to rise over the bay. Simon finally gets a clear view of the fort. He looks at the ramparts of the fort and can see soldiers upon them. He is shocked to see that the uniforms the soldiers are wearing are blue. Then he looks up at the flagpole in the fort, where he sees a huge American storm flag flying.

"Francis! It's our troops! For God and country, we won! The sons of guns did it!" Simon shouts cheerfully.

Simon cheers loudly, and the whole crew begins to cheer as well. Francis looks through his spyglass and sees the remains of the American flag flying defiantly over the fort. He drops his spyglass, and it falls off the ship and into the water. He puts his hands in the air and cheers. Simon and Francis hug each other, and then Francis Scott Key does the thing that will make him a legend in American History. He asks Simon a question.

"Major, do you think that the brave defenders of Fort McHenry and also the brave soldiers of this amazing country deserve a song?"

"Yes sir. They certainly do."

Francis Scott Key pulls out a piece of a letter, puts the letter down on the rail of the ship, and jots down a few verses.

> Oh, say can you see by the dawn's early light
> What so proudly we hailed at the twilight's last gleaming,
> Whose broad stripes and bright stars through the perilous fight
>
> O'er the ramparts we watched, were so gallantly streaming?
> And the rocket's red glare, the bombs bursting in air,
> Gave proof through the night that our flag was still there.
> O say does that star-spangled banner yet wave
> O'er the land of the free, and the home of the brave.

Simon walks over and looks at what Francis has written.

"Tell me what you think, Major," Francis says.

Simon looks at the letter and is amazed by the verses. "Wow! This is very impressive, sir. I like it."

"Thank you. And I have some good news for you." Francis turns to his crew. "Gentlemen, set sails. We are moving back to Baltimore Harbor."

Francis shouts to his crew. Simon smiles and looks down toward the fort. He fills with joy knowing that he will soon be reuniting with his unit. He reaches into his pocket, pulls out a wedding ring, and holds it in the palm of his hand.

"Well, Celestia, I have a birthday present for you, darling," Simon says.

But before he can pop the question, he will have to first apologize for his actions that got them separated in the first place.

What the soldiers of the Seventy-Sixth Pennsylvania go through that day—most importantly the staff of the Seventy-Sixth—are the most emotional moments in their lives.

CHAPTER 20

A REUNION OF TEARS

Baltimore, Maryland
Fort McHenry
September 14, 1814
8:00 a.m.

The USS *President* sails into the port of Baltimore. The ship enters a docking point and is tied into place. Before Simon sets off, he walks over to Francis.

"Francis, I would like to thank you for coming to my rescue, sir. And good luck with publishing your poem."

"Thank you, Simon. And it was my pleasure to rescue a fellow patriot. Hope to see you again."

"That would be nice. Goodbye, sir. And what are you gonna call the poem?" Simon asks.

"'The Defence of Fort M'Henry'!" Francis says

"I like it. It has a ring to it. Till we meet again."

Simon and Francis shake each other's hand.

Simon leaves the ship and walks up the dock. He looks at Fort McHenry, and then he hears drums behind him. He looks down the street and sees a unit wearing green coats and bearskin caps marching toward the fort. Simon holds his chest, relieved that they survived the battle. Simon walks down the street and he waits for them to pass. He can see that they are the Seventy-Sixth. But he wants to wait until they enter the fort. A few

tro*

minutes later, they enter. Simon walks a few paces behind them. He enters the barracks, and there he is noticed by Major Armistead.

"Who are you?" Major Armistead asks Simon.

Simon turns around and sees the major right behind him. Simon salutes the major. "Sir, my name is Major Simon Smithtrovich. I am the commander of the Seventy-Sixth Pennsylvania Keystone Grenadiers, sir. I was taken prisoner by the redcoats a few weeks ago. I was on board a truce vessel. I was exchanged for British prisoners. We had to wait for the fighting to stop before we were allowed to head ashore, sir."

"So you are the commanding officer of the Seventy-Sixth. Well, sir, please let me shake your hand. Your unit did a hell of a job defending Hampstead Hill for the past two days. They withstood the hellfire of Major General Robert Ross. They stood side by side with the militias and the regulars. They all did a hell of a job."

The two shake hands.

"Thank you, sir. Do you know what happened to Robert Ross during the fighting?"

"He was killed by a rifleman at North Point. Did you know him?"

Simon is shocked. He does not show any emotion, but he is sad on the inside. He takes a deep breath. "Yes, I did. That is horrible to hear. I bet that sent waves through the redcoats. Now, sir, where would my unit be?"

"I will take you to them. Follow me, Major."

"Thank you."

They walk out of the barracks and see the Seventy-Sixth standing up on the ramparts, watching the ships of the British navy leave the area one by one.

"They are up there. Till we meet again, Major."

Simon walks up right behind them. They do not hear him approach.

"That is a beautiful sight," Timmy says.

"I know Simon would be very proud of us all. I just wish he were here by our side," Celestia says.

Simon breaks his silence. "God save the brave Seventy-Sixth," he says quietly.

They turn around and see Simon right behind them.

"Simon!" they all shout.

216

Celestia, Brittany, Daisy, and Timmy gasp and rush to hug Simon. All of them engage in a group hug.

"Simon, we thought you were dead!" Timmy says.

"I knew you were still alive," Daisy adds.

They begin to ask Simon a bunch of questions at once.

"You guys, slow down! I will answer all your questions at a later time. But first there is something I need to do."

Simon turns his attention to Celestia. They both know what they need to do.

"Celestia, can I speak with you?" Simon asks.

"Yes. We do need to talk," Celestia says.

Simon takes her hand and leads her over to the middle of the rampart. He then takes both of her hands. All the grenadiers of the unit back off, and all the fort's defenders are about to be witnesses to an emotional moment of forgiveness.

"Celestia, I cannot begin to say how sorry I am for what I said to you back in camp. A normal sorry cannot cover for it at all. It's just so stupid. I just want you to know that." He begins to cry. "I am so sorry, Celestia, for all those horrible things that I have said to you. The truth is, I cannot win this war without all my friends—especially the most important one, and that is you." They are both crying by this point. Simon's voice begins to crack as he continues his apology. "After we win this war, you have the right to hate me, and I will be alright with that, because I have been the worst friend. I broke your heart. You were right about me being a terrible leader. I just want you to know that I am so, so sorry!"

Simon is trembling all over. Celestia steps closer to her commander. Simon stares at Celestia, and his eyes become glassy. Simon sniffs twice with a pause of a few seconds in between. Both of them try to keep their composure, but it is tearing at the seams. It is only when Celestia closes the gap between them and hugs Simon that the dam finally bursts. Celestia and Simon begin to blubber like infants. Simon is so weak in his legs that he collapses to the ground. Celestia falls to her own knees and holds Simon. Both of them completely break down.

Daisy says quietly to herself, "That's right, you two; Let it all out."

They hug each other tightly, not having a second thought about letting go.

"I never should have put you in so much danger. Please forgive me? It's all my fault," Simon says.

"It is not your fault, Simon." Celestia says as she sobbed.

"No, Celestia. It's my fault! I never should have yelled at you like that," Simon says as he was bawling his eyes out. "I was coming to say I was sorry. I got shot in my hand, and they took me away. I was never going to shoot you. The lobsters I saw in the woods were the ones that captured me. I never should have put you all in so much danger. I wanted to tell you all what happened, but I was afraid that the lobsters would hunt you all down. I wouldn't have been able to live with myself if they captured you all. I was so awful to all of you because I couldn't bring myself to speak my damn mind. I'm sorry! Sorry! I'm so sorry! I wished they would have just shot me dead for what I said to you."

Celestia holds Simon out to meet his gaze and yells, "For God's sake, Simon! I already lost twenty more grenadiers; I am not gonna lose you too! I know how much it hurts. You are not the one who is suffering. Things might not be the same, but we need to stay together. The Seventy-Sixth needs you, Timmy needs you, Brittany needs you, my sister needs you, and our nation needs you, but most of all, I need you. Having my first command of this unit was great, but it was too tough for me to have that much blood on my hands. I cannot do this alone."

They look at each other, and Celestia dries his tears and then her own.

"I just don't understand," says Simon. "Why are you not mad at me? I cannot believe that you can still like a monster like me. You should hate me for all those terrible things I said to you and for putting you in such great danger."

Celestia puts her finger on Simon's lips. "Simon, look at me." Simon looks at Celestia, and they look deep into each other's eyes. "Don't you ever say that to me again! You must understand that even the best of friends fight once in a while, but not even the kind of fight we had that day can tear our relationship apart. You learned that friendship is everything, just as your training has helped us survive to see this glorious morning. And what you did up in Canada—that was not your fault. You were just doing what you thought was right. I know why you didn't tell us; you were just trying to protect us. I know that you protected us out of love. You are my best friend, as well as the best leader we have ever had."

Simon continues to sob as though his heart is breaking. Celestia strokes his back and tightens her hold as Simon unleashes a year's worth of locked up emotion.

"Shh! Shh! I've got you, sir, it's okay. It's okay." Celestia says softly.

Simon continued to apologize, words tangled in a knot of mucus and mental pain. The more he continued to apologize, the more he cried. He tries to stop crying, but the pain inside of his heart and soul keeps the tears rushing out of the destroyed dam that was his eyes.

"I tried to stop myself from saying all those terrible words, but I didn't know how. Sitting on a ship, miles away from y'all made me worry so much that I wanted to throw up. Why have I been given a second chance? I don't even deserve it."

"You do deserve it, sir, Celestia says while rubbing Simons back. "If you didn't deserve it, fate would have made a different outcome for you. But you're here, alive and breathing, with a second chance that you absolutely deserve."

Some of the other grenadiers are shocked by what they are witnessing. Privates Jessica and Devin Little talk among themselves.

"I never ever seen the major cry like this before," Devin says, sounding puzzled. "I know we have been here for only a month, but from what all the vets told me, he has never cried for all the losses that this company has suffered."

Jessica holds her chest with her hand. She is becoming emotional as well, but she is strong enough to hold it together. "I have seen this happen before. Our cousin's parents had a moment like this. The tears that Simon is shedding are tears of regret, pain, and loss. And he is also crying for all his comrades he has lost in all his years of service. God, it hurts me to see them both like this." Jessica lets one tear drop from her eye.

Devin grabs his sister's hand and hugs her.

For many of the grenadiers, it is a moment of sorrow and amazement. They have never ever seen their own commanders break down in this manner.

As if Simon has run out of tears, he finally regains his composure and cools down. However, he felt hollowed out from unleashing year's worth of tears, not only for the pain that he caused in the past few weeks, but from all the death and destruction he has witnessed as a soldier.

"I'm alright. Thank you, Celestia. I really needed that."

"You're very welcome, sir. I want you to know that what has happened in the past is now in the past. Are you finished, or are you preparing to throw a third assault from the United States Tear Army?" Simon chuckles at her joke. Celestia then puts her hands around the back of Simon's neck. "And I cannot think of anyone else I would want to fight a war alongside. You are my true love forever. I read your letter, and it was the most romantic letter anyone has ever written to me. You are the one for me, and that can never change."

"Oh, Celestia, I love you more than I love my own freedom! And I am just so glad to see all my grenadiers again," Simon says in a normal tone.

Simon hugs Celestia, and she pats him on the back.

"And you melt my heart more than a raging fire surrounded by a million barrels of black powder on a hot summer afternoon," Celestia says.

"Aww!" the grenadiers of the Seventy-Sixth exclaim.

Feeling as if the time is right, Simon prepares to pop the question to Celestia.

"I want to ask you something I've wanted to ask from the first second I laid my eyes on you—a question that is long overdue." Simon kneels on one knee, and the other soldiers of Fort McHenry and the Seventy-Sixth take notice of what is happening. Simon pulls the ring out of his pocket. Celestia holds her left hand over her mouth as she begins to tear up. "Celestia Rose of the brave Seventy-Sixth, will you marry me?"

Celestia tries to catch her breath, and then she begins to cry again. "Oh, Simon! Yes. Yes, I will," Celestia says.

Simon stands up and puts the ring on the ring finger of her left hand. They look at each other and kiss for ten seconds. The Seventy-Sixth and other defenders of Fort McHenry cheer and clap. Timmy and Daisy run over to them, and they all cheer.

"By the way, Celestia, happy twenty-fourth birthday," Simon reminds his new fiancée.

"Aww! Thank you, sir. And by the way, where did you find this ring?"

"When I was in the British camp, a British sergeant gave me this ring as a gift. And it is a ten-carat diamond ring."

Celestia, Brittany, Timmy, and Daisy are shocked by the size of the stone.

"This is what I have wanted to give to you for a long, long time. And now, for standing up in the line of duty against a tough and determined enemy, Celestia, you are being promoted to the rank of captain. Sergeant Miller, you shall take the rank of second lieutenant. And First Sergeant Daisy Rose shall become a first lieutenant."

"Sir," Brittany asks, "would it be okay if I kept my rank? I am here to serve you lot, not to be above you."

"You can keep your rank, Drum Major Benson. Congratulations to all my Keystone grenadiers. For keeping up the fight while I was away," Simon says to his unit.

Celestia rallies the staff and the whole unit as well. "Gather round, my friends. I have something to say." The whole unit gathers in a massive group, and Celestia speaks to her comrades in arms. "From now on, no more fighting between us. We stand together for more than freedom. We stand for friendship!"

Celestia puts her hand in the middle of them. One by one, they all do the same.

"For friendship!" they all say. Then they all shout out, "Keystone grenadiers forever!"

Later that day, around 4:00 p.m., the parade ground inside the fort is being set up for the military wedding. Soldiers and civilians arrive and take their seats in the middle of the fort. Simon and Timmy wait at the makeshift altar. Celestia hasn't had time to find a wedding gown, and she has decided to wear her new military dress uniform. Daisy and Brittany are helping her get her uniform on.

"You look amazing! I am sorry we couldn't find a dress," Daisy says.

"It is okay. Thank you very much. I cannot believe this day is finally here. I am so glad that you are here to celebrate it with me, Daisy. I would like to thank you, Daisy."

"For what?" Daisy asks, holding on to Celestia's dress bearskin cap. She is fixing the fur and making sure the green plume is straight.

"When my heart was broken, you stayed by my side. You comforted me when I needed it the most. I'm glad to have a little sister like you. I love you, Daisy."

Daisy puts Celestia's bearskin on her sister's head and smiles. "I love you, too."

"Will you be walking me down the aisle?" Celestia asks.

"No. Someone very special will have that pleasure."

Just then a man in an American Continental officer's uniform walks up right behind Celestia, and she turns around.

"Father! Oh my God!"

Daisy and Celestia hug their father. Their father's name is Frank Rose; he was a colonel who had served under General Washington during the Revolutionary War from 1775 to 1782. He had been wounded twice.

"I didn't know you were supposed to hug your commanding officer in the army now! Stand at attention!" Frank says to his daughters.

Both of them back off and stand at attention and salute their father.

Frank smiles. "I am just kidding. I'm so happy that you two are okay. How are my two favorite soldiers doing?" he asks.

"Very great, Father. We both are glad you could come," Celestia says.

"That uniform still fits you really well, Father," Daisy says, observing her father's uniform.

"I may be in my fifties, but I can still appreciate the style. My oldest daughter is marrying a military officer. Congratulations. I will have the honor of walking you down the aisle."

"You will be able to see the man of my dreams, Father," Celestia says with happiness.

Just then Frank turns his attention to Brittany. "Drum Major Benson, I have a surprise for you, and you can thank your commander for this."

Brittany sees her mother, Sarah, and she runs over to her. They hug each other very tightly.

"Honey, it is so great that you are still alive. Have you seen some action up on that hill?"

"How did you know I was up there?" Brittany asks.

"Well, I watched you lead your corps down the street three days ago. I tried to get your attention, but you and your corps were singing. I am so very proud of you."

"Thank you, Mother. I always remembered that phrase you taught me: 'The second you open your eyes on a new day, stand up and fight to seize your victory in any way.' I need to get to my corps. We have a wedding to begin."

The Seventy-Sixth marching band and the Evans Company drum and fife corps set up their instruments. All the soldiers and townspeople take their seats. Simon makes sure his uniform is good to go.

"Is my bearskin on straight? How about my green sash, Timmy?" Simon asks.

"Sir, you are perfectly fine. This is supposed to be a happy day for all of us. Where do you two plan on spending your honeymoon?"

"Well, that is a good question. We already decided earlier this morning that we will spend it with you guys. I may have been gone for just a few weeks, but it feels like I have been away for three years."

They both laugh, and then the wedding begins. Twenty Keystone Grenadiers marched down the aisle on both sides. Celestia stands at the doorway. The guards prepare to open the door. Drum Major Benson stands up, walks in front of the band, and directs the band to play the wedding march. The band begins to play. The soldiers and civilians look behind them. The guards open the door. Flower girls walk down the aisle, throwing flowers down onto the floor. Celestia begins to walk slowly down the aisle, escorted by her father. Every grenadier she passes salutes her. Simon looks at her and cannot help but smile. Daisy begins to tear up. She pulls a tissue out of her pocket and wipes a few tears from her eyes. Celestia stands right beside Simon. They look at each other with happiness.

The priest begins to speak. "Dearly beloved, we have gathered here to celebrate the union of two brave soldiers, Captain Celestia Rose and Major Simon Smithtrovich. The strength of their commitment is clear. These two brave officers have answered the call to arms along with thousands of brave American patriots from across the nation. The power of their love is undeniable. Celestia and Simon, do you take each other to love and honor, in good times and bad, in sickness and health, till death do you part, as long as you both shall live?"

Simon and Celestia look at each other dead in the eyes, and they both gulp.

"I do!" Simon says.

"I do!" Celestia says.

"May we have the rings please?" the priest asks Timmy.

Timmy hands Simon the ring. Simon takes it and puts it on Celestia's ring finger.

"By the power of the right hand of God and the strength of American freedom, I now pronounce that they are husband and wife. You may kiss the bride."

Simon and Celestia kiss. The whole fort erupts in clapping and cheering. The twenty grenadiers that graduated within four days gave a salute to the newlyweds. The fort defenders fire fireworks into the sky. The fort's cannons are fired as a salute to their marriage. The night sky is lit up by fireworks. But it is not an attack; it is a celebration.

Along with the wedding, the whole city celebrates the victory over the British. Inside the fort, dancing and music fill the night. Soldiers and civilians dance the night away. Simon and Celestia dance in the middle of the fort as piano music fills the air.

"What a beautiful night, honey. I never thought that this day would come," Celestia says.

"Tonight my heart is bursting," Simon says. "I am the happiest major alive. Hey, look up there." He points to the sky.

Through the fireworks, they both spot another shooting star soaring in the sky.

"You should make a wish, darling," Celestia says.

"What more can I wish for? What do you wish for?" Simon asks.

"Well, how about when this war ends … Do you want to have a family?" Celestia says.

"That would be a great thing to do. I think that wish has been partly granted in a way. Everyone in this company has been the family I have always wanted to have.

"That is very sweet of you to say, sir."

Just then Frank walks over to the new couple, and Celestia introduces her father to Simon.

"Honey, I would like to introduce my father, Colonel Frank Rose. Father, this is our commanding officer of the Seventy-Sixth, Major Simon Smithtrovich."

Simon salutes her father, and he salutes Simon.

"Colonel," Simon says, "I would like to say that it is a great honor to meet you, sir. I thank you for your service, and I would also like to say that you have raised two great soldiers."

"Thank you very much, Major. I have given them every known training that I was given during my time under Washington. I know we have just met, but you look like the best man for my daughter. Thank you for taking care of my daughters."

They shake hands just as a salvo of fireworks erupts into the sky. The whole city of Baltimore is celebrating the victory. All the soldiers and civilians stand up on the ramparts of Fort McHenry. The Seventy-Sixth and the other defenders gaze up at the sky as the night fills with fireworks. The staff lock arms and watch the fireworks explode in the sky with the stars shining brightly.

Simon looks down at the bay where he witnessed the battle unfold.

This is definitely a night to be remembered—and not just by the Seventy-Sixth. It is to be remembered by the brave defenders made up of soldiers and civilians of the city of Baltimore, Maryland, for making a stand against the best trained and most professional army in the world.

The Seventy-Sixth Pennsylvania stay in Baltimore for the rest of the month, until they are given orders to march down to the southern states for defense. The British plan to attack the south and cut the country in half. But one man will make a stand at the city of New Orleans, and his name is Andrew Jackson.

CHAPTER 21

THE SEVENTY-SIXTH PENNSYLVANIA KEYSTONE GRENADIERS BACKSTORY

July 4, 1808, to August 1, 1811
Philadelphia, Pennsylvania, to Washington, DC

Years before the events outlined thus far in this book, the Seventy-Sixth Pennsylvania was created. Their story begins on Independence Day in the birthplace of the Declaration of Independence, where the Battle of Brandywine Creek took place on September 11, 1777; where the Americans commanded by General George Washington fought against General William Howe, who disobeyed General John Burgoyne in refusing his request to come up to aid him in the Hudson campaign. Howe and Washington battled at the creek, and a tactical flank that Howe used at the Battle of Long Island in 1776 broke Washington's forces. At the end of the battle, one thousand American soldiers and five hundred British soldiers were wounded or killed. Washington was forced to retreat north. He had to give up the fight and had to give up the city of Philadelphia.

Simon Smithtrovich was born January 8, 1790, in Philadelphia, Pennsylvania. He was raised in Chadds Ford, Pennsylvania, with his mother and father.

On the thirty-second birthday of the United States of America, Simon is heading into the city with Timmy, Celestia, Daisy, and Brittany. They want to be with Simon when he enlists in the army. They walk over with him to a recruitment table near Independence Hall. They walk up to it, and the recruiting sergeant sees them and gives his welcome.

"Welcome to Philadelphia. Are you interested in joining the United States Army? Because once you take this coin, you will be making a promise to serve and protect our great nation. You will be paid an army wage of five dollars a week, and you will be able to keep or sell any gear of any enemy soldier you kill. You will be trained to be a soldier who will feel no fear; and that fear that you ignore, you will unleash upon your enemy. Now, would you all like to serve our nation?"

Simon steps forward, looks back at his friends, and hugs them all.

The second recruiting sergeant speaks to them.

"Are you all good friends?" he asks them.

"Yes, Sergeant," Simon says. "We are great friends. I will be the only one that you will recruit today. My friends are here to support me." Simon grabs the feather pen and signs his name upon the list. He notices that he is the only one who has signed up to be in the army. "Good lord. It does look like I am the only one who is signing up today, Sergeant."

"That is true. Not much has been happening, so we have not had many enlistments. Now here are your five dollars. You are now a member of the United States Army, Private Smithtr ... Smithtro ... Smithtroi ... Um, how do you say your last name?"

People had always had this problem with his last name. Simon chuckles.

"My name is Smith-tro-vich. Everyone has always had a hard time saying the name. It is not a big deal to me at all, Sergeant."

"Thank you, Private," the Sergeant says.

Simon turns. "Well, my friends. Till we meet again. I will write to you when I get the chance."

They all have one final group hug, and then they all leave. The sergeant takes Simon outside the southern part of the city to a training camp. As they walk to the camp, Simon does not speak. Then he spots the camp. He can see the pounding of drums and hear the shouting of commands.

The sergeant says to Simon, "Private Smithtrovich, this is your time to quit, because once you cross that white line, there is no going back. Are you sure you want to be a soldier?"

Simon answers in a sure tone. "Sergeant, my father served in the Second Pennsylvania during the revolution. I have learned that you must never give up during a battle. I have been an apple farmer ever since I was ten years old. If I had given up on my crop during the summer of 1805, when I was fifteen, my family wouldn't have had any fruit to eat. I was sick with a fever, but I sucked it up and managed to save my family business. I will not fail here, Sergeant."

"That is what I want to hear, Private Smithtrovich."

They both walk into the camp, and the sergeant takes Simon to the quartermaster. There he is issued his uniform, which comprises a shako, a regimental blue coat, white trousers, and black lace-up boots. He is issued his cartridge box, a bayonet, and his Brown Bess musket.

The quartermaster asks Simon, "Have you ever fired a musket before, Private?"

"Yes sir. I have fired one every day since I was a young lad," Simon says.

"Very good. Make your mark or sign your name on this paper, and then you can begin your training, Private."

Simon signs his name upon the paper, and then he is taken to his tent. There he changes into his uniform. He walks out of the tent and sees what he looks like with his uniform on.

"Well, this beats the hell out of farmer clothes," he says to himself. "Well, Simon, there is no turning back now."

A sergeant major walks over to him. Simon immediately stands at attention with his musket at the position of order arms. The sergeant major stands five feet in front of him. He checks his uniform to see if it is in order. Simon does not talk or move a single inch. Then the sergeant major introduces himself to Simon.

"I am Sergeant Major Kevin Cooper; I am your senior drill instructor. Starting now, you treat me with the highest respect. You will obey all my orders immediately and without question. If you obey all my orders, I will train you to be the finest NCO in the army."

"Permission to speak, sir?"

"Permission granted, Private."

"I thought this was a regular soldier's training, sir. Did I sign up for officer training?"

"That is correct, Private. I will train you to become a Noncommissioned officer. You will be able to command your own platoons of men, and if you stay long enough and you are able to prove your worth on the field, you can become a commissioned officer in this army. Do you understand, Private?"

"Yes sir," Simon says.

Throughout the next several weeks, Simon is trained on the uniform code of drill, which is called "school of the soldier." He learns how to do weapon drills, how to march, and how to execute battle formations with other recruits.

In the seventh week of his training, He is taught how to use his musket. Simon is brought to the firing range, where three watermelons are set up upon a wooden bench.

"Prove yourself, Private. Take out those watermelons. Three rounds a minute."

Simon takes position as if the musket has just been fired.

"On my command, you will prime and load. Load!"

Simon primes and loads his musket within fifteen seconds. He aims and fires and shoots the first watermelon. He then loads for his second shot, which takes him twenty seconds. He aims and fires, hitting the second watermelon. This left him only thirty-five seconds to fire his third shot. Sergeant Major Cooper is expecting Simon to choke on loading the third shot. Amazingly, Simon manages to load and fire again. His final shot hits its mark. Sergeant Major Cooper checks the watermelons to see if Simon hit them. He sees a musket ball hole in each of the watermelons, straight in the middle.

Sergeant Major Cooper walks over to Simon. "Congratulations, Sergeant Major Smithtrovich. You have proven to me that you can fire three rounds a minute. The one question that needs to be proven in the field, though, is whether you can stand against the enemy."

Through the following years, Simon is stationed at Pittsburgh, Pennsylvania, as a drill sergeant. There he trains soldiers that will soon become Keystone grenadiers. On his first day in camp at Pittsburgh, Simon has not made any friendships with his men. But they soon become more than a platoon of soldiers. They become a group of friends.

October 5, 1808
Pittsburgh, Pennsylvania

That night at the camp, Simon and his platoon are sitting by the fire, talking about what to expect once they march off for their first battle.

"I bet this will be a hard campaign. Those savages actually live up to their name," Simon says.

Some of the other soldiers think it will be nothing at all.

"I bet you are all glad that I am here because I plan on taking out all the Mohawks all by myself," one regular says with confidence.

They all laugh, but some know that their first battle could possibly be their last. Simon walks out of the tent to get some fresh air. He then sits outside the camp, looks at his musket, and uses a knife to carve his state motto on the wooden stock. Halfway through his little design project, a soon-to-be-great friend notices Simon. The sergeant sits right next him. Simon does not notice the sergeant sitting there as he focuses on his crafting.

"What are you working on, Sergeant Major?" the sergeant asks Simon.

Simon jumps and almost stabs the sergeant by mistake.

"Sergeant, good God! You scared me! I am sorry," Simon says.

"That is all right, Sergeant Major. I didn't mean to scare you. I was just curious about what you were working on," the sergeant says.

"I am engraving our state motto on the butt of my musket so that if I ever begin to lose faith on the battlegrounds, I can just look at my stock, and it will remind me of what I am fighting for."

Simon finishes his crafting and shows it to the sergeant. The stock has the motto engraved into it.

"That is very impressive handiwork, Sergeant Major. What is your name?"

"Sergeant Major Simon Smithtrovich, Sergeant. I come from Chadds Ford, Pennsylvania."

"What did you do back home, Sergeant Major?"

"I was and still am an apple farmer. I crop the best apples on the eastern side of Pennsylvania. I have some apples in my knapsack if you want to try some, Sergeant."

"I would like to try one of your apples, Sergeant Major."

Simon takes off his knapsack and opens it. He opens his personal apple sack, takes out one of his apples, and hands it to the sergeant.

"Thank you, Sergeant Major."

"You're welcome."

The sergeant takes a bite and is amazed by the great taste. He gasps in delight.

"Sergeant Major, this apple is heavenly. How in the world do you produce such great apples?"

"I am sorry to say, Sergeant, but that is a question I don't even know the answer to myself. I guess my apples are touched by the gentle hands of God himself."

"I bet those apples come from the garden of Adam and Eve."

They both laugh for a few seconds at the joke.

"Sergeant, what is your name?" Simon asks.

"My name is Sergeant Greg Sumter, and I was born in Lancaster, Pennsylvania."

"That is very interesting, because that is where my father met my mother. What are the chances that my new buddy is from the same town where my parents met each other?"

"I guess there's a first for everything, Sergeant Major."

October 6, 1808

The next morning, Simon is training his platoon on marching drills. They are marching down a dirt road. As Simon marches with his platoon, he can see that one soldier is falling behind. He speaks to his sergeant of the guard.

"Sergeant of the guard, keep your dressing, and keep the platoon moving. A soldier is falling behind."

"Yes sir!" the sergeant shouts

What Simon does not know is that the private who is falling behind has several blisters on his right foot. Simon breaks ranks, marches to the rear, and speaks to the soldier. "Come on, Private. Let's get a move on. Hup one, hup two, hup three, hup four. You call that marching? I have seen a family of ducks march better than that!" Simon says.

"I am marching as fast as I can, sir," the private says through the increasing pain.

Simon notices the pained expression on the private's face and sees he is marching funny.

"Private, take care; halt! Sit down and take off your gaiter and boot on your right foot."

The soldier takes off his gaiter and then slowly removes his boot. Simon is shocked to see several severe blisters on the man's foot.

"Holy mother of God, Private! How long has this been going on for?"

"About three weeks, sir," the private said.

"Private, a good soldier always takes care of himself or herself in the field. Otherwise it would cost the soldier his or her life. These look like they could be very close to being infected. I am not a doctor, but one will have to decide whether you will lose your foot or not. I will carry you back."

Simon slings his musket and lifts the private and begins to carry him back to camp.

The private begins to shed a few tears. "Sir, I do not want to lose my foot," the private said sadly. "I have always wanted to serve in the army. I promise I will take better care of my feet, sir."

"We will try to save it. If providence decides to give you a second chance, then I hope you learned your lesson. I need every man in the field, and I can see potential for you to be a great soldier." Simon grabs a cloth from his pocket and wipes the soldier's tears off his face.

They reach camp, and he takes the soldier to the medical tent. He places the soldier on the bed, and then a surgeon walks over to Simon.

"We were marching back to camp, and this one was apparently not taking care of his feet," Simon says. "How bad is his foot?"

The surgeon checks the soldier's foot. "This soldier needs to be off his foot for a bit till it heals. It will be about one to two weeks. Another week of this and we would have to cut off this man's foot."

The private sighs, relieved that he is not going to lose his foot. "Thank you for helping me, sir. Thanks to you, I can continue my dream of being a soldier."

Simon sits on the second empty bed on the left side. "My dear private, you must understand that I would never leave anyone behind on the road, let alone the battleground. An American soldier should never be left to march on his own. Our willpower and our passion to maintain our nation's freedom is in our hands. Yes, I have not seen battle yet, but when it comes, we need to march onto the field as one man. Otherwise all the blood that our families shed during the Revolutionary War will have been for nothing. Do you have any family members that fought against the redcoats?"

"Yes sir. My father and my oldest brother served with Daniel Morgan's rifle corps at Saratoga and in Cowpens. They are both credited with twenty kills each on the lobsters, sir."

"That is very impressive. I thank you and your family for their service to our nation. Now you will get the chance to serve. Before I go, what is your name, Private?"

"My name is Private Ryan Williams, sir," he says.

"That is a very good, strong name, Private Williams. I wish that you get better and soon will be back with the platoon. Rest easy, friend. I will come and see you every morning before drill."

Simon gets up and leaves the tent. He heads back to the platoon. The sergeant of the guard salutes Simon as he approaches him. Simon stands at attention and salutes.

"Sir, how is the injured soldier?" he asks Simon.

"Private Williams will be off his feet for two weeks. We must continue without him. He was not taking care of his feet. I am making a new order that takes effect immediately. If I catch anyone not taking care of his feet, I will make sure he shall never march again. A good soldier should always look after his weapon, whether it be his musket, sword, pistol, or even his own personal weapon, if you know what I mean." All the soldiers laugh. "The next thing that a soldier should always take care of is his uniform. The next should be his own body, and that includes his feet. Marching in the hot, dirty dust can be a greater enemy than any bullet fired during battle. And the most important thing that a good soldier should take care of is his comrades in arms all around him." Simon's soldiers in the platoon look at each other, and they know he is right. "We all are marching together into the same fray. We must depend on each other to watch the backs of the soldiers in front of us. When the cold steel hits the hot meat, we must stand our ground and never show the enemy any fear. Trust within yourself as you trust your brothers. Understood?"

"Sir, yes sir!" the platoon shouts.

Through the next two years, Simon's platoon trains hard to prove themselves on the battleground. Soon, in June of 1811, all the training was to be put to the test, for Simon's platoon of seventy regulars were to march to join the Fourth US Infantry. After one month of marching through Ohio and into the Indiana backcountry, the platoon reaches General William Harrison's camp. Simon and his platoon march into the camp. Simon helps his men set up their tents, and then he reports to General Harrison's headquarters. Simon enters his tent and introduces himself.

"Sir, Sergeant Major Simon Smithtrovich reporting as ordered."

"Welcome to Indiana Territory, Sergeant Major. How is our outfit?"

"Sir, my men are ready to march at your command. You just tell us where you want us to go. We will take the fight against the savages."

"Have you ever fought against the Indians before, Sergeant Major?" General Harrison asks Simon.

"No sir. But my men are not the kind of soldiers that fight in lines. We have trained in that style, but I trained my men to fight Indian style. Other officers will say that we are just parade-grounds soldiers. We may like to be on a parade ground from time to time, but do not be fooled, sir; we are the toughest sons of bastards that you could ever wish to have in a battle."

"That is something that I am glad to hear, but I hope you are ready to back up your words with musket fire. I will be sending your platoon down south on a scouting mission, and you will have a battalion to escort you. Understood?"

"Yes sir!" Simon says.

"Dismissed!"

Simon exits the tent and returns to his men, who are eager to know when they will have their first orders.

Sergeant Greg Sumter walks up to Simon. "Sir, what are our orders?" he asks.

Simon smiles and pats Greg on the back. "We will be going on a scouting mission down south. We will be aiding in the battalion. In a few days, we will be on the front lines. I will tell the rest of men. Form them up, Sergeant."

"Yes sir!" Greg shouts.

Sergeant Greg Sumter forms the platoon, and then Simon explains their marching orders.

"My friends, we have our first orders. We will be supporting the First Battalion in a scouting mission in the southern backcountry. We will be in the first platoon leading the march. So while you are marching, be on your guard. The Indians will possibly attack us at a clearing just ten miles off, near a red-brick mansion. We are to rally there with an Indiana Territory militia, and we will march ten more miles south. And that is all I know. And one more thing: there are to be no drums. It is my personal order, and I know that it is not like us to not march to music. But that is why I trained you to march without music."

One of the snare drummers lowers his head, and Simon walks up to the drummer.

"Hey, my friend. Don't feel down. How about this? I will let you play the marches until we get to the mansion. It will help the battalion keep their spirits up. What do you say, huh?" Simon asks the drummer.

The drummer looks up and smiles. "Thank you, sir. That means a lot to me."

Simon pats the drummer on his shoulder. He then paces back to his post. "Now, when we get to the mansion, the commander of the Indiana Territory militia will escort us the rest of the way. We march at first light, and we expect to arrive before noon. Understood?"

"Yes sir!" his platoon shouts.

"That will be all. Platoon, dismissed!"

They salute, and the platoon breaks ranks.

Simon's platoon waits for the next four days, eager for the fight. On July 5, 1811, they finally got their chance. For many American soldiers, it will be their first and last taste of battle.

July 5, 1811
Indiana countryside
Early morning

The battalion under the command of Major Franklin Thomas begins the march out of camp. Simon's platoon is at the front of the column.

Simon stands right beside his second in command, and they prepare to lead the march.

"Good morning, Sergeant Major. It is a fine morning," Greg Sumter says to Simon.

"Good morning to you. Are we ready to move out?" Simon says.

"Yes, we are, Sergeant Major. On your command, sir."

"Very well. First platoon, to the front! Forward march!" Simon shouts.

The first platoon snare drummer plays a brisk drum cadence as they march down the road. The whole battalion marches onward into the forest, completely unaware of what is waiting for them at the clearing.

By noon the battalion from the Fourth US Infantry is marching through dense forest. Simon is starting to have a terrible feeling in his gut. He feels as if they are being watched by an unseen foe. And his suspicions are correct. Little do the battalion know that they are being hunted by Mohawk Indians that are waiting for them to reach the clearing, which is about one hundred yards ahead and stretches in all directions.

Once the battalion marches into the clearing, the Indians cover the rear and aim their muskets and rifles. Simon's gut feeling begins to get worse, and he sees movement in the trees to the left. Before he can say or do anything, a shot rings out from the trees. The bullet strikes a young drummer boy directly in the head. It exits the right side of his head and narrowly hits the fifer right beside him. The left side of the fifer's face is splattered with his friend's blood. The battalion halts, and seconds later a second shot is fired from the right flank and kills the fifer. The men of the battalion look around in all directions, trying to see the hidden foe firing upon them. Simon aims his musket at the left flank but is unable to see any of the Indians. Seconds later, a loud battle cry fills the air, and the whole battalion fills with terror and fear. A third shot is fired, then another, and then another. Finally the Mohawks unleash their fury upon the American battalion. As his comrades fire blindly into the forest on both their flanks and to the rear, Simon takes the time to fix his bayonet in case the hidden enemy should charge at the battalion. Simon is filled with fear, but he manages to keep his mind straight.

"First platoon," he calls out, "do not fire unless you see the savages. Fix your bayonets! Prepare to defend yourselves!"

His men fix bayonets and aim their muskets. They do not fire until the enemy comes out of the bushes. A few of the Indians try to charge Simon's platoon, but his men stay disciplined and shoot down five charging Mohawks.

Simon watches as the other American soldiers fire randomly into the trees. Major Franklin Thomas tries to rally his men and keep them from panicking. A few minutes later, Major Thomas has his horse shot out from underneath him and falls to the ground. The weight of the horse breaks his right leg. He screams out in sheer pain and pulls out his pistol shoots an Indian visible within the trees.

Simon sees his commander on the ground being crushed by his dead horse. He turns to Sergeant Sumter and orders him to get the platoon to the mansion. Sergeant Sumter and the platoon make a mad dash up the road, and a few other American regulars follow them. Meanwhile, Simon rushes over to Major Thomas and, with the help of two other comrades, manages to free the major. Just as they free him, the Indians charge forward with tomahawks in hand. They charge into the clustered American soldiers. Some of the American soldiers are able to bayonet the Indians but are soon overwhelmed by the sheer numbers. The Mohawks begin to kill the American soldiers in the most horrible and gruesome manner. They hack away at the soldiers' arms and legs. A few of the Mohawks throw their tomahawks at the soldiers. One regular is hit directly in his face with a tomahawk. An American captain attempts to defend his head with his right arm until it is hacked off. The Indian warrior then splits open the captain's head. The officer falls to the ground with his head laid open to the mouth.

The rear ranks of the battalion are killed within ten minutes. The foot guards make a mad dash up the road. Simon and three other regulars help Major Thomas to his feet and support him as he hobbles on his left foot. Simon lets the three other men carry him while he shoots down any Indian that approaches them. The Mohawks follow the retreating American soldiers up the road. Simon is running low on bullets. He checks his cartridge box and sees that he has only five rounds left. Just as he looks up, he sees an Indian charging at him with a tomahawk. Simon tries to fire, but he has forgotten to reload his weapon. The Indian tries to hack away at Simon, but Simon dodges every swing from the Indian. Simon thrusts his musket and bayonets the Indian in the chest. But he gets the bayonet stuck in the Indian's ribs, and that is a bad thing. The Indian falls to the ground and takes the musket down with him. Simon is now unarmed. Just because he is not armed, that doesn't mean he is going down without a fight. Another Indian charges at him with a war club. Simon manages to throw the Indian off balance and throw him onto his back. Simon grabs the war club and beats the Indian's head to pieces. Blood and flesh fly everywhere. Simon throws down the club and wipes the blood from his face with his sleeve. He picks up a Long Land Pattern Rifle and sees several cartridges upon the ground. He grabs a handful and puts them in his pocket. He then takes off running down the road, trying to catch up with his commander. Along the way, he can see his comrades' mutilated bodies lying dead upon the road. He is horrified by the evil sights of war. One soldier has had both of his eyes gouged out of their sockets; some of the bodies have been ripped open from end to end. Simon puts his hand over his mouth and his nose so he does not inhale the infernal smell of death. He trips over a body lying in the road. He looks at the young American boy and sees that the boy has been scalped. The boy's hair has been ripped off the head, and the blood has spilled out onto the boy's face. Simon almost throws up at the hellish sight. He gets up and manages to clear the woods. The rest of the battalion takes cover behind a stone wall in front of the red-colored mansion. Simon vaults over the wall and runs over to his commander. He sees that he has not only suffered a broken leg but has also been shot three times in the chest. One of the bullets has gone clean through his heart and out through his back. He is bleeding so badly that his blue coat is starting to look like a red coat. He is breathing very heavily, and Simon knows he is not going to last much longer.

As the commander grows weaker, he issues his last orders.

"Simon Smithtrovich, you are now in command. You're a major now. Defend this wall until those bastards are erased from the face of the earth!"

Major Franklin Thomas takes his final gasp of air and dies in Simon's arms.

The men of the battalion look to Simon and wait for a command. Simon cocks his rifle and stands at the stone wall. They all soon hear the Mohawks' battle cry, and Simon calls to his men. "Wait until they are within fifty yards, then unleash your fire and we shall charge them with bayonets!" Simon shouts.

One hundred Mohawks charge from the trees. Simon orders his men to fix bayonets, and they prepare to open fire.

"First Battalion, make ready! Take aim! Wait for my order!" Simon shouts.

The Indians run like hell toward the stone wall and fire upon what is left of the battalion. Their bullets skim the stone wall, but the regulars aim with precision. Simon waits for the Mohawks to get close enough that his soldiers can inflict heavy damage. Once the Indians are within fifty yards, the battalion opens fire with deadly effect.

"Fire!" Simon shouts.

The sixty men of the battalion fire a volley into the charging Indians. The volley cuts down half their numbers. Now that the odds are in favor of the regulars, Simon stands upon the stone wall and shouts to his men to charge. The regulars vault over the wall and charge forward with their bayonets. The Indians stop and begin to run. But they are not going to get away that easily. Simon's men cut down the last of the Mohawks with their bayonets. The regulars shout and curse. They stab wildly, as if they are an evil entity.

After one hour of intense combat, the battle is over. Only fifteen Mohawks manage to escape back into the woods. Simon and his men discover the carnage upon the field and down the road near the ambush point. The grass and the dirt are covered in massive amounts of American blood.

"Let's gather their weapons and find any ammo that you might need," Simon says. "Put pickets down the road. We are not leaving our brothers behind."

Just then the front-line Indiana militia of the Fourth Regiment marches toward them, coming from the same direction in which they entered. They see their dead comrades' corpses on the ground and fear that they are too late. Just then Simon and what is left of the battalion approaches them. The captain of the third company runs to Simon.

"My God! What the hell happened here? Where is your commander?" Captain Thomas Scott asks Simon.

Simon responds to him, his breath short, "Our commander is dead. I am Major Smithtrovich, and I was put in command. We need to get our men out of here before another attack comes. Do you have any wagons?"

"How many of the men are dead or wounded, sir? And we have sixty militiamen, Major. We will have to wait till the main body arrives."

"How long will they take to march here?" Simon asks.

"Three hours, sir."

Simon sighs. He knows that in two hours it will be dark, and fighting an enemy force in the dark is more dangerous than fighting in the daylight. The Indiana militiamen break ranks and form pickets around the area. After the first hour of waiting, five wagons arrive.

"Put the dead and wounded on the wagons," Simon says. "Put as many of them on as you can. We must be out here before dark."

Simon helps put their commander on the first wagon alongside ten other dead regulars. Ten minutes later, they manage to put most of the dead and wounded on the first set of wagons. Simon looks up and sees that the sun is very close to setting. He has to make a choice that could mean the difference between life and death. He could tempt fate and wait for the second load of wagons and risk being ambushed again. But then he remembers the red mansion just up the road. He makes his choice to take the rest of men and the Indiana militia to the mansion and settle there for the night.

"Captain Thomas," Simon says, "there is a mansion just up the road. Gather your men, and we will settle there till the dawn. We are way too exposed out here. I also saw they have a big barn where we can tend to our wounded. Gather the pickets, and we will make for the mansion."

"Yes sir."

Captain Thomas does not have to send other men to get the pickets. The unthinkable that Simon was fearing happens. All of a sudden, all the militia and regular soldiers can hear gunshots coming from down the road. The pickets are in a state of panic, and they are not running from Mohawks this time.

One of the pickets runs past his comrades, screaming at the top of his lungs. "Loyalists! They're loyalists, dammit! There are too many of them!" the soldier shouts. The pickets wildly fire back down the road.

Simon stops one of the retreating pickets. "Calm down, Corporal! Now tell me how many there are and how close they are."

"I guess there might be fifty of them, and I do not think they pursued us, sir. Is there any place that we can go for cover, sir?"

"Yes, Corporal," Simon says calmly amid the panic of the second ambush of the day. "There is a mansion just up the road. Just get your comrades to form a rear guard. We need to cover the wagons so we can get the wounded to the mansion."

The regulars and the militiamen form a rearguard as they make their way to the mansion. Five militiamen man the wagons and ride up the road. Simon and his men march on all sides of the wagons, keeping an eye out for any tory militiamen. Twenty Indiana militiamen watch their comrades' backs as they march up the road. The sun is finally in its setting phase, and the area around the forest is beginning to become hard to see. The American forces move at a normal pace but stay alert. Simon can see an owl upon a tree branch, and the owl hoots. Despite the danger all around them he feels a sense of happiness and joy. That happiness will turn into terror as the final battle of the night comes.

The American forces manage to get to the mansion, and the landowner spots the American soldiers and runs outside to help them. The landowner walks up to Simon and speaks to him. "Who are you lot?" he asks.

"Sir, I am Major Simon Smithtrovich, 4th Infantry Regiment, may we use your barn to house our dead and wounded for the night?"

"Yes, you can. I saw you defend my home and I am very grateful for that. This will be my way of thanking you. I heard more gunshots. Are there more of the savages out there?"

"The pickets are saying they're a Tory militia. Sir, do you have a basement?" Simon asks the landowner.

"I do, but with your permission, this is my land and I aim to defend it, sir. I was a regular in the revolution."

Simon smiles and hands him the second musket he is carrying in his left hand. Simon signals his men to bring the wounded into the barn. The wagons are sent to the barn, and once they are put in the barn, the men close the barn doors with a few surgeons inside to tend to the wounded.

Meanwhile, at the stone wall, Simon's regulars and the Indiana militia wait for the attack to come. The clouds up in the sky block the moon's light, but after one hour the clouds pass and the moonlight shines upon the ground. The moon is close to the earth that day, and its brightness enhances visibility on the ground by sixty to seventy yards. The American forces guard the stone wall, and some of the riflemen of the Indiana militia are mounted on the mansion's third-floor balcony. One rifleman is looking through his spyglass, and he soon spots a black figure walking through the field. He tries to make out what he is seeing, and then the figure aims his musket and fires.

The rifleman shouts to his comrades down below at the stone wall, "To arms! To arms! They are coming, Major!"

Simon and his mixed battalion stand ready to defend the stone wall. The loyalists charge forward with their muskets.

"Battalion, make ready! Present! Commence fire!" Simon shouts.

The whole stone wall erupts with red and orange musket flashes that light up in the night. The volley cuts down eighteen Tory militiamen. The loyalists return fire, and their first volley hits five American soldiers. The stone provides perfect cover against the loyalist volleys. Every shot that is fired from every musket lights up the night. The landowner is right next to Simon, and the man tries to fire another shot, but he takes a musket ball to his chest. Simon does not see him until he reloads his musket. Simon then drops his musket and tries to stop the bleeding from the man's chest. Sadly, the man took a bullet directly to the heart, and he is dead within seconds. Simon closes the man's eyes and continues to defend the wall.

"Sergeant," Simon says to Sergeant Sumter, "remember when you said that there is a first for everything?" Simon asks.

"Yeah, what about it?"

"Well, I was just expecting Indians. That is just one thing. But British loyalists? This is definitely a first."

Simon and Greg stand up and fire at two charging loyalists. They manage to kill them both, and then another disastrous event happens in the field. Some sparks from the Tories' muskets land upon the dry grass they were advancing through. The dry grass catches fire. The flames quickly spread, and some of the Tories began to catch on fire themselves. Fifteen Tory militiamen manage to get out of the field. They have had enough of the battle, and they drop their weapons. They put their hands up in the air and get down on their knees.

"They have surrendered. Hold your fire! Stop firing!" Simon shouts to his men

The Americans stop firing, and the battle is finally over, with the Americans claiming victory.

"Get their weapons and find some rope. We need to tie their hands," Simon says to his men.

They step over the wall and rush to get the loyalists' muskets. Then several Indiana militiamen grab rope and tie the hands of the loyalist prisoners. Simon walks over to them and tells them what will happen to them.

"Gentlemen, you are now prisoners of the United States Army. We will take you to our commander in the morning. You will be shot down if you try to escape. Do you all understand?"

None of them speak a word for a few seconds, and then one loyalist speaks out to Simon.

"Sir, will we be on parole?" he asks.

Simon walks over to him and kneels down.

"If you give us no trouble tonight, I will think about it. Now, are you gonna cause us problems, or should we just kill you all right now?"

"No sir," the loyalist says to Simon.

The Indiana militiamen take the Tory militiamen into the mansion and put them in the basement. Simon rallies ten guards and gives them watch for the night.

"Three-hour shifts. Two men each shift. If they try to escape, kill them. Understood?"

"Yes sir!" the guards respond.

Simon heads back outside and heads to the barn. He sees the surgeons tending to his wounded brothers. Simon then speaks to them to let them all know that will be alright.

"Rest easy tonight, my friends. The enemy has been destroyed. You will be home soon to be with your families."

He then sees a young boy who is dying from his wounds. Simon sits down right next to the boy and gives him a drink of water from his canteen. The boy drinks and then coughs. The boy grabs Simon's hand and grips it hard, for he is in severe pain.

"Shh, my friend. Take it easy and tell me what your name is," Simon says.

The boy responds with a weak voice, as he has only a few minutes left to live. "My name is Private Tyler Mercer. I am scared, sir. Can you sing me a tune, sir?"

"I will sing to you, my friend."

Simon begins a verse from a song set to the tune of "The British Grenadiers" called "Free America":

> Torn from a world of tyrants, beneath this western sky,
> we'd form'd a new dominion, a land of liberty;
> The world shall own their masters here, then hasten on the day.
> Huzza, huzza, huzza, huzza, for brave America.

The boy closes his eyes and dies. Simon stands up and grabs a blanket and covers the boy's lifeless body. Then he exits the barn and goes outside and gazes at the stars. He then feels a sense of relief. He has survived his first battle. He sets out his sleeping blanket upon the ground, and his men set up right beside him.

"You did good today, sir," one of his men says to him. "I hope we get to fight more battles under your command, sir."

"Thank you. I am glad to have fine men like all of you by my side."

They all then fall asleep under the stars. Simon's battle experience was more than what he was expecting. He now has a new perspective, and he has a terrible nightmare during his sleep. The nightmare is sort of a premonition. His dream shows a building engulfed in flames one minute, and then he is standing upon a rampart, fighting against what appears to be British redcoats. What he does not know is that the dream or nightmare is about to come true in the next few years.

July 8, 1811
7:00 a.m.

On the morning of July 8, 1811, the sun was shining brightly upon the area. Simon and a few of the regulars awake from their deep slumber. They can hear the birds singing up in the trees. Simon stands up and picks up his musket, and then he hears the sounds of drums approaching the mansion. A relief party of the main body of the Fourth Regiment is coming to retrieve what is left of Major Franklin Thomas's battalion. They have been expecting the battalion to have been wiped out, but they are in for a surprise. They come across the mansion, and the first thing they see is a scorched field covered with burned and charred loyalist bodies. The sight of the burned bodies makes one American soldier throw up. Simon and Captain Scott walk over to the relief party. Their commander is Major General William Harrison, who is the governor of the Indiana Territory. He dismounts from his horse and walks over to Major Smithtrovich and Captain Scott. Simon and Thomas salute General Harrison. Harrison salutes them both back, "Well, Sergeant Major Smithtrovich, I can see that you are all right. Where is Major Thomas?" Just before Simon speaks, his men rally around him to support him. "Sir, I regret to tell you that he is dead, sir. We were ambushed as we crossed that clearing just one hundred yards down the road. Mohawks attacked us with great force and with strong numbers. Nevertheless, we managed to beat them back. The major gave me his rank, sir."

"Sir, Simon is telling the truth," one regular says. "We all heard him, and this young officer helped us beat the savages back."

Captain Scott adds to the conversation in support of Simon. "Once we got the wounded on the wagons, sir, a group of loyalists attacked us, and we managed to wipe them out as well. We also took fifteen prisoners as evidence, sir."

As if on cue, the loyalist prisoners are brought out of the basement and presented to General Harrison. Harrison looks at the loyalists and then turns his attention back to Simon.

"Well, the evidence is true then. Very well then, Major Smithtrovich. Well done. You and your men will be relieved. Your battalion has earned the right to stay or to head back home." Harrison mounts his horse, and his troops take over the loyalist prisoners.

Simon and his men feel great joy that they have earned the right to go home. Simon turns to his men and gives a small speech to them.

"Gentlemen, I can honestly say that I have never served with a better group of men. I may have commanded you for just a short time, but I would take you sons of guns into battle again. I do hope that by the power of providence we shall meet again. I hope that you lot go on to live great lives. Till we meet again, friends." Simon salutes his men, and they salute him back. "May providence be with all of you," he says.

They all break ranks, and Sergeant Sumter gives his goodbyes. "I will miss you, Simon. I hope that we do meet again," he says

"This is just a temporary leave. I am not quitting the army. I will come back when I am ready. I will write to you. I will miss you too, Sergeant."

They hug each other, and then Simon takes his leave. Later that day, he manages to hitch a ride with an American cavalry supply convoy that is returning to Philadelphia.

August 1, 1811
Chadds Ford, Pennsylvania
Midday

A few weeks later, Simon returns to Chadds Ford Pennsylvania. He was given a ride by a carriage driver from Philadelphia to take him to his home. As Simon can see his house, he takes a whiff of the air, and he can smell his home apple trees. The carriage rolls to the front of Simon's home.

"Welcome home, Major," the carriage driver says to Simon.

Simon gets out of the carriage and pays the driver for taking him home. The carriage driver rides off, and Simon looks up at his home. He then looks at his apple trees. "*Now that is strange. Who in the world has been tending to my farm?*" Simon wonders to himself.

Suddenly he hears a female voice behind him. "The least you can give us is a thank-you, Simon!" the female says.

Simon turns around and sees Celestia, Daisy, Timmy, and Brittany standing right behind him.

Simon runs over to them, and they welcome him with open arms. They all laugh with joy.

"Did you all tend to my farm for the past two years, you guys?" Simon asks.

"Yes, we did. With the help of your parents. We helped deliver the harvest. You were right about this being the best farmland in the eastern side of the Commonwealth of Pennsylvania," Timmy says.

"And for that I shall thank you very kindly," Simon says with happiness. "You guys are the best friends any soldier could ever have. I missed you guys so much."

"We missed you too, Simon," Daisy says

"That uniform really makes you almost attractive, Simon," Celestia says. "Are you an officer?"

"Yes I am. I started out as a sergeant major. Then, during a battle against the Mohawks and against a group of loyalists, our commander was killed, and he gave me his rank. I had to help defend my comrades. I would like to say that I still have my commission, and I am able to return to duty anytime I want. However, unless a war breaks out, I will stay here with you guys."

Simon's parents walk up behind Simon so quietly that he does not hear them.

"Yes, that is true," Timmy says, "but how about your parents?"

Simon turns around and sees his parents. "Mom! Dad!" Simon shouts with joy.

He hugs them both tightly. All three of them begin to tear up. They hug each other for a minute.

"I missed you guys so much. My friends were telling me that they were helping you two with the farm. And again, I am very grateful for that."

"We missed you too, Simon. Look at you, my son. You are an officer," Simon's mother says.

"Just like your old man. What rank are you, son?" Simon's father asks.

"I am the rank of major. I am happy to tell you that I will be staying home for a while. They told me that I can return to service anytime I want to. Unless there is a war that poses a major threat to our nation, I will stay put. I missed you all, and I also missed my apples—or should I say 'our apples,' since you guys helped my family keep our business alive. You all are now a part of my family."

They all engage in a group hug for a few seconds, and they then all head into the house to eat dinner. As the sun sets on that day, Simon and his friends are sitting out on the porch and the sky is rich with beautiful colors of orange and red, mixed with dark blue clouds.

"What a beautiful day it has been. I really missed the nights here," Simon says.

"Not much has been happening here, Simon," Timmy says.

"We were hoping that you would make it home soon," Daisy adds.

Celestia sits right next to Simon and wraps a blanket around him. "Simon, we have been wanting to ask you this question for the past five months. When that sergeant asked us if we all wanted to join the army, we all really wanted to go with you."

"Really? You wanted to come with me?" Simon asks his friends.

They all nod.

"Yes, we did, Simon," she continues. And we were wondering, if another war breaks out or if you decide to return to duty, will you take us with you to fight alongside you?"

Simon looks at his friends' faces and thinks about the hell he endured. He thinks about saying no, but he knows in his heart that his four best friends are very tough and very loyal. He thinks about the full burden of a command. He stands up and walks to the railing.

"You want to serve our country?" Simon asks his friends.

"Yes, Simon," they all say in unison.

"I will ask you the following questions that I was asked. Wait till I am done to give a response. Are you willing to obey all my orders obediently, willingly, and without question? Will you stand your ground and fight against all that may one day, or anytime soon, with their muskets, bayonets, cannons, and banners, attempt to threaten and destroy our way of life? Will you march into the heat of battle despite the following hellish conditions that occur during that time: the roaring of muskets, the screaming of the wounded that litter the ground, the bullets that whiz all around you, the thick and dense smoke that chokes you and makes you want to vomit, and the roaring of cannons that makes you go deaf? And, most importantly, when the enemy is right in your face, can you face him, confront him, and kill him with your bayonet? Now you may give your responses."

The four of them think for a few seconds, and they stand up one by one and give their answers.

"No man shall call me a bloody coward," Timmy says.

"I would rather die than surrender," Brittany says.

Celestia and Daisy both stand up at the same time and speak in unison. "For virtue, liberty, and independence! We are in, Simon. Or should I say, sir?"

Simon smiles. "I am glad that you want to serve. I have a feeling that one day. America will face its next war, and we will either be invading an enemy nation or we will be facing our first invasion. Through the next few months, I will tell you about what I have learned and what I have experienced in my two years. And let me say that I sure as heck have seen a lot of things that one man can do to another man."

"Won't you have to get authority from Congress if you are going to create your own unit?" Timmy asks.

"That is correct, and since I am a major, I have the authority to command a force about the size of a company. The size of a company numbers from about a hundred to three hundred soldiers. When the time's right, I will ride to Washington and get permission from Congress to create the company."

Just then Timmy realizes he has forgotten to give Simon a welcome-back gift. He goes into the house and grabs the gift, which is wrapped in a blanket. He walks back out onto the porch and hands it to Simon.

"Simon, I am sorry, but I forgot to give this to you. It is a gift from your cousin over in France. This arrived here about two weeks ago."

"Thank you, Timmy," Simon says.

Simon has a cousin who is a soldier himself who is serving in the Imperial Army of France. Simon uncovers the blanket and finds that it contains the uniform of the Old Guard. There is a letter with it. Simon opens the letter and reads it out loud to his friends.

"Dear Simon, I have received your previous letter, and I am glad to hear that you are a soldier just like me. The war over here has been very hectic, as the English have been tearing our forces apart. The latest battle I fought was a slaughter. The Battle of Talavera was a sorry sight to behold. I was in the reserves guarding our emperor. We watched as seven thousand four hundred of our soldiers were killed or wounded. I am sorry that this didn't get to you any sooner. We are preparing for a campaign against the Russians. I hope you enjoy this gift I have sent you. It is a uniform of the Old Guard. I wish you the best of luck to your service in the American army. Signed Captain Charles Young of the Old Guard. Vive la France! May 1, 1811."

Simon puts the letter down and checks out the uniform.

"You have a cousin in the Old Guard? That is very interesting to hear," Brittany says.

"Yes, I do. Charles Young has been serving in the Old Guard ever since 1803. His first battle that he was engaged in was the Battle of Austerlitz in 1805. He had the honor of carrying the imperial eagle ever since then." Simon tries on the bearskin cap, and it is a perfect fit. He chuckles. "How in the world did he know the size of my head?" Simon says.

They all laugh, and then the clock strikes nine.

Daisy yawns and stands up. "Well, sis, it looks like it is our bedtime. Simon, we are very glad to have you back. We will see you in the morning."

"I believe it is that hour of twilight," Simon says. "Thank you, guys, for taking care of the land.

"You're welcome," they reply in unison.

They all head back into the house and go to sleep for the night.'

Throughout the next several months, Simon and his best friends live the lives of apple farmers, and on the side, Simon teaches his four friends the ways of the soldier. He teaches them everything he has learned and what history taught the young American nation during the wars that were fought.

The tensions of war are rising between the Americans and the British. Great Britain interfered with American shipping on the high seas for the past decade, and now the tension has begun to reach a boiling point. There is also the impressment of American sailors by the Royal Navy to serve in the fight against the French. Over a thousand American sailors were forced to serve in the Royal Navy. But it doesn't stop there. In the Mississippi valley, the Indians are being encouraged to attack the American settlers who want to explore new territory. The British want to have some control of the valley, and the Americans know that the British are responsible for these attacks. On June 1, 1812, President James Madison, the architect of the Constitution, puts the Constitution on a dangerous trial. He becomes the first president to ask Congress to declare war. He cites the issues on what the British have been doing on the land with the Indian attacks and their personal attacks on the high seas. Not everyone wants the war to happen, largely because of the economic problems that will ensue. Nevertheless, on June 18, 1812, President Madison got the war that he and his war hawks had been wanting. But two days prior to the declaration of war being signed, the English Parliament revoked the law of impressment. It takes six weeks for the news to reach Washington. It is too little, too late. The United States has entered its very first nineteenth-century war.

CHAPTER 22

BORN OUT OF ASHES AND BLOOD

Chadds Ford, Pennsylvania
June 18, 1812
Early morning

On the morning of June 18, 1812, Simon and his future staff awakened and prepared to ride to Washington. Simon dresses in his military uniform, while his friends dress in their finest civilian clothing. They expect to have a nice and pleasant ride to the American Capitol, but what happens within the next hour will be the final straw that will give birth to the Seventy-Sixth Pennsylvania. Simon grabs his Brown Bess, and they all prepare to leave. Simon's father rushes into the house in a manner of confusion and panic.

"Simon, I was outside checking the northern apple trees, and I saw a group of men coming down the road. They are armed with muskets," he says.

"Father, how many men are there?" Simon asks.

"I do not know. Maybe fifty or sixty?"

Simon rushes to the front door and sees the group of men coming down the long stretch of road that leads to his homestead. Simon turns to his parents and his friends.

"Everyone, listen to me. This could be an American militia. Do not say a word, and do what I say. Now, stay on the porch and do nothing. I will handle this."

They all step outside and see the group of men come close to their home. Simon cocks his musket and fixes his bayonet to the muzzle. He steps off the porch, and the group of men stand twenty yards away from the house. The men see that Simon is armed, and they cock their muskets.

"Good morning, gentlemen," Simon says. "What in the world are you doing on our land? Are you an American militia?" he asks them.

One of the men, who is dressed in red uniform, walks up to Simon. "Good morning. My name is Major Jack Zander of the York Canadian Militia. We came to buy some apples. We will pay you in British pounds. We heard that you have some of the best apples in the land that you lot call Pennsylvania."

"My name is Major Simon Smithtrovich of the US Fourth Infantry Regiment. I do have the best apples in the state of Pennsylvania. And as for selling them, I regret to say that I do not sell to people who disrespect our flag and who are allied with those who impress our sailors into illegal servitude."

"Major, my men are very hungry," Major Zander pleads. "Do not think of this from a military perspective. Think of this in a human-to-human manner. We have not had food for two days, sir."

Simon does not give in. "I am sorry, sir. If you had American dollars, I would be happy to feed your men. I will give you some milk and a few chickens; then I want you to get off my land. And if you do not leave, I will force you off. Unless you want to have the whole American nation after you lot for harassing an American military officer, you had better take what I am offering to you and march off my land."

Jack fills with anger, and when Simon turns around, Jack grabs his pistol and hits Simon in the back of the head with it, knocking Simon out. Simon falls to the ground unconscious.

Simon's parents and friends run off the porch and run over to them. The militiamen aim their muskets, but the major holds his hand up in the air.

"Do not fire!" Jack shouts to his men.

Simon's friends shout at Jack.

"You bastards!" Timmy shouts.

"What the hell is wrong with you, flapdoodle?" Celestia shouts.

"You'd better leave now like the meaters you are!" Daisy shouts.

253

Jack decided that if he could not buy the apples, he would just take them.

"Men, half of you take the apples and set fire to the house and barns. The other half keep your muskets aimed on these Yankees. Move it!" Jack shouts

The men grab the baskets near some of the trees, and they hitch the wagons and begin to take all the apples they can get their hands on. Simon's parents and his friends stay with Simon under gunpoint. They can only watch as their farmland is ravaged. Then a few of the men pitch torches and set the house on fire.

Jack walks over to them and utters that this was an act of vengeance. "I bet that bastard told you all his little war stories. This is for killing my brothers in Indiana," he says with a vengeful tone.

Just as they begin to burn the house, Simon comes to. The first thing he sees is his home, his barn, and the orchard going up in flames. Simon sits with his family and friends as the men leave the area. Simon fills with hate and pure anger. Celestia and Daisy help him to his feet. Simon is still in a daze from being hit hard in the back of his head. He almost falls, but they help him stay on his feet. Once he gains his balance, he breaks free and rushes back into the house, which was engulfed in flames. He rushes to the back of the house and he grabs his cousin's uniform, grabs a folded American flag, and also grabs four muskets from the closet. He then rushes out the door and gives his friends each a musket. Just then he looks behind his friends and sees another group of men marching toward the burning farmland. But this time the men that are marching toward the farm are wearing American uniforms and carrying a regimental Pennsylvania flag. Simon did not recognize them at first but then realized who they were.

"Now who in the hell are they, Simon?" Celestia asks.

Simon smiles. "Those are my men—my old unit!" Simon says with joy.

He rushes over to them and sees his old war buddy and one of his best men leading the platoon.

"Greg Sumter—I'll be damned!" Simon says.

"Hello, sir. I am so sorry that we didn't get here in time. We have been tracking down those Canucks for the past several days. We were coming to get you, but apparently we were too late," Greg says.

"Well, it is okay. I can always rebuild my home. I am just glad my family and my friends were not harmed. Now, do you know where these bastards are heading?" Simon asks Greg.

"They are marching north. If we move now, we can ambush them and reclaim what is rightly yours."

Simon's friends and parents gather right behind him. Simon turns to them. "You guys, I know this is happening too fast. I am not the only one who lost his home. You guys shared this home with me and my family. I am asking you if you are ready to begin your journey by serving alongside me?"

Simon's friends respond without wasting a second.

"Simon, this is not a conversation. Just take us to where the hell they are and we will show them what an apple farming family can really do!" Celestia says.

"This is not even a question!" Timmy says.

We are more than friends, Simon. We are a family!" Daisy says.

"Why are we even talking about this?" Brittany adds.

Simon turns to his parents, and they hand him the bearskin cap. Simon's mother says to Simon, "Go now, and make our family proud. We will be fine. We shall ride to our parents' home in the city. Come to us when the battle is over, and do be careful."

Simon takes the bearskin cap and replaces his shako. He puts the cap on and hugs his parents. "I love you both very much," he says to them.

"We love you too." they reply.

Simon turns to his friends, and Timmy hands him the folded American flag. He then hands it to Greg. He and three other regulars unfold the flag and find that it is the flag that has the number seventy-six where the stars would normally be. This flag was called the Spirit of Seventy-Six. This was a hand-sewn flag that represented the original flag, which was also called the Bennington flag. This flag represented the birth of the Declaration of Independence on July 4, 1776.

"Sergeant, put this on a pole. This is our flag, and I declare that today the Seventy-Sixth Pennsylvania Keystone Grenadiers are born out of the ashes. Once we catch those Canadians, we will be baptized in their blood," Simon says.

"Huzzah!" his men and friends shout.

"Sergeant Sumter, you said that they were marching north?"

"Yes sir," Greg says.

Simon had the ideal location to ambush the enemy militia. There was a small road that led into a clearing that stretched one hundred yards from side to side. This battle would take place in a near copy of the road where he and his men were ambushed in Indiana.

"We will ambush them the same way the Mohawks ambushed our battalion," Simon says. "This time we will make sure that no one will survive to tell the tale. And I have a promise to keep to you all. As a reward for your help, I will let you eat all the apples we manage to reclaim. My friends of the brave Seventy-Sixth, let's go get those sons of bastards!"

The Canadians were marching north down a main road thinking that they were out of danger, but what they didn't know is that Simon and his company were sneaking down a secret dirt path that circled to the west. The dirt road connected to the main road about six miles away from Simon's homestead. It was a long route, luckily it was out of sight of the Canadian militia. The Canadian militia were marching themselves into a trap and there would be no escape.

One hour later, the Canadian militia is making its escape down within the dense Pennsylvania forest. The militiamen march toward the ambush point, completely unaware that they are in for a painful and deadly surprise. Just three hundred yards down the road, the Seventy-Sixth are waiting for the militia to march into their sights.

Simon and his best friends are kneeling side by side with their muskets aimed. Simon tells his men to keep the leader of the militia alive.

"No one touch the one in the red uniform. That bastard is mine. Do y'all hear me?"

"Yes sir!" they say quietly.

A few minutes later, the militia is almost near the point. Simon whistles to the half his men on the other side of the clearing. Sergeant Sumter whistles back to Simon, and they wait for the militia to enter the kill zone. One of the wagons that the militia is hauling has one of the wheels snap off. The militia halts the march to repair the wheel. The militia is now in the kill zone, and Simon orders his men to prepare to commence the ambush. He whispers to them just loudly enough so that they can hear his commands but the enemy cannot hear them hiding within the trees.

"Seventy-Sixth, make ready! Take aim!"

Simon whistles to Greg in such a way as to repeat the same command. The Canadian militiamen hear the whistling, and they can already tell that something is wrong. Some of them aim their muskets in various directions. Major Jack Zander stands in front of his men and he looks down at the trees down the road. All the militiamen begin to get scared, and then, with one mighty breath, Simon screams at the top of his lungs to his men to open fire.

"Fire at will!"

The Seventy-Sixth opens fire from both flanks of the road. The crackle of the volley roars like a clap of thunder. Major Zander sees the white musket smoke for a split second, and he takes a musket ball to the groin. Blood erupts, and some of the worst pain imaginable rushes through his body. He looks behind him to see several of his men on the ground, either dead or wounded. Sergeant Sumter and his squad open fire on the militia. Their volley cuts down almost all the rest of the Canadians. Greg then fixes his bayonet and charges out of the trees. The last ten militiamen fire upon him, and Greg takes three musket balls to the chest. Simon can't see Greg through the smoke, and all he can hear is the sound of men screaming. Greg's squad charges at the remaining militia with their bayonets. Upon seeing their officer upon the ground, the squad breaks ranks, and they go blood drunk. One of the American regulars kicks a militiaman down so hard that the militiaman smacks his head on the ground. The skull of the Canadian cracks open, and blood spills out onto the dirt. The man is dead within seconds. Another regular thrusts his bayonet into the militiaman over and over again. The regular stabs him about eight times before stabbing him directly in the skull. After a few minutes of close-quarters combat, there are only three enemy militiamen left standing, cornered by the apple wagons. Simon brings up his team, and the Seventy-Sixth reload their muskets and aim at the remaining militiamen. The militiamen throw down their muskets and surrender. Celestia and Brittany grab their muskets and toss them behind them.

Simon looks around but he does not see Sergeant Sumter. "Where is Sumter?" he asks. Then he sees him upon the ground. He rushes to his lifeless body. Sergeant Sumter bleeds out from his wounds. Simon then hears Major Zander crying out from being shot in one of the worst places to get shot. Simon growls and then runs over to him and grabs him. He then drags him with a mighty surge of energy. He throws him hard against the wagon. Zander's body slams into the wagon, and his men cover him. The militiamen begin to beg for mercy.

"Please don't kill us! For the love of heaven and earth. Please spare us!" One of the militiamen cries and begs.

Simon fills with hate and pure anger. He looks at his best friends, and they all nod once to each other. They aim their muskets as the militiamen continue to scream and beg for the Seventy-Sixth to spare them. Without a moment's hesitation, Simon and his friends execute the Canadian militia and their commander. The Seventy-Sixth have fought their very first battle and come away victorious. No one says a word as the regulars gather the militia's weapons and others gather the apple baskets from broken wagons. They leave the bodies of the enemy militiamen to rot in the sun. Two regulars climb up on the wagons and mount the horses the wagons are hooked to. The Seventy-Sixth Pennsylvania marches toward Philadelphia with the reclaimed apples.

About two hours later, the Seventy-Sixth marches into the city and stops in front of Independence hall. Simon and his new company reap the bounty that they reclaimed from their enemies. Simon walks over to the first wagon, pulls back the blanket, and says to his unit, "Ladies and gentlemen, I am very impressed with your efforts today. I have a promise to keep, and now here is that promise." His apples are still in perfect shape. "Eat up and enjoy, my friends. That is an order." He smiles as he picks out four apples and gives his best friends one apple each. They all eat the apples. Simon's men are very amazed at how great the apples taste.

"Sir, these are the best apples I have ever tasted. My compliments, Major," one regular says to Simon.

Simon smiles. "Thank you, Corporal. I am a man of my word, and that will never change."

Then a civilian walks over to the Seventy-Sixth. "You guys need to hear this," he says. "President James Madison and Congress have declared war on Canada and England." He shows Simon a paper. Simon then passes it around to his men so they may read the news. Simon then takes a bite out of his apple and thinks about what the next move will be for the Seventy-Sixth. He takes off his bearskin cap and gets the idea of what the uniforms will be. Their next stop will be Washington, where they will get the supplies for uniforms and weapons.

The next day when they arrive in Washington, Simon and his staff manage to get authorization from Congress to raise the Seventy-Sixth. Congress gives them extra money so they may purchase the materials to create the uniforms they shall don for the war. But for the next three months, the recruits of the Seventy-Sixth Pennsylvania will undergo nineteenth-century-style training. They will learn how to march, how to move, how to think, how to use their weapons, and how to act like professional soldiers. They will do this no matter the weather, in the day and at night, which will keep them alive during the fighting.

June 21, 1812
Philadelphia, Pennsylvania

Three days after their first battle, the Seventy-Sixth Pennsylvania had recruited over three hundred civilians. It is now up to the staff to train these civilians into elite Keystone grenadiers. On the morning of June 21, 1812, Major Simon Smithtrovich and his staff were ready to begin training these civilians. In his tent, Simon is getting dressed in his brand-new grenadier uniform. He looks at himself in the mirror as he is buttoning up his coat. He puts his green sash on the right side of his body. He takes a deep breath and speaks to himself in his mind.

"I pray that what our families fought for three decades ago will be worth all the blood that will be spilled in the coming struggle. May our efforts not be in vain as we pick up our colors once again and lift them high so that they fly as high as the stars. May providence be with us all, now and forever."

Simon makes the sign of the cross, and then Celestia walks into the tent and salutes him.

"Good morning, Major. How is the Major doing today?" Celestia says to Simon.

Simon turns around and salutes First Lieutenant Celestia Rose. "Good morning, Lieutenant Rose. I am doing just fine. Just a little bit nervous about this command. How are you doing, ma'am?

"I am doing just fine, sir. Do not be afraid, sir. We have faith in you, sir. If you do this just as well as you harvest the greatest apples, then you can lead this company into a victorious battle, sir."

Simon and Celestia step out, and he sees the rest of his friends dressed in the new uniforms. They salute Simon, and he salutes them back.

"Good morning, everyone," Simon says.

"Good morning, sir," they say to Simon.

"I am glad to see you all so healthy this fine morning. How do you all like your uniforms?"

They give their opinions one at a time.

"Sir, these uniforms are outstanding," Timmy says.

"I love my uniform. It is very lightweight, and I love the lace style on this coat," Daisy says.

"I really love mine, sir. The lace pattern is very appealing for my taste," Brittany says.

"I am glad you like them. I figured that if we are going to die, then by the living Lord, we will die in style," Simon says.

Simon and his staff walk over to see the whole company standing on the training grounds. There are several blue-coated corporals and sergeants that will help train the new recruits.

One sergeant sees the staff approaching them. "Company, attention!" the sergeant shouts.

The recruits stand to attention, and the sergeant about-faces and salutes Major Smithtrovich. Simon salutes the sergeant.

"All the recruits are present and accounted for, sir," the sergeant says to Simon.

"Thank you, Sergeant. You may take your post," Simon says.

The sergeant takes his post on the right side of the company. Simon walks three paces forward and introduces himself and his staff. He then begins to preach about the outfit's mission and why they are here.

"Good morning, everyone. My name is Major Simon Smithtrovich, and this is my staff. I commend you all for volunteering for service in the United States Army. This unit that you volunteered for is called the Seventy-Sixth Pennsylvania Keystone Grenadiers. The men you see behind me and my staff are soldiers that served alongside me in Indiana against the Mohawks and the Shawnees. This company was formed three days ago, when Congress declared war on Britain and Canada. We are not a regular force of grenadiers. We are an irregular force, and what that means is that we play by our own rules of engagement. We do not belong to any other established unit. Now, a regular unit would form up in a massive column and stand like sitting targets. That type of tactic is not to be used in every single battle. We believe that the right tactic must be used in the right battle so that we can beat any enemy force that thinks it can fight against us. The redcoats believe that the manly thing to do is to fight in a massive battle line. They believe that hiding behind bushes and trees is cowardly. Those British officers are a bunch of fools who think like that because deep down they are just a bunch of overdressed monkeys who carry the pot for the pompous king."

The men laugh at the insult. Celestia rolls her eyes, and Daisy shakes her head. Timmy smiles and scoffs.

"Damn right about that, sir," Brittany says.

"Now, did anyone have any members of their families fight against the lobsters during the Revolutionary War?" Simon asks the new recruits.

Half of the recruits raise their hands. The whole first rank have their hands raised. Simon walks down to the first rank of men and begins to ask them questions. Simon begins with the first recruit in the first rank.

"You, lad. What was the reason you joined my company?"

"Sir, I joined because I want to fight against the lobsters, sir."

Simon moves on to the second recruit in line.

"How about you? I bet you couldn't march fifty paces without getting tired."

"Sir, I am here to serve my nation, sir. I have wanted to serve ever since I was a little kid, sir."

"Have you ever fired a musket before, dear Private?" Simon asks the second recruit.

"I have held one but never fired one, sir. I hope that I get the opportunity to do so, sir."

"Do not worry, Private. You will have that chance soon enough."

Simon moves down the first rank and observes the other ranks. He sees one of the recruits whose bearskin cap is missing the plate on its front. Simon stops and looks at the man's cap.

"Private, there is something wrong with your uniform. I just cannot put my finger on it. Does your coat have a missing button? Is one of the sleeves longer than the other one? First Lieutenant, can you please come over here and help me out here? I am having a really hard time with this private."

Celestia comes to Simon's side.

"First Lieutenant Rose reported as ordered, sir. What seems to be the problem here, sir?" she says to Simon.

"Well, Lieutenant Rose, I may have hurt my eyes, because I cannot find the reason why this private's uniform is out of sorts. This is just so very confusing. Do you know why this man's uniform is out of sorts?"

Celestia begins to do the same act. She looks over the man's uniform and speaks in the same tone. "Bloody hell, sir. I do not know what is going on here, sir. His buttons are not loose. Hold on a minute." She then takes the man's bearskin cap off his head and shows it to Simon. "Sir, the plate on the front of his bearskin is missing, sir."

Simon's tone turns serious. "Private, where in the hell do you lose your plate that displays the American eagle? I have paid for these uniforms, and you were just issued these caps just three hours ago."

"Sir, the plate kept falling off the cap, sir," the private says. "I have it in my pocket, sir." The private pulls out the plate, and Simon tries to fix it, but it is broken beyond repair.

"I am sorry, Private. We will get you another cap when we get the chance," Simon says.

Simon inspects the first rank, and then his staff joins him in inspecting the rest of the company. After the inspection is finished, Simon gives his final words of inspiration before his staff begin drills for the new recruits.

"Recruits of the Seventy-Sixth Pennsylvania, I am here to tell you a few words, so listen well. Our families have fought their heart and souls on those bloody fields. Some of those fields are the following: Lexington and Concord, Bunker Hill, Long Island, Trenton, Brandywine, Saratoga, Monmouth Courthouse, Cowpens, and Yorktown. Thousands of our comrades have shed their blood fighting tyranny. They have all done their duty. Let us now rise and carry on where they have left off. I will not send you lot out to die like cows for slaughter. Here in my company, we are all equal, for we stand and fight for the same motto. We are not a ragtag military anymore. We will show those lobsters and our families. Many brave men and women have died not only for our state but also for our nation. We shall fight in their stead until we declare to the whole world that we Americans are a free nation and are endorsed by the living God himself. May God bless us all, and God bless these United States of America."

The recruits utter a massive cheer that can be heard from the city. Simon looks back at his staff, and they stand right beside him.

"Sir, that was a great speech," Timmy says.

"Sir, shall I begin to drill the recruits?" Celestia asks Simon.

"First Lieutenant Rose, First Sergeant Rose, and Drum Major Benson."

"Sir," they say in unison.

"You may begin drilling the recruits. Lieutenant Rose, you will take the first platoon. First Sergeant Rose, you will command the second platoon. Drum Major Benson, you will take the recruits that are in the third platoon, who are in your corps marching band. Sergeant Miller, you will stay with me, and we will teach them how to load, aim, and fire their muskets."

"Very well, sir!" Timmy says.

"I will train the men till they can march in their sleep, sir," Celestia says.

"I will not sleep until my platoon can do the same, sir," Daisy adds.

"Sir, my corps will play music so bloody loud that the enemy will turn tail and run. Our drummers will sound louder than a thunderstorm, sir," Brittany says

"Very well. To your platoons you go," Simon orders his staff.

The female staff CO and NCOs take command of their platoons. For the next several weeks, the recruits are trained in the school of the soldier.

During the second week of the training, Simon writes in his diary about how the recruits are trained under his staff.

> Dear diary: This will be the first entry in this diary. I never expected to have a force of over three hundred soldiers. The special thing about these men and women is that they are all from the same state—Pennsylvania. They are learning very quickly. Whenever they make a mistake, they make no excuse, and they manage to learn from their mistakes. They are very keen to learn everything we teach them. I have never seen such spirit and passion from normal people who are willing to defend this country. They still have a lot to learn, and they seem to never know when enough has been learned. They hunger for the knowledge of battle, and that, I am afraid, cannot just be taught. That lesson has to be learned upon the battlefield itself. When that day comes, I hope that my grenadiers will be able to fire three rounds a minute and will stand their ground, proving to the lobsters that the Seventy-Sixth is a force that will forever haunt them in their sleep.

On August 18, 1812, the Keystone grenadiers completed their training and began their march into the lower regions of Canada.

September 1, 1812
Lower Canada

In the forest fifty miles east of Niagara Falls, a detachment of Canadian voltigeurs are marching down a dirt road. They are escorting two wagons. The wagon in the front holds ammunition and black powder. The second wagon holds uniforms and some acquired food. Thirty voltigeurs are marching on foot, while two are manning the wagons.

Up on the right side of the hill, Celestia's and Daisy's platoons are waiting to ambush the voltigeurs. They have their bearskin caps off their heads so they will not be spotted. Some of the men use their caps as bipods so they can have better accuracy. As the enemy marches into their sights, Celestia's and Daisy's grenadiers cock their muskets and take aim.

Celestia whispers to her men, "Start with the officers first. The rest pick off the footmen."

The Voltigeurs pass into their line of sight. Without thinking, the Seventy-Sixth ambushed their first Canadian supply detachment of the War of 1812. The Seventy-Sixth fired on the convoy, and their first shots cut down fifteen enemy soldiers. The convoy is completely taken by surprise, and the Voltigeurs scramble for cover behind the ammunition wagon. That wagon holds six barrels of black powder, and if it were to blow up, the whole road would be scorched in a fiery blast.

Although the voltigeurs' upper bodies are not visible, their legs and their feet are visible through the wagon's wheels. Daisy and Celestia aim their muskets at the voltigeurs' feet. Celestia takes a shot and manages to hit one soldier's left foot. The soldier falls to the right side of the wagon, and one grenadier finishes the soldier off with a musket ball to the head. The Keystone grenadiers use the same tactic, and it is effective. The voltigeurs fire randomly into the woods. The bullets skim the trees and the rocks. Seven of the voltigeurs hiding behind the second wagon try to make a run down the rear road. The grenadiers on the right flank fire but manage to cut down only two of the retreating enemy soldiers. The remaining five run as fast as they can down the road, but they run into a firing line of the Seventy-Sixth.

Simon and his men fire a volley into the five voltigeurs. The five voltigeurs are instantly cut down. Back at the main ambush point, there are still six Voltigeurs alive. They are hiding behind the wagon, and they, too, try to make a run for it up the road. Timmy and his squad on the opposite side of the road make sure that they do not escape. They rush out of the trees and form a firing line in front of the first wagon.

"Fourth platoon, make ready! Present! Fire!" Timmy shouts.

They fire a volley into the backs of the retreating enemy soldiers. The six men are riddled with musket balls in their backs and the backs of their heads. The convoy's soldiers are all killed, and their supplies are captured by the Seventy-Sixth. The Seventy-Sixth regroup near the wagons.

Simon speaks to his grenadiers. "Great job. Now, if anyone needs supplies or ammo, now is the time to get them. We will be moving out in five minutes. First platoon, gather the supplies. Second platoon, form a front and rear guard. Keep an eye out for possible incoming forces."

The grenadiers of the first platoon begin to go through the wagons. The second platoon forms the guards, and they keep an eye out for more convoys coming from up or down the road. The Seventy-Sixth staff regroups between the wagons, and they discuss how the first battle went for the unit.

"That was a textbook ambush. However, we do not even follow a book," Simon says.

"Sir, what are we going to do about the bodies?" Daisy asks.

Simon looks at the lifeless voltigeurs. "Let these be a warning for their comrades. They will know that more of their blood will be spilled. Sergeant Miller, gather their muskets and their ammo pouches."

"Yes sir!" Timmy says.

Sergeant Timmy Miller and his men take the enemy muskets, and the Seventy-Sixth finish gathering as many supplies as they can carry. They form up and march back to their camp.

On the way back to the camp, Simon informs his men that more is to come. "Keystone grenadiers, this is just the beginning of our campaign. There will be more glory to earn and more Canuck blood to spill. The more ambushes we perform, the more dangerous it will become. But rest assured, my friends, you will not ever be captured by them."

September 5, 1812
New York Countryside
Ten miles from the border of Pennsylvania
Noontime

On a warm and sunny day late in the summer of 1812, an American detachment of the Pennsylvania militia is marching through an open field to a hedgerow. Their objective is to hunt down a Canadian artillery battery hidden in the woods. The Pennsylvania militiamen number seventy men. They are spread out about twenty-five feet apart. They all look toward the trees to see whether there might be Canadian skirmishers waiting to ambush them. The tall grass makes it quite difficult to spot anything beyond twenty yards in front of them. The sun beating on their heads is beginning to take its toll on the militiamen. Some of the men are almost out of fresh drinking water. A few have empty canteens. Little do they know that they are walking into a trap.

Just one hundred yards in front of the militia, a Canadian battery that has six-pound cannons is waiting for them. Plus they have a small company of Canadian regulars at their disposal. The Canadian artillerymen are well hidden in the underbrush. None of them make a sound. The second lieutenant who is in charge of the battery watches the militia move closer and closer through his spyglass. The Canadian officer raises his right hand high in the air—his signal for his battery to prepare to open fire. The artillerymen with the linstocks wait for the command to fire the cannons. Once the Pennsylvanian militia begins to cross into the hedgerows one hundred yards away from the battery, the Canadian lieutenant swings his arm down, giving the command to open fire. The artillerymen fire the cannons, and the brush explodes in white smoke and flames. The militiamen are caught out in the open. Several militiamen are blasted into the air by the cannon fire. The rest of the militiamen take cover in the hedgerow to their rear. They lie down and return fire with their muskets. With their first shots, two artillerymen are killed.

While the artillerymen reload their cannons, the Canadian regulars take a position near the rim of their hedgerow. They fire into the Pennsylvanian militia. Their first volley wounds five of the militiamen. Both sides are locked in a blind battle because of the smoke that is obscuring the hedges on both sides. Neither side makes any type of advance across the field. Both forces want to hide their numbers, not knowing how many enemy soldiers they are facing.

The artillerymen manage to reload their cannons. The regulars clear the firing line for the artillery, and the battery fires another barrage of solid shot into the militia's position. One of the cannonballs flies toward a tree and ricochets off of it. One unlucky militiaman is maimed by the cannonball. The militiaman loses both of his legs. He falls to the ground in severe pain. He looks at his legs, and all he can do is scream at the top of his lungs. His fellow comrades are terrified by the sight. One of them takes out his pistol, aims at the man's head, and puts the man out of his misery.

The battle rages through the afternoon, with neither side gaining any ground. Both sides have lost more than ten men each. The militiamen are beginning to assume that they are going to lose the battle, but they are about to receive some unexpected help. A half mile away from the battle, the Seventy-Sixth Pennsylvania is marching down the same road the Pennsylvania militia crossed just a few hours prior. Sergeant Timmy Miller looks to the east and sees black smoke rising over the trees. Sergeant Miller steps out of rank and runs up to Major Smithtrovich.

"Sir, look to the east. There is black smoke rising over the trees. I think there is a battle happening," Timmy says.

Simon looks toward the east and sees the black smoke. He then orders the Seventy-Sixth to halt.

"Seventy-Sixth, take care; halt!" Simon commands the company.

The Seventy-Sixth halt their march. They all begin to hear the crackle of musket fire and then the roars of cannons in the distance. Simon pulls out his spyglass and tries to make out what is happening. At first the smoke makes it very difficult to spot any soldiers. Seconds later he sees the flashes of cannon fire, and then he is able to make out a Canadian flag. He then looks in the direction of where the cannons are firing. He can see Pennsylvania militia pinned down in a hedgerow. He puts his spyglass in his knapsack and prepares the Seventy-Sixth for battle.

"Seventy-Sixth, prime and load your firearms!" Simon commands his company.

The Seventy-Sixth load their muskets, which takes twenty to twenty-five seconds. When the muskets are loaded, they shoulder their muskets. Simon takes a position on the right side of the company. He unsheathes his saber and positions it to carry saber, with the sword being held in Simon's right hand with the blade touching the right side of his chest while pointing up. He looks toward his company.

"Seventy-Sixth, right face!" Simon shouts.

The company performs a right face, turning towards the east.

Simon then calls out, "Drum Major Benson, would you kindly play 'Chanson de L'Oignon'? Let us give a salute to the Grande Armée and the Old Guard."

"Yes sir!" Brittany says joyfully.

"Seventy-Sixth, Charge your bayonets!" Simon shouts.

"Huzzah!" the grenadiers of the Seventy-Sixth shout loudly.

They level their bayonets, now ready to attack.

Simon performs an about-face that faces him toward the fray. With a loud, commanding voice, he orders, "Seventy-Sixth Pennsylvania, to the front. Forward march!"

Drum Major Benson blows her whistle. She whistles for a mark time / forward march (a moderate whole note and four quarter notes). A trumpeter plays the bugle call of the march, and then the whole band plays the march as they begin their advance. The snare drummers play the first verse of the march. The whole company began to sing the whole song in french. The Seventy-Sixth males would sing the first and second verses while the females would sing the chorus's.

> "J'aime l'oignon frit à l'huile,
> J'aime l'oignon car il est bon.
> J'aime l'oignon frit à l'huile,
> J'aime l'oignon, j'aime l'oignon.
> Au pas camarades, au pas camarades,
> Au pas, au pas, au pas,
> Au pas camarades, au pas camarades,
> Au pas, au pas, au pas.
> Un seul oignon frit à l'huile,
> Un seul oignon nous change en Lion,
> Un seul oignon frit à l'huile,
> Un seul oignon un seul oignon.
> Au pas camarades, au pas camarades,
> Au pas, au pas, au pas,
> Au pas camarades, au pas camarades,
> Au pas, au pas, au pas.
> Aimons l'oignon frit à l'huile,
> Aimons l'oignon car il est bon,
> Aimons l'oignon frit à l'huile,
> Aimons l'oignon, aimons l'oignon.

Au pas camarades, au pas camarades,
Au pas, au pas, au pas,
Au pas camarades, au pas camarades,
Au pas, au pas, au pas."

(Written by the French Old Guard, 1800's)

The militiamen hear the marching music and the singing coming from their rear. The Canadian artillerymen and the infantry hear the march as well. The lieutenant pulls out his spyglass and soon spots the Seventy-Sixth marching straight toward them. He orders his battery to elevate their cannons and fire upon the Seventy-Sixth. The cannons open fire, and the shells soar over the hedge and straight to the marching Keystone grenadiers. The Keystone grenadiers stay in formation as they begin to get barraged with cannonballs. The Seventy-Sixths Corps Marching Band marches right behind the infantrymen. They play their music with pride and with honor as they brave the cannon fire. The Pennsylvania militia are stunned and confused as to how the Seventy-Sixth is marching parade style while being bombarded. The shells explode all around the Seventy-Sixth. Some of the Canadian soldiers are astounded by the advancing menace. They have never seen something so impressive and yet very scary to the cores of their hearts. One Canadian soldier with his eyes wide open can only stand spellbound at what he is gazing upon. The Canadian officer is scared for once in his life.

After marching through eight hundred and eighty yards of open ground, the Seventy-Sixth disappears into the hedgerow. Then a problem befalls the Canadian artillery battery. They have no more cannonballs. Now it is up to their infantry to repulse the Seventy-Sixth and the militia. The artillerymen pick up some of the regulars' muskets and form a battle line. But the Seventy-Sixth is not about to let them form their ranks. Simon quickly commands his company to fire on the enemy line.

"Seventy-Sixth, take care; halt! Make ready! Take aim! Fire!" Simon shouted to his grenadiers.

The Seventy-Sixth aim their muskets and fire upon the Canadian regulars. The volley cuts down two thirds of the enemy regulars. A few of the regulars fall out of the brush and come into view. Then the Seventy-Sixth and the Pennsylvania militia do the unthinkable.

"Seventy-Sixth, charge!" Simon shouts as he points his sword forward.

"No quarter!" First Lieutenant Celestia Rose shouts as she charges forward out of the hedge, instructing her platoon that no prisoners are to be taken. The Seventy-Sixth charge out of the hedge with their bayonets at the ready. The Canadian regulars themselves step out of their hedge and make an attempt to repel the Seventy-Sixth. The Seventy-Sixth screams a bone-chilling battle cry that makes a few of the Canadian regulars retreat from the fast-approaching green line. A few of the Canadian regulars manage to fire just a few shots. Those few shots hit their marks. Five Keystone grenadiers are hit. Four out of five are wounded. The fifth grenadier takes a musket ball to the throat, and it snaps the spinal cord. Any communication from the brain to the heart is cut off, and the grenadier is dead before his body crashes to the ground. The grenadiers crash into the enemy regulars and begin to bayonet any remaining Canadian soldiers.

A few brave Canadian regulars try to fight off the Seventy-Sixth, but to no avail. Many Canadian regulars are cut down. The last remaining Canadian soldiers retreat into the woods, leaving behind their wounded and dead comrades. Many wounded crawl toward the woods, but they do not make it far. Many are shot or are bayoneted in their backs. The Seventy-Sixth, despite the order of no quarter being commanded of them, do not pursue the retreating Canadian soldiers. They stand at the edge of the woods and they stand victorious. They cry out in jubilation and for their survival. The battle is finally over. The Seventy-Sixth retreats down across the field, back to the militia hedgerow. Despite the great victory, the Seventy-Sixth have also suffered their first casualties and their first fatality. Simon and the staff, along with the first platoon, help carry their dead and wounded off the field.

First Sergeant Daisy Rose gives the battle report to Simon. "Sir, we have four wounded. I regret to say that we have suffered one grenadier death. The name of the deceased is Private Bill Marcus."

Simon then sees Private Bill Marcus being carried by three grenadiers. He is put onto a wagon in the hedge. Simon walks over to the lifeless body of Private Bill Marcus. He gazes upon the lifeless face, which is covered in blood. Simon then looks down and spots a red rose. He picks the rose and he places it upon the private's uniform. Simon then salutes Private

Marcus, and he salutes their wounded grenadiers as well. Simon then calls to his company.

"Seventy-Sixth, reform at color!" Simon shouts to his grenadiers.

The Seventy-Sixth reform their ranks, and Simon walks over to Daisy. "First Sergeant Rose, do you know how to drive and handle a wagon?" Simon asks her.

"Yes sir!" she says.

"I want you to escort our wounded and dead brothers behind our column."

"Yes sir. As you command."

Daisy mounts the wagon and waits for the company to march. The Seventy-Sixth reform their ranks and begin to march back home.

This time, in a salute for their fallen comrades, the Seventy-Sixth's marching band plays "The Keystone Grenadiers" at a slower pace as they march down the road. The mood of the Seventy-Sixth goes from victorious to bitterly sad for their first fallen comrades who marched and braved the heat of battle—those who gave it all for the pursuit of freedom for everyone in the United States.

A week later, the Seventy-Sixth finally return home to the city of Philadelphia, where they will give their first fallen grenadier an honorable funeral.

September 10, 1812
Philadelphia, Pennsylvania
Delaware River

On a warm and sunny day on the northern outskirts of the Delaware River, the Seventy-Sixth gather to send off their first fallen grenadier, with the family of Private Marcus attending the funeral. The funeral begins with the song "Amazing Grace" being played by the Seventy-Sixth Corps Marching Band. The band plays with honor as the casket is bestowed upon a wagon. After the song is played, Simon steps in to give a few final words for Private Bill Marcus. He takes a deep breath, trying to hold back tears.

"Private Bill Marcus was more than just a soldier. He was a friend, like a part of the family that makes up the Seventy-Sixth. He was a brave soldier who was loyal to the cause of freedom and liberty. He came to our company as a citizen of this nation, and he died as a grenadier. We will honor his sacrifice for the country. And in honor of his service to his country, we will give him one final salute."

The staff command five grenadiers from their platoons to fire a volley as a salute to their fallen brother.

First Lieutenant Celestia Rose's squad fires a volley first. First Sergeant Daisy Rose's squad fires a second volley. Finally, Sergeant Timmy Miller's squad fires the final volley. Then Private Marcus's family mounts the wagon, and they ride down a road that has grenadiers lining both sides.

"Grenadiers, present arms!" First Lieutenant Celestia Rose shouts with a loud commanding voice.

The Keystone grenadiers salute their departing brother as the wagon goes by. The Seventy-Sixth may have lost their first grenadier in the heat of battle, but this is not going to be their last. Many more of their grenadiers will die in many more battles to come. The Seventy-Sixth stay in the city for one month; then they are to march back into the fray. From October 1812 to March 1813, the Seventy-Sixth continued to engage Canadian military forces. The Seventy-Sixth engages in open-field battles and takes several small forts in the upper and lower parts of Canada. The grenadiers lose very few, but with each death, they suffer. The losses break their hearts but strengthen their will to keep up the fight.

April 20, 1813
Near the border of Pennsylvania

The Seventy-Sixth is stationed near the border of Pennsylvania. This was the final stop before the grenadiers were to march on home for a break from the war. But there was to be one final battle that they would fight. However, Major Smithtrovich was to be the only one who would be engaged in the Battle of York.

Simon is asleep in his tent. The grenadiers are resting for the day, for they have nothing on the schedule. A post rider carrying orders for Major Smithtrovich enters the camp. The rider dismounts from his horse and sees the Seventy-Sixth. He walks over to them.

"I am looking for the commanding officer of the Seventy-Sixth Pennsylvania. I have a letter for him from General Henry Dearborne."

Celestia walks up to the rider. "I am second in command. Our commander is in his tent. I will give him the letter."

The rider hands Celestia the letter, and she then runs to Simon's tent. Celestia enters the tent and sees Simon lying asleep on a bed. She walks over to him and sits on the bed.

"Major. Major, you have mail." She taps on his arm, and then she slaps his arm.

Simon wakes up and jumps out of the bed. "I am awake!" Simon says.

Celestia hands him the letter. Simon looks at it and opens it.

"Who is this letter from, Lieutenant?" Simon asks Celestia.

"A post rider said it was from Major General Henry Dearborne," Celestia says.

Simon opens the letter and sees the following written:

> To Major Simon Smithtrovich of the Seventy-Sixth Pennsylvania. You and you alone are to report to Sackets Harbor post haste. This is an official order, and this is not negotiable. If you do not show up by the end of the week, then you will be brought up on charges for disobeying your superior officers. Signed, Major General Henry Dearborne.

Simon was extremely confused by what the letter was ordering him to do.

"Major, what does the letter say?" Celestia asks.

Simon looks at her. "I have to report to Sackets Harbor post haste, and that means right now. The thing is that it just means me. Celestia, form the company. I need to inform them about what is happening."

Celestia stands up and exits the tent. Simon grabs his Brown Bess and reads the letter one last time to make sure he didn't misread the letter. He confirms he is reading it correctly. He crumples the letter and throws it on the bed. He then exits his tent and goes to address his company.

Celestia commands the company to form their ranks. "Seventy-Sixth Pennsylvania, fall in!" she shouts.

The Seventy-Sixth form their ranks and stand at attention. Simon puts his bearskin cap on his head and informs his grenadiers that he will have to leave for a little while.

"Ladies and gentlemen of the brave Seventy-Sixth, I have just received orders that I have to report to Sackets Harbor. Orders from Major General Henry Dearborne himself. I have no idea when I will return. I will give my following orders now, before I go. I want this company to remain here till I return. And until I return, First Lieutenant Rose will be in command. I want you all to respect her command, and if I hear that you don't, there will be hell to pay. I hate to leave you all. I will return, and I will pray for you all to be safe and protected. Grenadiers, till I return."

Simon turns around, and the post rider speaks to him. "Sir, I will escort you to the harbor."

Simon mounts a horse and looks one last time at his company. He salutes them all, and his company salutes him in return.

Simon and the post rider begin their journey to the harbor. It takes them a day and a half to ride to Sackets Harbor. Once they arrive, the rider escorts Major Smithtrovich to Major General Henry Dearborne.

The general is finishing inspecting the troops. After the regiments break ranks, the post rider brings Simon over to him.

Major General Dearborne sees the post rider bringing Simon over and meets them halfway. Simon stands at attention and introduces himself.

"Sir, Major Simon Smitrovich, Seventy-Sixth Pennsylvania Keystone Grenadiers, reporting as ordered, sir."

Major General Dearborn salutes Simon. "Welcome to Sackets Harbor, Major. I am sorry to let you know to ride here on such short notice."

"It is not a problem at all, sir. I just wonder why I have been ordered to come here, sir."

General Dearborne knew that question was going to be asked, so he cuts to the chase and explained why he ordered Simon to come here.

"Major, I needed the best officers in the US Army here, and your name came up. I have been hearing reports about your grenadiers raising hell all around Canada. The reason I brought you only is because I want you to fight alongside the First American Rifle Regiment. They will be the tip of the spear for the invasion of York. You will ride across with them when the attack begins. Understood?"

"Yes sir!" Simon says.

"Report to them, and their commander will fill you in on the rest. Don't worry; they already know you are coming. They are on the end of the camp. They will be wearing green uniforms. I must attend a meeting. Till we meet again"

General Dearborne leaves Simon, and Simon is stunned and confused like a duck that has been hit on the head.

"This doesn't make any damn sense. I still do not know why in the hell I am here," Simon mutters to himself. He then walks through the camp like a lost puppy. Other American soldiers look at Simon as though he is a leper. Simon reaches the end of the camp, where the First Rifle Regiment is encamped. He sees an officer sitting on a rock, cleaning his rifle. He walks up to the officer.

"Good afternoon, are you the commanding officer of this regiment?" Simon asks.

The officer looks up at Simon and then stands up. He smiles at Simon and puts his hand out. "Yes I am. My name is Captain Benjamin Forsyth."

They shake hands. Simon introduces himself to the captain.

"I am Major Simon Smithtrovich, commander of the Seventy-Sixth Pennsylvania. I was ordered here to fight alongside you by Major General Henry Dearborne."

They sit down and have a conversation about how things were going to be different from there on out.

"Now, I know you are the leader of this regiment," Simon says. "I was ordered to fight with you, not take command. I just want to make that clear."

"I understand that, my friend. Any greencoat is allowed to fight by me." Simon then takes his bearskin cap off and combs his hair. "I can see that you are a grenadier. What are you supposed to be, the American equivalent to the French Old Guard?

Simon looks up at him and chuckles. "You hit the hammer right on the bloody nail." Simon stops combing his hair and hands his bearskin cap to Benjamin. "It is the same cap the Old Guard wears, except the plate has the American eagle and the seventy-six on the bottom." Benjamin hands Simon his cap back, and he puts it back on the rock. "I still do not understand why I was ordered here in the first place. I mean, if there is gonna be a battle, then I shall fight, but it just feels different without my company." He heaves a sad sigh.

The captain pats Simon on the back. "I am guessing that you and your company are very close?" he asks.

Simon nods twice. "We are like a family. This is the first bloody time I have ever been away from them. I gave them my word that I will return. And before you ask, I am a veteran of only seven battles in this fight for our freedom. I will prove it on the field, because I believe that actions are more proof than spitting out nonsense."

"We are honored to have you here, Major," Captain Forsyth gladly says to Simon.

Through the next few days, Simon spends time with the First Rifle Regiment. He gets to know them, but every day he misses his fellow grenadiers. The American invasion is to take place on April 23, but a storm delays it. The squadron finally departs on the next day. Then, on April 27, 1813, there occurs the Battle of York (York being the British capital of upper Canada). This battle would become one of the fiercest of the war and is the battle that leads to the burning of Washington just one year later.

CHAPTER 23

GREEN AS THE GRASS

The Battle of York, Canada
August 27, 1813
Early morning

The American forces, which comprise fourteen ships and 1,800 American soldiers, are bearing down on the city of York, Canada. Major Simon Smithtrovich is to be with the US First Rifle Regiment that day, and that regiment is to be in the thick of the fighting. The first American ships, carrying three hundred soldiers, landed 6.4 kilometers west of the town. On one of the first boats, Simon is sailing over to the shore with the commander of the US First Rifle Regiment under the command of Captain Benjamin Forsyth.

Simon has a short conversation with the captain.

"Thank you for letting me fight alongside you. I just don't know why Major General Dearborne wanted me to come on this campaign. I miss my fellow grenadiers."

"You're welcome, Major," Captain Foryth replies. "It always seems like we get dangerous missions. Have you fought in the woods before, sir?"

"My Keystone grenadiers have been fighting like guerrilla fighters ever since the war started. I have been teaching them how to fight in line whenever we need to."

Simon notices that he forgot his musket at the main ship. He has no weapon, but the riflemen are not going to let him fight the redcoats without a proper weapon. One of the soldiers hands him an 1803 Harpers Ferry rifle. Simon takes the rifle, and then Captain Forsyth gives him a quick lesson on loading it.

"Now this is a little bit different, but it is loaded in the same way as a musket. Along with the powder and bullet, You must use a small piece of patch material that you wrap the bullet in so it will have a seal, and that patch has grease on it. You want to have a great seal on the ball so you can have great accuracy. You don't have to use the patch, but we recommend you do use it. And this wooden ramrod is more sensitive and can break easily, so be careful with it. And you pour the powder in the flash pan, and then you are ready to fire. Do you think you can handle that?"

"I will do my best," Simon says. "This is pretty interesting to know the difference between the musket and the rifle."

A few minutes later, their boat and four other boats of riflemen land, and Captain Foryth gives Simon a battle buddy to stay with him and to make sure that nothing happens to him.

"Now, Simon, you will be with Sergeant Dennis Hrin. Sergeant, it is your job to stay by his side; and you are to do the same, Major. Do you two understand?"

"Yes sir!" Sergeant Hrin replies.

"Yes, Captain," Simon says.

The British grenadiers, of the Eighth Regiment of foot, which is under the command of Captain Neal McNeal, prepare to make their stand within the forest. They are accompanied with Mississauga and Enjibway Indian warriors that are on their flank. They know that the Battle for York is going to be won or lost here. And there is another danger the redcoats are facing here: the Americans declared that any white man fighting against them with Indian allies would be executed on the spot if he was to be captured or found wounded on the battlefield.

The riflemen move into the brush as quietly and smoothly as possible. Captain McNeal and his grenadiers are waiting in the middle of the forest two kilometers south of the fort. Simon has his rifle, and Sergeant Hrin is by his side. They move slowly through the woods, going from tree to tree. The whole regiment is now in the forest. The American riflemen spot the redcoats about one hundred yards in front of them. Captain Forsyth holds his left hand in the air as a signal to halt. The riflemen take a knee and scramble to the nearest cover, whether it be a tree or a bush. Simon and Dennis hide behind two thick trees that are close together. Simon looks between the space that separates the two trees. He can see the British soldiers' red uniforms, which make them stick out like a sore thumb. He makes sure that the redcoats cannot see his black bearskin cap. He takes it off and removes the hackle plume and puts it in his knapsack.

Sergeant Hrin watches Simon put his plume away and then looks at Simon's bearskin cap. He asks Simon, "Why do you grenadiers wear those bloody bearskin caps anyway?"

Simon looks up at his cap and chuckles. He quietly answers Dennis's question with an answer he has said over a hundred times. "Short, sweet, and to the point, we wear these because it makes us scarier and because this is what I and my staff voted to wear. And I have a cousin who is a soldier in the Old Guard."

"Well, okay then. That is a good answer for me. I just figure it is very heavy to carry upon your head all the time," Dennis whispers.

"That is right, and it makes us look taller and more intimidating," Simon says.

7:20 a.m.

One of the American riflemen aims and opens fire upon the vanguard of the British grenadiers. The first shot hits a redcoat directly in the lung. The Battle of York has now begun. Both sides commence firing at will from the cover of the trees. But unlike the blue-coated American regular soldiers who fight on open fields, The redcoats are facing a force that has a very bad reputation in the American army. Captain Forsyth's men are very skilled at this particular business. Their style of fighting is to fire from cover, unlike regular soldiers. They are wearing green uniforms, to camouflage them among the trees. The British soldiers are wearing red coats and can be spotted from miles away.

It must be stated that during the previous two wars fought in the American heartland, the British suffered heavy losses in battles due to enemy soldiers attacking them from cover while they stood in line formations. Some such battles were Braddock's defeat during the French and Indian War, Lexington and Concord, Bunker Hill, Saratoga, and Kings Mountain during the revolution. Many people believed the British military wore red uniforms because it hid the blood when a British soldier was shot or stabbed during battle, but that is entirely false. The true reasons that the British wore red uniforms are that the red dye was cheap and it required less work in the dyeing process. And during the era of muskets, the redcoats wore red because when the battles were raging and the smoke was obscuring the views of military commanders, they had a hard time trying to identify their troops on the field. But the British had an easier time spotting their men on the field because the red uniforms stood out more clearly through the smoke of battle. The Grand Armée, on the other hand, wore blue uniforms during battle, and sometimes the commanders had trouble spotting their own regiments or companies that were fighting on the battlegrounds. The only way commanders could spot their forces on the field was by their flags and through the fog of war.

Simon and Dennis stay together, and they begin to pick off the redcoats at will. Simon aims his rifle at a redcoat that is 110 meters away from where he stands. Simon fires the rifle, and his bullet hits the redcoat. Simon is very impressed with the range of this rifle. He begins to reload his rifle, and he decides not to use the patch but just load it the original way. Dennis loads his rifle the way he was taught. The redcoats decide to push closer toward the riflemen, and that is a terrible mistake. For every single step the redcoats march, a comrade is shot and killed. Captain Neal McNeal leads his men, but the way he leads his men today is the wrong way to do it. The riflemen believe that if one kills the enemy commander or all the officers, one is cutting off the head of the snake. Captain McNeal is very well known by his men because he leads by example.

"Come on, my brave grenadiers!" Neal shouts to his men as he swings his sword. "For the honor of Great Britain! Follow me, lads!

His men follow him closer and closer to the American riflemen. Dennis and Simon spot Captain McNeal and aim their rifles. They wait for the British captain and a redcoat sergeant major who is standing right next to Neal to halt. Simon takes aim at the NCO, while Dennis aims for Captain McNeal. The way the captain is behaving in the battle makes him an easy target for the riflemen. Captain McNeal halts his men, and the sergeant major aims his musket. Simon breathes slowly and pulls the trigger. The Sergeant major takes the bullet right between the eyes. Seconds later, Dennis takes his shot, and he kills Captain McNeal with a rifle bullet right between the eyes. The British grenadiers are horrified to see their commander dead upon the ground. There are no officers commanding them now. The redcoats fix their bayonets and decide to charge at the riflemen. The riflemen aim at the charging redcoats and unleash a devastating volley. The British grenadiers are cut down in great numbers. They are without a leader, and their forces are being destroyed by the American riflemen. They are stunned and demoralized as they begin to retreat from the forest.

"Whoo-hoo! They are running, boys!" Captain Foryth shouts to his men. The riflemen chase down the grenadiers and fire right into the backs of those retreating redcoats. Simon has one last bullet loaded in his rifle, and he kneels and takes aim at a redcoat.

"Stop! Darn you! Turn around!" Simon says to himself.

The redcoat turns around and fires his musket. Simon does not flinch as he fires his last shot, and he makes it count. The redcoat is hit in the neck, and the shot cuts the spinal cord. The redcoat is dead before he falls to the ground. Simon exhales and stands up, and he observes the carnage that he and the riflemen have caused. Dennis regroups with Simon.

"Not bad for a grenadier," Simon says to Dennis.

"You did all right, kid," Dennis says.

Simon looks at Dennis confusedly. "Kid? I am twenty-three years old."

"I am thirty years old, Major. In my family, you would still be considered a kid. Since you did so well, I will let you keep that rifle."

"Thank you very much, Dennis. Do you have ten more rounds? I am out of ammunition."

Dennis reaches into his ammo pouch and hands Simon ten more cartridges. The First Riflemen have done their job well, and now they are to wait for the rest of the reinforcements, which are being led by General Zebulon Pike. The British commander General Sir Roger Hale Sheaffe knows that the battle is a loss and makes the choice to retreat. Before he makes his retreat, though, he orders his men to burn a sloop of war and to sabotage the powder magazine inside the fort. The British leave their flag up as a ruse to confuse the American soldiers that are two hundred yards away.

1:00 p.m.

The riflemen are sitting near the northern edge of the woods that is two kilometers away from Fort York. While General Pike is questioning British prisoners, the unthinkable happens. The fort's powder magazine, which is housing three hundred barrels of black powder, explodes. A massive explosion erupts from the fort. The blast throws debris over five hundred yards away. Hundreds of American soldiers are blown off their feet. Simon is blown to the ground by the shockwave that travels away from the fort. Thousands of pieces of shrapnel strike American soldiers. Soldiers who are one hundred to two hundred yards away from the fort take the full force of the blast. A massive mushroom cloud soars into the sky and is visible for miles. The initial force travels at five meters per second and is powerful enough to perforate eardrums and hemorrhage the lungs of Pike's soldiers, who are massed outside the fort, waiting for the official surrender. Large rocks, twisted bits of metal, and pieces of timber rain down for thirty seconds after the initial explosion. When the blast is over, General Pike and thirty-seven of his fellow soldiers are dead. An additional two hundred and twenty-two were wounded. Now the American soldiers are to have at their mercy the city of York. The US forces march into the city, and in retaliation for the death of their commander and their dead and wounded fellow soldiers, they raid and burn the town. The whole city is turned to char and ash. This marked the campaign that would lead to the Battle of Bladensburg, Maryland, and then the destruction of Washington.

CHAPTER 24

THE SMITHTROVICH HONEYMOON

The New Orleans Campaign, Part 1
Baltimore, Maryland
September 17, 1814
8:00 a.m.

The Seventy-Sixth are still stationed in Fort McHenry, and they are soon given orders to march down south to their final battle. Just after morning inspection, Simon and Celestia prepare to go on their honeymoon. They are in the officers' barracks, grabbing their weapons and their knapsacks.

"This is going to be great, honey," Celestia says to Simon. "I am going to show you where we fought to defend the city. I will take you to Hampstead Hill, and I will take you to North Point. This is gonna be so romantic."

"It seems that warfare is very romantic to you," Simon says.

"Remember, Simon; we fell in love because of war."

"That is true, and if we do win this war, we can rebuild the house and continue creating the best apples the whole world has ever seen," Simon says.

"I would love to do that. I love you, Simon."

"I love you too, Celestia."

They hug and kiss each other.

"Are you ready to go?" Simon asks Celestia.

"I am ready, Simon."

They both walk out of the barracks, and their unit is outside waiting to say goodbye to them. "Seventy-Sixth Pennsylvania, present arms! Timmy commands the unit.

The Seventy-Sixth advance their muskets in a saluting position. Timmy and Daisy stand in formation two paces in front of the company. They salute their commanders. Simon and Celestia stand at attention and salute the unit.

"Major Smithtrovich, have a great time on your honeymoon, sir!" Timmy shouts to Simon.

"Captain Rose, have a great time on your honeymoon, ma'am!" Daisy says to Celestia.

"Thank you," Simon and Celestia say in unison.

Simon and Celestia climb aboard the carriage that is waiting for them outside the fort's main gates. Thus, their honeymoon has begun. They drive away from the fort. Their first destination will be the city of Baltimore.

"I guess today we can also forget about the war?" Simon asks Celestia.

"Well, sort of, sir." Celestia says.

"Honey, you don't have to call me sir. Just call me Simon. Today we are a newly married couple just spending personal time with each other. And all I want to do today is spend time with you, for you are the love of my life."

"Aww, Simon. I'm glad to be with you today. I just wonder if they cleared the grounds of the dead and wounded? That would really spoil the moment of this occasion."

"I agree. That would be a very non-romantic thing to see when cruising with the most beautiful woman ever. I just wish I could have seen you commanding the troops. I bet you looked like a great leader."

"Aww, Simon. You are going to make me faint."

Simon laughs, and Celestia rests her head on his shoulder as they enter the city. A few minutes later, they reach Hampstead Hill. Some American soldiers are still stationed at the hill. Simon steps out on his side of the carriage and walks over to Celestia's side. He opens the door and offers his hand, which Celestia takes. She steps out of the carriage, and they both put their bearskin caps on their heads.

Simon says to the carriage driver, "Can you wait here? I will pay you double the amount when we get back."

"Very well, sir," the driver says. "Enjoy yourselves, you two, and thank you for serving our country."

"Thank you," Simon and Celestia say in unison.

They both walk into the camp and approach the rampart the Seventy-Sixth are stationed at.

"This is where we fought against the lobsters," Celestia explains. "They came at us with multiple assaults, and with the night's dark, it made it very difficult. Nevertheless, we stood as firm as the tallest mountain in the whole world, and we bloodied them so badly that they retreated. Brittany was the only one who was wounded."

"Yes, she told me yesterday that a bullet skimmed her mace and cut her right cheek. You did the right thing by giving the corps muskets. I kind of felt bad having them in the rear lines. I knew that you would one day have to take command without me. I am glad that the training that I gave you all really kicked in when it needed to."

"Well, Simon. You trained us well, and I speak on behalf of the company when I say thank you!"

She then takes Simon to the spot where she slept outside.

"This is where I slept after I read that letter you wrote to me," she says.

Celestia pulls out the letter and shows it to Simon.

"Right. I remember writing this. It was hard for me to write this, because I was wondering if I was ever going to return from Canada. I'm glad that you liked what it said."

Celestia kisses Simon, and they hug each other.

"I was touched by what it said. It made me realize that you were telling me the truth all along. I hope that we never fight like that ever again," Celestia says.

"Never shall we do that again. Let's not think about that. We must think happy thoughts. Let us make our way to North Point."

They cross over the redoubt and begin their walk toward North Point. They hold hands the whole way down. Soon after one hour, they reach their position. The forest has trees in it that have been cut in half. Simon is shocked at the sight.

"I am very impressed. You guys survived this?"

"Yes, we did." Celestia says.

Throughout the day, Celestia explains to Simon everything that the Seventy-Sixth endured during the Battle of Baltimore. Simon picks out some flowers for her, and they go to the Old North Bay and skip some rocks. From North Point to the defense of Hampstead Hill, it takes four hours to explain everything. When they get back to the hill, they watch as the sun begins to set upon that great day. They both go and sit on the rampart and gaze up at the sky. They hold each other's hand and watch as a shooting star soars through the sky. Once it gets too cold, they both go into the tent and fall asleep. The next morning, they will begin their march down to their final battle. The question is, will the Seventy-Sixth survive to see the end of the War of 1812?

CHAPTER 25

AT A CROSSROADS

December 22, 1814
Border of New Orleans

As the Seventy-Sixth are marching down a road toward a crossroads that will lead them straight to New Orleans, they can hear distant drums coming from their right flank. As they approach the crossroads, Celestia spots a faint glimpse of what appear to be redcoats. Celestia tries to make out the possible enemy forces marching on the other side of the trees. Some of the other grenadiers also see the redcoats marching toward the crossroads.

"Sir, I do believe that there are redcoats marching toward the crossroads," Celestia says to Simon.

Daisy puts her hand over her right ear and hears them singing.

"I can hear them singing too, sir," Daisy says.

Drum Major Benson waves her mace baton up and down very fast. "Corps, silence your cadence!" she shouts.

The Seventy-Sixth Corps Marching Band stop playing their music, and they can then clearly hear the drum and fife corps of the redcoats' unit playing just on the other side of the trees, across the road. A company of the Forty-Third Regiment of Foot is marching toward the same crossroads. They are singing a tune called "Take the King's Shilling." The Forty-Third's drum and fife corps plays the march.

Oh, my love has left me with bairnes twa.
And that's the last of him I ever saw.
He joined the army and marched to war.
He took the shilling; he took the shilling, and he's off to war.
Come, ladies, come; hear the cannon roar.
Take the king's shilling and you're off to war.
Well did he look as he marched along
With his kilt and sporran and his musket gun.
The ladies tipped him as he marched along.
He sailed out by, he sailed out by the Broomielaw.
Well the pipes did play as he marched along,
And the soldiers sang out a battle song.
'March on, march on,' cried the Captain Gay.
For king and country, for king and country we will fight today.
Come, laddies, come; hear the cannon roar.
Take the king's shilling and you're off to war,
Well, the battle rattled to the sound of guns,
And the bayonets flashed in the morning sun.
The drums did beat, and the cannons roared,
And the shilling didn't seem, oh the shilling didn't seem much
worth the war.
Well, the men they fought, and the men did fall,
Cut down by bayonet and musket ball,
Many of these brave young men
Would never fight for, would never fight for the king again.
Come, laddies, come; hear the cannon roar.
Take the king's shilling and you're off to war.
Die in war …
Die in war …
Take the king's shilling and you're off to war.

(Written by the British Army/Royal Navy, 18th-19th century)

Both sides approach the intersection, and they spot each other. The Seventy-Sixth and the Forty-Third prepare for a close-range showdown. Both unit commanders give their commands simultaneously.

"Forty-Third, take care; halt!" Colonel Robert Rennie shouts to his men. "Forty-Third, left face! Forty-Third, make ready! Take aim! Hold fire until ordered!"

"Seventy-Sixth, take care; halt! Seventy-Sixth, right face! Seventy-Sixth, make ready! Take aim! Fire on my command only!" Simon shouts.

Both sides aim their muskets at each other. They stand only fifty yards apart, and at that close range, the casualties would be very great. Both sides eye each other, not wanting to take a loose step.

Simon is thinking that the redcoats do not want to fight. He says to Timmy while he is still aiming at the redcoats, "Second Lieutenant Miller, do we have a white flag?"

"Yes sir. Why though, sir?" Timmy asks.

"If they were going to shoot us, their commander would have given the order already. Let us talk to their commander," Simon says.

"Very well, sir," Timmy replies.

Timmy disengages and walks to the back wagon. He brings out the white flag. Simon returns his musket and orders his staff to come with him.

"Seventy-Sixth, staff to me. Grenadiers, no one will fire without my order. Is that understood?"

"Yes sir!" the Seventy-Sixth shout.

Simon and his staff hoist the flag, and Colonel Robert Rennie sees that they want to parley. They meet in the middle of the intersection. For a few seconds, both sides say nothing. Then Colonel Rennie speaks.

"I guess I shall speak first. My name is Colonel Robert Rennie of His Majesty's Forty-Third Regiment of Foot. Who shall you lot be called?"

"Sir, my name is Simon Smithtrovich, major of the Seventy-Sixth Pennsylvania Keystone Grenadiers. This is my staff. We seem to be at a bit of a crossroads, so to speak."

Colonel Rennie chuckles. "That we do, Major. So do you wish to fight today for passage to our destinations? Our forces are about the same size, and my men have not seen combat for quite some time."

Simon looks at his men, and his soldiers say nothing, but Simon feels their fear. He knows that neither his troops nor his staff want to have a battle today. "We are not to do battle today, sir. My grenadiers are exhausted, and I would not put them through that. A battle after a long march across several states would be just silly."

"Very well then," Colonel Rennie replies. "I agree with you, Major. Our men have been on the march for three nights straight. But the buggers are brave. Would you allow my men to march on by first?"

"Very well, sir. Your regiment marched here first, so it is only fair. And it seems that you and your men like to sing. Our grenadiers love to sing as well. I usually do not compliment enemy soldiers, but for your regiment I can make an exception. You guys do sound great."

"Thank you, Major. We believe that singing helps our men's morale. We would love to talk more, but we must be on our way. Till we meet again."

Colonel Rennie and the Seventy Sixth's staff salute each other and return to their units. The Forty-Third prepare to march, while the Seventy-Sixth wait for them to cross the road first.

"Forty-Third, right shoulder arms!" Colonel Rennie shouts. "Forty-Third, right face! The Forty-Third will prepare to advance! Regiment, forward march!"

They begin to sing again. The British drum major spots Drum Major Benson, and he salutes her with his mace. Brittany smiles and salutes the redcoat drum major back. They sing a march that is set to the tune of "The British Grenadiers."

> Eyes right, my jolly field boys,
> Who British bayonets bear,
> To teach your foes to yield, boys,
> When British steel they dare!
> Now fill the glass, for the toast of toasts shall be drunk with the cheer of cheers, Hurrah, hurrah, hurrah, hurrah for the British bayoneteers!
> Great guns have shot and shell, boys,
> Dragoons have sabers bright.
> The artillery fire's like hell, boys,
> And the horse like devil's fight.
> But neither light nor heavy horse nor thundering cannoneers
> Can stem the tide of the foeman's pride like the British bayoneteers!
> The English arm is strong, boys;
> The Irish arm is tough.
> The Scotsman's blow, the French well know,
> Is struck by sterling stuff.

And when before the enemy their shining steel appears,
Goodbye! Goodbye! How they run, how they run from the
British bayoneteers!

(Unknown date origin, written by the British army)

The Forty-Third Regiment of Foot marches out of sight. Brittany taps her right foot to the beat of the drums. The grenadiers of the Seventy-Sixth Pennsylvania are very impressed with the discipline and the high spirit of the Forty-Third.

"Those British sure do know how to march and sing with pride," Simon says. "We have our own version of that one. Drum Major Benson, would you please play our march?"

"With honorable and humble pleasure, sir!"

Drum Major Benson blows her whistle to order the regiment to mark time and begin a forward march.

The drummers and fifers begin to play their own march that's set to the tune of "The British Grenadiers."

"Seventy-Sixth, sound off!" Celestia shouts.

Born in a world of freedom, beneath this western sky,
We forged a new company, a company of warriors.
But when our newfound freedom begins to fade away,
The company marches toward the fray, the Keystone grenadiers.
To those who wear the bearskins and broke thy infernal chains,
Thy blood that shall be spilled let never be in vain.
Should England empty all her force, we'll fight her any day.
God bless those who call themselves the Keystone grenadiers.
Whene'er we are commanded to break the enemy line,
Our leaders march with sabers and we with bayonets.
We throw Britain off the hills and toward the deep blue sea,
Cheering with glee, proud to be, a Keystone grenadier.
And when the war is over, back to our homes we march.
Our families cheer, 'Hurrah lads, here come the Seventy-Sixth!
Here comes the Seventy-Sixth, my dears, our noble grenadiers.
With blood, sweat, and tears, the Keystone grenadiers.
Some future day shall hail us the masters of the land
and giving laws and freedom to subject France and Spain;

A nation o'er the ocean spread shall tremble and obey,
The brave, the brave, the brave, the brave, the Keystone
grenadiers.

(Written by, The Keystone Grenadiers, June 18th, 1812)

One hour later, the Seventy-Sixth spot, the American camp, and with their drums beating and their colors flying proudly, they march onward into it. But before the Seventy-Sixth enters the camp, a sentry stops them and begins to question them.

"Halt! State your orders," the guard says to Simon.

Simon pulls his orders out of his pouch and he hands them to the guard. The guard reads the orders and hands them back to Simon, but he still wants to know who they are.

Simon begins to rant. "Are you questioning me, soldier? You are looking at a higher rank. My name is Major Simon Smithtrovich, and we are the Seventy-Sixth Pennsylvania. We were ordered by the president to march here and aid General Andrew Jackson in the defense of New Orleans. We have marched over a thousand miles to fight in a battle that could end this bloody war. And once we arrive, you dare to question a higher-ranking officer? You are lucky I choose to not have you court-martialed. Now, are you going to let us march on through, or do you have any other questions for us?" Simon is right up in the soldier's face as he speaks—so close that the soldier can surely smell Simon's breath. The soldier chuckles and steps backward two paces.

"You may enter the camp, sir," the soldiers said.

Simon gets back in formation and marches his men into the camp. He marches to the officers' tent with his men, and there they see the commander of the American southern district, Old Hickory himself, Major General Andrew Jackson. The Seventy-Sixth march toward the inspection ground, where General Jackson will inspect them. Once they get to the ground, Simon commands his unit to halt.

"Seventy-Sixth Pennsylvania, take care; halt!" he shouts.

The Seventy-Sixth stops marching.

Celestia shouts, "Seventy-Sixth, left face! Order arms!"

They perform a left face and order their muskets on the right sides of their bodies. The Seventy-Sixth Pennsylvania stand at attention, as tall and straight as Christmas nutcrackers. Simon and his staff hold their places, not speaking a word. General Andrew Jackson observes them and is impressed by their formation. He gets off his horse.

"Will the commanding officer of this company please take two steps forward!" he says.

Simon shoulders his musket and marches two paces forward. He salutes General Jackson. "I am Major Simon Smithtrovich, commander of the Seventy-Sixth Pennsylvania Keystone Grenadiers. And this is my unit's staff. Staff officers and noncommissioned officers to me—double time!"

His staff walk to his position and stand in the order of their ranks.

"Staff, give your ranks and names. Staff, sound off!" Simon shouts.

"Sir, my name is Captain Celestia Smithtrovich. Second in command of the Seventy-Sixth Pennsylvania, sir!" Celestia says. She salutes with her sword, and General Jackson salutes her back.

Daisy goes next. "Sir, my name is First Lieutenant Daisy Rose. Our captain is my older sister, sir." They salute each other.

Timmy then gives his introduction. "Sir, my name is Second Lieutenant Timmy Miller, sir!" Timmy orders his musket and salutes with his right hand. Jackson salutes him back.

Jackson turns his attention to the Seventy-Sixth Corps Marching Band. Drum Major Brittany Benson salutes Jackson with her mace.

"Sir, my name is Drum Major Brittany Benson, leader of the Seventy-Sixth Corps Band, sir."

They salute each other, and Jackson walks back to his guards and remounts his horse. He then speaks to the Seventy-Sixth.

"This will be your area for encampment. It is good to have you here. So far it looks as if you are the only Pennsylvania company here so far. I salute you all for marching this far. Did you see any redcoats on your march down here?"

"Yes sir," Simon says. "The Forty-Third Regiment of Foot is the unit that we ran into just outside the border of New Orleans, sir. We parlayed, and no shots were fired. But their numbers are high."

"Nevertheless, sir. We are a company of hardened grenadiers," Celestia says. "You just let us know when you want us to take the fight to the lobsters, sir."

General Jackson smiles. "Set up your camp. Major Smithtrovich and Captain Smithtrovich, there is an officers' meeting at 5:00 p.m. tonight. Be there, because we will be discussing a plan of action."

"Yes sir," Celestia says.

"We will be there, sir," Simon adds.

"Very well then. Do not be late." General Jackson rides off back into the camp.

Simon turns to his troops. "Set up your tents. Tend to your food and water supplies. I want an ammo count within one hour. Seventy-Sixth, fall out."

The Seventy-Sixth break ranks, and they begin to set up their camp. Within one hour, their camp is set up. Simon is sitting in his tent, cleaning his weapon, when Celestia steps inside and sits right next to him.

"Hello there, honey. What are you doing?" Celestia asks Simon.

"I am just cleaning my rifle."

Celestia looks and she notices that he hasn't brought his Brown Bess.

"Where in the world did you get that?"

"When I was at York. I forgot my musket on the ship, and I was given this to use. I was allowed to keep this and brought it over with me. I still have my Brown Bess, but I wanna use my rifle again."

"Well, I came to tell you that the meeting is in thirty minutes. We should march off to the tent. The general did tell us to not be late."

"Very well. Let me do a quick check."

Simon checks his rifle and finds it is all clean. Then they both grab their bearskin caps and make sure that their uniforms are in perfect order. They collect their weapons, kiss each other quickly, and then make their way to the meeting. Along the way, they see fellow soldiers socializing with each other. They are joined by one other officer from the Beale rifles. The officer introduces himself to Celestia and Simon.

"Good afternoon. My name is Captain Thomas Beale of the Beale rifles. What unit do you guys command? I see, though, that you two are grenadiers."

"Nice to meet you, Captain Beale. We are grenadiers. My name is Major Simon Smithtrovich, and this is my wife," Simon says.

"I am Captain Celestia Smithtrovich. It is nice to meet a fellow officer."

"Nice to meet you two as well. What unit do you command?"

The Seventy-Sixth Pennsylvania Keystone Grenadiers," Celestia says.

"Whoa. You are from Pennsylvania? I have to give you guys some credit for marching this far down here. You guys look like Napoleon's Old Guard."

"Thanks. Can you show us where the officers' tent is? We are still new here," Celestia says.

"Sure, I will take you there. Follow me."

Captain Beale escorts them to the tent.

"So you are a rifleman I guess, Major?" Captain Beale asks Simon.

"Well, I kind of am one, because during the Battle of York, I forgot my musket, and one of the soldiers from the First US Rifle Regiment gave me this rifle. It took me a while to learn how to use this weapon."

"But my husband has taught us how to shoot the eye out of a squirrel from two hundred yards with a musket," Celestia says. "How many riflemen do you have in your unit, Captain?

"Not that many, but every single man in my unit is equal to one hundred redcoats. We have had skirmishes with them for the past two weeks, and they are relentless. No matter how many we kill, they just keep on marching toward us. It's like they respawn from the deepest depths of hell."

"We both know how that feels," Celestia replies. "We went through that same thing at Bladensburg. Those were redcoats that we never faced before, but we sure learned a lesson from them. And thus that lesson will be that we will never underestimate the lobsters again."

Soon they reach the officers' meeting, where dozens of high-ranking officers from the army, marines, and militia units have assembled. General Andrew Jackson walks into the tent, and all the American officers stand at attention. He then walks to the front of the tent, where a map is posted on a board.

"At ease," General Jackson says.

All the officers stand at ease, and General Jackson lays out the battle plan.

"It's a pleasure to have you brave soldiers alongside us. For you all who do not know my name, let me make this very clear. I am Major General Andrew Jackson. I am here to tell you all that we must be ready to fight. From what I have heard about the Seventy-Sixth, as well as many other units that have marched into my camp, they are battle-ready and itching to end this war. We will wait till we hear for more intelligence. Now, who here is ready to end this bloody war?"

The officers cheer.

"Tomorrow night we will launch a raid on the British camp. Now, I want the commanding officers of each regiment to pick fifty soldiers from their units to take part in the attack. We will take them by surprise or we will perish. From what our scouts have reported, this camp is the majority of General Edward's Pakenham's force. Tomorrow night, there will be no fooling around. If our attack goes according to plan, we could end this bloody conflict once and for all. Be ready by 5:00 p.m, tomorrow night. Commanders, take charge of your units and report to me before five. Dismissed!"

All the American officers fall out. Simon and Celestia marched back the Seventy-Sixth Pennsylvania, once there, they talked to the whole unit, soldier by soldier, asking them if they wanted to take part in the attack. After one hour, the fifty grenadiers have been chosen for the night attack. And the fifty that are chosen include the twenty grenadiers who were trained in only four days.

Simon and his staff brief the chosen fifty grenadiers so they know what to do for the attack tomorrow night.

"Chosen grenadiers, listen up, and listen well," Simon says. "Tomorrow is the night that we will show the American forces, as well as the British tyrants, why we are called Keystone grenadiers." He turns to Celestia. "Captain, do you have the ammo count for all our Grenadiers?"

Celestia takes a piece of paper out of her pocket, on which the ammo count is written. She reads it with a worried tone. "Sir, all the men have about ten rounds per grenadier."

Simon's eyes open wide, and he shakes his head. He knows that ten rounds will not last long during a battle. "Well then, we must steal some ammo from the enemy. I am issuing an order that I rarely give you all. Tomorrow we will invade the enemy camp. And I mean that I want you all to break into their tents and steal their ammo. We will define the meaning of the word 'raid.' Every grenadier will be in charge of himself or herself during the raid. Steal not just ammo but also any food or other supplies you will need. Do you all understand the orders?"

"Yes, sir" the grenadiers reply loudly.

"Very good. Captain Smithtrovich has something very important to tell you. Captain, you have their attention." Simon steps back.

Celestia pulls out a red, white, and blue lace cord along with a twelve-inch hackle plume. She holds the plume in her right hand and the cord in her left hand. "Now, since this is winter, do not let this weather fool you. The days are shorter than they are during the summertime. I want you to wear these red, white, and blue cords and plumes on your bearskin caps. The darkness can cause confusion, and I think that might happen during the battle. This will help other American regiments distinguish friend from foe. Do y'all understand my instructions?"

"Yes ma'am!" they reply.

She hands each of the grenadiers a cord and a plume. After receiving their orders, the company breaks ranks and begins to fix their suppers and engage in other leisure activities.

December 23, 1814

4:50 a.m.

In the tent, Simon and Celestia are sleeping, but Simon is tossing and turning, having a terrible nightmare. In the nightmare, Simon is standing with his company, and they are marching with bayonets fixed and ready for use. Then they collide with a British regiment. Bloody hand-to-hand fighting ensues, with both sides hacking away at each other. The screams of the wounded are deafening. Everywhere Simon looks, he has a British soldier in his face. For every single redcoat he kills, another one tries to kill him. Hundreds of musket shots are fired, and the pounding of drums fills the air. The blood splatters everywhere, and dismembered bodies litter the ground all around him. Then he hears a voice calling for help. He knows it is Celestia's voice. Then he sees her. She is being dragged with a sword to her throat by a man whose face is blackened with powder. Then a barrage of cannon fire rains down upon the American and British soldiers. Simon hears the heart-piercing emotional scream of Celestia. Then a cannonball explodes in front of Simon.

Simon wakes up with his heart beating like the pounding of a bass drum. He looks over at his sleeping wife, who is still fast asleep. Simon begins to sniffle, and that is enough to wake his wife up. She looks over at Simon, who has tears running down his face. She gets up.

"Simon, what's wrong?"

Simon hugs her tightly and begins to lightly sob.

"Simon?"

"Oh, Celestia!"

Simon continues to sob. Celestia hugs him as she tries to comfort his scared heart.

"Shush, Simon. Tell me, what is wrong?"

"Oh, God. It was horrible. We were fighting in the English camp, and all I could hear was your voice. You were calling for help. There were hundreds of redcoats all over the place. I couldn't find you, and when I did find you, a British soldier in a yellow coat had a sword against your throat, and the last thing I heard was you screaming."

Simon tries to cry softly so he does not wake his other soldiers. Celestia hugs her terrified husband, and then she pulls a cloth out of her knapsack and hands it to him.

Simon takes it and wipes his tears from his eyes.

"Oh, honey, it was just a bad dream. I am actually not surprised. I can understand why this is happening."

Simon looks at her and sniffles, trying to hold back more tears.

"You have been a soldier for almost seven years," she says with a soothing voice. "You are starting to have nightmares because you have experienced all the carnage war brings." She grabs Simon's hand and he could feel her warmth.

"That could be why this is happening and why I seem to be scared about this raid." Simon then looks outside. It is still dark. Celestia lights a candle and puts it on the table right between them.

"Oh, look at me, 'Major' Simon Smithtrovich, blubbering like a baby in front of my wife. I guess my time as a soldier is coming to an end."

"Simon, it is perfectly normal for soldiers to have nightmares like that. That is a way of army life."

She puts her hands on Simon's shoulders, and they both lock eyes with each other.

"Look, Simon; being a leader is very hard, and the fact that you're upset means that you're taking your role seriously. Being scared doesn't make you a weak soldier. It makes your will even stronger. And if we are meant to die in battle, I swear we will go down together. We are not going to be away from each other. From now on, we will always be together. Because this is what the good Lord intended this to be."

Celestia brings Simon closer to her, and she wraps her arms around him.

"I love you more than I love my own freedom, Simon. Don't you ever forget our love."

"I love you too, Celestia."

They kiss for ten seconds. Their cheeks blush redder than an apple. They moan, and they hug each other with their eyes closed. When they pull apart their lips, they still have their hands wrapped around each other. Each of them can see the blush in the other's cheeks.

"Now we have two more hours till morning. We need all the rest we can get. But this time I will hold on to you, and I will not let go." Celestia says.

They hug each other as they fall asleep. Celestia asks Simon one more question before they drift off.

"Simon?"

"Yes?"

"Promise me that you will never stop loving and caring for me, just as you care about the health of our loyal grenadiers."

"It's a promise, my love."

Simon kisses Celestia one more time on the cheek and they finally fall asleep in each other's arms.

What Simon didn't realize is that the dream he had that night will happen in reality at the following battle. But the final weeks of the War of 1812 are coming to an end, and so are the days of the Seventy-Sixth Pennsylvania.

CHAPTER 26

PREMONITION OF WAR

The New Orleans Campaign, Part 2
December 23, 1814
7:30 a.m.
American encampment

On the morning of the day of the raid, everyone begins to cook breakfast. Daisy, Timmy, and Brittany are eating their breakfasts when they notice that Simon and Celestia are not awake yet. Brittany looks at their commanders' tent and sees it is still closed.

"I wonder why they have not woken up yet?" Brittany says.

She puts her plate down and is about to walk over to the tent when Daisy stops her.

"Maybe we should wait to see if they wake up on their own," Daisy says. "One time I disturbed them, and my sister made my whole day a living hell. She made me march around the whole encampment fifty times. My feet felt like they were going to fall off. I love marching, but not forced marches."

Brittany thinks that scenario through in her own mind and realizes that would not be fun at all.

"That is a great idea," Brittany says. She sits back down and finishes her food.

In the tent, Celestia and Simon finally awaken. They look at each other and say in unison, "Morning, honey."

"How are you feeling now?" Celestia asks Simon.

Simon yawns and wipes his eyes. "I feel much better now. I just hope that bloody dream never happens again. Of course, I cannot make that a promise. You are right about what you said last night."

"What am I right about, sir?"

"That being upset does not make me weak. It assures me and you that our roles as leaders are being taken seriously. I just don't know why I get so bloody emotional."

"My guess is that you are very open-hearted and you really care about all of us. I am sorta the same. Sometimes I used to cry myself to sleep because I was worried about my sister's safety during the early parts of this war. I made a promise to my father to keep her safe, and I have never broken a promise in my whole life."

They both begin to put their uniforms on. They wait until they are outside to put their bearskin caps on their heads. Before they went to bed, they put the American-colored cords and hackle plumes on their caps. They both can see that all their fellow grenadiers have done the same. They look at each other in amazement.

"Wow! That really gives our bearskins a very nice touch," Celestia says. "I think we should keep this new look."

"I agree," Simon says. "I like this, and as I have always said, if we are going to march toward the musket and cannon fire, we shall die like grenadiers in fine attire."

A few fellow grenadiers walk over to greet their commanders.

"Thank you for the accessories for our caps, commanders," one grenadier says.

"They look very stylish, ma'am. I bet those lobsters won't have any trouble seeing us in the fire and smoke, ma'am," one female grenadier says to Celestia.

"You're all very welcome," Celestia says.

"It was our pleasure," Simon adds.

They salute each other, and then Celestia and Simon join their staff for breakfast.

The staff salute their leaders, and they salute them back.

They all greeted one another.

Simon hands his fellow staff one apple each; they thank him as he does so.

"How did you both sleep last night?" Brittany asks.

Simon and Celestia look at each other. They are both hesitant to talk about Simon's nightmare, but Simon decides to tell them what happened. He has learned that hiding things from his fellow soldiers can lead to terrible fights, and he wants to avoid that at all costs. He takes a deep breath and explains what happened.

"It was a rough night because of one main reason. I had the worst nightmare I have ever had in my life. And what made it more terrifying was that my gut was hurting as if I had been shot by a six-pound cannonball. Bear with me here. I was leading the company into the British camp, and the first thing I saw was that the redcoats were being barraged by artillery. Then, a few seconds later, we were in a hand-to-hand battle. Blood was everywhere. Bodies were mutilated, and the cries of the wounded could be heard from miles away. Then I heard Celestia scream in a heart-wrenching way. Then something exploded at my feet. And then I woke up."

"Yikes! That sounds like a hell of a nightmare, sir. But you have to remember that it was just a dream, sir," Timmy says.

But Simon is still convinced that his dream was not just any ordinary dream. "But that is not the point. It felt so real. I just hope it is not a sign of terrible things to come. That is what is so bloody scary about this dream and every time I get that gut feeling, it has never, ever lied to me in my whole life."

Celestia puts her arm around Simon's neck, and his best friends sit next to him and all let him know that they are with him.

"Sir, you have nothing to worry about. We are with you. You have taken us this far, and we are still marching proudly alongside you toward the fray," Timmy says.

"We will always be marching right beside you," Brittany says. "We always have remembered the sacrifices that you have made for us. Wherever you march, we will be there marching too."

"We believe in you, and we will never abandon you, sir," Daisy says. "You are a bright shining fire from Liberty's torch that stands for freedom."

"Do not let that dream bother you anymore," Celestia says, "because we will always be here no matter what. We all love you, sir. And don't take our word for it; just ask our fellow grenadiers, sir." She points behind them.

Simon looks behind them and sees his fellow soldiers in formation, standing at attention. Simon smiles and stands up and walks toward his fellow soldiers. They all stand without a word of command. His staff follow close behind their leader. Celestia shouts a command to the company.

"Keystone grenadiers, present arms!" she shouts with a loud and stern tone.

The Seventy-Sixth salute by presenting their muskets in front of their chests. Simon stands at attention and salutes his fellow soldiers.

"My brave grenadiers of the Seventy-Sixth," Simon says, "never would I have thought that I'd be serving alongside such brave men and women. I haven't said this in a while, and I do apologize. I am very proud of you all, and I would never want to command a different company of grenadiers. Before we march out tonight, I just want to say ..." He thrusts his sword toward the sky, yells the battle cry, and shouts his own personal motto, which rings across the fields and swamps of New Orleans—a motto that will be remembered by all those there to hear the famous words. "For virtue, liberty, and independence! Never shall any foe destroy the power of friendship that shall unite this great nation forevermore!"

The men and women of the company utter a loud cheer. The color-bearers wave their regimental flag and their state flag. The wind catches the flags, and they billow high in the breeze. They hoist their muskets in the air, and their cheers are heard by the whole American camp. Simon looks at his staff, and they salute him. Simon turns around and salutes them by putting the handle of his sword in his face.

Just then Major General Andrew Jackson walks out of his tent and then looks at the Seventy-Sixth. He smiles, astounded by the high passion of the Seventy-Sixth. He thinks to himself, *"I have never seen a company with such strong loyalty and courage for a state, let alone the whole nation. These Pennsylvanians have two qualities that I strongly admire: passion and, above all, their courage for upholding their state's motto."*

He then walks down with several guards around him. Simon sees General Jackson coming toward them.

Simon about-faces. "Seventy-Sixth, attention! Right shoulder your firelock!" He about-faces again. "Staff, form on me!" The staff forms in order of rank. "Staff, attention! Staff, present arms!"

The Seventy-Sixth salute General Jackson. He salutes the Seventy-Sixth. He observes them for their great discipline.

"Major," says General Jackson, "stand your company at ease."

Simon salutes him. "Yes sir! Seventy-Sixth, stand at ease! Staff, stand at ease!"

The Seventy-Sixth stand at ease with their feet eighteen inches apart. The musket is on the right side of each body, the butt of each musket is on the ground, and a hand is grabbing the top of each muzzle.

"Major Smithtrovich, I admire the discipline of your company, just like many of the companies and regiments here. For this raid tonight, I need the best of the best. Is that your company of grenadiers, Major?"

"Yes sir. My grenadiers will not fail you. We have never failed to do our duty in the heat of battle, sir. We suffer small casualties, and yet we cause massive damage to our enemies, sir."

General Jackson smiles. "Major, you and your company may take the lead in the attack tonight if you want to."

Simon smiles and looks at his troops. They are all smiling, knowing that they are pleading not with their mouths but with their hearts. They want to prove themselves to Jackson. Simon looks at his staff, and they all nod to him once. Simon thinks for a few seconds, because deep in the back of his mind, the nightmare is still haunting him. Nevertheless, he still has a war to fight and a company to lead into the hellish elements of the war. He makes his choice.

"Sir, the Seventy-Sixth would be honored to lead the attack tonight. In honor of choosing us, sir. We would like to thank you in the way of the Seventy-Sixth, sir." Simon right about-faces. "Seventy-Sixth Pennsylvania, attention! Staff, to your platoons!" Simon shouts sternly.

"Yes sir! his staff shout, and they rejoin their platoons.

Celestia marches to the first platoon. Daisy marches to her second platoon. Timmy joins Daisy. Brittany stands with her corps marching band.

"The Seventy-Sixth will prepare to pass in review," Simon commands. "Captain Smithtrovich, you march the company in review."

"Yes sir!" Celestia shouts. "The Seventy-Sixth will pass in review. Seventy-Sixth, square formation! Seventy-Sixth, to the front! Forward march!"

First Lieutenant Rose repeats the same command to her platoon. Drum Major Benson gives her commands a little bit differently, since they are a band and not a regular infantry platoon or squad. She points her arms in a V shape with her mace in her right hand. She puts her left hand on her hip with her hands grabbing her hip like the beaks of ducks. She then moves her mace up and down in front of her face and blows her whistle to signal the platoon to mark time and begin a forward march. Jessica and Devin Little stand at attention. Devin plays a drum roll for ten seconds, and then Jessica plays a drum cadence at a brisk tempo. The Seventy-Sixth corps marching band marches forward about twenty paces and then performs a right pivot. The first and second platoons march in place till they are commanded to march forward. The company then marches in a square formation. The band marched in front of their commander. Brittany salutes Major Smithtrovich and General Jackson. They march with such passion and pride. The first platoon begins their pass.

Celestia commands her platoon, "First platoon, eyes left!"

The grenadiers face left as a salute.

"Eyes … front!"

The platoon face forward after they make their pass. The second platoon then begin to make their pass.

"Eyes … left!" Daisy shouts.

They face left and salute their commanders. Simon salutes them. Major General Andrew Jackson is very impressed by their parade-style marching. Once the company marches into their original posts, Celestia orders them to halt.

"Company, take care; halt!" Celestia shouts.

The Seventy-Sixth stop their review pass.

Simon marches two paces forward. "Company, right face! Stand at ease!" He turns to General Jackson. "My unit thanks you, sir."

"You are very welcome, Major," General Jackson says with a delighted voice. "I am impressed with your parade style. Now that I have seen this, I cannot wait to see your grenadiers' fighting style. Be ready one hour before six. Godspeed, you brave Seventy-Sixth." He then walks back to his tent.

Simon turns to his grenadiers, and they smile with excitement. Simon has trouble trying to come up with the words to say to his company. He mutters a bit, and then Celestia laughs. She takes the words right out of Simon's mouth.

"I believe what our commander is trying to say is that he is very impressed and he is glad that we have the opportunity to lead our forces into battle again."

Before she finishes, Simon finally gets the words for the last sentence.

"I am sorry, lads. What I was trying to say before my wife stole the bloody words from my mouth is that it was very unexpected for us to have this honor. Great job, all of you! Now that we have shown Old Hickory that we are partly parade-grounds soldiers. We must show him that we are the bloodiest and deadliest company of grenadiers in the United States."

The Seventy-Sixth and the other American forces are prepared for the raid, but what they do not know is that the attack will be one of the fiercest night attacks in the War of 1812.

2:00 p.m.
British encampment
Lacoste's Plantation

On the British side of New Orleans, earlier in the morning, General John Keane leads an advance guard of eighteen hundred men to the Lacoste Plantation. At this stage of the campaign of New Orleans, General Keane has enough soldiers to overrun General Jackson's whole army. The whole city is lightly defended by American forces. All they would need to do would be march three more hours, take the American soldiers by surprise, and overrun New Orleans. It was that simple. But Keane makes a mistake that will cost him greatly not just on that night but throughout the whole campaign.

One British sergeant major leads a squad of fifteen British redcoats from the Seventh Royal Fusiliers to a home. The home belongs to an American officer named Major Gabriel Villeré. The Sergeant Major walks up to the door and bangs on it.

"In the name of King George III, open the damn door!"

The Sergeant Major continues to bang on the door repeatedly. The officer inside grabs his pistol and stands near the back window. The redcoats bang at the door with their muskets, and just as they break down the door, Major Villeré fires on the first redcoat that enters the house. The redcoat takes the bullet to the head. The major escapes through the window. He takes off dashing for the American lines with the redcoats in desperate pursuit. They fire upon the major but miss him. Major Villeré manages to fire one more shot. He kills another redcoat with a bullet to the heart. He then manages to escape into the trees.

The sergeant major smacks his head with frustration. "Bugger that bastard! Now he knows the position of our bloody camp. Squad, fall back to camp. We must prepare for attack." The sergeant major takes his men through the woods and back toward the camp, where they are met by General John Keane.

"Sergeant Major Oliver Adams, what the hell was that firing?" Keane asks.

"Sir, a bastard American officer has escaped," Adams replies. "Permission to chase after the Yankee, sir?"

"Negative, Sergeant Major. You must remain here with your men. When that Yankee gets to General Jackson, they will attack us, so get your men ready to defend the camp. If you fail me again, I will have you flogged. Now get the hell out of my sight!"

Keane rides off, and Sergeant Major Oliver Adams fills with frustration. He then heads to his tent and sits on a log. He throws his musket against his bed. One of his men enters his tent.

"Sergeant Major, are you all right?" the redcoat asks.

Oliver turns to the redcoat and kicks him outside. The redcoat falls to the grass, and Oliver begins to rant at his men, yelling with enormous rage. "No, I am not mad. I am absolutely disgusted. How can you worthless bastards not be able to kill one puny Yankee? And you call yourselves soldiers of His Majesty's finest. You lot are scum and pure filth. I should have gone back to France when I was given the bloody chance. I was told that you buggers were the best in this bloody land of pirates. I was transferred to this bloody unit after my father died in Baltimore. I have to live up to his bloody expectations now, and I cannot do that if you bastards cannot kill one single Yankee prick. I should have you five shit-filled pukes flogged. Do any of you bastards have a brain in your thick skulls?"

None of his men answer, because they are scared to speak even a single word. Them not speaking just makes Oliver angrier.

"Give me a bloody answer, you filth! Are you British soldiers, or are you cowards? Answer me!" Oliver shouts

One redcoat has the guts to speak. "We are fusiliers, Sergeant Major," he says.

Oliver hears him and rushes over to the redcoat while he quivers with fury. He gets up in the redcoat's face and whispers in his ear. "That you are, no doubt about it. But I also know another thing that you and your brothers are." Oliver then screams at the top of his lungs directly into the soldier's ear, yelling so loudly that he almost punctures the man's eardrum. "You are filth! You are scum! You are worthless! You are a sorry excuse for an Englishman!"

The redcoat grabs his ear and groans in massive pain. He falls to the ground and cries out in pain from his ear.

Colonel Robert Rennie from the Forty-Third Regiment of Foot dismounts from his horse and yells at Oliver, "Sergeant Major, what in the Lord's name are you doing?"

"These men let an American officer escape from his home. Now the officer is running to warn General Jackson of the location of our camp."

Rennie picks the redcoat up from the ground, and two other soldiers take the wounded man to the surgeon. Rennie then turns his own rage to Oliver.

"This is not the way to treat fellow comrades in arms. I know that you are trying to take your father's place, but abusing fellow soldiers is not the way to do it. Your father would be disappointed in you if he saw you doing this. If you want to redeem yourself, do it on the battlefield. Now, I am here to tell you about the whereabouts of the Seventy-Sixth Pennsylvania."

Colonel Rennie grabs Oliver's coat and drags him to the officer's tent. He then shuts the flap and starts to yell at him. He speaks to him loudly, as he is mad at him, but he alternately speaks to him quietly about the Seventy-Sixth.

"What in the bloody hell were you thinking about abusing your fellow soldiers?" he bellows. Then, softly, he says, "The Seventy-Sixth is in New

Orleans." Again he shouts: "You are so bloody lucky that I do not have your sorry arse flogged for that!" Then he whispers, "I spoke to them myself. They number only one hundred. And the ones who killed your father are over there as well." he shouts, "I should just have you hanged, but we need every man we can muster to put the Yankees in the grave. I will not tolerate this kind of behavior in this army. Now, if I see this happening again. I swear on my honor that I will shoot you myself!" Finally, he quietly states, "If you want to defeat that company, then you must kill their leader. Get Simon away from his grenadiers and he will be all yours."

Oliver gives Colonel Rennie a small bag of money for his little favor that he had asked him to do. The Seventy-Sixth had walked right into a trap set by Oliver.

Oliver smiles in a sinister style, and the men shake hands.

"Thank you, sir. My father would be very pleased that you are helping me."

Just then the redcoat Oliver screamed at walks in.

"Colonel Rennie, sir. Corporal Brice Turner reporting." He walks in, and they begin to talk about the plan to trap the Seventy-Sixth and to remove Simon from his only help.

"I guess that worked really well. Sergeant Major, you sure as hell have a ferocious yell," Brice says as he rubs his ear.

"I am very sorry for that, Corporal. How is your ear?" Oliver asks.

Brice makes a joke by pretending that he cannot hear him. They all laugh, but not so loudly that the other officers can hear them.

"I will be alright," Brice says. "Now we all know what the plan will be?"

"Yes. Once the barrage begins. Brice will grab Celestia and take her toward the house. Then I will bring Simon over to the house, and we will trap him inside. And finally, I will have my revenge for his company killing my father. Those bastards will pay dearly for my father's death."

After the plan is discussed, the colonel dismisses them with an angry voice.

"Now you bastards bugger off before I shoot you myself! Now!"

Brice and Oliver exit the tent and return to their own. They both loom at each other, and they both burst out laughing.

"Now that was truly something," Oliver says. "I am glad that you are willing to help me. I just hope this plan works. I have been waiting to pay that bloody bastard back since September."

"From what you told me about Simon when you captured him, Major General Ross decided to spare him when he confessed. I just don't understand why you didn't kill him when you had him cornered at the Potomac River. You could have just said that he was fighting back and he accidently fell onto your bayonet."

"It is not that simple. We had orders, and now I have my father's rank. I can put our plan into action. Just stay out of the camp, because they will bombard the camp before their infantry marches in. Are you with me, Brice?"

He stands up, stands at attention, and salutes Oliver. Oliver stands at attention and returns the salute.

"Let's kill these Yankee Doodles!" Oliver says.

CHAPTER 27

"BY THE ETERNAL, THEY SHALL NOT SLEEP ON OUR SOIL!"

December 23 1814
American encampment
3:00pm

Before we continue the story, I would like to present a little background information about the American commander of the Seventh US Military District, Major General Andrew Jackson. He was forty-seven years old at the time of the battle of New Orleans. He originated from Tennessee, and his abdominal will; his hot, fiery temperament; and his battle-hardened guts earned him the nickname "Old Hickory." Andrew Jackson is one of my favorite military leaders in American history. He had all the right reasons to hate the British. And it all started during the American Revolutionary War. First his brother died of heat exhaustion after the Battle of Stono Ferry in 1779. Two years later, at the Crawford family home, Andrew Jackson and his brother Robert were captured by the redcoats after refusing to clean a British officer's boots. The officer slashed Andrew with his saber in the face. His mother and two brothers died in captivity, and they contracted smallpox during that time.

During the following decades, he was looking for vengeance on the British, and the War of 1812 gave him his chance for payback. In early 1814, President James Madison denied him the role of general, which was

done without Madison's permission. Nevertheless, Andrew Jackson was the only American general capable of the defense of New Orleans. On December 1, 1814, He arrived in the city and declared to the citizens of that city that "they will drive their enemies into the sea or perish in the effort!" He began to act on preparing the city's defense. Jackson's army was the most diverse American force ever created during any war the United States has ever fought. Andrew Jackson created an army of soldiers from every background. Andrew Jackson had the ability to recruit the average man off the street to pick up a musket and make him stand and fight against any foe. The following defenders were at the battle of New Orleans: American regular soldiers, US Marines, militiamen, frontiersmen, French-speaking Creoles; Indians, and Pirates. And the most famous pirate of them all that fought for the Americans was named Jean Lafitte. (We will get to him later in the story.) But the question remained: would these Americans stand and face down the wrath and might of the British military? The Battle of New Orleans would answer that question. Jackson would find out the answer. His ragtag force of four thousand men would face off against eight thousand redcoats who were heading their way.

On December 12, 1814. American fishermen spot the British armada off the coast of Lake Borgne. When the news reaches the city, the citizens panic, but Jackson does not. Instead he puts the whole city on lockdown. This is one of the first times in history that martial law is used in the United States of America.

On December 14, 1814, the Royal Navy engaged an American gunboat flotilla on Lake Borgne. The Americans are outmanned and outgunned. They stand and fight back. The Royal Navy fires hundreds of cannons at the flotilla. The Americans fight bravely until the Royal Navy proves itself once again. The toll is two American officers killed and three dozen wounded, with more than eighty captured.

On December 23, they land and begin their march forward. They number over eight thousand British redcoats. Just as occurred at the engagements before the Battle of Bladensburg in Maryland just four months prior, the Louisiana militia harassed them upon their landing. A small skirmish with the militia drags on for almost an hour. The British suffer fifteen dead and ten wounded. However, the redcoats manage to capture several local militiamen in the fight. It slows, but does not stop, the juggernaut that is marching toward the city.

Back in the American camp, the American forces prepare for the raid, but they still don't know where the redcoats are camped—until Major Gabriel Villeré comes running into the camp. He collapses to the ground out of exhaustion. The American regulars rush to his aid and give him a canteen full of water. Major Villeré chugs the water down within seconds and finally catches his breath. He begins speaking in French, and the American soldiers cannot understand him. He cries as he tries to explain to the regulars.

"Les manteaux rouges sont dans la plantation de mon père."

He keeps saying the same thing over and over again.

"What in the bloody hell is he saying?" one regular says.

"I do not know; I only speak Spanish and German," another says.

The American regular soldiers help the major to his feet, and they walk to Jackson's headquarters. The three soldiers escort him, and then Simon sees the boy crying out and speaking French. He stands up and runs over to the major. Simon begins to talk to the boy in French.

"Quel est le problème?" Simon asks the major.

Monsieur, les homards sont sur la plantation de mon père et ils installent leurs camps au moment où nous parlons, monsieur. S'il vous plaît, où est le général Jackson?

"Êtes-vous sûr?" Simon asks.

"Sir, what is he saying?" Timmy asks.

"He says that the redcoats are at his father's plantation," Simon replies. "Captain Smithtrovich, get the grenadiers ready to march. I have to get him to the general."

Simon and the other regulars take the frightened major to Jackson. Once they reach his headquarters, the boy barges in and tries to get to him, but the guards hold him back. The boy continues to cry out in French.

"Veuillez me laisser passer. Les manteaux rouges sont à la ferme de mon père. S'il vous plaît pour l'amour de Dieu. Je dois vous parler général."

Simon tries to get the guards off of him and tries to calm the boy. The major gets past, and he then cries out to General Jackson, "Général, les homards sont dans la plantation de mon père. huit miles au sud d'ici. Ils sont des milliers."

"For the love of God, I do not speak French. Can someone please tell me what the hell he is saying?" General Jackson yells.

"Sir," Simon says, "He is saying that the British are eight miles south of here on his father's plantation." Simon walks over to the map and he points it out to him. "Right here, sir. It is just a one-hour march away. I've been studying the maps, sir. This right here is the Rodriguez Canal. There, sir, we can build a defense. The redcoats will have to take the canal if they want to reach the city. If we can harass the enemy long enough for our main force to begin to fortify the canal then we can tease the British with just our presence. They will be forced to march towards the canal. What are your orders, sir?"

General Jackson looks at the map. He then looks up at his staff. "Gentlemen, by the eternal, they shall not sleep on our soil. Have the burglar sound assembly and get the men ready to march. We will attack them before they can attack our forces."

The American forces prepare for the attack. They make sure that their muskets, rifles, pistols, bayonets, and swords are cleaned and ready. The grenadiers of the Seventy-Sixth prepare for the battle to come. Major and Captain Smithtrovich clean their muskets and shine their sabers. Neither of them say a word. Timmy melts his own plates to make several musket balls. Daisy cleans her uniform in a bucket of water. She then begins to shine the brass on her bearskin cap. Meanwhile, Brittany and her corps, along with dozens of American soldiers, attend the Mass in the camp. The priest speaks the final words of prayer for the protection of the American soldiers.

"May our Heavenly Father's glory and wisdom spread the seeds upon the earth. May it protect those brave men and women who fight for divine freedom. May they be safe from the horrendous, insidious evil that threatens our great nation, our daily lives, and our citizens. May it be banished forever by the right hand of God. In the name of the Father, the Son, and the Holy Ghost. Amen."

The American soldiers make the sign of the cross.

"Before you dismiss, let us sing 'Old Hundredth,'" the priest says.

A Pianist plays a song on his piano. All the American soldiers begin to sing.

> You faithful servants of the Lord,
> sing out his praise with one accord
> while serving him with all you might
> and keeping vigil through the night.
> Unto his house lift up your hand,
> and to the Lord your praises send.
> May God who made the earth and sky
> bestow his blessings from on high.

(Written by, Thomas Ken, 1674)

The Mass ends, and the priest dismisses the American soldiers.

"Go now to your regiments, and go in peace; glorify the Lord by your light," the priest says.

"Thanks be to God!" the American soldiers reply.

The American soldiers leave the Mass and the return to their units. Private Jessica and Private Devin Little walk back to the camp together. They both worry for each other's safety. Brittany marches with them and gives them direct orders for the battle to come.

"You two will stick next to me like clay, "Brittany says. "Our corps will march together, and we will be in the rear this time. Major Smithtrovich gave me the order just before we left for church. If anything should happen to me, I want you two to take the rest of the corps and run to the rear of the line. Understood?"

"Yes, Drum Major," Jessica says.

"Yes ma'am," Devin says.

Brittany pats them on their backs. "Now, play a march to get the soldiers' morale higher than the stars in the sky. Play 'Over the Hills and Far Away.'"

"Yes ma'am."

Jessica and Devin begin to play the march. Some of the American soldiers sing some of the verses. As they march back to camp, dozens of soldiers form up right behind Brittany and her corps. She looks behind her and is amazed to see dozens of her fellow soldiers marching. The American flags and the regimental colors of various states billow high above the column.

> O'er the mountains' dreary waste to meet the enemy we haste. Liberty commands, and we'll obey. Over the hills and far away. Whoe'er is bold, whoe'er is free, will join and come along with me to drive the British without delay. Over the hills and far away.
> O'er the mountains' dreary waste to meet the enemy we haste. Liberty commands, and we'll obey. Over the hills and far away. On fair Niagara's banks we stand with musket and bayonet in hand. The British are beat; they dare not stay. But take to their heels and run away.
> O'er the mountains' dreary waste to meet the enemy we haste. Liberty commands, and we'll obey. Over the hills and far away. O'er the mountains' dreary waste to meet the enemy we haste. Liberty commands, and we'll obey. Over the hills and far away.

Simon and Celestia hear drums approaching their tent. They step outside to see their fellow soldiers singing loudly and proudly. The energy of men and women whose will and passion for freedom are strong soars through the air. Simon looks on as his grenadiers begin to form their ranks. Simon spots General Jackson on his horse, and Jackson nods to him. Simon nods back, and he and Celestia march to the front of their company. General Jackson was telling him to form ranks. The Seventy-Sixth forms into ranks. The whole company is taking part in the attack. Simon and Celestia take their posts and wait till the whole regiment has formed.

Once they are formed, Simon gives the command to advance: "The regiment will take care to advance! Regiment, to the front! Forward march!"

The American force, which numbered fifteen hundred American soldiers, began the eight-mile march to the Villeré plantation. The drum and fife corps play their music during about half the march toward their target. The rest of the march is all about stealth and taking the redcoats by surprise.

Just two miles from the British camp, the American Regiments break off and divide into their independent companies.

On the Mississippi River, a fourteen-gun ship named the *Carolina* travels parallel with the infantry down the fog-shrouded water while the infantry marches on the land. They begin to close in on their target. The redcoats, who are sleeping in their tents, are totally unprepared for what is about to hit them. The Seventy-Sixth crosses a small field and goes into the trees. A few minutes later, Simon and Celestia lead the Seventy-Sixth down a pathway with only the British campfires to light their way. They move slowly down a dirt trench, moving in a row, making sure they do not make a sound. In a few minutes, they have a clear view of the camp, and they wait for the rest of the American forces to be in position. Simon and Celestia kneel in the trench and note the camp. They speak quietly to each other.

"Those bastards are already sleeping?" Simon says. "Why in the hell would they have lights out already? It is way too early to be sleeping."

Celestia looks up and can see the campfires are still lit. But there are no redcoats to be seen. But then she hears snoring. "You've got me, sir. I can hear them snoring," she whispers

They can see the ship *Carolina* in position and ready to fire upon the camp.

All the American soldiers are in position to attack.

December 23, 1814
7:30 p.m.

The guns of the *Carolina* open fire. Several shells explode right on top of tents. The explosions blast the tents sky high. British redcoats emerge from their tents in massive panic. They scramble to grab their muskets and meet the enemy. More shells fall from the sky, and the British are overwhelmed. Several shells strike dozens of redcoats. One redcoat grabs his buddy, and they try to take cover any way they can. A shell explodes right between them. They both fall onto the ground. One redcoat looks up and sees his buddy's head right next to him. The shells scream as they fly into the camp. The British soldiers cannot see where the cannon fire is coming from. A group of five redcoats is trying to hide, but everywhere they run, a shell explodes in a fiery red-and-orange blast. The *Carolina* fires round shot and grapeshot into the camp. The redcoats begin to panic.

One shell blows several British soldiers away. Shrapnel from the shell strikes them all over their bodies. One redcoat and his comrade are running when a shell lands right between them, and they lose both of their hands. Blood sprays out of their maimed arms. Several British soldiers hide in their tents, and the shells hit the tents. The tents skyrocket into the air in fiery blasts. Dozens of redcoats are lying on the ground with the most ghastly and gruesome wounds. Arms and legs are severed from the lifeless bodies. The redcoats are horrified to see their disfigured comrades on the ground, either dead or crying out the most bone-chilling cries. The American infantry watches as multiple explosions erupt all over the landscape.

Simon is kneeling on the rim of the ditch, not moving a single inch. The only things in his body that are moving wildly are his own eyes. In his mind, he is watching some type of interactive painting that depicts a terrible barrage of shells that begin to destroy the British camp. Celestia and Daisy are standing on the right side of their commander, and they are both amazed yet absolutely terrified of the barrage. They both gaze up into the sky as a shell rains down, striking a lone redcoat. The shell pierces his chest, and the concussion of the blast causes the soldier's body to erupt in a shower of blood, flesh, and bone. They both look away, not believing what they have just seen. They both take one more glimpse of the battle, and they both witness a terrible scene of cannonballs. One of the balls hits the ground and skips, striking three redcoats. The first one is decapitated. A second redcoat who is just ten yards behind that one is struck in the leg by the cannonball. The leg is completely torn off his body. And five yards away, the final British soldier is struck in his chest, which is blown completely open. The soldier gasps as he looks down and watches his own guts spill out of his body. He falls to his knees, and with the force of his knees hitting the dirt, his own heart falls out of his chest. The soldier falls backward, and one of his comrades comes to his aid. All the helper can see is his friend's ribs sticking out of his body.

Timmy stands with his hand over the flint, ready to cock the hammer and open fire when the command is given. He then sees a group of five redcoats trying to escape the hellish cannonade that is slaughtering their men. Timmy can only see a shell that explodes in front of them in a fire-filled blast. When the smoke from the blast clears, Timmy cannot see the redcoat bodies. He thinks he has just witnessed five enemy soldiers literally erased from the earth itself.

Brittany and her corps stand just about one hundred yards away from their comrade's battle stations. They can see only the flashes of the explosions. The sound of the screaming redcoats fills them all with pure horror. Brittany shakes her head and begins to feel sorrow for those experiencing the complete and utter hell that was coming from the river. The artillery barrage finally stops. The first phase of the battle is over. The remaining redcoats think that the attack is over, and all is quiet for a brief five minutes. During those five minutes of silence, the American infantry prepares to begin the second phase.

The Seventy-Sixth are accompanied by a platoon of US Marines under the command of Major Daniel Camrick. The Seventy-Sixth and the marines prime and load their muskets. While they load their firearms, three platoons of the Ninety-Third Highlanders, the Forty-Third Regiment of Foot, and the Fourth Foot run to aid their fallen and severely wounded brothers in arms.

Simon peeks above the brush and sees that a squad of forty-five redcoats from the Fourth Foot are in their range. He ducks back down and signals a private, by whistling like a bird, to communicate with the other American companies that now surround the British camp. The redcoats hear the call but think it is just a random bird. Twenty seconds later, another bird call comes from the northern side of the camp. The call is made by a rifleman from the Beale rifles. The call sounds through the whole woods, and the redcoats grab their muskets and form defensive formations around what remains of the camp.

Among the redcoats are Sergeant Major Oliver Adams and his friend Corporal Brice Turner. They both stand ready for the second attack.

"Where the hell are the Yankees? I cannot see anything," Corporal Turner says to Oliver. Oliver aims his Brown Bess at the trees. All he can see is darkness, but he knows the American's are out there.

"Do not let the dark blind you," Oliver says. "They are out there, and so are the scums that killed my father."

Just then four shots are fired from the redcoat lines. And before the redcoats know what is upon them, the American forces burst from cover and unleash a devastating volley. The Seventy-Sixth join in the volley a little late, but they make their shots count.

"Open fire!" Simon shouts.

The Seventy-Sixth opens fire with a massive volley. The shots from the American forces cut down dozens of redcoats. The whole forest erupts with muzzle flashes, and the British are enveloped in a hailstorm of musket balls. British soldiers are shot all over their bodies, from their heads to their feet. Several redcoats take more than ten musket balls to their bodies. One redcoat is shot five times in the chest. He falls onto a fire pit, and the fire begins to burn his uniform and his flesh. He rolls around on the ground in pain from the flames that are melting his skin.

The American infantry bursts from cover. The American and the British begin to fire frantic volley after volley into each other. The chaos begins with both sides firing blindly into the darkness. Simon sees the US Marines charge forward with their bayonets fixed. Simon unsheathes his sword. He looks to see that his men have already fixed their bayonets without even being ordered to.

Simon shouts to his troops, "Charge your bayonets! Seventy-Sixth Pennsylvania, advance!"

The US Marines and the Seventy-Sixth scream a loud battle cry. They run like hell at the men of the Ninety-Third and the Fourth with their bayonets. Some of the redcoats from the Fourth Foot stand firm along with all the men of the Ninety-Third, while a few others flee from the sight of enemy bayonets. The American forces roll onto the British camp like a piece of paper. Bayonets and swords clash in vicious hand-to-hand fighting. Simon and his grenadiers clash with the Fourth Foot in a bayonet battle. Several redcoats of the Fourth are bayoneted. Celestia and Daisy fight against several redcoats with their bayonets. Celestia fights fiercely until a sudden blow from the butt of a musket causes her to fall to the ground, and she is then forcibly grabbed by Corporal Brice Turner. He is taller and stronger than she. Celestia tries to scream to Simon to have him come and save her, but it has little effect; the sound of musket fire and the screams of soldiers drown out her call for help. Brice drags her to the Villeré plantation, where Sergeant Major Oliver Adams is waiting for her.

Brice restrains her while Oliver puts a cloth in her mouth. Celestia tries to break free, but she is not strong enough to do it. She is then tied to a chair, and Brice holds her hostage near a destroyed house on the right side of the Villeré household. Back in the fray, Simon cannot find Celestia.

"Celestia! Celestia! Where are you!" he shouts.

Then he spots the Villeré house and fights to get to it. Three redcoats try to stop him but are easily fended off by Simon. Simon slices them with his eagle sword. Once he is closer, he looks to his right and sees Celestia tied to a chair. He runs to her, but a grenade bounces off the ground and explodes. The concussive force blows him back away from the entrance. He takes a fragment of shrapnel to his left shoulder. He crashes on the ground and struggles to stand up. He looks up and sees Oliver.

"Well, well, well, if it isn't Simon Smithtrovich himself," Oliver says to him.

"Oliver, is that you?" Simon asks weakly as he stands up.

"Yes, it is. You betrayed our hospitality. I and my father offered you friendship, and you bastards took him away from me."

Oliver punches Simon in the chest and in the face. Simon ducks to dodge a punch, but he gets kneed in the face. And then he gets punched so hard that he falls to the ground. Simon manages to stand up again, only to suffer another punch. The force is so hard that it sends him flying six yards away. He lands on the ground, and the fall stuns him for a few short seconds. Oliver dashes over to him and delivers three more savage punches to the face. Simon manages to block one blow and deliver two punches of his own. Oliver then grabs Simon, headbutts him once, and throws him another six yards away. Simon manages to grab his pistol and tries to fire at Oliver. Unfortunately, the gun is not loaded, so he turns it and uses it as a club. Simon puts up a fierce defense, landing several blows to Oliver's chest and face. Oliver kicks the pistol out of Simon's hand and continues to overpower him. They both have a brutal fistfight that leads into the destroyed house. They both brawl just twenty yards from where Celestia is being held at gunpoint by Brice. Celestia spits the cloth out of her mouth and yells at Simon.

"Come on, sir. Kick the shite out of that lobster!" she shouts.

Brice punches her, and Simon tries to run to her, but Oliver grabs him and throws him against a weakened brick wall. The wall collapses on his legs, pinning him. He tries to break loose, but Oliver kicks him one more time in the face. Then he grabs Simon by his hair and speaks to him in an angry tone.

"Let me tell you something before I stab your brain. I was glad that you saved me at Lundy's Lane, but you should have killed me when you had the chance. Because after I kill you, I will finish off your best friends. I will kill them in the most gruesome manner possible. I will do it slowly and make sure that every minute of it is very painful. I will kill the woman you love. I will cut off her head and put it on a lance for every one of my men to see."

Simon growls as he fills with rage. Suddenly a shot is fired. Celestia looks to her left and sees that Brice has been shot in the head. His body falls to the ground. Celestia looks outside and sees Daisy standing in a firing stance, the muzzle of her musket smoking. Oliver sees that his friend is dead and thrusts his bayonet at Simon. Simon grabs it with a very firm grip. Simon's right eye gazed upon the cold steel that was hovering close to his right eye. Simon was already feeling tired and almost too weak to fight back. He thought he was going to die. Suddenly, his whole life was flashing before his eyes. He remembered every single moment with his family and his friends when they were kids. He then remembers his early military career and fighting his very first battle. He remembered singing to the young lad who was dying before his very own eyes. He remembered seeing his best friends faces when they wanted to enlist and come along with him to the war that brought them closer than ever before. He remembers all the good and bad times that the Seventy-sixth have been through. He mostly remembers his own wife. The fact that he and Celestia were married, he was not ready to go down like this. Leaving his wife that he loved and cherished with all his heart and soul. Simon then remembered what Celestia had said to him the night before.

"And if we are meant to die in battle, I swear we will go down together. We are not going to be away from each other. From now on, we will always be together."

With that specific phrase within his mind, Simon was able to muster up a hidden strength that he never even knew he had within his body.

"You will never lay one finger on her, you demon!" Simon shouts with rage.

They both struggle for a few seconds, but Simon manages to break the tip of the bayonet. He takes the broken tip and thrusts it into Oliver's right eye. Oliver screams out in terrible pain as blood spills out of his eye socket. Simon manages to break free. He grabs Oliver and throws him outside through an unbroken window. Oliver lands on several pieces of broken glass that pierce his back. He stands up and tries to run, but Simon stops him. Simon savagely punches him multiple times in the chest and in the face. Simon shouts and curses with every blow he lands on Oliver With every punch Simon lands on Oliver's face, Oliver's teeth fly out of his mouth. Daisy and Timmy run over to Celestia and cut the ropes with their bayonets. They set her free, and they watch as Simon beats on Oliver. Celestia spots Corporal Turner's blunderbuss, which has a bayonet. She picks it up.

"Simon! Catch!" she shouts.

Simon turns around, and Celestia throws the blunderbuss to him. Simon catches it and begins to club Oliver's back and chest. Simon runs out of breath, and Oliver tries to get up and run, but with one last surge of brute strength, Simon kicks Oliver in the face. The force of the kick stuns Oliver, and with one massive, quick thrust, Simon bayonets Oliver in his chest. Oliver falls to his knees, breathing very heavily. Simon looks down at Oliver and cocks the blunderbuss. Bloodied and bruised, he gives his words of farewell to Oliver.

"Now let me tell you something, Oliver. I saved you because I had compassion for you. But now I realize you are one of those who fight for vengeance. I would say, 'Death to thy tyrants, whose blood is filled with thy hate!' My regards to your father. And I want you to know that I really wanted to be your friend. Unfortunately, I changed my mind."

Simon pulls the trigger, and the blunderbuss discharges. The blast blows out Oliver's back in a fine shower of blood, bone, and flesh. A huge amount of blood spills out of Oliver's back. Simon pulls his bayonet out of Oliver's body, and Oliver's body falls to the ground. Simon kneels and closes Oliver's open eye. He then falls to the ground himself and faints from exhaustion. Just then a British artillery barrage is unleashed on the American forces. The redcoats counterattack. The two sides exchange fire with muskets almost touching. Friendly militiamen lose sight of the enemy and fire into their own men. Celestia runs over to her husband, who is out cold. Several militiamen and grenadiers of the Seventy-Sixth help carry Simon to their original positions. The redcoats begin to gain the upper hand, and the Seventy-Sixth's staff tries to figure out where to retreat to.

"Captain, where is the rallying point?" Timmy asks.

Celestia tries to think amid the battle unfolding around them.

Major Daniel Camrick says, "Captain Smithtrovich, take your troops and fall back to the Rodriguez Canal. Make it fast. My marines will cover you. Go!"

The Seventy-Sixth run out of the ditch, and they begin to retreat to the canal. Several soldiers carry their leader's body. Simon wakes up right as they near the canal. He is in great pain and is weak. He is having a hard time staying awake. All he can see is his comrades carrying him back to the main lines. Celestia looks down at her wounded husband. His face is bruised and bloodied from his wounds and from the beating he suffered. His men manage to get him to the surgeon. They rush him into the tent and they put him onto a bed. As they put him on the bed, Simon groans in great pain. Two surgeons begin to tend to his wounds. Simon suffered several blows and shrapnel to his shoulder and to his leg. The metal is sticking out of his body. The surgeons remove the fragments. Simon is awake but is in so much pain that he is not able to respond. He feels all the things the surgeons are doing to him. Celestia and the staff watch as their commander is tended to. Celestia is upset greatly to see her husband so torn up. She exits the tent and begins to tear up. She puts her hand over her face and cries softly. Daisy comes out and puts her hands on Celestia's shoulders and tries to get her to go back in the tent, but Celestia is hesitant.

"Celestia, your husband needs you right now," Daisy says.

"I just cannot see him like that. It's all because of me," Celestia says as she cries.

Daisy hugs her frightened sister. "Celestia, look at me." Celestia looks at her sister. "You need to be a strong officer as well as a strong wife. He gave everything he had to make sure that you were not harmed, but he expects you to be as strong and brave as you would be in battle. Now I am saying this as a sister: you march back in that tent and you kneel down and stay right next to him. Do you understand me, Celestia?"

Celestia nods, and she and Daisy go back into the tent. Celestia kneels next to her husband. She holds his hand, but for a few moments Simon does not grab hers. But when the surgeons are finished sewing his wounds. Simon grabs his wife's hand and coughs. He is fully awake, and Celestia laughs thankfully.

"Simon, can you hear me?" she asks.

Simon turns his head and looks at Celestia. He smiles with happiness.

"Honey, I'm okay. Thank God that you all are all right. Thank providence you are okay, Celestia. Are the troops okay?"

Timmy comes to his side. He tells him good news about the company.

"Sir, the company is alive. We have had no casualties. Do not worry about that. The only thing you need to do is recover, sir. We will stay alongside you the whole night, sir."

The surgeon comes over to Simon. "Major, we have managed to take out the shrapnel that was in your leg and shoulder. You are badly bruised, and I have checked your teeth. Every tooth is right where it should be. You will be up and fighting again within a day or two. Tomorrow night, we can try to walk, but I am giving you direct orders to stay in bed for tonight and for the rest of the day tomorrow."

The surgeon leaves the tent to go to the second tent and to help tend to the other American wounded. Simon then remembers what Oliver was saying about his father. Oliver's voice echoes throughout his mind.

"Sergeant Major Harry Adams is dead? Timmy, I just killed his son. When did his father die?"

Timmy kneels. "Sir, at Hampstead Hill. We were defending the hill, and he and his marines charged at us. We fired a volley into them, and he was shot in the neck. I saw it all happen."

"Well, who shot him?" Simon asks his friends.

Celestia begins to cry again. Simon looks at his wife.

"Honey, do not be mad at me, but I am the one who killed him. Please don't be mad at me!" Celestia says as she sobs.

Simon rises and hugs her. He brushes his hand against her hair and tries to calm her down.

"Oh honey," Simon says. "Shh, shh, shh. I am not mad at you. You never could have known. I am not mad at you."

Celestia looks at her husband, confused about why he is not angry. "Why are you not mad at me? It is my fault that you are hurt. I don't understand."

Before she can finish, Simon puts his finger on her lips. "I am not mad. I am actually proud of you. I know it hurts to hear that he died, but he was still a lobster nonetheless. He was an enemy of the nation. I am just thankful to God that you are okay, as well as the rest of the company."

Simon wipes the tears from his wife's eyes. She smiles, and they both hug each other.

"I love you, Celestia."

"I love you too, Simon. Now we are going to go check on the company. I will be back in an hour. You relax and get some sleep, sir. We will see you in the morning."

Simon and Celestia kiss, and then staff exit the tent. Simon closes his eyes and gets some much-needed sleep. Celestia and the staff walk off to tell the company about the condition of their commander. They walk to their troops' tents, and the troops rush over to their officers, anxious to know whether Simon is okay.

"Is the major okay, Captain?" one grenadier asks.

"How bad is he hurt, ma'am?" another grenadier asks.

"Is he going to be able to fight?" Jessica asks.

"Is he gonna leave us, ma'am?" Devin asks.

All the grenadiers ask similar questions all at once. Brittany blows on her whistle loudly for five seconds. All the grenadiers stop talking.

"Thank you, Drum Major," Celestia says to Brittany.

"I have always wanted to do that," Brittany replies.

"All of you will be able to rest easy tonight," Celestia says. "Major Smithtrovich is recovering from his wounds. He will need to be in bed for a few days. He is okay and will be back in action soon. I know we are all worried, but he would want us to keep marching on. Now, we had a long and bloody day. Let us all get some sleep and tomorrow get in formation at eight hundred hours. Good night, my grenadiers."

"Thank you for telling us, ma'am," Jessica says.

"Good night, ma'am," Devin says.

The rest of the grenadiers say good night to their officers. They all salute, and they all return to their tents. Celestia and Daisy head to their tent. Celestia looks at the medical tent.

Daisy taps on Celestia's shoulder. "You should go and be with your husband. It would be great for him. I do not mind at all."

"You don't?" Celestia says.

"Not at all."

They hug each other, and Celestia heads back to the medical tent. She enters and sees that Simon is sound asleep. She holds her chest and pulls another bed right next to him and lies down on it. She takes his hand gently to let him know that she is next to him. He gently grips her hand but keeps his eyes closed. Celestia falls asleep right beside her husband, and they both sleep soundly through the night.

The battle itself lasts till three in the morning. The night attack is a success for the Americans. It causes great damage to the southern British invasion force. In this battle, the Americans suffered 24 dead, 115 wounded, and 74 missing in action. The British suffered 46 dead, 167 wounded, and over 50 missing in action. However, the British would argue that this was a tactical victory, for they defended their position. This attack gave the American forces the time they needed to fortify the Rodriguez Canal, which would be the location of the final, and the bloodiest, battle of the War of 1812.

CHAPTER 28

HEART-TO-HEART

New Orleans Campaign, Part 3
New Orleans, Louisiana
American Encampment on the Rodriguez Canal
December 24, 1814
8:00 a.m.

On the morning of Christmas Eve, The American forces are reeling from the previous night's attack. Some of the American forces are helping to construct the redoubts that will be called Line Jackson. In Medical Tent Number 1, Celestia and Simon are sleeping. The surgeon comes and quietly checks on Simon's wounds. Celestia wakes up and looks down at Simon. The surgeon removes his bandages carefully and checks on the stiches. Celestia looks at the wounds and can see that the skin around the stitches is covered in blood. The surgeon begins to clean the blood, but Celestia wants to do it herself. She puts her hand out, and the surgeon hands her the wet cloth. Celestia pats on the blood and on the wound as softly as she can. Simon can feel Celestia cleaning his wounds. He pretends to still be asleep. Once she finishes cleaning the blood off Simon's leg, she begins to clean the blood off his shoulder. She looks down at his face, and then she leans down and gently kisses him on his lips. That kiss is enough to finally wake him up. Simon opens his eyes, and all he can see is his wife's beautiful face.

Celestia sees that he is awake. She takes his right hand and holds it with a gentle touch. "Good morning, honey."

"Good morning, sweetie," Simon replies.

"Are you in any pain, Simon?"

"Just a little bit, but not enough to keep me out of the fight," he says weakly.

"Do you know what today is, Simon?"

Simon thinks for a few seconds, and then he remembers. "Yes, I know. It is our first Christmas Eve, and soon to be Christmas Day, as husband and wife."

Celestia smiles, knowing that is the case.

"You're right. I hope that the lobsterbacks will let us spend time with our men and, most importantly, with each other. Do you have anything in mind, Simon?"

Simon smiles, and they both grab each other's hands and gazed into each other's eyes.

"I can give you a little early Christmas gift that shows you what I have in mind," Celestia says. She winks twice, and Simon knows what she wants to do. They move slowly together, and they both begin to kiss. Simon opens his eyes for a few seconds and sees her cheeks blushing red. Their tongues begin to dance inside their mouths. They both begin to moan. Thankfully they are the only ones in the tent. A massive great feeling courses through their bodies. They pull apart, and Simon runs his fingers through Celestia's hair. Just before they can continue, Daisy enters the tent with a basket of fruits. Simon and Celestia look up at Daisy. Their eyes are wide, and they chuckle a bit.

"Don't try to hide it, you two. I heard all the moaning. There is nothing to be ashamed about. Your husband and wife," Daisy says. They all laugh for a few seconds. "Anyway, I am glad that you are okay, sir. I just brought you two some breakfast. So eat up, lovebirds." Daisy puts the basket of fruit on the table.

"Thank you, Daisy. Happy Christmas Eve," Simon says.

"Happy Christmas Eve, sir," Daisy replies, and then she leaves the tent.

Celestia and Simon both sit up, and they begin to eat their breakfast. Celestia takes a banana, and Simon takes his favorite fruit—an apple, of course. They both begin to eat.

After they eat their breakfast, Simon says, "Honey, can you help me stand up? I want to try to walk."

Celestia is thinking that Simon is rushing his recovery. She still wants him to stay in bed. But she is willing to help him if he feels he is ready.

"Are you sure you want to try to walk? The surgeon told you to stay in bed," she says hesitantly.

Simon pushes his blanket away from his chest and uses his hand to get his body up. Celestia stands up and grabs his hands as Simon makes his first attempt to stand. He can feel the pain in his leg. He groans with pain, but he makes an attempt to stand. Amazingly, he is able to stand on his own two feet with the help of his wife. She still hangs on to him, and then she lets go. He stands still for a few seconds as he slowly takes his first step, and Celestia holds her hands close to him in case he falls. Then he takes his second step, and then another. Celestia is amazed at how her husband is able to walk without any trouble. Just then the surgeon comes and checks on him, and he sees that Simon is standing and walking.

"How are you feeling, Major?" the surgeon asks.

Simon smiles with happiness and gladness. "I feel some pain, but not enough to keep me down. I can thank you, sir, my friends, my grenadiers, and my lovely wife."

Celestia blushes, and the surgeon smiles.

"You are welcome, sir. But maybe you should use a cane just in case," the surgeon suggests to Simon.

He hands him a walking cane, and Simon uses it to stand up.

"Thank you, sir," Simon says.

Simon grabs his coat and walks out of the tent with Celestia by his side. She stays close to him just in case he should fall.

"Simon, take it slowly," Celestia states. "If you feel like you're gonna fall, just tell me."

"I will let you know, but so far, so good," Simon says as he slowly walks step-by-step. They walk toward their encampment. The grenadiers are eating their meals as they see their leader walking toward them. Some of them put their food down and walk over to see their wounded leader. One comes up to Simon and is happy to see him alive and well.

"Praise to the heavens above. Thank God you are okay, sir. How are you feeling, sir?" the grenadier asks Simon.

"I am feeling like a bit of a mess, but on the other hand, I feel great that everyone made it out of the fight unscathed. I wish I could say the same for myself."

"Sir, you must remember that your efforts were not in vain last night," the grenadier replies. "Because if you didn't fight for your wife's safety, she would have possibly died or been taken prisoner by the lobsters. You saved her life, and your leadership helped us live to spend Christmas Eve with you, sir."

"You are right, Corporal. Thank you for telling me that."

You're welcome, sir," the grenadier says.

"I have a mission for you, Corporal. I want you to see if you can find some wine. Tonight we are gonna celebrate Christmas the Seventy-Sixth's way."

"What kind of wine do you want for the men, sir?"

Simon thinks for a moment. "I know I was raised in a barn and I harvested apples, but tonight we are going to have grape wine."

After hearing Simon speak those words, Celestia decides to be funny. She taps on his head. "Umm, sir, did you suffer some brain damage? I thought you were an apple farmer, not a grape farmer." She chuckles.

Simon laughs and explains that tonight must be a night to never forget. "No, my brain is okay. I am just saying that tonight we shall cut cards with the devil himself. Corporal, gather some of the men and head into the city and see if you can find some grape wine. I am sure that there is a winery in the city. Let me know if you found anything when you return."

"Yes sir!" the corporal says as he takes his leave. He then gathers some of the men, and they make their way to the city.

Brittany and her corps are sitting together as they discuss the Christmas carols they will play that night. Brittany writes down the songs on a piece of paper.

"Okay, so far we have 'Joy to the World.' What other songs can we come up with?" Brittany asks her corps. They think hard but can't come up with any tunes.

Celestia and Simon walk behind the corps. The group see their leaders, and they stand up, but Simon puts his hand up and says, "As you were. Happy Christmas Eve, everyone."

The corps members return the sentiment.

"What are you guys up to?" Celestia asks the corps.

"We are trying to come up with Christmas songs to play tonight," Brittany says. "Do you two have any songs in mind?"

Celestia and Simon think for a few seconds, and then it hits them.

"'Auld Lang Syne'!" Celestia says.

Daisy remembers that name, and she jumps up and hugs her sister. "I'm glad you know that one. That was our father's favorite. We will do that one without a doubt."

"I have heard of that song. I remember you two sang it back in 1807. If you two want to sing it together tonight, that will be great." Simon says.

Daisy and Celestia look at each other.

"So how about it, little sis?" Celestia says. "You and me? Just like old times." She smiles and hugs her sister. They feel the joy of Christmas bringing them closer to each other than ever before.

"But this time, Celestia, let us write our own words. And we will dedicate this song to our fallen comrades who couldn't be here tonight."

"That is a great idea. Drum Major Benson, we will help you learn the words to the song, and we also know instruments to play for the music.

"Let us get to work." Brittany says.

Simon and Timmy take a walk together and converse.

"How are your wounds, sir?" Timmy asks.

Simon feels his wound on his shoulder, and it stings him. "I will make it, Lieutenant. Do you miss your family, Timmy?"

"Every single day, sir. I know that they are watching me from up above. And now I have a family down here, and it is the Seventy-Sixth Pennsylvania, sir."

As they walk through the camp, they see their soldiers engaged in other menial activities. Timmy begins to describe how being a soldier has changed his whole life.

"At first I was very skeptical about being in the military. I never found that being a soldier was really worth my while. But when you took me and the girls under your wing, I found out that war not only brings pain and death but also brings you and your comrades much closer than ever before. It bonds complete strangers from all over and turns them into reliant friends that will watch your back as you do the same for them. It is amazing to see a war unite ordinary citizens into men and women who are willing to fight and die for a common cause. I never knew that a company of brave and loyal Pennsylvanians would march over a thousand miles for freedom and for equality in America. In other words, sir, I am glad that you took me and our friends with you. I am glad to be your friend, Simon."

He then puts his hand out in front of his body.

Simon looks at the hand and shakes it. "Thank you, Timmy. You are a great friend. Can you help me to my tent? I need to lie down if I am going to be able to attend tonight's party."

"Yes, I will help you, sir," Timmy says.

Timmy helps Simon to the other side of their camp. Once they get to his tent, Timmy helps him sit on the bed.

"Now, if you need anything at all, sir, just let one of the men know, and they will help.

Simon decides to crack a joke. "Jeez, Timmy, you are starting to treat me like a grandpa."

They both laugh, and Timmy walks away. Simon reaches into his knapsack and grabs his diary. He opens it to a clean page and begins to write.

Dear Diary: Through the last four months, many things have not changed at all. I am glad to be fighting with those that are like my family. In fact, they are my family. Though I can be killed on the field, the bond that I and my grenadiers hold deep in our hearts is something that can never ever be killed. I know I have said this once before, but I must write it down once again. There are so many horrible and gut-wrenching atrocities that one man can do to another man. I will say that I am not innocent in that matter. I have done so many of those terrible things myself. I hope that Jesus himself will forgive me and my fellow countrymen for our sins that we all have committed in this bloody war. I will say that I am afraid to realize that my time is coming. I hate to say it, but I had a nightmare back during my time in Indiana that I was going to die on the battlefield. If it shall be my destiny to die defending my country, then it be that. I will not fear it, and I will not stop fighting till I take my final breath of the great American air. That is worth fighting for.

Simon puts his diary back in his knapsack and then takes a quick snooze.

Christmas Eve
5:00 p.m.

The men and women of the Seventy-Sixth Pennsylvania prepare for the Christmas party of their lifetime. That night is to be a magical night of great moments for every American soldier that will take part in the famous battle of the War of 1812.

In Simon's tent, he does his hair and shaves his facial hair off. During his shaving, Major General Andrew Jackson makes a quick stop to ask him a question.

"Major Smithtrovich, it is General Jackson."

"Come on in, sir," Simon says.

General Jackson enters Simon's tent. "Merry Christmas, Major."

"Merry Christmas to you, General."

"I am inviting you and your staff to dine with me and my staff. Would you and your officers attend?"

Simon finishes shaving his face. He wipes the shaving cream off his face with a towel. "Thank you, sir, but I have to deny the invite. I and my staff are going to spend this night with our men, sir. We have had this planned for the past two weeks. We went and hunted and bought our Christmas meals right before the night attack. Right now, my men are cooking us three pigs, and we were able to get some fine grape wine. I hope you do not mind, sir."

General Jackson smiles; he doesn't mind at all. In fact, he is grateful that Simon and his staff are celebrating Christmas as a company.

General Jackson sits on the bed while Simon puts his dress coat on. General Jackson takes notice of Simon's dress uniform.

"That is a nice coat, Major," General Jackson says.

"Oh, thank you, sir. This is the coat that I wore on my wedding day."

His coat is dark green with black epaulettes and heavy lace on the front of the coat. On the bearskin cap, he still has his American-colored cord and hackle plume.

"Well, I shall not keep you waiting, Major. I wish you a merry Christmas, and I would like to thank you and your grenadiers for your service in the American army.

Simon finishes getting his uniform on, and he salutes General Jackson.

"Thank you, sir. I wish you a merry Christmas and a happy New Year, sir."

Jackson puts out his hand instead of saluting. Simon shakes it.

"And to you as well, Major," Jackson says. But before I leave, I must ask you—how much ammunition does your company have?"

"Sir, we have only about three to four rounds a grenadier, sir. We also don't have enough flints and we're low on gunpowder. If we go to battle again, we will have to turn into marksmen and target the officers. Is this the same with the other regiments, sir?"

Jackson sighs, knowing that what Simon has asked him is true. The American forces have more soldiers than munitions.

"Unfortunately, that is the case, Major. But by the eternal, we shall defend this city and drive those redcoat rascals into the river or the swamp," General Jackson boldly states. He then leaves the tent.

Simon looks at himself in the mirror. He holds his bearskin cap in his right hand as he checks to see if his uniform is perfect. He makes sure that his epaulettes are fitted properly and that his gaiters are in line with each other. He makes sure that every button on his gaiters is buttoned.

Celestia and the girls are in Daisy's tent, getting themselves ready for the party. Their dress uniforms are the same, but Brittany's uniform is a bit different. Her epaulettes are red, along with the lace on the front of her coat. Daisy and Celestia are helping each other with their makeup. Once Daisy's makeup is finished, she helps her sister with hers.

Celestia sits in the chair and closes her eyes and crosses her legs. "Take your time, Daisy. But I am letting you know now—nothing too fancy, but just enough blush to make it last through the whole night. You hear me?"

"Yes, darling. I will make you look like the most beautiful soldier in the entire camp."

Daisy gently brushes the powder onto Celestia's skin. Brittany watches through the tents' flaps and sees Timmy walking toward them. She exits the tent and speaks to him.

"Good evening, Lieutenant. Merry Christmas."

Timmy smiles. "Merry Christmas, Drum Major. Are Celestia and Daisy ready?"

Celestia hears Timmy outside the tent and responds to his question. "We are almost ready. Daisy is helping me with makeup. Can you go and see if the major is ready himself?"

"Yes ma'am. I will go and check on him." Timmy about-faces and heads to check on Simon.

Simon is finally ready for the night ahead. He pulls out a piece of paper on which is written a speech that he and his staff are going to give to the company after dinner. He quickly reads it in his mind, and then Timmy calls from outside the tent.

"Sir, it is Second Lieutenant Miller. Are you ready to go?"

Simon puts the paper in his pocket and walks out of the tent.

"You look very nice, sir," Timmy says.

"Thank you, Timmy. As do you. Are the ladies done with their makeup?" Simon asks.

"Your wife has sent me to get you. Follow me, sir."

As they both walk to the females' tent, they notice a massive fire that is cooking the unit's Christmas dinner. Three big pigs are cooked over an open flame, and the sweet smell of ham makes Timmy's and Simon's stomachs gurgle.

They both pat their bellies and simultaneously say, "I'm hungry! How about you?" They both laugh and snicker.

A few minutes later, they reach the ladies' tent.

"We are here, and we wait for you three to finish," Timmy says.

"Take your time, but please do not take so long," Simon says.

Timmy snickers at the comment.

Celestia calls out to Simon and Timmy, "Simon and Timmy, are you two already drunk?"

"No, honey, we are both sober … for now."

They both laugh.

Brittany walks out first.

"You look amazing, Drum Major Benson," Simon compliments.

"Thank you, sir; you look very handsome yourself."

Celestia steps out, and Simon is amazed by how beautiful his wife looks. She has a touch of blush on her white-powdered face. Simon's heart races, and he walks over to his wife.

Celestia holds out her hand, and Simon kisses it. Celestia blushes.

"You ladies look very beautiful tonight," Simon says.

"Thank you, sir. You men look very handsome tonight."

Simon and Timmy bow, and the ladies curtsy. Simon holds out his arm, and Celestia locks her arm with his. Timmy offers his arm to Daisy. Daisy and he lock arms.

Just then Simon reveals a surprise for Brittany. "Oh, Brittany, I have an escort for you as well. I talked to this man earlier today. He has told me that you two have met before. Drum Major Mattson" The soldier comes and stands right beside Simon, and Simon introduces him to Brittany. "Drum Major Benson, this is Drum Major Ivan Mattson of the US Marines. He has agreed to be your date and your escort tonight."

Brittany is excited to see him. She puts her hand out, and Drum Major Mattson kisses it.

"Ma'am," says Drum Major Mattson, "I am honored to spend time with you, and I would like to get to know you. I sure hope you don't faint on me this time. May I have your permission to have that opportunity?"

Brittany blushes and smiles. She extends her arm and gives him the chance.

"You have my permission, sir. I would be glad to be with you. I won't faint this time. However, I'm not making any promises. Now that we have our dates, it is time to celebrate."

The gentlemen escort their ladies down to the center of the camp, where all the other grenadiers, dressed in their finest uniforms, are waiting for their commanders to join them. The other grenadiers see them coming toward them. One grenadier cheers with joy.

"Hallelujah! Now the party can now begin."

Private Devin and Private Jessica Little begin their piece of music. Jessica plays an Irish flute, while Devin plays his snare drum. They fill the air with a magnificent serenade. The Seventy-Sixth staff are spellbound by the energy of their grenadiers. The grenadiers have such happy faces that they look as if they have won the war.

The company cook informs the company the ham is ready to eat. Some of the men insist that the staff get served, first but Simon speaks to the troops.

"My fellow grenadiers in arms, we will wait till you all are served first. This is our Christmas gift to you all from your own staff. This is for all the valiant efforts in the heat of battle. You have done what your country has asked of you time and time again."

"I *command* that y'all go first," Celestia says.

"It would be an honor if you all went first," Daisy adds.

"I am willing to wait," Timmy states.

"Corps, you all have proved yourselves. I am commanding you to go first," Brittany tells her corps.

The grenadiers feel flattered that their commanders want them to be served first.

Privates Jessica and Devin Little walk up to Brittany. They salute her, and she salutes them both back.

"That is very nice of you, ma'am," Jessica says.

"We do not know what to say, ma'am," Devin adds.

Brittany steps forward and puts her hands on their shoulders. "Do not say another word. Just go and eat up. We need to have the energy for tonight."

The Seventy-Sixth corps marching band files in line, and the cook cuts them each an equal portion of the ham.

"Do not forget," Simon says. "On the left side of the table, I have packed my apples from my family's farm. Each of you can have one if you choose. So eat up everyone, and enjoy."

One by one, the grenadiers are served their meal, which consists of two big slices of ham, two pieces of bread, and an apple. The grenadiers sit down on rows of logs that face each other. They all take their seats, and once all the soldiers have been served, the staff are served their meals. Simon and Celestia sit with their platoons. Daisy and Timmy sit with their platoon. While Brittany and Ivan sit with the corps marching band, They are all enjoying the fine meal that has been presented to them. The grenadiers are all enjoying themselves, and that is just the first event of the evening.

"Gentlemen, how are your meals tonight?" Simon asks.

"The meal is very great. I am loving this meal, sir," says one grenadier.

"This is the best meal I have had in weeks, sir," another says.

"Are your bellies full yet, my comrades?" Celestia asks her platoon.

"Very delicious, ma'am," one of them replies.

"This is heavenly, ma'am. Thank you all for the great meal, ma'am," another states.

Brittany and Ivan begin to get to know each other while they eat their meals.

"So Ivan, where were you born?" Brittany asks him.

"I was born in Charleston, South Carolina. The date was November 10, 1789. I was raised there until I was eighteen years old. I joined the marines when the war began, and I have been in a few battles. For example, I was at Bladensburg and Fort McHenry."

Brittany gasps. "Were you inside the fort when the bombardment was occurring?"

Ivan nods as he finishes his meal. He wipes his face and tries to remember, but every time he does, he is reminded about the hellish conditions that made him feel as though he was not going to live.

"Bear with me on this, because I have never told anyone else about this. As soon as the first shot was fired, I saw the first bomb soaring through the sky as if a space rock were hurtling toward us. The shell didn't strike the ground but exploded about one hundred feet above the fort. The roar of the explosion was so deafening that I thought I was going to lose my hearing. Our men rushed to the cannons, and with one word from Major Armistead, the batteries commenced firing solid shot. I and my comrades were ordered to hide behind the walls on the western side of the fort. We ducked down, and all we could see and hear were the bombs exploding all around us. I saw the bombs blast massive craters in the grass. That was about eighty or ninety feet in front of us. Some of my brothers wanted to run back into the fort. One marine who was right next to me tried to run, and I had to restrain him. He was screaming in pure fear and panic. We hid behind that wall for the whole afternoon and until the next morning. I was so scared that I did not have the urge to sleep for the next two days. I am glad that none of my friends were wounded or killed, but if those redcoats made me realize one thing, it is this: Those who are willing to defend their freedom and liberty must be ready to face the music of war. And the instruments that are played in the symphony of battle are the instruments that will test you to see whether you are willing to stand and fight for those you love and cherish the most."

Brittany is spellbound by the story. Ivan takes a deep breath and sniffles. He then takes a piece of cast iron from his pocket. That is the material the bombs were made of. He holds it in his hand and looks at it.

"At midnight a shell arced over the wall and exploded. This piece struck the wall, and I saw the sparks fly right past my head. It bounced off the wall to my left and landed right next to my foot. This is a souvenir that almost killed me that night."

He hands it to Daisy, and she looks at it. She can feel the weight even though it is a small piece.

"Yikes! This almost hit you? My God almighty!"

"You know you're the first person I have told this story to," Ivan says. "I guess that makes you very special?"

Brittany blushes and grabs his hand. Ivan looks at her face.

"I guess it does," she replies. "And I can smell bravery from a mile away. And I can smell that great scent all over you. I feel bad that you went all through that hell. Look at this on my cheek."

Ivan looks and can see a scar from when she was shot in the face during the Battle of Baltimore.

"Did you get shot in the face?" Ivan asks.

"Yes, I did. I was in Baltimore as well. We were stationed up at Hampstead Hill. We had to face the fury of the British infantry at North Point. We suffered thirty-nine casualties at the end of the day. But the next night, during the bombardment, Colonel Arthur Brooke launched his infantry at the hill. I was fighting alongside my corps, and my mace was on my right on the redoubt. A bullet struck the part of my mace which is called the crown and cut my face. A layer of skin was ripped from my cheek."

"We both seem to have almost met our fates that day. I'm sorry that happened to you," Ivan says.

"I am sorry that almost happened to you as well," Brittany replies.

They take each other's hands and look deep into each other's eyes. They both realize once they touch that there is a connection between them. For both of them, it is love at first sight. Ivan moves in closer to Brittany, and she moves toward Ivan.

"Do you believe in love at first sight?" Ivan asks.

Brittany smiles, and she answers with a kiss. Ivan's eyes open wide, and he then closes them. They kiss for twenty seconds. Devin and Jessica, along with the rest of the corps, witness the sight of love. Devin holds his chest, while Jessica smiles.

"Aww!" Jessica exclaims.

Brittany and Ivan pull away, and their cheeks are blushing as red as Simon's apples.

"That was very romantic," Brittany says.

"That sure was. I can see that you are a woman that is worth fighting for—a woman I would want to be with till the earth reaps its bounty."

Brittany holds her chest as she begins to sniffle. "You really think that about me?"

They hug each other. Brittany cannot lose the smile; it is glued to her face.

"I would fight for you. I would march a thousand miles for you. I would most definitely die for you," Ivan says with a soothing, romantic voice.

Brittany begins to shed tears of happiness. "Ivan, you're going to make me faint. That was the most romantic thing anyone has ever said to me. I can see now that your feelings are true. I know we just met, but you seem to be my prince. I am very glad I met you." She tries to hold back a sob that is itching to escape.

They are now a couple, but their relationship will soon be put to the test in the final battles of New Orleans.

Daisy and Timmy are the only staff officers not connecting on a serious love level. They want to stay friends. Deep down in their hearts, they have feelings for each other, but they do not want to admit it. They are both shy when it comes to loving other human beings because of one reason: during war, if you get too close to someone as a friend or in a love relationship, you might just lose that friend during battle. Tonight is the night that will determine whether Timmy and Daisy will take their relationship to the next level.

After all the grenadiers finish their meals, Simon stands up and gives an announcement regarding the next event planned that night.

7:45 p.m.

"Keystone grenadiers, may I have your attention please?" Simon shouts. All the grenadiers look at Simon.

"I know that Christmas Eve is not a celebration without Christmas carols. Now let us all gather by the fire and sing the songs we all know and love."

All the grenadiers stand up, and they all gather by a huge stock of wooden logs.

Timmy pours some gunpowder out and ignites it. Within seconds, the logs are ablaze with flame. The heat is very warm for all the soldiers. But before the carols can begin, the staff speak some words that they want to say to the company. Celestia stands up and gives a speech to the unit, and while she speaks, the cook gives all the grenadiers a cup of grape wine.

"Seventy-Sixth Pennsylvania, I would like just to say that tonight … I cannot thank you all enough for all the great things you have done for this nation. We have been through the thickest and the roughest patches of this war. We have done the impossible, and it wouldn't have been possible without you all. At the beginning of this war, we had three hundred grenadiers, and now we have one hundred eleven. Through the past two years, one hundred eighty-nine of our brothers and sisters have gone up to heaven." Celestia begins to tear up, and some of the other grenadiers begin to shed tears. Celestia soldiers on. "Those brave souls knew the true meaning of honor and sacrifice. They marched a thousand miles. For freedom and friendship, we salute our fallen friends. That is all I have to say. Now our own commander has something to say. Major?"

Simon stands up and pulls out a paper. "Thank you, Celestia. Now I want to say this to you all. I want to say that no matter what the new year shall bring, whether on the battlefield or within our own ranks, I am honored to have led this group of patriots like you all into battle. We are all sons and daughters of Pennsylvania. We have had our great and our bad times. Nevertheless, we have beaten the odds, time and time again. This is something that I never told you all from the beginning, and now I feel it is the time to do it. I only have my parents left in my family, because the other side of my family are loyalists. But you all have opened up my heart to friendship, and that is something that I never really wanted until

343

I created this unit. I could not have done what I have done without you all. You have changed my life in a massive way, and tonight I am proud to say to you all that I can call the brave and loyal soldiers of the Seventy-Sixth members of the Smithtrovich family! I will cherish your friendship forever till the day that I die. One more thing I want to make very clear is that when the next major battle comes, if I should fall, do not feel sorrow, and do not let the pain halt your advance. Just march on and never, ever end the fight for the glory of Pennsylvania."

All the grenadiers cheer and clap.

Daisy Rose stands up and gives her speech dedicated to her men and to her older sister. "I want to say that I love you all. You all have been the best of friends that I could ever want—especially my sister. Without her, I could not have survived to see the stars up in the sky tonight. In the middle of the battle at North Point, I lost myself amid all the chaos around me. But one woman came to my side and made me realize that she would protect me from all the harm that shall come our way. I will always be thankful, and I would never trade her for another sister in the whole world. She is my whole world, and I will love her forever. To the best sister in the world."

Daisy raises her cup and toasts Celestia. Celestia stands up and walks up to her. They hug each other tightly.

"Oh, Daisy, I am touched. I love you too, little sister."

Brittany then steps up and prepares to give her speech to the company and to her corps. "Tonight I am proud to say that I am very glad I had the chance to march with you all across this great nation. You all have been a great group of friends. If I were given the chance to join another company, I would say to hell with that! My heart belongs to the warriors of the brave Seventy-Sixth. I would also like to say to my friends in the corps band that you are the bravest bunch I have ever had the privilege of commanding. As Major Smithtrovich just said to us, we are a company of brave warriors marching headlong into the fray as a family. We stare the lobsters dead in the eye and say, 'for virtue, liberty, and independence!' We shall stand firm like mountains, and we will maintain our newfound freedom till the earth reaps its overdue bounty. I want to say that tonight I have found someone that has truly become my rock. We both fought on the same battlefield but at different parts of the battle. We both were wounded at the same time. We both have the same rank, and we both command a corps of musicians who love to march to the beat of the same cadence. I want to say that Drum Major Ivan Mattson is now my heart and soul."

Brittany waves to him to stand right beside her, and he joins her. He then speaks about his feelings for her.

"As Brittany just said," Ivan states, "we both seem to have a lot in common. And she has absolutely become my princess. I pray that one day when this bloody war finally ends, we both can begin another chapter in our lives and raise a family. I will stand with her in battle, and I will defend her from every ounce of harm that dares to come between us."

They all clap for the both of them.

Timmy is next, but he is somewhat nervous. But he is feeling that the time to share his feelings with Daisy is now.

"Well," Timmy says, "I am not a man of many words, but tonight will be the exception. I would like to thank the Lord for the starry night and the chance to spend this season of Christmas with the ones I cherish the most. Although there are so many other American units that I could have enlisted in, this is the unit that caught my eye, for these reasons: One, the men and women of the Seventy-Sixth are true and loyal to the cause of freedom; two, this is a unit that fights for more than freedom for this great nation. They fight for the power of friendship that makes our families happy to be Americans. And three, the most important reason to me, because we stay true to ourselves. We fight for our grandchildren so they can be raised in a country that will accept them for what they want to be in their lifetimes. I love you all and will always cherish our friendships even after this war is over. I wish you all a Merry Christmas and Happy New Year."

The grenadiers clap, but Timmy holds his hands up and begins the second part of his speech. He turns his attention to Daisy. "Daisy, can you come and stand next to me please?" he asks. Daisy comes and stands right in front of him. "Daisy, we have known each other ever since we were just six years old. I have come to know you as a friend, a fighter, and a soldier. You have always been my nights dark and days light. Whenever the hot lead was flying all around us, we have always stood by each other's side, since the beginning of the war. We have never separated from each other, other than when we have fallen asleep at the end of the day. I know that you have the same fear as I do, but we cannot let that fear put a dividing line between our friendship. I am hoping that tonight that we can sew the wounds that we both have had inflicted on our relationship."

Timmy pulls out a promise ring and gets down on one knee. Daisy begins to cry. She holds both of her hands over her heart. "With this promise ring that I hold in my hand, I, Second Lieutenant Timmy Miller of the Seventy-Sixth Pennsylvania Keystone Grenadiers, promise to love and cherish our friendship and to always protect you from any harm that we will face when we go into battle. Will you, First Lieutenant Daisy Rose of the Seventy-Sixth Pennsylvania Keystone Grenadiers, accept this ring?"

"Oh, Timmy! I will accept this ring!" Daisy says as she holds back her cries.

Timmy stands up and puts the ring onto her ring finger. They kiss each other, and the whole company erupts in cheers. Brittany looks to her corps and nods to them to begin to play the first Christmas carol. Jessica plays the Irish flute, and the rest of the corps play their instruments. The first song they play is "The Messiah's Coming Kingdom," known commonly as "Joy to the World." All the grenadiers put their arms around each other and sway from side to side.

> Joy to the world; the Lord is come!
> Let earth receive her King!
> Let every heart prepare Him room,
> And heaven and nature sing.
> Joy to the earth, the Savior reigns!
> Let men their songs employ
> While fields and floods, rocks, hills, and plains
> Repeat the sounding joy.
> No more let sins and sorrows grow,
> nor thorns infest the ground;
> He comes to make his blessings flow
> Far as the curse is found.
> He rules the world with truth and grace,
> and makes the nations prove
> The glories of His righteousness
> And wonders of His love.

(Written by, George Frideric Handel, 1719)

Celestia, Daisy, and Brittany stand side by side. Celestia speaks to the company.

"This is a song that I and my sister have been singing every Christmas Eve, and tonight we want to sing it to all of you."

"We decided to change the words and make them match the time of day, since we are in a war," Daisy says.

"This song goes out to all the one hundred eighty-nine comrades in arms who have given their lives for freedom and for friendship. The song is called 'Auld Lang Syne,' which means 'times long past.'"

(Song was written by, Robert Burns, 1788)

Jessica plays her Irish flute while he lightly taps his drum. Another grenadier plays his trumpet.

"When comrades cannot be here, havin' marched a thousand miles, we sing a tune to honor them to remember Auld Lang Syne," Celestia sings in a clear voice.

Daisy joins her in the second verse. "So take your glass and raise them high, just as the rising of the sun, and honor we will those gone before as we salute Auld Lang Syne. As we salute Auld Lang Syne."

Brittany joins in, and now it has become a trio. They all sing with heart and pride on the first chorus. All the grenadiers lock arms and sway from side to side. "For comrades not here, my friends, havin' marched a thousand miles for freedom and friendship, we honor the Auld Lang Syne."

They take a fifteen-second instrumental break, and then Brittany takes the lead on the third verse. "Our paths shall cross again one day. In time we shall reunite. For family we shall remain, over the hills and o'er the main. So take your glass and raise them high, just like the rising of the moon, and honor we will those gone before as we salute Auld Lang Syne."

Then the whole company helps them sing the final chorus. They all sing with great energy. The whole American camp can hear the Seventy-Sixth sing the song. "For comrades not here, my friends, havin' marched a thousand miles for freedom and friendship, we honor the Auld Lang Syne. For freedom and friendship, we honor the Auld Lang Syne."

The whole company erupts in cheers. Some of the grenadiers even fire off their muskets into the darkness. Throughout the rest of the evening. The Seventy-Sixth spend time singing more carols and telling stories to each other.

The next two weeks will go by fast, in that period of time, the soldiers of the American forces cherish the days. What the grenadiers of the Seventy-Sixth Pennsylvania do not know is that they are about to suffer a tragic loss, for the battle of New Orleans will go down as the bloodiest battle of the War of 1812. In the Battle of Bunker Hill, the redcoats suffered over a thousand casualties and captured the hill after three assaults. In this case, history could repeat itself; but the question remains: will the United States accomplish the impossible, which their fathers and grandparents at Bunker Hill failed to do?

CHAPTER 29

A FIRST TIME FOR EVERYTHING

New Orleans Campaign, Part 4
Rodriguez Canal, New Orleans, Louisiana
American encampment
December 25, 1814
Christmas Day

It is Christmas Day for the American, British, and Canadian Armies, although a war is on. Some of the fighting is called off for the rest of the day as a Christmas truce. The Seventy-Sixth Pennsylvania awaken and are amazed to see snowflakes falling from the sky. Celestia and Simon step outside and are awed by the sight of their first snow of the year. The snow is light but is thick enough to see the shapes and designs of it. Celestia holds out her hand and catches a decent-sized snowflake in the palm of her hand. Simon opens his mouth and catches three snowflakes on his tongue. Celestia wraps her arms around Simon's chest.

"Merry Christmas, Celestia," Simon says.

Celestia kisses Simon on the cheek. "Merry Christmas, Simon."

Timmy and Daisy walk out of their tent and are amazed by the wonderful flakes falling from the clouds above. The sight of snow is a true sight of Christmas. Today is a day to spend personal quality time with each other, but they still have to be on alert. The staff gather around and all wish each other a joyous and merry Christmas.

"Today there will be no drills," Simon says to his best friends. "Nothing today but just having fun. Those are my orders for today. Merry Christmas, everyone."

The staff breaks off, and Simon and Celestia decide to take a stroll down to the ramparts. The snow continues to fall gently to the ground.

"You will get a part of your gift in a few minutes. Then, on New Year's Eve, you and the whole unit will get the gift," Simon says.

"I cannot wait. But for you I shall wait," Celestia says.

They reach the rampart, and there is no other fellow soldier to be seen.

They look beyond the foggy field in front of them. The fog is so thick they can't see beyond forty yards. They stand close together as they gaze at the foggy grounds.

"I hope that today will be very romantic, Celestia thinks to herself. *I hope that this will be perfect. I now have my chance to make this fantasy come true."*

Celestia wants to have an appetizer before the main course is given to them later. She looks around to see if anyone else is around. Once she sees that they are alone, she grabs Simon's hand. They look into each other's eyes.

"Did I ever tell you how handsome you look in that uniform?" Celestia asks erotically.

Simon knows what she wants to do, but it is too early. Celestia gently rubs her hand on the right side of his cheek.

"I guess maybe a few times. I know what you're thinking, and I am flattered, but we are out in the open. We should find some cover."

Celestia puts her finger to his lips, and Simon stops talking.

"It is okay, sir. We are perfectly fine here. The other soldiers do not come down here till about nine in the morning. We have one more hour till then. We have that long to have an opening act."

Simon then smiles and kisses her hand. Simon takes her hand and asks her for a dance. What Celestia doesn't know is that Simon, Brittany and the Littles hatched a plan last night before they went to bed. Hidden in the fog, they both have their instruments with them. As Simon says those words, Brittany directs them to play a slow love march they wrote. They call it "The Fog of Love." Jessica plays her fife while Devin lightly taps on his drum. Celestia hears the music and looks out toward the fog.

"Celestia?"

"I would love to dance with you, honey," Celestia says.

Celestia smiles, and they move to the spacious section of the rampart and begin to slow dance. Simon twirls Celestia around twice, and they hug each other very closely. They close their eyes and kiss. Celestia begins to lose feeling in her legs. They both moan when they kiss. They both were very aroused. The feeling is so strong that Celestia has a tear run down her face.

"Oh, Simon. I love you," Celestia moans.

"Shh. Don't cry. I love you, too," Simon says. They pull each other closer as they continue to kiss. Celestia begins to moan pleasurably as if the feelings inside her are hurting her. She begins to feel weak in her legs. She keeps herself up on her feet, but with every kiss and feeling the warmth of her husband's body, she is growing even weaker.

"Simon, I cannot feel my legs," she says weakly.

Simon pulls his face back. "Do you want to take a break? I will be okay if you want to."

"Yes," she replies. They both take a seat. Then Simon calls out to Brittany and the Littles. Celestia looks behind them and sees them walk out of the fog.

"Merry Christmas," Brittany and the Littles say to their commanders.

"Merry Christmas, you three. Thank you for helping me out this morning."

Brittany and the Littles salute Simon.

"It was our pleasure," Devin says.

"It is so wonderful to see a couple in love," Jessica says. "Love and friendship will never be destroyed by those lobsters."

They all begin to head off, but Celestia wants to know the name of the song. "Brittany," she asks, "what was the name of that song?"

"That was called 'The Fog of Love.'"

Brittany and the Littles walk back to the camp.

Simon and Celestia sit on top of the rampart and stare at the fog. They begin to have a conversation about their history.

"Would you have believed that we would be here together?" Celestia asks Simon.

Simon does not answer for a few seconds but finally speaks up. "Celestia, you remember that nightmare that I had a few days ago?" Simon asks.

"Yes, I do; why do you ask?"

Simon had dreamed about something else that night as well, and the two of them were in his dream. Simon takes a deep breath and holds both of her hands.

"Celestia, I am not going to lie, but ..." He hesitates, fearing that he will upset his wife.

"Simon, we are married. You can tell me. Is there something about the dream that you are not telling me?"

"Yes, there is. Hear me out on this. Well, in that dream, you and I were battling on this very redoubt, and all we could see was thousands of British soldiers. It looked like there were millions of them. We fired volley upon volley into them. When the lobsters returned fire, you and I kept getting shot. The next thing I knew, we were both on the rampart with our backs on it, and we were bleeding from several wounds. The next thing I saw was the faces of our grenadiers. They had pure sadness in their eyes, and then the nightmare was over." He looks over at Celestia.

"Simon, you know that is a dream that some soldiers have. But if we are going to die in battle, we will fight and die side by side. We will stay together no matter what the lobsters throw our way. Now let us forget about that and think happy thoughts."

Simon smiles, and they hug each other. Then Simon asks a funny question.

"Have you ever noticed that we have very sensitive emotions?" Simon asks.

Celestia snickers and then laughs so hard that it hurts her stomach.

Simon shakes his head and crosses his arms. "See? Prime example," he says with a chuckle.

Celestia cools off and answers the question.

"Absolutely, sir. But I want to say this straight out. I want to give you my gift to you. May I have your permission, sir?"

Simon knows what she is talking about and is ready for what is about to come.

"Yes, I would love to, ma'am. Lead the way, honey."

They both walk back from the ramparts and head up toward their camp. Simon spots Timmy and tells them to not disturb them.

"Second Lieutenant Miller, we do not want to be disturbed for the next two hours."

Timmy is confused for a few seconds, but then he realizes what they are about to do.

"Go get 'em, sir. Good luck, sir," Timmy says.

They shake hands, and Timmy stands guard over their tent. Simon enters the tent, and a few minutes later, all Timmy can hear is the sound of Celestia and Simon moaning.

"Oh, Simon. I love you so much," Celestia moans.

"I love you, too, honey!" Simon says.

When Simon and Celestia finish making love after an hour and a half, they look at each other and ask each other the same question: "How was that, honey?"

"That was a great first time. I love you, honey," Simon says.

Celestia kisses Simon's sweaty mouth one more time. "I love you too."

They get dressed, exit the tent, and go back to their duties.

"So how was your first time, sir?" Timmy asks.

"Words cannot express what I have just experienced. Thank you for guarding us. Simon says as he wipes his sweat off his head.

After lunch, Celestia and Simon see a large group of their American regular troops at a table near the chow tent. They walk over to see that Daisy and Timmy are engaged in an intense game of chess.

"Ah! The game of chess. Who is winning here?" Celestia asks.

"So far it is tied. But they haven't made a move in ten minutes," Brittany says.

They both have their kings in check, and they both eye their pieces that are still standing. Timmy makes a move for his rook, but he hesitates. He puts his hand back down, and then Daisy tries to attempt a move but realizes that it would cost her the game.

Simon stands and studies the board, and he realizes that they can't make a move without being checkmated. He knows that the game is a tie. Simon whispers this into Celestia's ear. She looks at the board and sees that he is right. They do not say a word, for they do not want the players to figure it for themselves.

Ten minutes later, with Daisy and Timmy still not having made a move, Timmy finally realizes it is a tie.

"If either one of us moves anything, our kings will be exposed," Timmy says.

Daisy notices this after a few seconds, and she stands up and puts her hand out to Timmy. "A fine battle, Lieutenant," she says.

Timmy smiles and stands, and they shake hands.

"A fine battle indeed, Lieutenant," Timmy replies.

They salute each other in honor of a great match. The grenadiers cheer.

Later that day, the Seventy-Sixth Pennsylvania takes it easy, celebrating Christmas. What they do not know is that the American Garrison has a plan for New Year's Eve. They are going to make a statement to the British that if they want to take New Orleans, they will have to bleed for it.

December 31, 1814
New Year's Eve
Six hours till midnight

American regimental commanders, including Major and Captain Smithtrovich, are passing out sheet music to their men, for they are going to sing a tune to the British who were opposing them. By November 1814, Francis Scott Key's poem "The Defence of Fort M'Henry," now known as "The Star-Spangled Banner," had gained popularity in the United States. Now the American garrison at New Orleans is ready to sing it to the redcoats. All the American soldiers learn the words, while the drum and fife corps and marching bands learn the music. Brittany is teaching her corps marching band the music.

"Band, to the ready!" Brittany commands.

The corps stand at preattention but not at full attention.

"Seventy-Sixth corps, ten hut!" she commands.

"Hup!" her corps shouts in unison. They stand at the position of attention.

Now, have you practiced the sheet music I gave you last week?" Brittany asks her corps.

"Yes ma'am!" they shout.

"Really? I hope you all did, because we will not be playing as a corps. We will be playing as an orchestra with the other regimental bands. There is no room for being one or two notes behind on this one. We need to show those lobsterbacks that we Americans are here to stay. And if they want to win this battle, then by God, they will have to bleed for it. Do you understand me?"

"Yes ma'am!" the corps shouts.

"Good. Now, this will be the longest song we will have ever played. We only have time for one run, so show me that you have rehearsed this."

Brittany stands at attention. "Corps, roll off!" Brittany commands.

The band ready their instruments to play.

Drum Major Brittany Benson blows her whistle in a four-second note, and then she blows four quarter notes. The corps begins to play the song.

The snare drummers play a drum roll and are followed by the brass and woodwind players.

With their bodies in perfect posture, and with no facial expressions, some of the American regulars stop and watch as the band plays.

"That sounds very good," one American regular says.

"Good? They're astounding!" another says.

Brittany directs the band with her hand movements. Brittany eyes her corps as they enter halfway through the song.

"Never shall I doubt this noble corps ever again," Brittany thinks to herself.

Just then Drum Major Ivan Mattson walks with a few other marines to see where the music is coming from. They turn into the Seventy-Sixth's camp, and he sees Brittany directing her corps. Ivan's friends are impressed by the discipline of the Seventy-Sixth Corps Marching Band.

"Whoa, Ivan. You were not joking. They do sound very great," one marine says.

"Yes, they do sound very great, but you lot are very great as well. I wonder how we would sound when we are combined?" Ivan thinks out loud.

"We will not know till tonight, sir, but I bet we will sound like nothing those redcoats have ever heard before," another US marine declares.

"That we definitely will," Ivan says.

The Seventy-Sixth corps marching band finishes the final notes of the song.

"Corps, order arms!" Brittany commands.

The corps order their arms. Brittany is impressed by their performance.

"Comrades, you have nailed it. I am very proud of you all. Gather here a half hour before midnight. Drink plenty of coffee to keep you awake. Corps, dismissed!"

The corps breaks ranks, and Ivan comes and talks to Brittany.

"Wow, Brittany, that was very impressive. My compliments," Ivan says.

"Thank you very much, Ivan. We always strive to be our best."

"Would you like to go on a walk with me? There are some people I want you to meet."

"Sure. I would like that," Brittany kindly says.

They walk down to the US Marine encampments. Ivan is curious about how she trains her corps.

"How in the world do you do it?" Ivan asks Brittany.

"Do what?" she says.

"Train your corps. Because I was given command after my friend was killed at the Battle of Bladensburg. He was our drum major at the time. He was known only by his last name, Morrison."

"I am sorry to hear that. How did he die?" Brittany asks.

"Well, we marched with Commodore Joshua Barney, and once we formed our ranks, a volley erupted from the trees. I was looking at Drum Major Morrison for a few seconds. Sadly, I watched as he was shot in the head. I saw the back of his head explode. Then I had to take his command and help get the corps out when it came time to retreat. I was honored to take the command, but I didn't want it to happen that way."

"You know, "Brittany says, "I actually remember seeing you at that battle. I and my sister were leading our platoons into the final line of defense, and I think we were marching right behind you. I heard your corps playing quite fine marches."

"Thank you. Like you just said, we strive to be the best," Ivan says jokingly.

They both laugh at the fact that Ivan threw her comment right back at her. A few minutes later, they reach the US Marine camp. Ivan takes

Brittany to see his corps. Once they reach the band's tents, Ivan calls to his men.

"Detail, fall in!" Ivan shouts. He then blows on his whistle for six seconds. His corps falls into ranks. "Detail, attention! Ivan shouts.

The corps stand with feet together and parallel; stomachs in; chests out; shoulders back; elbows frozen, slightly bent; chins out; eyes facing above the horizon with pride; instruments parallel to their spines; and hands in loose fists. Not a single word is spoken.

Brittany observes their great posture and attention to detail.

"They look like they were very well trained," Brittany says. "The question I want you and your corps to answer is, How do they sound?"

Ivan smiles and takes his post about seven paces from his corps.

"Detail, roll off!" Ivan commands.

"Up!" his corps sound as they raise their instruments.

Ivan raises his hands. "Corps, play 'Yankee Doodle'! And!" He moves his hands as he commands his corps. The drummers and fifers play "Yankee Doodle." Brittany gets moved by the tune and begins to tap her left foot. She then begins to move her head up and down to the beat of the march. Once they finish playing the march, Ivan directs them to play a tune that Brittany is very familiar with. He blows his whistle the same way Brittany does with her corps.

The band begins to play "The British Grenadiers." Ivan looks back at Brittany and can see the sweet smile upon her face. Brittany begins to sing the lyrics in her head as the marines play the march. Ivan signals his corps to stop at the end of the song. He circles his hands and then points outward with his arms in the shape of a V.

"Detail, stand at ease!" Ivan commands.

The corps stands at ease. Ivan about-faces, and he salutes Brittany with his mace. Brittany marches toward him and stands six paces away from him. She stands at attention and salutes Ivan with her mace. They hold the salute for five seconds and then stand at ease.

"Drum Major Mattson, I am very impressed with your men. I salute you and your corps as noble soldiers of music."

"Drum Major Benson, would your band want to accompany our band tonight?" Ivan asks.

Brittany shoulders her mace and marches four paces. She then salutes Ivan and gives her answer. "The Seventy-Sixth Corps Marching Band would be honored to accompany you," she says with great pride.

Brittany and Ivan looked at each other, and Ivan asked a very important question to her.

"Brittany, may I offer my strong arm for your protection?"

Brittany's eyes open wide, and she then blushes. Brittany steps back one pace and puts her left hand in front of her body. Ivan kneels on his right leg and kisses her hand three times. Brittany puts her right hand in front of her mouth.

"Aww, sir!" Ivan's men say.

Ivan quickly looks back at his men and sternly says to them, "Detail, dismissed!"

His men break ranks. Ivan stands back up on his feet.

"I am touched, Ivan. That is very sweet to offer your protection. I trust you," Brittany says.

They hug each other tightly. Then Brittany tells Ivan something that she has been waiting to tell a man. "Ivan, I am glad to tell you that you are my first love. I am so glad that you are the first. I honestly hope that you are the only one."

Ivan pulls his head back, speechless. His heart is bursting with emotion.

"I am really your first love?" Ivan asks.

Brittany turns away for a second. She then looks back at him and moves in close to him. Ivan closes the gap. They both close their eyes and kiss. Their maces drop to the ground, and their tongues dance together inside their mouths. Ivan moans once, and Brittany moans a few short moments later. They rub each other's back and head. After they both pull their heads back, all they can do is smile at each other.

"That is my second time doing that kind of a kiss," Ivan says.

"I guess there is a first time for everything. Would you want it to happen again?" Brittany asks Ivan.

They both pick up their maces. Ivan smiles and escorts Brittany to his tent. Brittany takes off her bearskin cap, and Ivan takes off his shako. They both lie down on the bed.

"May I have your permission? Ivan asks.

Brittany feels herself becoming very aroused. Brittany nods once in agreement and begins to make love. After an hour of making love, they finally finish, panting hard.

Ivan stands. "Well, that was a hell of a first time.

"Brittany puts her coat back on. "That is right; no doubt about it. I am very touched that I mean that much to you.

They both get their uniforms back on and sit on the bed.

"Thank you," Ivan says.

Brittany hugs him. "You're welcome," she says as she buttons her coat. "I will see you later tonight. Can you escort me back to the camp?"

"I would love to," Ivan exclaims.

They exit the tent and put their hats on their heads. Ivan puts out his arm as an escort. Brittany happily takes it, and Ivan escorts Brittany back to the Seventy-Sixth's camp.

A few minutes later, Ivan has escorted Brittany back to the camp. Just before the two take separate paths till the night comes, they give their parting words.

"I just want you to know that's what we did today … I would have never done that with anyone else. You must be very special," Ivan says.

"I can say the same thing about you. You are very special to me. Till we see each other tonight," Brittany says sadly.

They do not want to part ways, but duty is calling, and they must answer. They let go of each other's hand and walk away.

Brittany runs through the camp and tries to find Celestia. She spots her near the chow tent and runs up to her in a state of panic.

"Captain, may I have a word?"

"Um, sure?" Celestia says with a confused tone.

Brittany and Celestia head to Brittany's tent and close the flap.

"You are not gonna believe what happened!" Brittany says, sounding panicked.

"Whoa! Whoa! Calm down. Now tell me what happened!" Celestia exclaims.

Brittany takes a deep breath and then explains. "Now, before I tell you this, I am trusting you with this because you are like family to me, ma'am. You know that other drum major, Ivan Mattson?"

"Yes. What about him?" Celestia says.

Brittany hesitates for a few seconds and then finally spills her guts. "He and I went through our first time. And it was amazing!"

Celestia is confused but is also proud for her as well. "Well, you should be proud of yourself. If you love him, then there is nothing wrong with that at all. It is humanly normal, that experience."

"I guess you're right, ma'am." Brittany says with an accepting tone. She knows that she liked it. Then Celestia lets her know her little secret about her and Simon.

"Between you and me, including my sister, I and Simon went through our first time on Christmas Day. And It was so bloody amazing. And you helped me with your marching song that you played for us that day." Celestia chuckles and giggles.

Brittany's eyes are wide open, and she nods rapidly. "That is really great, ma'am. I am very proud of you two. I guess it is true what they say; there is always a first time for everything, right?"

"That is right, Drum Major. Now, let us get ready for tonight. I will let you get your hair fixed, because seriously, it is a bloody mess."

Brittany feels her hair all out of place. Celestia leaves the tent, and Brittany then begins to fix her hair. She grabs her hair comb and begins to gently brush her hair. It takes her about fifteen minutes to fix her hair. She sits on her bed and prepares to take a quick snooze. She gazes at the top of the tent. She then closes her eyes.

Back in the US Marine camp, Ivan is doing the same thing. He is lying in his bunk, deep in thought. He is not against what happened. He is all for it, and he decides that he will take it to the next level in their newly formed relationship. But he will wait till after the war. However, they have the same question in their heads: Will they both live to the end of the war?

CHAPTER 30

"THE STAR-SPANGLED BANNER" IS SUNG

New Orleans Campaign, Part 5
Rodriguez Canal, New Orleans, Louisiana
Half an hour till midnight
December 31, 1814

The whole American garrison, comprising four thousand regulars, marines, militias, and special forces, is waiting for the New Year. All the bands from each unit gather at the front of the redoubt alongside their regiments. The Keystone grenadiers gather in the middle alongside the US Marines.

General Jackson steps onto the redoubt and speaks to his garrison. "Tonight, my comrades in arms, we shall let the lobsters know that we are here to stay. They do not pose a major threat. We will be singing 'The Star-Spangled Banner,' which Francis Scott Key wrote while watching the brave defenders of Fort McHenry. I want all the color-bearers to stand with their commanders on the redoubts. Company commanders, join up and form a single-file line from left to right."

Every color-bearer from all the units at New Orleans brings the flag of their state and the Stars and Stripes. The Seventy-Sixth bring their flags forward, which include the Pennsylvania state flag and their regimental flag with the big "76" on it. Simon and his staff stand side by side with their flag-bearers. They see dozens of American flags billowing in the breeze upon the redoubts.

Back in the rear ranks, about fifty yards from the redoubt, dozens of regimental marching bands form their ranks. The Seventy-Sixth and the US Marine marching bands form their ranks right beside each other. Brittany stands at her post, and then Ivan stands at his post. They look at each other and shortly speak with each other.

"Lovely night, isn't it?" Brittany says.

"I agree. How are you doing?" Ivan asks.

"I am feeling good. Listen; I am actually happy about what happened today. I am happy we got to spend personal time together."

They smile at each other, and then General Jackson rides by checking the ranks of the bands. All the soldiers stand at attention when he rides by each of the corps.

Back at the redoubt, the Seventy-Sixth stands amazed, seeing all the flags.

"My God, this is so amazing," Simon says. "There must be a hundred flags here. Those lobsterbacks are sure in for a show."

"I cannot believe this," Daisy replies. "This is gonna be so darn patriotic it is not even funny."

Celestia stands upon the redoubt and is awed by the awesome spectacle.

"I never knew that we would live to see this day come. Let this be a day for all of us to remember."

Timmy stands right next to Daisy, and he has one thing on his mind. "I know the redcoats will be able to hear us, but how in the world are they going to be able to see us?" he asks his friends.

"I am pretty sure the general has that covered, Timmy. Let us all just enjoy this moment together as a company."

Celestia then grabs Simon, Daisy, and Timmy, and she pulls them close to each other.

"We are more than a company. We are all a family!" Celestia declares.

Just as they are about to begin playing, a British light company is patrolling near the American redoubt about 120 yards away, and they are trying to see what the Americans are doing. Leading them is Colonel

Robert Rennie, who leads sixty-five men from the Forty-Third Regiment of foot.

"Platoon, halt; take a knee," Rennie commands his men.

His men take a knee and see the American forces upon the ramparts. They are stunned to see the Americans' flags.

"Hmm, I wonder what those Yankees are doing?" Colonel Rennie says.

He and his men observe the American soldiers with their flags.

"What the bloody hell is going on here?" one redcoat says out loud.

"Damned if I know!" another one says.

Just one minute before midnight, the bands are ready to play and the color guards have their flags presented. Several American cannons are pointed upward toward the sky, loaded with handmade rockets.

"Gentlemen, we are here tonight to let those lobsters know that if they want to take New Orleans, they will have to step over our cold and dead mutilated bodies. Artillery commanders fire the rockets. It is time. Drum majors, commence music. And my friends, let us celebrate our new year.

"Cannons one through six, commence firing!" An artillery commander commands his battery.

The rockets fire into the sky and explode, and rocket glares shine bright in the sky. Three rockets are fired, and each rocket is of a different color. The one on the right flank is red, the middle one is white, and the one on the left flank is blue. The band's drummers start a loud drum roll, and then the rest of the band play their music.

The Forty-Third Regiment can see the American colors waving on top of the ramparts.

Rennie's fellow soldiers are shocked by the musical score and the light show. The whole American garrison begins to sing "The Star-Spangled Banner." They all sing out with pride and lots of energy. The redcoats are able to hear the whole song.

O say can you see by the dawn's early light,
what so proudly we hail'd at the twilight's last gleaming,
whose broad stripes and bright stars through the perilous fight
O'er the ramparts we watch'd were so gallantly streaming?
And the rocket's red glare, the bomb bursting in air,
gave proof through the night that our flag was still there,
O say does that star-spangled banner yet wave
O'er the land of the free and the home of the brave?

On the shore dimly seen through the mists of the deep
Where the foe's haughty host in dread silence reposes,
what is that which the breeze, o'er the towering steep,
as it fitfully blows, half conceals, half discloses?
Now it catches the gleam of the morning's first beam,
in full glory reflected now shines in the stream,
'Tis the star-spangled banner. O long may it wave
O'er the land of the free and the home of the brave!

And where is that band who so vauntingly swore,
That the havoc of war and the battle's confusion
A home and a Country should leave us no more?
Their blood has wash'd out their foul footstep's pollution.
No refuge could save the hireling and slave
from the terror of flight or the gloom of the grave,
And the star-spangled banner in triumph doth wave
O'er the land of the free and the home of the brave.

O thus be it ever when freemen shall stand
Between their lov'd home and the war's desolation!
Blest with vict'ry and peace may the heav'n rescued land
Praise the power that hath made and preserv'd us a nation!
Then conquer we must, when our cause it is just,
and this be our motto - "In God is our trust,"
And the star-spangled banner in triumph shall wave
O'er the land of the free and the home of the brave.

(Written by Francis Scott Key, November 1814)

The flares die out, and the whole redoubt goes from day back to night. The Forty-Third are amazed by the power of their enemies' passion for freedom and liberty. But Colonel Robert Rennie is not taking the bait.

"Patriots' pride is a foolish errand. Don't worry; We will all have our chance to stab those Yankees in the chests with their own flags. Platoon, fall back to our lines."

The Forty-Third's first platoon retreated back to their lines.

Little does Colonel Rennie know that when the final battle comes, he will regret his words.

The whole American garrison unleashes loud battle cries at the British lines, and then the American lines fall as silent as the night sky.

At the British lines, all the British soldiers have been awakened from their slumber. They all heard the Americans singing—seemingly to them, from their point of view. Colonel Robert Rennie and his men return to camp, and he goes to Major General Sir Edward Pakenham's tent. He makes sure his uniform is presentable and then asks for permission to enter the tent.

"Sir, Colonel Robert Rennie reporting. I need to inform you about the enemy position, sir."

General Pakenham gives Colonel Rennie permission to enter his quarters.

Colonel Rennie salutes his commander, and then Rennie explains the location of General Jackson's line of defense.

"I have the position of the Yankees. They are here, on the Rodriguez Canal. They have built defensive earthworks from the cypress swamp to the Mississippi River. I am guessing that they have about one garrison of regulars, mostly a large portion of pirates and untrained militiamen, sir."

"Very well. We have enough artillery pieces that we can use against them. This is what we will do tomorrow. Since today was New Year's Eve, I bet those Yanks will probably be very dead drunk. When the dawn's first light shines, we shall pound them until they abandon the redoubt or beg for mercy, and then they will swear their allegiance back to Wellington."

"Very well, sir. How about our numbers?" Colonel Rennie asks.

General Pakenham pulls out a book that lists the regiments and their commanders. He begins to read them one by one to Colonel Rennie.

"We have several regiments here with us. First off, we have a demi-battalion from the Ninety-Fifth Rifle Brigade. That means that they have five hundred men in the battalion, Colonel. We have the Kings Own Royal Regiment, the Seventh and Twenty-First Royal Fusiliers, and the Eighty-Fifth Bucks Volunteers, including your Forty-Third Regiment of Foot. We also have the Ninety-Third Highlanders. We can use the Fourteenth Light Dragoons to help guard against an infantry attack, should that come in the near future. We have the First and the Fifth West Indian Companies here as well."

"Sir, that numbers our forces up to almost eight thousand men," Colonel Rennie says.

Just then the rest of the British staff enters the tent—General Samuel Gibbs, General John Keane, General John Lambert, Colonel William Thortan, and Lieutenant Colonel Thomas Mullian. Once they all are in the tent, Sir Edward Pakenham calls his council of war. They discuss the battle plan for what would be the final showdown.

"Gentlemen," Sir Edward Pakenham explains, "we have a chance to end this bloody war right here. Now, tomorrow we will begin our attack with a mass bombardment of the American redoubts. We will pound them with our cannons and our Congreve rockets. We must make every single shell count. Once we have destroyed their ramparts, we must overrun their position with a full-on assault."

General Samuel Gibbs is not so sure about the infantry attack.

"Permission to speak, sir?" General Gibbs asks.

"Permission granted, General Gibbs."

General Gibbs takes a deep breath and shares his worries about the infantry attack. "Sir, I know we outnumber the Americans three to one. But with all due respect, sir, Why sacrifice the lives of our soldiers when we can demolish their redoubts like a heap of dry leaves."

General Pakenham begins to rant about how immature and pathetic the United States is, since the nation is still in its childhood. Many British still believe that if they win the war, the Americans can be brought under the iron fist of the British.

"Because, General Gibbs, I was sent here by Wellington himself to end this ridiculous war. My mission is to bring peace and prosperity to this land—to bring these Yankees back to their rightful place in history.

If we win this war, the American dream will be crushed before it reaches adulthood. This godforsaken land of pirates and rebels will either bow before our duke or their children will be his servants. Their American women or their bloody whores will be his slaves. But their men will either be wearing our red jackets and the pipeclay pants or they will be hanging from the neck above the streets of London."

"Sir? Don't you think that you are being too harsh?" Lieutenant Colonel Thomas Mullians says.

General Pakenham slams his fist on the table. His staff jump, and they all take a step back. He then looks up at Colonel Mullians, his face full of anger and rage.

"By God, you shall not question me! We are here as servants of the duke. Are you questioning my brother-in-law?"

"No sir!" Colonel Mullian says.

Sir Edward Pakenham cools off, and he then gives his final orders to his staff. "Have the batteries set up before first light. No battery shall fire without my order. Those who do not obey my orders, I swear by God that they shall be given three hundred lashes by my own hand. Staff dismissed!"

His staff leave his tent. He then sits on his bed and puts his hands over his face. He groans with disbelief that his own officers would dare question his orders.

CHAPTER 31

TRUE OFFICERS VERSUS OVERDRESSED POSH, POMPOUS OFFICERS

Now before I get back on with the story, I want to talk about how officers from the British and American armies were back in the eighteenth and nineteenth centuries. Unlike the officers of the present day, who fight with their men in the heat of battle, many officers from European armies would sit back on their horses and let their men march toward their deaths. Many British officers were true officers that served and led their men in many terrible battles. The men of those true officers looked up to and respected the officers, such as Major General Robert Ross. He led his troops from the front, and he was well respected.

In the British military, many officers died leading their men in battle. They died in battle in many ways that people today might think of as a complete waste of fine men. But some of these officers that served were serving because they wanted to impress their wives and show that they were better than the men under their command. When they wanted to impress the ladies, they would talk about how the thrill of battle was so glorious and how honorable it was. But when they actually saw battle for the first time, they would retreat and leave their men to die, or allow a braver officer to lead the regiment into battle. Many officers ranking from lieutenant to colonel would take command of training camps and would help train civilians and turn them into professional soldiers. But a few officers would go over the top to train their men and maintain discipline.

During the Napoleonic Wars over in Europe, many Irishmen served with the British Army to fight against the French. But for eight hundred years, the British and Irish had held a deep hatred for each other. Some of the Irish recruits would be mistreated during training. If they so much as made one misstep during parade ground drills, they would be abused by being punched or kicked until they bled. Some even had their bones broken. Others were shot for disobeying orders.

Many British recruits would be called "scum" or "filth of the earth" to degrade them to break them down so they could be turned into soldiers.

There may have been some officers that were corrupt, but many were gentlemen and were honorable, such as Arthur Wellesley, the first Duke of Wellington. He bought into the British Army but soon became an officer who commanded enormous respect from his men. He had won a notable victory against Emperor Bonaparte at the Battle of Waterloo on June 18, 1815. He and his forces had to face the wrath of the Grand Armée. At 7:00 p.m., as a last-ditch effort, Bonaparte sent his Old Guard into battle. The Old Guard was known to be invincible, but that was the day they were to be proven wrong. Wellington gathered what was left of his forces to stand in the center of the line and make a final attempt to beat the French. When the Old Guard got close, Wellington uttered his most famous phrase: "Now, Maitland, now's your time!"

The British forces fired a devastating barrage of musket fire into the Old Guard. Hundreds of French grenadiers fell to the dirt within a few seconds. Then, to make matters worse for the French, the Prussians arrived to aid the English. Together they made the Old Guard break and run. Wellington and his allies accomplished the impossible.

In most cases, there was a payment system in the army; one could pay into the army to receive a commission. One had to be sixteen years old to be able to qualify, and every man always had to start at the lowest rank, which would be the rank of ensign. He would have to put his check into horse guards but would have to wait till a spot was open for him to become an ensign. He needed to have friends in high places in order to have free commissions, which indeed there were. This promised young men the chance to lead men into battle or march them upon the parade grounds. But it was up to the commander-in-chief whether one would have a free commission or not.

Some officers got the commission either by having friends in high places or by having proved their skills, tactics, and authority on the field. However, when it came to battle, some officers never actually even saw a battle. But some of those officers lied about fake experiences, just trying to impress their families and the ladies, as I stated earlier. Sometimes they were relieved of their command, or, even worse, they actually saw a battle.

Battle was where it really showed whether an officer would lead his men by example or turn tail and run like a coward. If you were an officer and you retreated without orders from your senior officer, you would either lose your commission or you would be court-martialed. If you were found guilty, you would be flogged or, worse, hanged or shot for cowardice in the face of the enemy.

Now, there were many types of military officers during the eighteenth and nineteenth centuries. But many of those officers served as true gentlemen. Many officers who were truly respected by their men served in the eighteenth and nineteenth centuries.

Moving on to American officers, I would like to note that these American officers I will mention are my favorite American officers of the time. I like these officers for their great achievements and their great mistakes during the American Revolutionary War.

Colonel Henry Knox, a Boston bookseller, was an American artillery commander. He took his men to Fort Ticonderoga and brought back its artillery to help liberate the city of Boston. Knox and his men marched and sailed cannons over three hundred miles, all the way back to Boston. Throughout his military career, he was respected by General George Washington. He used his engineering skills, which he taught to his artillerymen. Throughout the rest of the way, he was the commander of artillery.

Nathaniel Greene was known as George Washington's most trusted general. He was a major general in the Continental Army during the Revolutionary War. He was a former Quaker and had served alongside General Washington throughout the whole war. During the war, in the south, Major General Nathaniel Green commanded the American southern army after one glory-hungry officer stole credit from General Benedict Arnold and Colonel Daniel Morgan after the defeat of General John Burgoyne at Saratoga. That officer, Horatio Gates, or Granny Gates, was the one who commanded the northern army during the Battle of Saratoga in 1777. In 1780, General Gates fought against General Lord Charles Cornwallis, the British commander in the south. Gates and Cornwallis battled at a piece of land called Camden, South Carolina. The battle was bloody and vicious. When the American forces were beginning to lose the battle, Horatio Gates who rode south to gain glory. He took off on the fastest horse in his army and rode two hundred miles, all the way back to Hillsborough, without even stopping. And he then became the butt of every mean-spirited joke in the US Army. He had proved himself a loser. He was completely outwitted and outmaneuvered. He marched with three thousand men at Camden and lost half his forces. Gates would face court-martial. After the defeat, Washington was able to send General Nathaniel Green to command the southern divisions. Washington even said, "If I were to fall in battle, I would want General Greene to take command of the army."

General Greene had a can-do attitude, and he would never accept defeat at the hands of the enemy. But he would have to face command of an army that had only eight hundred soldiers fit for duty. Greene needed a miracle to keep his army from destruction, and it came in the form of a rough-and-tumble American colonel named Daniel Morgan. He was a backwoods soldier who had served with the British as a wagoner. He had once received five hundred lashes for punching a redcoat officer. When the American Revolutionary War began, he raised a corps of riflemen called Daniel's Rifles. And at the Battle of Freeman's Farm, his corps ambushed Burgoyne's Army and killed six hundred redcoats in just one day.

Down in the south, General Green and Colonel Morgan devised a plan to split their forces. They wanted to split the British army in two. Greene marched his forces southeast, while Morgan marched his men to the southwest. And as if on cue, Lord Cornwallis split his army. He chased after Green while Colonel Banastre Tarleton chased after Morgan. Both sides moved through the roughest terrain in the eastern seaboard. All four generals, who were gifted and ambitious, were now engaged in a game of cat and mouse. Both armies engaged on the fringes of their forces. The American plan was to draw the British away from their supplies and their troop reinforcements. The British became more frustrated with every single mile of rough terrain. Then Daniel Morgan needed to fight against

Colonel Tarleton's legion. He had six hundred men, and half of them were militiamen. They were the same militiamen that fled from Camden without firing a single shot back in the Revolutionary War. American militiamen broke their ranks and retreated from the field at such battles as Long Island, Kips Bay, Princeton, Brandywine Creek, and Camden. But on the eve of the famous battle that would begin to shift the war in the south, he visited with his men and said the following words to them: "Just you wait, my lads. You will be back home to kiss your sweethearts. You will be able to hug your children and your families close."

January 17, 1781
Cowpens, South Carolina

On a mild winter morning at a field called Cowpens, Colonel Daniel Morgan attempted a new tactic that had never been done in the war. He was going to finally learn how to use militias against the redcoats in open battle. Like others before him, Morgan put his militia forces out front. They would be the first line to meet Tarleton's charging redcoats. The militiamen were hiding in the thick grass instead of standing in a row. And this time he told his men to fire just two volleys. When the British got close, the militiamen opened fire. The first shots picked off fifteen dragoons and checked the first cavalry charge. Their second volley cut down twenty foot soldiers. They then retreated from their positions, and the second line was a line of veteran militiamen hiding in the trees. They had the same orders to fire twice and then withdraw. The British redcoats continued their march forward. However, for every forward pace they marched. They were harassed by snipers on both their right and left flanks. The riflemen fired relentlessly into the British lines. Once the militiamen reached the third line, they stood with Morgan's regular soldiers. The British fired a devastating volley into the third American line. Over seventy American soldiers fell to the ground. The British moved in with their bayonets. Both sides clashed, and Tarleton's legion began to slice American soldiers with their sabers. Colonel Morgan's plan was now in the balance. An order for the American forces to regroup was misheard as a call to retreat. The remaining regulars and militia began to panic and retreat from the grounds. But Morgan himself stepped in to steady their nerves and save his men.

"Form! Form, my brave fellows! Give 'em just one more fire and the day is ours! Old Morgan is never beaten!" he shouts.

When the British thought they had earned a replay of Camden, they believed that the American forces were running, so they chased after them. All of a sudden, the British forces found themselves facing the well-directed volleys of Morgan's regulars. Colonel Tarleton had landed right in Morgan's trap. The Continental forces fired with alarming force. The volley cut down scores of British infantry soldiers within seconds. The sight of the American volley fire and their vicious battle cries sent the redcoats running for their lives. The redcoats scattered and retreated. Tarleton tried to rally his men, but within one hour of fighting, the battle was in favor of the American forces. Some of the redcoats tried to surrender but were met with bayonets to their chests. Tarleton had chased Morgan all across the southern states, and he was defeated by Colonel Daniel Morgan at Cowpens. Most of the redcoat detachment was killed, captured, or wounded. Only a handful managed to flee, including Tarleton himself. He will escape, soon he'll rejoin Cornwallis's army and he was thirsting for vengeance. After rejoining Greene's army, Colonel Daniel Morgan was given the right to home by Greene himself.

However, the war was not over for General Greene; the chase was far from over. His enemy was not going to stop chasing him until they made him stand and fight. But like a boxer who realizes that his opponent hits with greater force, General Greene continued to lead the British deeper into the backcountry. General Greene learned early in the war, during the battles of New York and Brandywine Creek, that keeping the army away from a major confrontation was very important. He knew that if he could buy himself and his forces some time, they could get more reinforcements and more supplies. The redcoats were having a hard time trying to keep up. Greene's force was like a mirage that disappeared as they drew near.

For months the cat-and-mouse chase zigzagged across the south. Both sides often trailed each other by one hundred yards. The redcoats knew that they had to destroy some of their necessaries to keep up. On one night, the redcoats pitched a massive bonfire and burned wagons, tents, clothing, wine, tobacco, fine china, silver, and cask upon cask of rum.

With the load now lighter, the redcoats began to move at a faster pace. Greene had to make a risky move in order to trick his predators. He split his army, sending one branch toward the upper Dan River while his main force moved east toward Taylor's Ferry. Amazingly, Green's plan worked. He moved his whole regiment of two thousand men across the river. The chase was now over, and now the American army could finally rest. But soon he moved back across the river and fought against the redcoats at the Battle of Guilford Courthouse. Both of these officers outsmarted British officers by thinking outside the box, and they would be remembered as part of American tactical history.

Now back to the main story.

CHAPTER 32

AN ORCHESTRA OF ARTILLERY

The New Orleans Campaign, Part 6
Rodriguez Canal, New Orleans, Louisiana
American encampment
January 1, 1815
Dawn

The American forces, including the Seventy-Sixth Pennsylvania, awaken from a deep slumber in the predawn mist of New Year's Day and begin their first day of defending Line Jackson with the US Marines. All the grenadiers and marines march over to Line Jackson. When they reach the redoubt, the fog is extremely thick and dense. The staff stand with their troops upon the line and try to see anything through the fog. Simon grunts because he cannot see anything.

"Fog! Fog! And more bloody fog! I swear!" Simon says with frustration. He shakes his head, scared that the redcoats intend to attack. He knows they will not be able to see the British approaching them.

His staff are having no luck either. They scan the whole area, but they do not see anything but fog.

"This blasted fog had better lift soon," Celestia says with a worried tone. "I have a bad feeling about it."

Daisy puts her spyglass down and looks at her sister. "What is there to worry about?" she asks.

"I am worried that the redcoats will attack us today, since last night was New Year's Eve."

Brittany knows what Celestia is talking about. She wants to think from the perspective of the enemy regarding what they want to do. She then begins to explain what she would do in a scenario like this. "If I were Sir Pakenham, I would take my troops and launch an attack on the enemy for just one reason. He probably believes that we're all dead drunk right about now."

Timmy nods, agreeing with what Brittany has just said. "That is the capital idea. Just like Washington at Trenton. The Hessians were so damn drunk that we caught them with their breeches down."

More and more American soldiers take their positions at the redoubt, and American cannons are placed all along it. The Keystone grenadiers guard the artillerymen who are rolling the cannons onto the firing line. The US Marines roll out their cannons at the number 3 battery. Six eight-pound cannons are lined in a row facing toward the foggy field.

Simon continues to stare at the fog. He stares at it as if he is mesmerized by it. He had never seen such fog in large areas before in his entire life. Timmy stands on his right, and they gawk at the fog.

"It is truly something what the fog can conceal," Timmy says. "I feel like this fog is actually hiding something."

"I have my same suspicions, Lieutenant," Simon says. "Those lobsters may try to probe our lines. They might try to poke at us and see what our true strength is."

"I agree, sir. But the one thing that concerns me is that we do not know their true strength." Daisy says with a bit of concern.

"You know, something tells me that they will attack us. They will not throw their entire force at us; they will send a company to scout our line. We have a strong line, but I have seen General Jackson's map, and it seems he is weak on the right flank. No doubt the redcoats will try to strike up the middle and cut us in half."

Andrew Jackson rides to the redoubt and checks on each of his soldiers. He stops at the number 3 battery, stands up on the redoubt, and calls to his men.

"Here is where we will plant our stakes. And we will not abandon them until we drive those Redcoat rascals into the river or the swamp."

Brittany and Daisy, along with three other US Marines, roll the ninth cannon into position. They finally get into position, and they both stand with their backs to the field.

"You know what?" Brittany jokes. "If this is called a six-pounder, you would think it would weigh only six pounds."

"I agree," Daisy says with a laugh.

The rest of the Seventy-Sixth form up at redoubt number seven. The American forces are watching the line and having regular conversations with each other. Most are eating their breakfast. They are totally unaware that just a few hundred yards in front of them, the redcoats are placing large amounts of cannons for a surprise attack on the American line.

Major General Edward Pakenham and his staff are riding up and down the artillery line. They stop in front of the main battery, which is made up of eight twelve-pound cannons. The royal artillerymen prime and load their pieces and wait for the command to fire. The fog is causing problems for the British as well. The visibility is becoming troublesome. General Pakenham has a choice to make.

"Gentlemen, we must make a choice. Either we wait for this bloody fog to lift or we let fate decide the victory for us," he says to his staff.

Some of the staff have different opinions about what to do next. They are all divided.

"Sir, we have all the bloody day to let this fog lift. If we attack now, we might just be wasting all our ammo. I suggest that we wait until the fog lifts," General Samuel Gibbs suggests.

"Sir, we must attack those bastards now while they are still weak," Colonel Robert Rennie says to General Pakenham. "I have seen those bastards with my own eyes, and their redoubt is lightly defended. If we bombard them now, we can take out a few of their regiments. We must pound them hard and fast. But as I am very cautious, we will need to have enough ammo to cover our soldiers when they advance, sir."

Pakenham knows that Rennie is telling the truth. He agrees with him, but they are all still cautious.

"Colonel, you are as right as rain," Pakenham says. "However, I will not make any foolish moves until this fog is gone."

As if on cue, the fog begins to lift toward the river. General Pakenham looks through his spyglass and has the whole American redoubt in full view.

He sees American soldiers building the redoubt and setting up artillery on the wall.

General John Keane has a bad feeling in the pit of his gut. He rides forward on the right side of General Pakenham. He has a feeling that this attack will fail.

"Sir, I must tell you right now that both the artillery and the infantry attacks will fail, sir," he says.

General Pakenham looks at him with disbelief. "Why in the world do you think that, General Keane?"

General Keane takes a deep breath. He then begins to explain what was going to happen during the battle to come. "Sir, I believe that Colonel Rennie is wrong about their defenses. I have read that George Washington and his rebels fortified Dorchester Heights in just one night. The whole city of Boston was under the sights of over a hundred twenty cannons. And just three years ago in Spain, our forces were attacking a lightly defended French fortress. We waited till morning to attack, which was a major mistake on our part. We woke up to see that they had received thirty more cannons and seven hundred more men in just one night. Those Yankees have a lot of cannons, sir. The difference is that ours are in the open. They will pick off our pieces one by one. And when the infantry attack begins, should we actually get to that point, I fear that this battle will be just like Bunker Hill. Those are Jackson's men on that canal. When our Infantry begins their march, they will be under heavy fire from the Yankee cannons. If we don't have enough scaling ladders, then we won't be able to storm their rampart. Troops will come under heavy fire when they attempt to storm Jackson's line. General Jackson will not turn tail and run like General Winder at Bladensburg. Sir, this battle is going to be very different from the battles we fought in Spain. The only chance we have to either cut Jackson's line in half or we attack on their right flank, where they are the weakest. However, it still won't be enough, sir."

Sir Edward Pakenham thought to himself for a few seconds, wondering if what he was hearing from his subordinate was actually the truth. However, his professionalism as an officer in the British army leaves him with a strong confidence that this attack will not fail at all.

"We are going to do our duty for the king and country. Keep the faith within yourself and within our great King George. We will remove those yankee's no matter what the cost. Now, gentlemen, to your regiments."

"Yes sir!" Pakenham's staff say. They salute General Packenham and return to their units. The general pulls out his sword and stares intently at the American redoubt.

The fog begins to clear for the American forces. Simon and his staff see the fog lift. Celestia looks one more time through her spyglass and spots a terrifying sight.

"Major, come over here right now!" Celestia shouts to Simon.

Simon is checking on his men, and when he hears his wife scream, he rushes over to her as fast as he can. He reaches her and sees the fear in her eyes.

"Honey? What is wrong? What did you see?" Simon asks.

Celestia stutters and can't speak plain English. Simon then looks through his glasses and sees dozens of British cannons and Congreve rockets aimed at their positions. He is shocked to see that many cannons aimed in their direction. He freezes for a few seconds, and then General Jackson rides up on his horse behind the Seventy-Sixth.

"Major Smithtrovich," Jackson asks, "what is all the screaming about?"

Simon turns around and looks at him.

Seconds later, the British commence their attack.

Major General Sir Edward Pakenham shouts his order to the batteries: "For king and country, open fire!"

Simon runs to General Jackson and, with a mighty heave, throws himself and General Jackson to the dirt. A volley of hot lead rains down from the sky. Dozens of explosions erupt all around Line Jackson. Several shells blow up right in front of the number 7 battery. Most of the American soldiers rush to take cover behind the redoubt. Others fall flat upon the ground. The Seventy-Sixth takes cover behind the redoubt. Their bearskin caps fall off their heads. They use their hands to cover their heads from exploding soil and hot lead. Simon and General Jackson are down in the dirt. They both look up at the sky and can see shells exploding up above.

Simon looks at Jackson. "I am sorry I yanked you from your horse, sir."

General Jackson pats Simon's shoulder. "Don't worry about it. You did the right thing, Major."

They both crawl to the wall and duck. Simon looks up, but then a shell lands near the wall, and he ducks back down.

"Jesus, Lord! I knew this was going to happen!" Simon said as he shouted in panic.

Celestia and Daisy are both at the wall. A shell flies toward them, and they both duck with their hands over their heads. The shell lands about twenty feet away from them but does not explode. They both look up real quick to see the shell smoking. They both look at each other and slowly duck back down behind the rampart. Timmy and the rest of the men duck. Brittany and her corps duck behind several trees. They are trapped near the trees. The shells keep them stuck. They all hunker down, and they know that they have to wait it out now. Simon risks his life running back and forth along the line, making sure that the men are staying down. Regimental commanders order the men to man the cannons.

General Jackson stands up and begins to run through the lines. "To arms! To arms! Infantry, take cover! Artillerymen to your batteries. Return fire! Fire at will!"

The shells explode in fiery blasts. Flame and earth explode and shoot up into the sky. One American cannon crew tries to load their cannon. Unfortunately, a shell lands and blows their cannon apart. The five American blue coats are struck by shrapnel. The American forces manage to return fire. Their body parts get blown apart by the shell. Blood splatters on American soldiers near the blast. Then the Congreve rockets are fired. The rockets soar through the sky toward the American lines. The scream of the rockets is terrifying.

Andrew Jackson calms his terrified men. "Don't mind those rockets. They are mere toys to amuse children!" he shouts.

Simon returns to his staff but sees that Brittany is missing. He looks around for her but doesn't see her. "Where the hell is Brittany?" he shouts.

Celestia looks around and sees her corps hiding in the trees. Simon removes himself from cover and runs to rescue her. Ivan spots Simon running to the trees, and then he sees Brittany and her corps trapped there. He makes the sign of the cross and takes off running toward the trees. They both run together. Shells land all around them, but neither of them is hit. They run about seventy yards to the swamp, and then they finally reach them.

Simon urges Brittany and her corps to run back to the line. "Brittany, is anyone wounded?" he asks.

"No sir!" she says.

Ivan runs to her and hugs her. "We need to get to the redoubt. Can your corps run?"

Brittany smiles and calls to her corps. "Get ready to run! On the major's command. Stand ready!"

They all get ready to run like hell back to the line. Simon takes a deep breath and shouts at the top of his lungs, "Run!"

With that word, they all make a mad dash through the field. They have to dodge more flying lead. Amazingly they manage to make it back to the redoubt.

The artillery barrage duel goes on for more than three hours. The American forces manage to return fire. The shells fall from the sky on the British cannons. The cannonballs land all over the British positions. One English battery of seven cannons is slowly being destroyed one cannon at a time. As one cannon at the left side of the battery is reloading, a shell from the American lines bounces upon the ground three times before it decapitates the artillery officer of the battery. His head explodes into pieces, and blood and flesh shower his fellow artillerymen. Seconds later another cannonball skips upon the ground. The ball maims several artillerymen. They fall to the ground as they see their own blood spill out onto the grass. One by one, the American artillery silences over 75 percent of the British artillery. After hours of constant barrage that sounds like a terrible thunderstorm, the American and British cannons finally fall silent. The American forces emerge from cover to see the surrounding area smoldering from the cannon blasts. The Seventy-Sixth emerge from cover and see dozens of shell craters all around them. The earth is scorched, and the smoke from the craters is shooting high into the sky.

"Jesus Lord!" Daisy exclaims.

Celestia stands up on the wall and shouts to the company, "Seventy-Sixth, sound off!"

All the Keystone grenadiers sound off to let them know that they are okay.

Simon runs up and down their ramparts, and a few minutes later he reports back to his staff.

"You are not gonna believe this," Simon says, out of breath. "We have not suffered any casualties."

"Oh, thank the Lord," Celestia replies.

Timmy looks up to the northern section of the rampart and notices five soldiers in blue coats, US Kentucky regulars, who died in a British cannon blast. Simon and his staff run over and see the grisly aftermath.

"Holy shite! Poor lads. They didn't know what hit them," Timmy says.

The regulars' bodies are mutilated. Their heads have been ripped off, and their chests and legs have been carved out like scoops of ice cream. What is left of their bodies is swimming in a pool of blood and flesh.

"God rest their souls. And you did not let me finish. I was saying our unit did not suffer any casualties. I was going to say the US Kentucky regulars suffered five fatalities," Simon said.

The sight of the corpses makes some of the men want to throw up. The smell is too much for one American regular, who takes one whiff and then passes out.

Simon and his staff are very fortunate to have not been killed, but they feel very sorry for their poor comrades in arms.

"You know that could have been us, right? Come on; let's get back," Celestia says.

Simon and his staff return to their positions.

Back at the British lines, General Pakenham and his staff see whether any of the cannons survived. A royal artillery officer runs up to General Pakenham and gives him some bad news.

"Sir, I regret to inform you that most of the artillery pieces have been destroyed," the officer says. "We have several rockets left to use. Worst of all, sir … we have over one hundred fifty men dead or wounded, sir."

General Pakenham closes his eyes and growls under his breath. "Thank you. Tend to the wounded."

"Yes sir!" the artillery officer replies.

The British begin to clear the field of the wounded and the twisted bodies of the dead. The British have been defeated twice, and now they will put their hope into the phrase "The third time's a charm."

Unfortunately, that will not be the case during the final battle. The American and the British forces prepare themselves for what will be known as the bloodiest battle of the War of 1812.

CHAPTER 33

THE THIN LINE JACKSON

The Battle of New Orleans
The New Orleans Campaign, Part 7
Rodriguez Canal, New Orleans, Louisiana
January 8, 1815
Dawn

The morning arrives, and a thick blanket of mist covers the whole battlefield. The clear blue sky is barely visible from the ground. The sun shows in small patches through the mist. The whole American force stands at the ramparts, ready for the battle to start. The Seventy-Sixth stand alongside the US Marines. Simon walks back and forth between his men, making sure they have ammo and keeping their morale high. He pats soldiers on their shoulders.

"Keep yourselves steady, men," Simon says as he crosses through the lines. "Do not be scared by the mist. This is a blessed mist given to us by the Lord himself."

He reaches the middle of their section of the redoubt. There he is surprised to see his fellow staff and several soldiers of the Seventy-Sixth. He taps on Celestia's shoulder, and she kisses him. Simon is confused by the sudden kiss.

"Aww. What was that for, babe?" Simon asks.

Simon partially forgot that today is his Twenty-Fifth birthday.

"How could I forget my husband's birthday. Happy birthday, Major," Celestia says.

The others there wish their commander a happy birthday.

"Happy birthday, sir!" Timmy says.

"Happy birthday, Major," Daisy adds.

"How old are you today, sir?" Brittany asks Simon.

Simon uses his fingers to count backward.

"First off, thank you, everyone," Simon says. "And I am twenty-five years old today. And the only gift I want from all of you is to bring not only me but America a great victory that will end this bloody war once and for all."

"Huzzah!" the entire Seventy-Sixth cheers.

As the rest of the American forces continue to reinforce the redoubt, Simon pulls out his diary.

> Dear diary: Today will be my last entry that I shall possibly write in this diary. Today is the day that we fight what could be the last battle of this war. This war was not supposed to last this long. I have seen so many things that one man can do to another man. However, I have done some of those terrible things myself. I pray that today will be the final battle. If I shall fall today, I hope that my men will have the Lord's protection. And most importantly for my best friends and my beloved wife, I am proud to have fought alongside such great warriors who are not afraid to defend their rights. And today I am glad to take part in this battle even if just for one whole minute. I hope and pray that one day our future American citizens will remember this day, and that honor, bravery, valor, and sacrifice reign not only for the Americans but also for the British Army today. I write these words for generations of Americans to remember: Never shall any foe destroy the power of friendship that will unite this nation forevermore! I hope that our future grandchildren will remember, that what we fought and died for was not in vain. All I want for my grandchildren and for all Americans to do is remember our sacrifices!

Simon closes his diary and puts it in his haversack. He stands up and heads back to his position on the center rampart. Celestia and five other

385

Keystone grenadiers are praying. Celestia is holding a Bible. They all are praying the Our Father and Hail Mary. Celestia finishes the prayers and gives last-minute orders.

"Now, gentlemen," she says, "we must protect one another today. None of you will retreat. Keep an eye on your ammo, and be sure to make every bullet count today. But most importantly, you will keep your fellow soldiers motivated and calm. Is that clear?"

"Yes ma'am!" they reply.

Simon prepares to give his orders to his company. He calls to his men to gather around him, and he stands on the rampart.

"Keystone grenadiers, I have our orders." He takes a quick look at his grenadiers and can see the war has changed them. "Grenadiers in arms, the US Marines will be stationed on our left, while the Forty-Fourth Regiment of Foot, Beale Rifles, and Seventh Infantry will be posted to our right, all the way to the river. We will be stationed here. This is the middle of the line. We are directly in the center. We must hold the center for good reason. If the redcoats break through the center, they will cut our force in two. General Jackson believes the main attack will be here in the center. We must hold this center. Now, today can be the battle that means the difference of this nation reaching maturity, or it can be the end of our freedom. I cannot stress enough that today is a day on which we must not retreat. Do you all understand that?"

"Yes sir!" the Seventy-Sixth shout.

"Good. I have another thing to say to you all. I see how this war has changed our nation for all of us. Many of us came to fight because we were tired of working on the farm. Some wanted to fight because they thought war would be a new adventure for them. I was an apple farmer for many years, and I never knew that I would be standing here with you all. There are a few of you here today that fought alongside me in Ohio and Indiana. Some of those men who fought with me are up in the clouds. Today they are looking down at us, and that is what they have been doing ever since then. Many of us have come to fight because we have families who want to carry on the military tradition. We are here to let not only the British and the Canadians, but also the rest of the world know that America cannot be ruled by a king or a duke. We will not bow to anyone who dares to wear a crown. We will not surrender to those who threaten our families with

The Forgone War
tyranny or those who want to oppress us as slaves for a king or persecute
us for having different beliefs. That is what our nation has been fighting
against since 1775. We Pennsylvanians are fighting to preserve not only
our state but also our families. We are fighting for our homes, our flag,
and the future generations of American citizens. Today I ask only one
thing from all of you. Should we win this day, when you return home, I
want you to let the whole world remember what happened here today. I
do not wish tribute—not through song or poem. When you all return to
your families, tell them all about the thin American line. Tell them what
those men and women stood for. Tell them what they bled for and what
they died for. And let those redcoats know about the strength, heart, and
courage of an American who is not afraid to stand toe-to-toe against ten
thousand tyrants who threaten our own way of life!"

"Huzzah!" the Seventy-Sixth shout.

"Grenadiers, what is our motto?" Simon shouts to his company.

"Virtue, liberty, independence!" the grenadiers shout.

They shout those three words five times. The sound of the battle cry
can be heard through the whole rampart. Major General Andrew Jackson
can hear the battle cry, and it gives him chills up his spine.

Thirty minutes later, American regulars, marines, and militiamen are
building extra fortifications using cotton bales, wagons, and other types of
defenses. Some are cooking and eating their breakfast. But the defenders
of New Orleans have a big problem. Owing to the fighting during the
last two weeks, many American defenders have little to no ammunition,
few flints, and little gunpowder. General Jackson checks on his men.
Many of them say that they have no flints or gunpowder. He rides over
to the number 7 battery, where the US Marines and the Seventy-Sixth
Pennsylvania are stationed. Simon sees General Jackson, Simon and his
company salute General Jackson.

"As you were, lads. Major Smithtrovich, how are your men and
provisions?"

"Sir, we have one hundred eleven soldiers at your command. But
we have only five rounds each, and some of my soldiers do not have
musket flints. But we will not let that stop us, sir. My grenadiers are great
marksmen, sir."

387

"I am aware of that, Major. About 65 percent of our forces do not have enough powder or flints. We will have just enough supplies once Jean Lafitte gets here."

Right now, the American forces were trusting their lives to a pirate and his crew, who were to get them the supplies needed to defend the city of New Orleans.

"Do you really expect that pirate to come to our aid, sir?" Simon asks General Jackson.

"Major, if he does not come to help, by the eternal, my hair will turn gray."

They both laugh. General Jackson rides off to check on the rest of the line.

"Major," Celestia says to Simon, "if you want my opinion, I bet those pirates are back in the city. They're possibly looting it, for God's sake."

Just then several marines escort a wagon full of cotton bales to their spot on the line, and two more bales are sent over to the Seventy-Sixth's position. The wagoner to whom the cotton belongs complains about his cotton being stolen. "Hey, that's my cotton, dammit. I will report this to your commanding officer!"

Simon grabs the man and gets up right in his face. "Listen to me, buddy. That cotton will not belong to you if the lobsters take the city. Now, if you want to have it back, then take a musket or go complain to the British. Make your choice!"

The man cools off and agrees to defend it. "I will join you lot on the battle line."

Simon lets go of the man and walks over to Timmy. "Lieutenant Miller, give this man a musket."

"Yes sir!" Timmy says. He grabs a musket that is lying on the wall, and he gives it to the wagoner. "Here you go. Now don't go shooting yourself or any one of our men."

The wagoner sees a group of militiamen and falls in line with them. They walk down to the number 6 battery.

Simon takes his bearskin cap off and scratches his head. "Bloody civilians!"

Brittany stands right beside him with a canteen full of milk. "Major, do you want some milk? It will give you strong bones."

"No thank you; I already had my breakfast," Simon says.

"Very well. I will drink it myself." Brittany takes a gulp but spits it out. "Jesus! This is spoiled! That tasted like donkey shite." She wipes her mouth with her sleeve and dumps the milk out of the canteen.

Simon scoffs, and Brittany looks at him. They lock eyes, and then they both begin to laugh.

On one section of the American battle line, the governor of New Orleans, William C.C. Claiborne is helping his civilian soldiers get the gear they need to defend the city. Several American soldiers have a single station. One soldier is handing out a musket to each civilian. The second one is handing out five to ten musket cartridges. The third is giving out powder horns and paper-wrapped powder. The governor and his fellow secretaries give each of the civilians a dollar for their service to America. General Jackson rides over to the governor.

"Governor Claiborne, how many citizens have you recruited?" General Jackson asks.

"Three hundred, General Jackson." C.C Claiborne said.

"That is more than I thought. I am impressed."

Just then an American regular gives General Jackson a letter. "Read this letter, sir; it is urgent." The soldier runs back to his place in the line. General Jackson opens the letter and reads it. He crumples the letter and throws it to the ground.

"What did the letter say, sir?" Governor Caliborne asked General Jackson.

"Report from the lines. The last of the damn powder is gone. I only hope Lafitte gets here soon. If he doesn't, then we are going to have one hell of a melee."

An American patrol is scouting the British positions. Three American cavalrymen ride blindly through the fog and dismount from their horses. They begin to slowly walk through the mist.

"It is so dense I cannot even see beyond my own damn nose," one American soldier says.

The three cavalrymen take cover in a crater left there from the bombardment just seven days prior. They look around, and for a moment they do not see anything. But then they hear snare drums playing in the distance.

"Is that our troops?" one American soldier asks.

One cavalryman looks behind them, and the sound of the drums is in front of them.

"That is definitely in front of us. It has to be the redcoats," the soldier says.

Just then they get a glimpse of the British Union Jack poking out of the mist. Then they see another one, and then another. Before long, dozens of British flags are waving in the mist. The American scouts can see massive columns of British redcoats marching straight toward them. One of the cavalrymen aims his musket, but his friend grabs it and forces it to the ground.

"Don't fire, you fool! You want those bastards to know we're here?" one of the American soldiers says quietly.

General Sir Edward Pakenham rides in front of his men, and he holds his right hand in the air.

"Battalion, halt!" he shouts.

The British halt their march. Over eight thousand British soldiers halt as they await the command to advance on Line Jackson. General Pakenham rides back and forth in front of his men. His men stand as straight as a pole and stare straight forward at the fog. He then rides back to his staff to discuss the battleplan.

Sir Pakenham rolls out a map and indicates where his regimental commanders will attack.

"Look at those pathetic Yankees," he says. "Do they think that they can stop us? Lord Wellington destroyed the terror of Europe. Now it will be a great honor to destroy the American cowards that took our colonies away from us four decades ago. I do not expect much from Yankee doodles. Now here is the plan. Colonel Mullians, you will lead the first charge. You will be joined by a company of the Ninety-Fifth Rifles as a defensive skirmish line that will cover your advance. The Forty-Fourth will be on the right flank. The Twenty-First Fusiliers will be right behind you. The Fourth Regiment will be on your left. Do you understand?"

"Yes sir!" Colonel Mullians says confidently. They will be dead to the last man, sir. My men will not relent until every Yankee is either bowing to our king or facing our cold steel."

"General Gibbs, you will follow behind with the fusiliers. You both will be attacking the center. General Lambert, you will follow the attack from the left with the Seventh and the Forty-Third."

General Lambert salutes his commander, sure that his men will not fail him and England. "Yes sir. We will not fail you," he says.

"General Keane, you will command the Ninety-Third Highlanders and support the center from the far left. You will also dispatch small companies from the Seventh, the Forty-Third, and the First West Indies to attack the far bank of the Mississippi. Our scouts have noticed that their right flank is open, and you shall be able to take them by surprise."

"As you wish, General. My men will crack their bloody ramparts open like a rotting wound," General Keane says.

"Very well then," Pakenham replies.

Soon the fog begins to lift once again. For the British, the American ramparts are visible once again. They can see the American soldiers scrambling to finish building the last of the fortifications.

Sir Pakenham points toward the American lines with his spyglass. "We will first bombard them with cannons and rockets to soften them up. Now, godspeed to you all, and return to your units. The attack will begin shortly." They all ride away to their units. Pakenham views the American lines and feels a chill crawl up his spine. "It is such a pity to send great men to their deaths. May God forgive me for this terrible day that will unleash pain and death that can bring us victory or bring us total defeat."

The redcoats prime their Congreve rockets and prepare to open fire.

The American cavalrymen rush back to Line Jackson. Some of the American soldiers open fire upon the scouts, but once they get close, the American soldiers stop firing. The American cavalrymen report back to General Andrew Jackson.

"What did you lads see?" General Jackson asks them.

The cavalrymen are in a state of panic, having just seen thousands of redcoats.

"Sir, they are coming this way, just six hundred yards away, all the way from the swamp to the river," one of them states. "There are thousands, general."

General Jackson pats the first cavalryman on his back and hands him his coffee he was drinking.

"Take a sip, all of you. It will help get rid of the smell of black powder from your noses."

All three of the cavalrymen take a sip of the coffee. They go and grab muskets and take their position upon the line.

Back on the British lines, the British are preparing for the opening bombardment. A loader rams a rocket down into the barrel of a cannon, and its fuse is lit. Ten Congreve rockets are fired, and they fly toward the American lines. The American defenders duck for cover as the rockets fly over their heads. The Seventy-Sixth stands firm, not moving a muscle, knowing they will not be hit. Simon and his staff watch as the rockets fly a few feet over their heads.

General Andrew Jackson eats an apple while the rockets fly overhead, laughing at the pitiful excuse for artillery. "Be not afraid of those rockets, my lads. They are mere toys in the hands of British children."

An American bugle call sounds amid the rocket fire. The American soldiers begin to cheer. Jean Lafitte and his crew come out of the swamp carrying much-needed supplies. They carry musket flints, bullets, cannonballs, dozens of powder kegs, muskets, and one twelve-pound cannon. Jean Lafitte walks up to Andrew Jackson, where he is warmly welcomed by him.

"Sorry we took so long, General," Lafitte says. "It's just that we are not accustomed to traveling by land."

"It is all right, Mr. Lafitte. You may be a tad late, but you are very welcome to our lines," Jackson says.

Jean Lafitte looks up at the sky and sees rockets soaring over their heads. "What a nice reception you have prepared for us," he says.

General Jackson chuckles and pats Lafitte on his shoulder. Just then Major Smithtrovich runs over to General Jackson and sees Jean Lafitte.

Simon looks behind the pirate and sees his whole crew carrying supplies to the lines.

"By God," Simon says. "You lot are sure a damn sight to see. Thank you for aiding in the cause, Lafitte."

"It is our pleasure," Jean says.

"Major Smithtrovich, place these men at the number 3 battery," Jackson orders Simon.

"Yes sir. The battery is just on your right." Simon points it out to Jean Lafitte.

Jean Lafitte turns to his men. "Gentlemen, get the supplies to the soldiers. Make it fast, lads."

His pirate friends begin to distribute the supplies to all the American soldiers. A dozen pirates give the US Marines, the Keystone grenadiers, and the rest of the American soldiers ammo, powder, and flints.

Lafitte hands five musket flints to Timmy and Daisy. "Here you guys go; I got some flints for you all."

"Pirate flints?" Daisy says.

Timmy smiles as he fixes the flint to his musket. "Those lobsters will never know the difference."

Two more pirates bring three large musket cartridge boxes to the Seventy-Sixth's position. Several other pirates bring kegs of black powder.

"Where in the world did you guys get all this powder?" Timmy asks one of the pirates.

The grenadiers are filled with joy. The whole American line now has the supplies it desperately needed.

Simon and Celestia take a handful of cartridges and place them in their pouches.

"This is so amazing!" Celestia says happily. "We now have more supplies than we could ever want. Ha ha ha ha!"

After all the supplies are given out, the defenders have to deal with the next problem—the fog. The fog gets thicker with each passing minute. No one can see what is in front of them. The fog is still too thick for clear vision. Daisy tries to look through her spyglass. Celestia stands right next to her and looks to see whether the redcoats are marching toward them or not.

"Bloody hell, Celestia I cannot see a damn thing," Daisy says in frustration. "The fog is so thick I can barely see ten yards in front of the rampart."

Celestia grabs her spyglass and looks downfield. She can't see anything at all. "If this damn mist does not lift soon, the red bastards will march toward us and take us by storm."

As if on cue, the mist begins to lift. The sun shines upon the American ramparts. Just as the mist lifts, Celestia sees a massive number of British regulars forming their battle lines. The British drums are beating "The British Grenadiers." The march can be heard through the American lines. Celestia drops her spyglass and is shocked to see the massive force of redcoats. She is frozen with fear. The whole American line can see the massive number of British soldiers stretching from the cypress swamp to the Mississippi River. The Seventy-Sixth are stunned to see the large numbers of redcoats. Nevertheless, they stand ready and are prepared to fight the biggest battle of the war. Celestia stands with her men as they look at the redcoats. The whole American force takes positions at the ramparts. General Jackson stands upon the ramparts and looks through his spyglass at the British Army.

Simon calms his grenadiers. "Stand fast, lads. This will be a day that will be one to tell your children and grandchildren of—a day of glory!"

Simon and his staff stand together, looking down at the massive columns of the redcoat lines. Simon grips his musket, Celestia makes a sign of the cross, and Daisy fixes her bearskin cap and checks the pan on her musket. Brittany sets her mace on the wall and looks for a musket. Just then a soldier hands her one. She notices that the soldier holding the musket is Drum Major Ivan Mattson. Brittany takes it, and they salute each other.

"Permission to join you on the battle line?" Ivan asks Brittany.

Brittany looks over at Simon, and he looks at them both. Simon sees Ivan and motions them both to join them on the line.

"Permission granted," Brittany says.

They both walk to the wall. Timmy fixes his bayonet onto his musket. Simon looks at Timmy and sees that his bayonet is fixed.

"Timmy, do you really think they're going to get that close?" Simon asks.

"Close enough to use the bayonet? I'll throw my musket like a spear if I have to."

They both laugh.

The US Marines want to stop the British rocket fire. General Jackson rides behind the US Marines and orders them to take out their rockets.

"Marines, stand ready to fire your cannon and target their munitions. Wait for my command to open fire." General Jackson shouts

The marine cannon crew primes their cannon to fire. A marine climbs up a tree and spots the British rockets through his spyglass. He gives a bearing by pointing his arm toward the British artillery.

"I can see where the rockets are coming from. I make it about six hundred yards. This is the bearing." The marine points his arm out.

Major Samuel Spotts's eighteen-pound cannon is primed and ready to fire.

"Sir, our cannon is primed and ready to fire," Major Spotts says to General Jackson.

"Fire the cannon!" Jackson shouts to Major Spotts.

Major Spotts points his sword forward and orders his artillerymen to open fire.

"Fire!" Major Spotts shouts.

Major Spotts's artillerymen light the cannon fuse, and the cannon fires. The shell flies out of the barrel. The cannonball flies over the redcoat infantry. The shell then strikes the British Congreve rockets. The ordnance explodes in a huge fireball. Dozens of rockets fly out in all different directions.

One of the British rockets strikes a British cannon, and the cannon explodes. The force of blast throws the cannon barrel onto a redcoat, crushing him. Three redcoats try to get the barrel off their comrade, but it is too hot. The redcoat tries to pull it off himself, but his ribs are crushed and he is in too much pain. Several other redcoats rush over and manage to get the cannon barrel off their friend. The redcoat looks at his coat and sees his ribs sticking out of his coat. He bleeds out and within a few seconds and dies.

The whole British staff can see the explosions, and that is the final straw for Pakenham. He smacks his knee and he blows up.

"God damn those bloody Yankee Doodle bastards! This has gone on for far too long. The time to end this bloody war is now. Gentlemen, return to your units and you shall attack. It is time to squash these Yanks like the worthless scum of the earth they are."

Back at Line Jackson, the American soldiers watch as the mushroom cloud rises into the sky, and they give a loud cheer that is heard through the British lines. The Seventy-Sixth cheer and shout. Simon and Celestia do not cheer but only smile. Daisy and Timmy calm their men.

Simon calls to his comrades, "They will send their Infantry next. Grenadiers, get ready and prepare to defend yourselves. No redcoat shall get inside our ramparts. You hear me? No one gets inside!"

"No one gets inside!" the Seventy-Sixth shout through the ranks.

General Jackson smiles as he puts his left leg on the left wheel of the cannon, with his sword in his right hand. He looks out toward the British line.

The redcoats prepare for their advance. The commanders give their orders to their units. Major General John Keane steps off his horse and walks in front of his men. He turns and faces them and gives his commands to his men.

"Ninety-Third Highlanders, prepare to fix bayonets. Fix your bayonets!"

The Ninety-Third Highlanders fix their bayonets onto their muskets.

"Shoulder your firelocks!"

The Ninety-Third Highlanders left-shoulder their muskets.

"Charge your bayonets!"

The Ninety-Third Highlanders charge their bayonets forward. They utter a battle cry. The Forty-Fourth Foot prepared their advance with Lieutenant Colonel Thomas Mullians riding behind his men. His men fix their bayonets to their muskets and charge them forward.

"The Forty-Fourth Foot will prepare to advance!" Colonel Mullians shouts.

The Twenty-First Fusiliers and the Fourth Foot fix their bayonets and prepare to march. General Gibbs rides back and forth in front of his lines, making sure the troops are ready. He rides in front of the Twenty-First Fusiliers marching band and gives his orders.

"Drum Major, you keep your music playing. You drummers keep drumming even if you have been shot. Is that clear?"

"Yes sir!" the British drum major replies.

In the rear with the reserves, General John Lambert rallies his men, and they prepare to march. All the British brigades are ready, and General Pakenham gives the order. A trumpeter sounds a bugle call that gives the order to move out. For five minutes, neither side makes a single sound or takes a single step. The whole area is completely silent.

Simon and his company are surprised by the pure quiet that fills the air around Line Jackson.

"My God, that is the loudest quiet I have ever heard in my life. This is quieter than just before the Battle of Bladensburg."

"Enjoy it while it lasts; it is always calm before the storm," Celestia states.

Timmy tries to find his pocket watch. He pats his pockets, not knowing that he lost his watch during the night attack.

"I wonder what time it is? Anyone know the time, because I think I lost my watch?" Timmy asks.

"Why do you care? We sure as hell are not going anywhere soon."

Timmy scoffs. "Well, you're sorta right and wrong, because if we die in battle today, we will be taking a seat at Jesus's dinner table tonight."

"Good point," Daisy says.

Just then Brittany's stomach growls. She rubs her gut. "Please don't talk about food. You buggers are making me hungry."

Simon and his staff along with a few other grenadiers laugh together.

The Americans stand by their cotton bales as they ready for the British assault.

Simon gives his orders to his grenadiers to load their weapons.

"Seventy-Sixth Pennsylvania Keystone Grenadiers, prime and load!" he shouts.

The Seventy-Sixth load their muskets.

Simon and Celestia look at each other.

"Celestia," Simon says, "if we shall fall today. I want you to know that I love you very much. And I am very grateful you are with me today."

"I love you too, Simon. If we do die today, we shall see each other again in the garden of the Lord."

They grab each other's hands, look deeply into each other's eyes, and kiss each other.

Timmy turns to Daisy. "Daisy, I really want you to know that I love you, too."

Daisy looks at Timmy and immediately kisses him.

Brittany and Ivan hug and kiss each other without speaking a single word to each other.

General Jackson looks over and he sees all of them kissing. He smiles and chuckles to himself. "Love birds."

The British Army begins its advance. Pakenham rides among the whole force. He cups his hands in front of his mouth to enhance his voice.

"The entire garrison will advance in line of attack! For the glory of England and our families. For the Duke of Wellington! For our great and noble King George III! Garrison, to the front! Quick march!"

The Forty-Fourth Regiment of Foot, Fourth, Seventh, Twenty-First, Forty-Third, Eighty-Fifth, Ninety-Third, Ninety-Fifth Rifles, Fourteenth Light Dragoons, and First and Fifth West India company begin their march to the American ramparts. The marching bands play their drums and pipes as they advance toward the American ramparts. Some drummers twirl their drumsticks in the air. The drums and bagpipes can be heard by the whole American line. The remaining British cannons fire one more volley toward the American ramparts. The cannons billow out massive amounts of black and white smoke. The shells land in front of the ramparts. The British garrison marches past the artillerymen. The artillerymen cheer for their fellow brothers. The British Infantry marches on past with pride and dignity. Their flags wave and their bayonet shine from the gleam of the morning sun. The smell of the artillery smoke can be smelled by all the British Infantrymen. One British soldier from the Ninety-fifth Rifles vomits because the smell of the smoke was too much for him. He wipes his mouth with his sleeve and keeps on marching alongside his brothers-in-arms.

Back with the British drum and fife corps from the Ninety-third Highlanders, a young drummer boy was beating his drum alongside the drum major. The boy was not even a teenager, he was no younger than ten years old. The boy looks up at the drum major who was thrusting his mace baton towards the sky, as he leads the corps from behind the infantry of the Ninety-third. The drum major looks down at the boy. He could see the fear in the boy's eyes. Deep inside his own heart, the drum major was scared as well, however he knew they had a duty to fulfill. The drum major winks at the little drummer boy and smiles. The little boy felt a sense of hope, he still felt scared, but not as less.

General Andrew Jackson stands behind Simon and his staff as they watch the massive British force moving toward them. All the grenadiers and marines watch as the fusiliers march toward them. The sound of the bagpipes fills the air.

"Out of all the music on earth, those bloody bagpipes are the worst of them all," Daisy says to her friends. "That music will make my ears bleed before the bullet does, by God."

Simon looks down at the rest of his company and then looks back at the advancing redcoats. He wipes the sweat off his head and fixes his hat. He then gives a prediction of how this battle will play out. "This is gonna be a repeat of Bunker Hill. No doubt about it. I hope we win this time."

All the American soldiers stand still, expressionless. Timmy is standing next to Simon and begins to quake in great terror.

"Jesus! I have never seen that many lobsters before, sir. For the first time in my life, I am very scared, sir."

Simon pats Timmy's shoulder and tries to calm his fears. "I feel the same way, my friend. They look like an inhuman entity. Don't worry, you will be alright."

Daisy and Celestia watch as the thousands of redcoats march toward them, and they begin to get scared as well.

"Steady yourself, sis. I'm scared as well. Just stay next to me and we will be okay. Understand?" Celestia says to her scared sister.

"Understood! May God have mercy on us all," Daisy says as she makes the sign of the cross.

The redcoats march within four hundred yards of the American ramparts. Hundreds of British Union Jacks are flying in the breeze. The bagpipe music can be heard by the American forces as it gets closer. Andrew Jackson stands upon the ramparts and looks at the redcoats. He begins to count quietly.

"One, two, three, four, five, six."

"General," Simon says, "the enemy is in range. Shall we unleash hell?"

"I will count forty seconds before firing," Jackson says.

"But the enemy is in range, sir. And every second we waste brings them closer by five yards, sir." He points at the enemy line.

"I know that, Major. I will count forty seconds. Fifteen, sixteen, seventeen, eighteen, nineteen, twenty."

The Keystone grenadiers begin to get nervous as they cock their muskets. The Forty-Fourth Regiment of Foot is three hundred yards away. They step high as they make their drummers drum so loudly that it makes the ground shake. American soldiers look all around them as the dirt begins to shake as if an earthquake is happening. Andrew Jackson then shouts an order so loudly that the commanders of other American units can hear it.

"My brave Americans, stand ready!"

The Seventy-Sixth Pennsylvania aim their muskets downrange. The US Marines and Tennessee, Kentucky, Louisiana, and Mississippi militias aim their muskets and rifles. The artillerymen push their cannons forward toward the rampart's walls. The naval soldiers and regulars aim their muskets and cannons at the redcoats. Simon and his staff aim downrange, using the walls of the ramparts as bipods so they will have better accuracy. Simon spots a British major on horseback riding in front the Forty-Fourth's drum and fife squad. He aims for his head. Celestia aims at the chest of a British lieutenant. Daisy and Timmy aim for the bagpipers. Just then the Seventy-Sixth marching band aim their muskets downrange.

"Ten more seconds, lads," Jackson shouts to his men.

As soon as the Forty-Fourth Regiment of Foot is one hundred yards away from the center American ramparts, the redcoats see the Americans.

Andrew Jackson slowly raises his sword high. "Thirty-five, thirty-six, thirty-seven, thirty-eight, thirty-nine, forty. They are near enough now, gentlemen. You may fire when ready!" After ten more seconds, Major General Andrew Jackson screams at the top of his lungs, *"Commence fire!"*

The whole American line, from the swamp to the outer banks of the Mississippi River, erupts with a massive volley of heavy iron cannons and thousands of small arms. The American ramparts are ablaze as over three thousand muskets and rifles open fire. The bullets fly through the air. The Forty-Fourth Foot is struck by the bullet hailstorm. The front guard of the Forty-Fourth Foot is instantly destroyed. British soldiers are shot multiple times with bullets and shrapnel from cannonballs. Bullets and cannonballs instantly cut down over a hundred British soldiers of the Forty-Fourth Regiment of Foot. The American defenders cut down hundreds of British soldiers with the first volley. British soldiers are shot in their chests, faces, legs, arms, and heads. Scores of redcoat officers are instantly cut down. The Seventy-Sixth fire into the faces of the Forty-Fourth Foot. Simon shoots a redcoat major in his right eye, and the bullet exits the major's head. Blood and flesh splatter the face of a British drummer right behind him. The drummer stops and tries to wipe his face but ends up getting shot in the chest. The drummer kneels on one leg, still beating his drum. The second rank of the Forty-Fourth Foot fills the gaps. The Forty-Fourth Foot and the Ninety-Fifth Rifles halt their advance seventy yards away from the American ramparts. They fire upon the American ramparts, but with the heavy smoke, they have a hard time identifying their targets. The Forty-Fourth Foot attempt to open fire upon the American center line. The Seventy-Sixth Pennsylvania and the US Marines, alongside a small platoon of American riflemen, reload and fire their small arms with great speed. They use a one-two system in which one man primes a musket with powder and a second loads the musket with shot and powder in the flash pan. He then passes it to the shooter, who cocks the hammer and opens fire.

The front and rear ranks of the Forty-Fourth Foot kneel and fire into the Seventy-Sixth's line. The bullets strike the dirt wall and miss. Both sides race to reload their muskets. The Americans beat the British to it, and they fire volley upon volley into the Forty-Fourth. Scores of redcoats from the Forty-Fourth are cut down by the volleys. Simon and his staff stay calm under fire. They reload and fire their muskets quickly. Simon puts a US Marine in his spot while he checks on the other men. He runs by his men, screaming out so they hear him. The gunfire is so loud that he has to scream.

"Keep up your fire! Pour into them, grenadiers! Keep an eye on your ammo. Reload and fire!"

Just then a bullet strikes the top of his right shoulder. Blood spills out. He puts his left hand over the wound. The pain is severe. Simon cries out in pain. Timmy and Celestia look behind them and see Simon on the ground. They run over to him.

"Simon, are you alright?" Celestia asks.

"Sir, stay down. You're wounded!" Timmy says.

However, Simon is able to ignore the intense pain and keep up the fight while he can still breath.

"Calm down, you two. I'll be fine in a minute. Go back to the ramparts and continue firing! Don't let up!"

Timmy heads back to the rampart. Celestia drops her musket and helps Simon to his feet. Simon is able to stand up, and he grabs a bandage from his haversack. He binds his arm. He and Celestia pick up their muskets. They get back to their positions and continue firing.

An American captain named Daniel Patterson comes running along, and he shouts to his men, "Shoot low, boys! Shoot low! Rake 'em!"

The Twenty-First Fusiliers march forward to aid the Forty-Fourth Foot. Major General John Gibbs watches as the Forty-Fourth struggle to hold their own. Soon the Twenty-First Fusiliers reach the Forty-Fourth Foot. The Twenty-First Fusiliers opt to raise their muskets and open fire instead of rushing American lines head on.

"Twenty-First Fusiliers, halt. Make ready! Take aim! Fire at will!" General Gibbs shouts.

The Twenty-First Fusiliers fire their volley in a massive poof of smoke. The US Marines return fire and begin to cut down dozens of the Twenty-First's front rank. The Twenty-First Fusiliers are soon under heavy musket fire. Dozens of British soldiers fall to the ground dead or wounded. General Gibbs rides forward to rally his men. The ground is covered with more redcoat bodies than blood. Wounded soldiers roll on the ground, crying out in pain. Another massive volley made up of one thousand muskets from the American ramparts fires into what is left of the Forty-Fourth Regiment of Foot. The volley cuts down hundreds of redcoats. All the American soldiers fire at will. The whole battlefield is covered with white smoke, and the sounds of the wounded fill the air. Every volley shakes the ground like a massive earthquake. The American fury is unleashed upon the Forty-Fourth Foot. One British soldier says during the battle, "In less time that one can write it, the Forty-Fourth Foot was literally swept from the face of the earth." Only small pockets of the Forty-Fourth Foot join with the Twenty-First Fusiliers, and they make a mad charge toward the Rodriguez Canal, but without extra ladders they cannot scale the ramparts, and they become easy pickings for the Americans pouring fire into the column.

The Ninety-Third Sutherland Highlanders march forward to within range of the American line. The officer at the front rank halts the Ninety-third. As he prepares to order them to fire, he raises his sword, but a bullet strikes him in the head. The men of the Ninety-Third stand there in their tight ranks. They are easy targets for the American forces pouring fire directly into the column. Every time a Highlander falls to the ground, another one steps forward and takes his place.

The Highlander's drum and fife corps hid behind the infantrymen. Unfortunately, that was not going to keep them out of danger. One US Keystone Grenadier finished reloading his Brown Bess and took aim. He tries to look for a british officer. But from the smoke, clouds of cannon and musket smoke, it almost made it impossible to spot any British soldier from fifty yards away. The Keystone grenadier soon spots the Ninety-third's drum and fife corps and takes aim. He breathes slowly, aiming with nice precision, he fires his musket. The bullet skims off a Highlander's right ear and the drum major takes the musket ball right between his eyes. The boy was splashed with the drum major's blood. The drum major falls to the ground dead. The boy fell to his knees and tried to get the drum major back on his feet. Seconds later, the little boy is shot in his right cheek and falls to the dirt. The boy's right cheek had an entrance wound about the size of an acorn. The boy looked up at the sky and all he could hear was the sounds of war. The boy spits up blood and he dies right next to the drum major.

Scores of the soldiers of the Ninety-Third are cut down until an officer runs in from the rear and orders them to retire to the rear. They retreat, but the front rank, which is facing the ramparts, is cut down. The others retreat from the ramparts, and some of the Americans stop firing at them and clap for them, acknowledging their discipline and order in the heat of battle.

Daisy spots General Gibbs, who is riding around on his horse in a demented rage. He is expecting Colonel Mullians to bring up his men, but they are nowhere to be seen. He shouts, "Colonel Mullians, if I shall live till tomorrow, I will see you hanging from one of these trees!"

Daisy reaches into her cartridge box and notices that she has no more rounds. She drops her musket and looks behind her and spots a dead rifleman. She kneels, closes the man's eyes, and picks up his Pennsylvania rifle.

"I'm sorry, but I need to borrow your weapon, my friend," Daisy says.

She finds that the rifle is primed and loaded. She walks back to her position, where she sees scores of redcoats firing into the American lines. Every time she tries to aim, bullets strike near her position. She braves the musket fire and takes aim for General Gibbs. Gibbs tries to rally his men, but his horse gets stuck in the canal. As he tries to get out. He notices Daisy taking aim and pulls out his pistol.

Celestia looks down at the canal, runs over to Daisy, and pushes her out of the line of fire. Daisy falls to the ground, and Gibbs fires his pistol.

The bullet strikes Celestia in her chest. She falls to the ground. Daisy watches as her sister cries out in pain. Daisy screams out in horror at the sight of her big sister being wounded.

"Celestia, *noooooo!*"

Daisy gets back up and aims at Gibbs, who is still trying to get out. A few seconds later, he manages to break free, but he is not quick enough.

Daisy aims at him. "To hell you go, you British bastard!" she shouts. She fires the rifle, and the bullet mortally wounds General Gibbs. Gibbs falls from his horse into the canal. She begins to cry as she runs over to Celestia and covers her wound. Celestia groans in pain but tries to get back up on her feet. She grips her musket and stands up slowly. Blood spills out of her chest. She looks at her wound. Daisy pulls out a bandage and wraps the wound up. Celestia stands and takes her place beside Simon. Simon looks at Celestia and notices that she has been shot.

"Oh, God. No! Celestia, how bad is it?"

"It's nothing, Simon. Just keep blasting those lobsters."

Both of them reload their muskets and continue to unleash their fury upon the redcoats.

The redcoats get cut down by the near hundreds. The green grass has turned red with blood. Both sides frantically and relentlessly fire, with less than one hundred yards separating them.

While the American left and center ramparts hold strong, the right flank on the Mississippi River remains in the open. The British right flank under General John Keane and Colonel Robert Rennie leads about two thousand light infantry toward the ramparts. The Beale Riflemen and the Seventh Infantry regulars wait for the redcoats to get close. Once the redcoats are at 150 yards, they fire with deadly fury. A massive volley of muskets and several cannons unleash a storm of bullets and solid shot. The Forty-Third Light Infantry suffers one hundred and twenty casualties in a few short seconds. Some of the wounded redcoats try to stand up, but they are too badly wounded and they get trampled by their fellow redcoats. The Riflemen target the British officers. Every few seconds, a British officer drops to the ground wounded or dead. General Keane tries to rally his men for the push into the ramparts, but a volley from the Seventh Infantry cuts him down, and he falls from his horse wounded. The Seventh Infantry and Forty-Third halt their advance and fire a volley that cuts down five American regulars and three riflemen. With the cover of the musket smoke, the British utter a loud battle cry. The Forty-Third and the Seventh British regulars make a mad dash through the canal and manage to storm the ramparts. Two redcoats manage to bayonet five American soldiers. The Seventh US regulars charge with their bayonets and begin to stab any redcoat that storms the ramparts. Colonel Robert Rennie grabs his pistol and climbs the ladder and storms the rampart. An American regular charges at him with his bayonet. Rennie fires his pistol and kills the Yankee. More British soldiers storm the ramparts. The American riflemen snipe at the Forty-Third. One rifleman takes aim at Colonel Rennie.

Rennie swings his sword in the air and screams to his men, "Come on in, lads! We'll kill 'em all. Wipe them out! Take them by storm! Charge!"

The American rifleman fires and hits Rennie directly in the heart. He falls to the ground, bleeds out, and dies. The Seventh US regulars are able to push the Forty-Third and the Seventh British regulars off of the ramparts.

Across the river, the American artillery open fire with their heavy cannons. Dozens of shells explode all around the Forty-Third and the Seventh. British soldiers try to take cover but are cut down by the shells. Redcoats lose their arms, legs, and even their heads. Blood and flesh spill out on the banks of the river. The Forty-Third and the Seventh Infantry retreat from the ramparts in mad panic. American regulars fire into the redcoats' backs. Some American regulars begin to cheer in victory. The Fourth Foot rallies with what is left of the Second Fusiliers and the Forty-Fourth Foot. The Seventy-Sixth fire relentlessly into the British lines. The cannon the marines have overheats. A cannon that is in reserve is brought forward onto the rampart. Daisy and Timmy aim their muskets and cut down two drummers still beating their drums. The drummers are both shot in the chest. One dies instantly, while the second one beats his drum with one hand and then dies a few seconds later.

Just then another young British drummer boy marches out of the smoke and looks down at the ramparts. The boy drops his drum and picks up a Baker rifle that was in the hands of a dead rifleman from the Ninety-fifth Rifles. The drummer boy aims the rifle and spots Celestia. Celestia spots the boy and aims her musket, but she has a memory of shooting Sergeant Major Harry Adams at North Point. She hesitates for a few seconds—long enough for the boy to take a potshot. Simon steps in front of her and takes the bullet directly to the chest. Two seconds later, a volley from the Fourth Foot wounds Simon and Celestia. Simon grabs the rampart wall to keep from falling. He is hit in the chest again, the two bullets shatter two ribs, and a bullet skims his head but doesn't penetrate his skull. Simon feels his chest and he could feel that ribs were broken. Celestia is hit in the chest and in the right shoulder. They both try to keep their balance and not fall to the ground. Daisy runs over and helps her sister. Timmy runs to Simon and holds him. Despite being wounded more than twice, he keeps commanding the Seventy-Sixth.

"Keep up the fire. Kill every red bastard in sight!" Simon orders. He manages to stay on his feet. He points to Celestia, who is having a hard time staying on her feet because the pain is becoming too much for her. "I can stand up, Timmy; just help Celestia!" Simon says.

Timmy runs over to Celestia and helps her up. Just then a soldier of the Ninety-Fifth Rifles sees Timmy and fires at him. The bullet wings Timmy's right arm. He cries out in pain. Another British volley is fired, and one bullet hits Daisy in her left hand. She grabs her hand but holds on to Celestia. She cries out in pain and she sees the bullet went right through her hand. A few of the British riflemen from the Ninety-Fifth are cut down. Fifteen minutes of the battle have passed, and the redcoats continue their attack. General Pakenham rides forward with a grenadier company from the reserves as they march toward the center.

As General Pakenham rides forward, he can see the field covered with red-coated bodies. The grass is as red as blood. After five minutes, he arrives at the center and rallies the redcoats for a final stand. He shouts a threat to the American lines, "We will hang your gutted bodies on the streets of England!"

Simon tries to keep his stance and loads his musket. He hears Pakenham's threat and screams his own threat as he takes another shot. "Shut the hell up and give us more lobsters to fry, you filthy red bastards!"

Then Celestia screams out to the redcoats, "You English bastards will burn in the hottest depths of hell!"

Timmy Miller spots one redcoat who was aiming at him. The redcoat pulls the trigger but nothing happens. He forgot to load his musket. The

British redcoat hurries to reload his musket. Timmy remembers that he had his bayonet fixed to his musket. Timmy positioned his musket like he was about to throw a spear. With one great throw, he threw his musket at the redcoat. The redcoat looks up in time to see Timmy's musket flying towards him. He is not able to get out of the way and Timmy's musket pierces the redcoat's chest. The bayonet lands in the redcoat's chest and punctures the redcoat's heart. The redcoat grips the musket and can only see the bayonet in his chest. He gasps for air. He looks up to see Timmy gripping the musket and pulling the bayonet out of the redcoat's body. The redcoat falls into the canal that was filled with blood. Timmy rushes back the rampart and vaults over it as fast as he could. He resumes his defensive position and continues to fire into the redcoats along with the Keystone grenadiers.

General Pakenham rides forward as he tries to rally his troops. He is shot in the knee by grapeshot. A few seconds later, a US Marine shoots the general's horse. He falls off his horse, but he manages to stand back up. His aide-de-camp gives him another horse. He continues to rally his frightened and panic stricken soldiers. General Jackson walks behind the marines. Just then, Pakenham's aide-de-camp is shot in the head.

Jackson has the chance to kill the commander of the British. He calls to the marines, "Marines, target their commander now! Fire double grapeshot. You may fire when ready!"

Five marines prime and load their eight-pound cannon. They load the cannon with two bags of grapeshot. Captain Patterson looks down the cannon's sights and aims it at Pakenham.

"We are primed and ready! Marines, fire the cannon!"

One marine fires the cannon, and the grapeshot is like a shotgun blast. The shot strikes General Pakenham in the lungs, spine, and arms. He falls from his horse, severely wounded. The grapeshot also cuts down a dozen redcoats surrounding Pakenham. The redcoats see their commander on the ground, dying in front of their eyes. Some soldiers begin to retreat, while a few others run over to his side. Five redcoats pick his body up and carry him away from the American ramparts. A small platoon from the Twenty-First Fusiliers covers their retreat, but not before firing one more volley. This time the shots find their targets and their shots will be fatal. The fusiliers fire upon the Seventy-Sixth Pennsylvania, and two bullets strike Simon, one in the lung, and a final bullet strikes him directly in his gut. One more bullet hits Celestia in her right shoulder and exits out the center of her back. Both of them fall down, mortally wounded. Celestia and Simon breathe heavily as their wounds gush blood. She looks at Simon's wounded body. Simon's green uniform goes from being green to being bloodred. A few Keystone Grenadiers break their ranks and rush over to their wounded commanders. Simon and Celestia try to stand back up, but they're in too much pain to stand. Two Keystone Grenadier's kneel down by Simon and Celestia.

"Sir, stay the hell down! You're wounded very badly. Please, stay down." One Keystone grenadier says to Simon while a fellow female grenadier is by Celestia's side. She urges Celestia to stay down as well.

"Ma'am, please stay down."

"Help me up, soldier. Get me up now! The battle is not over till every lobster is dead!" Celestia says as she tries to stand back up on her feet. The female grenadier forces Celestia to the ground and restrains her.

"Ma'am, for the love of God stay the hell down!" The female grenadier shouts. Celestia and Simon look down at their bodies and realize that they're mortally wounded. They knew that they were going to die. They both finally stay down with some of the grenadiers at their sides. A few of their grenadiers were shocked and left with sadness at the sight of their commanders so grievously wounded.

The whole redcoat force begins to retreat. The whole American line erupts not with muskets or cannons but with cheers of victory. The American defenders begin to taunt the British soldiers by yelling battle cries at them.

"Bunker Hill! Bunker Hill! Bunker Hill!"

The US Marines begin to use their own chant. "Washington! Washington! Washington!

The British soldier can hear the American's chanting and they feel embarrassed and humiliated. The remaining redcoats, who are now commanded by General Lambert, are ordered to retreat from the field.

When the battle is over, every inch of the field is covered with redcoat bodies and body parts. The British suffer 2,459 killed, wounded, captured, or missing; while the Americans suffer only 70 casualties. Soon after the fighting, General Pakenham bleeds out and dies before his body can be brought back to the British lines. On the Seventy-Sixth's position, Major Simon Smithtrovich and Captain Celestia Smithtrovich are dying from their wounds. Timmy grabs Simon's body and lays him right up against Celestia. Both of them lie on the ramparts with their backs against the wall. All the grenadiers gather around them and watch their commanders dying in front of them. Some of the men begin to shed tears and cry. Daisy and Timmy kneel in front of them. Celestia and Simon look up at the Seventy-Sixth and their best friends.

"My friends of the brave Seventy-Sixth," Simon says weakly, "I had a dream that I would be fighting alongside the bravest and most loyal patriots on this planet. That dream came true because of all of you. You are all the toughest bunch of Pennsylvanians I have ever had the honor of commanding. You all have done everything I have asked today and many more times before. Y'all have earned the right to go home."

Timmy kneels between them. He tries to hold back his tears.

"Timmy, Daisy, Brittany, everyone, thank you for everything; I will always cherish your friendships," Celestia says.

Daisy walks over to her dying sister, kneels, and grabs her hand. They grip each other's hands tightly. Blood spills out onto Daisy's hand. Celestia smiles, and then Daisy hugs her. When she hugs her, Celestia groans in pain. Then Celestia looks over at Simon, who is bleeding greatly from his wounds. Celestia begins to cry. The tears make her blood run in the trail of her tears on her face.

"I love you, Simon. I will see you in heaven. We will watch you all from heaven," Celestia says.

Simon then says, "We both will remember you all…forever!"

Celestia slides right next to Simon. She grabs his hand, and then they both take their final gasps of air. Celestia's head leans down onto Simon's shoulder, and they both take their final breath of American air that they proudly defended with their own lives and die from their wounds.

"Simon? Celestia? No!" Daisy shouts. Then she begins to bawl.

Daisy and Timmy wept along with the other grenadiers. Timmy drops his musket and falls to his knees.

Daisy has a major mental breakdown. She grabs Simon and Celestia and hugs them tightly, blubbering and shrieking like a banshee. "No! Simon! Celestia! Please wake up! Please, for the love of God! Don't go! I love you! Please!"

Timmy tries to pry Daisy off of them both, but he is not able to. Daisy holds on tight.

Jessica and Devin, along with Brittany, help Timmy pry Daisy off their dead leader's lifeless body. Daisy then hugs Timmy with a very firm grip as she blubbers uncontrollably. Brittany kneels and puts her hand on Celestia's heart. She then does the same to Simon. She definitely can tell with the touch that their hearts have stopped beating for sure.

"Y'all did really great. I will never forget you both. Rest in gentle and sweet peace," Brittany says. She stands up and salutes with her mace. Devin and Jessica walk over, and their hearts sink in pure sadness. Jessica and Devin hug each other. They cry hard in each other's arms. The blood from Celestia's and Simon's bodies flows on the ground in small streams. But the tears falling from the eyes of the Keystone grenadiers are beginning to flow like a raging river. The tears seem to be more plentiful than the blood shed that day. The cries from the Seventy-Sixth are louder than the muskets and cannons that are still being fired. The Seventy-Sixth may have lost few, but each fatality was a best friend or a family member.

Upon seeing the lifeless bodies of their commanding officers, some of the Keystone grenadiers break ranks and fire upon the retreating and wounded redcoats. Timmy grabs his musket, and the rest of the Seventy-Sixth grab their muskets and aim downrange. Timmy yells out with pure rage, "Kill any wounded redcoats that are still alive!"

The Seventy-Sixth fires one last major volley with one hundred small arms. Some wounded redcoats stand up and try to limp away from the battleground. However, they are instantly shot down by the Seventy-Sixth. Two dozen wounded redcoats are shot and killed. The Seventy-Sixth then drop their muskets and begin to lose their sense of discipline. But they soon get a grip and stand and look upon their fallen leaders. Sadness grips their hearts more tightly than the fact that they have won the battle of New Orleans.

Through the whole day after the fighting had stopped, the grenadiers of the Seventy-Sixth Pennsylvania stood guard over their fallen commanders, not moving a single muscle. Not a single word is spoken during the whole day. By now the blood has drained out of the commanders' bodies. After standing guard for almost twenty-four hours, the guards of the Seventy-Sixth are finally relieved of their position. A wagon is brought over, and Daisy and Brittany help put Celestia in it. Timmy and Ivan help put Simon right next to Celestia. The Seventy-Sixth form their ranks, and they march away from the ramparts. But this time like many times before there are no marches being played and no songs were sung. Another company of American regulars were marching to stand at the post where the Keystone grenadiers fought during the battle. The American regulars gazed at the faces of the Seventy-sixth and could see the sadness, not only in their hearts, but within their very own souls.

CHAPTER 34

"REMEMBER WHAT WE HAVE FOUGHT FOR!"

New Orleans, Louisiana
Line Jackson
January 9, 1815
Noontime

The Seventy-Sixth Pennsylvania prepare to bury their leaders on the battlefield. They dig one grave for the both of them. They were each given a coffin. The coffins are laid side by side inside the grave. American flags were wrapped over the coffins. The Seventy-Sixth attends the funeral. The remaining staff of the Seventy-Sixth prepare to say their final words to their fallen leaders. Daisy starts off with a speech to her sister.

"Celestia was not just our captain. She was a friend, a leader, and the best sister anyone could ever ask for. She was a woman who was not afraid to get her hands dirty. She was a brave soldier. She was a woman who always committed to the cause and never took anything from anyone. She will be missed by all of us, and may she rest in peace forever." Daisy salutes them and steps back.

Brittany goes next. She holds back a few tears, and then she speaks.

"I have never known any officer who valued music more than Simon and Celestia. They both believed that music is the best thing to keep a company together when the times get bad. They both helped us write our march that we have sung so many times. I honestly have lost track of how many times we sang it. Clearly it was never enough for them. It made us not only a company but also what we will always be forever till the end of time—a family. I will forever cherish their friendship till the day the earth shall claim its overdue bounty." Brittany salutes them and she steps back.

Timmy steps forward. He speaks with a heroic and motivational tone as he was giving his speech.

"'Remember what we fought for.' That is what he said to us at the beginning of the war. It is a simple order that any officer can give. He never wanted to have tribute. Simon wanted that to be his hope should he ever die on the field. And for all the many decades to come for this nation, for all who learn about what the American armies have done in this war, should any free American citizen or veteran step upon the land where we fought, or should our grandchildren visit any battleground, may they remember their ancestors who laid down their lives for virtue, liberty, and independence. This battle may be over, but the war to uphold our state's motto will never end. As long as there are those who will support everything and as long there are those who will lay down their lives to destroy tyranny and who are willing to keep the promise that America holds, which declares that all men and women are created equal under God, never again shall America have to bow to a man who dares call himself a king. Let those future warriors who will lay down their lives for the United States of America be blessed by the men and women who have gone before them, and let them know that they will never be alone to face those who bring evil to this nation. God bless our fallen comrades, and God bless these United States of America."

The Seventy-Sixth Pennsylvania cheer so loud that they know that Simon and Celestia, along with their fallen brothers and sisters, can hear them.

Brittany then directs her band to play "The Keystone Grenadiers."

"Let us all sing one last time in honor of our fallen leaders and the one hundred eighty-nine of our comrades who have laid down their lives. I shall take the first verse, then join in for the rest of the march."

The Seventy-Sixth Corps Marching Band stood at attention and began to play the march. The Keystone grenadiers encircle the graves of their fallen leaders. They lock arms and wait for their cue to sing.

Brittany has changed the words for the first and second verse. She takes a deep breath and begins to sing:

Defending the land of the free, let's all sing with honorable glee.
We fight for our motto with all our heart and soul.
We'll always be on our guard, from the night's dark to the day's light.
Hurrah, hurrah, hurrah, hurrah, the Keystone grenadiers.
To those who wore the bearskins, who wore the best array,
Ready to answer America's call at any time of day,
Never shall our eternal freedom be taken away.
Freedom's torch burning all the day, the Keystone grenadiers.

Brittany blows her whistle three times, and then the rest of the Keystone grenadiers join in the final three verses.

Whene'er we are commanded to break the enemy line,
Our leaders march with sabers and we with bayonets.
We throw Britain off the hills and toward the deep blue sea.
Cheering with glee, proud to be, a Keystone grenadier.
And now the war is over, back to our homes we go.
Our families cheer, "Hurrah, lads, here come the Seventy-Sixth.
Here comes the Seventy-Sixth, my dears, our noble grenadiers.
With blood, sweat, and tears, the Keystone grenadiers.

As they sing the final verse, They all lock arms and slow the pace of the song. They continue to sing in unison.

Some future day shall hail us the noble and the brave,
and giving peace and freedom to the United States,
A nation o'er the ocean spread shall strive and thrive,
O'er the land of the free and the home of the brave, God bless America!

(Written by, Drum Major Brittany Benson, January 9th, 1815)

The Seventy-Sixth finally bury their fallen commanders, who are not just military leaders but members of their families. The rest of the company paid their respects by saluting their fallen leaders one by one. The last ones to salute was the remaining staff of the company. Daisy stands over the grave of her sister. She slowly raises her hand and salutes. She sniffles and sheds a few tears. Timmy Miller then walks up and stands right beside Daisy. Timmy was crying softly, but managing to keep some of his composure. He stands proudly at the position of attention and salutes. He lowers his arm. Daisy then wraps her right arm around Timmy. Timmy looks at Daisy and wraps his left arm around her. Brittany, and the Little's stand side by side with their senior officers. All three of them stand at attention and pay their respects with a final salute. Jessica and Devil Little kneel down on one leg and touch the grave soil. Brittany kneels down and touches the grave soil. Timmy and Daisy both follow suit, kneeling down and touching the grave soil. They lock each other's hands and touch the soil together. They all give one final silent battle cry as they all speak in unison for their fallen leaders.

"For virtue, liberty, and independence, may you now rest in sweet and heavenly peace."

May 5th, 1827
The Miller Plantation
Morning

On the Miller plantation, Daisy and Timmy Miller awaken from their peaceful slumber. They both looked at each other and knew that the morning was going to be a very special day. Because they were going to do something great with their children. Daisy gets up from the bed and heads to their childrens bedroom. She slowly opens the door and can see their children who are just nine years old, almost ten in two months. She walked into the bedroom and leaned down between their beds. She kisses Celestia on the cheek and then she kisses Simon on the cheek.

"Good morning, my darlings." Daisy said with a sweet and soothing voice.

Simon gets up first and stretches his arms. He looks at his mother and smiles.

"Good morning, mommy." Simon Miller says.

Celestia Miller awakens and gets up from her bed and hugs her mother.

"Good morning, mommy. What are we going to do today, mommy?" Celestia Miller asked her mom.

Daisy hugged both of her children and informed them about how this day is going to be very special because you two are going to learn about your name sakes.

"Well, today we get to go plant something very special, I know how much you love helping daddy in the gardens. And you two are going to learn why you were named Celestia and Simon. You were named after your late uncle and aunt, Smithtrovich. But first, let's have some breakfast and then we will go into the gardens."

Down at the dinner table, Timmy Miller was setting the table for breakfast. Daisy and the children walk into the hall and take their seats. Timmy sees his children and goes to hug them.

"Ah, there's my two little soldiers. Did you two sleep well?" Timmy said excitedly.

"Yes, daddy." Simon and Celestia said at the same time.

Timmy kisses them both once on the cheeks and then goes to bring in the rest of the food to the table. They all sit down and have a conversation about the first part of their children's names sake. Daisy begins to speak the first part of the story.

"Simon, Celestia, you two are about to learn about how you two got your names. Now your mother and i have been wanting to tell you all about this, but we wanted to wait until you were old enough to fully understand. First off, your mother and I were soldiers back in the War of 1812."

Simon and Celestia Miller were amazed by the fact their mother and father were soldiers. They had excited expressions on their faces. Daisy continues the story.

"We were a part of a professional company of elite grenadiers called the Seventy-Sixth Keystone Grenadiers. Me and my sister, along with two dozen other women were in the unit. My sister's name was Celestia. I named you after my late sister. She was our second in command. Our senior officer was named Simon Smithtrovich. Timmy decided to name you after our commander. Both of them were very brave, noble, honorable and the most dedicated patriots that we could ever serve under, but most importantly, they were family. Your late uncle and aunt lead your mother and I in many battles. We were a sight to see on the battlegrounds. We had our good and bad times during that war."

Simon Miller then asks about what they became of them during the war.

"What happened to them, mother?"

Daisy and Timmy look at each other. Timmy decided to explain what happened to them.

"Well, bare with me on this. There was one battle down in the south. The Battle of New Orleans as it's now known. We marched all the way down to the city and fought against the British for a few weeks. On January 8th, 1815, just two years before you two were born, the main battle took place at a canal. Your mother and I, along with the company had to defend the city against the British and they outnumbered us, three to one. It happened in the early morning. The British sent eight thousand men towards us and we battled for twenty-five minutes. The company held the center of the line and we fought against them with every ounce of strength we had. When the battle was over, America came out on top. Sadly though, your aunt and uncle were killed in the battle. We buried them down near the battle line where they rest today. But for their honor and sacrifice they made for our company, for the army, and for our country, we decided to name you two after them."

Simon and Celestia Miller were surprised that they were named after war heros.

"Father, I have to say that was a great story. I can't believe that I'm named after your company's leader." Simon Miller says with gladness.

"However, that is only half of the story. We were not just soldiers, we were apple farmers. Your uncle owned the greatest farming land in Pennsylvania." Timmy added into the story.

"That's right. He grew the best apples anyone could have ever tasted. And that is why we will continue the family business. How would you like to become apple farmers, kids?" Daisy asked her children.

Simon and Celestia Miller raised their hands and said proudly.

"We want to be apple farmers!" They both said with glee and joy.

"Well, then that's great to hear. Once we finish our breakfast, we will go out and plant our first apple trees for the new season." Timmy says.

The four of them eat the rest of their breakfast. They head on out onto the new piece of land on the northern side of the Miller plantation. Daisy brings the children out from a shed. Simon and Celestia Miller were holding the seeds in the palm of their hands. They walk over to Timmy who was digging two holes. Timmy finishes digging the holes and turns to see his children holding the seeds.

"Okay now, the hole is dug. Now you two get to lay the seeds into these two holes. These apple trees are in the name of our company's leaders who gave their lives in the defense of our great nation. So, let's begin a new chapter in our lives. Kids, you do the honors."

Simon and Celestia Miller walk over to the hole and they kneel on their knees. They both hold the seeds over the hole. They both speak to their late uncle and aunt before they drop the seeds into the hole.

"Thank you for serving our country and protecting my mother, Celestia. I love you." Celestia Miller says.

"I will never ever forget you Uncle Simon, I love you." Simon Miller says.

They both flip their hands over and drop the seeds into the dirt hole. Daisy and Timmy felt touched and happy for their children for speaking those kind words about their late family members. Daisy kneeled down between her children and hugged them both.

"Awe, that was very nice to say that to them. I know they love you both with all their hearts and souls." Daisy says as she sheds a tear of joy.

Timmy kneels down and joins in the family group hug.

"That's very kind of you both to say. I love you all very, very much." Timmy says.

They all break off from the hug and they all take turns filling in the hole and watering the soil. They all lock arms around each other's shoulders and gaze upon the soil of what will become their new family orchard that would create the same kind of apples that Simon and his best friends had farmed before dropping the shovel and picking up a musket, to take to the battlefields that would transform a young nation into one of the most powerful and legendary nations on earth, the United States of America.

AFTERWORD

In the aftermath of the Battle of New Orleans, General Lambert held a council of war three days after the battle. They wanted to attempt to continue with the campaign, but they knew that it would be too costly. And when Napoleon Bonaparte escaped from Elba on February 26 of 1815, King George III knew that fighting in the United States was not worth it, because their forces would be needed in Europe. Many of the British regiments that fought in the Battle of New Orleans would go on to fight in the Battles of Quatre Bras and most famously Waterloo. The casualties at the Battle of New Orleans were light in comparison to how many the British Army would suffer during the Hundred Days Campaign, which marked the final days of Bonaparte's reign as emperor of France.

Major Simon Smithtrovich died at the age of twenty-five. He wanted to be remembered as an American officer who wanted not only to serve his nation but also to find the true meaning of friendship. He was given that friendship by his grenadiers, and he was given the best birthday gift by his family, the brave Seventy-Sixth—a great victory in the Seventy-Sixth's final battle during the War of 1812.

Simon's cousin, Charles Young, would fight at the Battle of Waterloo on June 18, 1815. Waterloo would be the final battle of the Napoleonic Wars. Charles Young marched into the battle at 7:00 p.m. The Old Guard was sent up the center of Wellington's line. Once they got close to the British lines, the British fired devastating point-blank volley's into the Old Guard. Charles Young was shot more than ten times in his chest, head, and legs. He was killed along with twenty-five thousand soldiers of the Grand Armée. Charles received a letter from Simon's parents about his cousin's death just two weeks before the Battle of Waterloo. Charles Young died at the age of twenty-seven.

Captain Celestia Smithtrovich died at age twenty-four. Celestia, her sister, Daisy, and Brittany lived on as the head female patriots of the Seventy-Sixth Pennsylvania. She kept her promise to protect Daisy and managed to keep her alive, though in doing so she made the ultimate sacrifice to keep that promise.

Daisy Rose and Timmy Miller were married five days after the Battle of New Orleans and retired from the Seventy-Sixth Pennsylvania. After the War of 1812, Daisy gave birth to two kids named Simon and Celestia, they were born on July 4th, 1817. For the rest of their lives, they lived at the Miller plantation. Timmy Miller died at the age of seventy-three on December 10, 1865. Daisy Rose died at age seventy-two just three days later, on December 13, 1865.

Brittany Benson and Ivan Mattson were married on July 5, 1815. They had twin children just three years later, on October 5, 1818. They named their kids Fred and Kevin Mattson. For the rest of their lives, they lived in the city of Philadelphia, Pennsylvania. Brittany Mattson died at the age of seventy on May 1, 1863. Ivan Mattson died at the age of seventy-one on May 2, 1863.

Francis Scott Key wrote "The Star-Spangled Banner," and it was published as a military song in November of 1814. In 1931, Congress made the song into the national anthem of the United States of America, and it is still sung by Americans to this day. Francis Scott Key died on January 11, 1843. The shattered flag that flew above Fort McHenry is displayed in the Smithsonian to this day.

Andrew Jackson became the seventh president of the United States on March 4, 1829. He died thirty years after the War of 1812 ended, on June 8, 1845. His legend as one of America's most famous generals not just for the War of 1812, but within the history of the United States lives on.

The Seventy-Sixth Pennsylvania Keystone Grenadiers faded into history, and they are remembered for their honor and valor in the second war of independence. The Seventy-Sixth were known as one of the most disciplined and patriotic companies of the early nineteenth century. Out of 300 soldiers of the Seventy-Sixth, only 109 survived the War of 1812. The Seventy-Sixth Pennsylvania disbanded on January 15, 1815. When the Keystone grenadiers returned to Chadds Ford, Pennsylvania, Simon's homestead and farm was never rebuilt and no one ever farmed on the land ever again. However, the only thing that was returned to Simon Smithtrovich's family along with all the families of the Seventy-sixth was the promise that Simon ordered his grenadiers to do. And that was to spread the word of the galant valor that the unit displayed along with all the American soldiers displayed throughout America's forgotten war. The surviving grenadiers met once a year on June 18 in Philadelphia, Pennsylvania for forty years straight. Private Devin Little was the last Keystone grenadier to die, he died in Lancaster, Pennsylvania on March 12th, 1867.

The War of 1812 began on June 18, 1812, and ended on February 17, 1815. The American and British members of their governments met in Ghent, Belgium, to discuss peace on Christmas Eve of 1814. It would take four weeks for the peace terms to reach America. The news of the war's end would come only after the Battle of New Orleans had ended. At the end of the war, the Americans had suffered 11,300 casualties, while the British and their Canadian allies had suffered a combined total of 8,600 casualties. This war has been known as the forgotten war in American military history. This war showed the world that the United States was to be known as a major world power. But many more terrible wars would put the young American nation to the test. The War of 1812 was known as the first invasion by a foreign military power in United States history. The War of 1812 was a military draw; neither side claimed victory. After the War of 1812, the British military never again attempted to invade the United States.

The War of 1812 has been forgotten by many citizens of our time. Many people do not realize how important the War of 1812 really was. This war proved to the world that America was a major world power and that it would be marked in stone. Nothing can ever be erased in our nation's history. Many more terrible wars and battles would challenge the young American nation: the defense of the Alamo by 187 brave Texans against a Mexican army that outnumbered them five to one; the great long walk of General Scott down the Rio Grande during the Mexican War; the disastrous American Civil War, which saw more American deaths than any American war to date; Colonel Theodore Roosevelt's Rough Riders' famous charge up San Juan Hill in the Spanish-American War; From Belleau Wood to the Argonne forest during the first Great War; the island-hopping campaign of the US Marines during World War II;. From Operation Torch to Operation Overlord in the European theater of World War II; America's second forgotten war, the Korean War; the Vietnam War; and the wars in Afghanistan and Iraq. And many more wars that our nation might face in the distant and unknown future.

Our freedom and liberty will never be free. It will always come with a cost. As long as there are men and women who are willing to pay that cost with their own blood, sweat, and tears, America will always remain forever free. Thanks to those—young and old, strong and weak, brave and true, noble and honorable, loyal and passionate—who lay down their lives and who put their lives on hold and leave their families to march, sail, or fly thousands of miles from their homes for the cause of liberty. Though millions of Americans have fought in many wars throughout history, we shall always remember and shall never forget those brave men and women who marched headlong into the fray in a war that will forever be known as 'THE FORGONE WAR'.

ABOUT THE AUTHOR

Nathan Smithtro, born June 18, 1998, which is the same day that the War of 1812 began and the same day as the Battle of Waterloo, in which Napoleon Bonaparte was savagely defeated by Arthur Wellesley, the first Duke of Wellington. Smithtro is an independent military historian that studies eighteenth- and nineteenth-century warfare and tactics. He has loved military history ever since he was in the fourth grade. During Smithtro's years in high school, he excelled greatly in history that was about eighteenth- or nineteenth-century warfare.

Smithtro has taken part in historical reenacting for the past five years. He has been a part of American Civil War reenacting with the Second US Sharpshooters, as well as World War II reenacting as a private in the Ninety-Ninth Infantry Division of the 393rd Regiment. He is now a member of the American Revolutionary War reenactment group, His Majesty's Forty-Third Regiment of Foot and the Second Pennsylvania Regiment.

Nathan Smithtro's future plans are to become more involved in the entertainment business and also to publish more books about America's famous wars and battles.